Mrs. Dukes' Million

Mrs. Dukes' Million

WYNDHAM LEWIS

GEORGE PRIOR PUBLISHERS

London England

Published in the United Kingdom 1980 by
George Prior Publishers
37-41 Bedford Row, London WC1R 4JH

ISBN 0 86043 505 9

CONTENTS

I

MRS. DUKES COLLECTS HER WITS

Mrs. Dukes was about sixty-five years old, her hair quite white, with rifts of red where it grew scarce, and although not exactly fat, she was lumpy in an expressionless, puzzling way. It was as though the fat within her case of clothes were loose and adrift, and like the contents of an ill-made bolster, would sometimes collect in one place, sometimes in another.

One evening she sat amongst her goods, the refuse of time – styled 'Bric-a-brac' on a large bronze plate without – and from her unlighted and sordid shop gazed out on the rather suspect and sluggish life of Marbury Street. It was the principal thoroughfare of that particular foreign quarter within a few minutes of Oxford Street, frequented by a rabble of waiters and barbers. Her husband on leaving her thirty years ago one morning, apparently for ever, had also left her this shop and house – a cruel legacy or substitute for himself. The house, chiefly its upper regions, provided her with its rent and a little nourishment – culminating in a haddock usually – for herself and her son Cole. The lodgers were kitchen hands, coiffeurs, or mysterious and sordid young gentlemen, interested in betting – all 'furriners' – hated, and known as 'dirty furriners,' to this not exactly spic-and-span old lady. The shop and its contents, uncompromisingly dusty and dilapidated, appealed to no artistic instinct in the world around; the perfect indifference felt towards it by everybody, Mrs. Dukes chivalrously took to herself. And she disliked everybody for ever so many reasons.

On this particular evening she was of a brooding humour, and sat longer than usual staring out of her shop, gradually grown quite dark. Then she got up, walked to the front door, which was at right angles to the door of the shop within, and stood for some time on her step. After this moment's more extended glance into the world without, she would every evening retire to her den at the back of the shop. On her way back now she stopped at the stair head.

'Cole,' she called. 'What on hearth are yew doin' down there? Come up, and help me clear this mess away!'

But Cole did not appear, and sounds of chopping were heard fitfully from the cellar. So she cleared up the 'mess' they had made at tea-time alone.

Her restlessness increased. She gradually became aware of it, and asked herself what it was uneasily. It seemed to go on growing mechanically, something worrying and vague in her head.

Suddenly in the middle of a kind of uneasy rambling waking dream, a fact quietly appeared in her mind. *Her new lodger's voice was changing!*

She sat quite still, the little drink she had prepared herself at her elbow, her mind a blank, collecting her wits as it were. It was as though someone had just said to her 'Your new lodger's voice is changing,' and she could not grasp what he meant, or see any sense in the observation.

The new lodger's voice was changing! Yes, there was the thought right enough that her mind had just given her, and the first moment of puzzled astonishment over, it had a startling and troubling effect.

It took possession at once of her mood 'en maitre,' and at once gave that indefinable restlessness a meaning. All the vagueness left her mind. She began to think with a sudden uneasiness about her lodger. This fact, that at first seemed incredible, established itself more and more in her mind, and seemed each minute more indubitable and yet utterly senseless.

But the fact remained. The young artist who had taken her second floor front a week ago up among the waiters and cooks, and who had quickly become friendly with her, and for whom she had now sat twice for her portrait – it was unquestionable that there was something strange about him. His voice was changing. He had lately used several expressions that were her personal property. She had not noticed it at first, or until now put all these unconscious observations into 'so many thoughts.' It almost seemed as though he were imitating her – her tones too – not very obviously; but still several times she had been vaguely conscious of it. His voice was changing, *and it was becoming like hers!*

Even this conclusion would not have had quite such an uncomfortable effect, had it not been that various other things about him served as a vague and troubling background to it. They were indefinable enough, and the impossibility of grasping them, and yet the feeling that many kindred things were there, gave this strange fact additional intensity.

Was she mistaken, was this a fancy? It must be: what a senseless fancy to have though! He couldn't be making fun of her, it wasn't that she felt. What did she feel then? She did not know, but she remained uncomfortable and angry, and determined not to sit for her portrait as she had promised, on the following day.

2
THE PORTRAIT

Mrs. Dukes in waking up the next morning was still resolved not to sit any more as model to Mr. Ernest Nichols.

When he came down at ten she feigned some obscure heart trouble. According to her, her heart was behaving just as though it were her liver. From her description of the symptoms the listener gathered that her heart was like a burning potato and was choking up one of her principal veins, which in its turn was communicating unwonted and disturbing tremors through her lower limbs.

'Oh no, I won't see the doctor, Mr. Nichols. It'll pass off sudden, like it came.'

'I have some stuff that'll put you all right, Mrs. Dukes. Just take a dose or two and you'll feel another woman.' And Mr. Nichols went on to say that he hoped she could give him just an hour or two, that she could have as many 'rests' as she liked, since the paint would be dry otherwise by the next day, and the portrait spoilt, he was afraid.

Mrs. Dukes had greeted him with, 'Do you want a model for the Witch of Endor, Mr. Nichols?'

'No, why?' replied he, watching her closely.

'Why, wouldn't I do? Look at me! Ain't I a beastly old fright this morning!'

'Ha! ha! ha!' laughed Mr. Nichols, with his boisterous bohemian laugh, with ringing appreciativeness, for every true bohemian is a lover of quaintness. And Mrs. Dukes was being quaint. Mrs. Dukes was not insensible to the flattery of the hearty bohemian laugh. In the gravest circumstances of life she had never yet been able to resist the temptation to be witty and whimsical. In this case the pleasure resulting from the ready and disarming laugh was the first step in her giving up the resolve of the night before.

So an hour afterwards she was sitting in Mr. Nichols' room, a foot or two away from his easel, at which he was working with a singular intentness.

Several diagrams rather than drawings of her head were pinned in a row on the wall. Each peculiarity, the exact position of her limbs, the relaxed muscles, the lines of the forehead were registered. The painting on which he was engaged also was rather like a *plan* of her head than a painting. It was very wooden, and could an artist have watched him at work he would have said that Mr. Nichols was making, not a painting, but an exact copy in colour of Mrs. Dukes' face. He seemed to be trying to get on his canvas the exact shade of rather violent sallow whiteness of which her complexion was composed.

With a last glance of intent summing-up at his sitter, and another at his canvas, he laid his palette and brushes down, and with his cheery bohemian voice sang out, 'That'll do, Mrs. Dukes for the moment. Draw your chair up to the fire and let's have a little chat. Then a quarter of an hour's more work, and it'll be finished.' Approaching her, he continued, 'Haven't tired you, I hope? We artists, once we get well into our work, forget all about the sitter's sufferings.'

He went over to a table and took up a coloured reproduction of a picture by some modern Swedish painter, and holding it up before Mrs. Dukes, exclaimed, 'What do you think of that, Mrs. Dukes? There's a pretty bit of loose chiaroscuro for you!' He made passes over it with his hand as though mesmerising the very ill drawn violet youth who made the principal figure in the picture; he half shut his eyes and cocked his head on one side.

'By gum, I wish I'd done that!' And he threw it back on the table, strewn with papers, art magazines, pencils, etc., with a brutal gesture, as though he hated it because he hadn't done it.

Again, here, to a witness of this scene of certain penetration and one thoroughly versed in art matters, Mr. Nichols would have appeared to be affecting the vulgarity, the manners of the bohemian artist, but with a conscious vulgarity, and with a purpose, and not merely as some outsider trying to be like an artist, and enjoying himself in mouthing a pseudo-technical slang of the studios. Besides, his painting of Mrs. Dukes and drawings on the wall, if not works of art, were at least extremely skilful diagrams, proving no small technical knowledge.

He was a short man with strong and rather large features, the lower part of his face hidden in a close tow-coloured beard, of the same colour as his hair. His face just escaped being handsome. It would have been reckoned so, as it was, had it not been for the intensity of his expression, which just turned the scales, and made him descend to the level of merely 'well-looking' men.

We have referred already to a person of certain penetration. No author can afford to be without a fellow of this sort. When the author feels that it would be conceited to claim so much penetration for himself, he just ushers in this person of certain penetration.

In the case of Mr. Nichols he would have had all his work cut out. For Mr. Nichols was a tough customer for the thought-reader. He would as we have said probably have concluded that Mr. Nichols was not what he seemed: that his grotesque expressions 'loose chiaroscuro' and so on, his unpleasant bluffness, were assumed. He would have summed Mr. Nichols up in the following way. 'That's a queer cuss – an odd, cold, fanatic kind of nature – a little off his head, with some sort of fixed idea, some obsession or other. His eyes have a kind of expressionless fixity, as though they were not *real* eyes. He seems to be looking at you from behind a mask. He looks like a man who has been living at a great strain for some time. His voice is the funniest thing about him. Occasionally when he's not playing the boisterous bohemian quite so much, his *real* voice seems to appear and it is quite expressionless, like his eyes. In summing up, he seems a very queer fish indeed. He seems an inhuman sort of person, using very good gifts of one sort and another to satisfy some quaint passion or other — or fixed idea, as I said. I should think that he was extremely dangerous — though *how* and *why* I couldn't say. And what he's driving at in painting that old woman I couldn't so much as guess. But he looks at her strangely!'

That is the way my little man does his work. I have now dismissed him, however.

Mr. Nichols was about thirty years old, although many people might have taken him for anything up to forty. His accent, or what of it one could recognise beneath his bohemian bluffness, was simple, but that of a well-educated man. His eyes were large, blue and mobile: very practical and sophisticated looking organs.

Having told Mrs. Dukes that she could have a rest, he was looking at himself in the glass that hung over his mantel-piece. He was frowning at himself, as though displeased with something he had just done; he looked at himself severely and disapprovingly in the face, at all events. Had my little friend 'of certain penetration' observed him at this moment, it would undoubtedly have confirmed him in his belief that Mr. Nichols was a madman.

'Oh Lord! Do I look like that?' drawled Mrs. Dukes. 'What've ye put that smudge o' yeller on there for? It looks as though I'd bin lickin' the mustard pot! Well! you have made me look an old cat!'

Mrs. Dukes had dragged herself before the portrait. She always appeared to drag herself and not to walk, as though her skirts were made of lead. Her head, with its heavy white

Roman outline, slanted up from her lax little body towards the picture. Her curiosity thoroughly satisfied, and quite disillusioned – she would never take an interest in the portrait again – she went back to the chair where she had been sitting, ignoring her lodger's invitation to 'draw up to the fire.' It was dignity and a feeling of fitness that made her refuse.

Mr. Nichols then continued chattily, 'You say you've been here for thirty years, Mrs. Dukes. Did you come from London originally?'

'Lord yes. I was born just off the Strand,' she replied promptly. 'And before I came to this ramshackle little 'ole I lived a very different life. Who'd ever 'ave thought that I should come to lettin' lodgin's to the nasty foreign lot what's all I can scarcely get 'ere?'

The young Swiss cooks rankled, rankled, in Mrs. Dukes' uneasy spirit.

'Why don't you brighten up your shop a bit? I'll paint a sign board for you: you'd do a much better trade then.'

'Trade! I don't want trade! It was my 'usband made me start with the shop downstairs; and then the fashion in old furniture passed, and I was left with all that stuff, good for nothin' but makin' a bonfire of! I 'ave things that money wouldn't buy once; I could sell them now but won't let them go for what some people 'as the cheek to offer!'

While Mrs. Dukes was finishing her outburst – conversation with her was a series of outbursts, varying in violence but not in kind – Mr. Nichols had got up and stooped over a large phonograph standing on the table in front of Mrs. Dukes. He left it, shrugging his shoulders and saying 'The confounded thing won't work any more. Ever since I had it down in your room the day before yesterday it has refused to work. I don't know what's the matter with it.'

16

'But it's movin',' said Mrs. Dukes.

'Yes, it moves all right, but it won't talk!' replied the lodger.

He then said, continuing their former conversation, in the voice of a practical man speaking with conviction: 'What you need Mrs. Dukes is someone who would put some money into the business, renovate your stock and do a certain amount of advertisement. But the question of a partner is a ticklish thing, always. Have you no old friend, no very old friend, whom you could trust?'

'No, I 'aven't any friends and don't want any. They're no good! I and Cole 'ave lived 'ere for the past thirty years and we 'aven't made a single friend in the district. That's the gospel truth! Not a single one! And what should I want goin' and renovatin' and spendin' money like that?'

The phonograph emitted just then a small and rasping sound. Mr. Nichols sprang to it, and again bent over it. 'I thought it had made up its mind to speak. But apparently not. I must take it to a musical shop and have it overhauled.'

Mrs. Dukes had caught once or twice already the new note in her lodger's voice. It was chiefly when they were engaged in a heated discussion that his voice took this tone.

And now he began speaking again. She started, and their eyes met for a moment, for the first few words could, not only in the words themselves but in the tone, have been spoken by her. It was as startling as a parrot.

'Good Lord, no; I don't say *that:* not to spend money, but to get someone else to. You've already spent your share. You already have a certain stock, but it wants renewing.'

She got up brusquely, and said in a suddenly energetic voice, 'Well, Mr. Nichols, 'ave you finished with me for to-day?'

'Why, I haven't quite; I just wanted to put a finishing touch to my canvas. Must you go at once?'

While he was speaking he had stooped down and shut the lid of the box. The whirring became almost inaudible.

'I don't know why yew want me, Mr. Nichols: I don't think I quite understands yew, ye know!'

Her lodger seemed at once to have divined the cause of her glance, and the sudden anger that had brought her to her feet.

He was very alert and grave. He prevailed upon her to give him ten minutes more, that he might put the 'finishing touches' to his picture. He seemed to do this not because there was really very much to do to it, but to break the fall, so to speak, of their amicable relations – not to let her go away at once, but by getting her to sit for a little time longer to disarm her anger.

She left without looking at the portrait, and was not responsive to Mr. Nichols' effusive thanks.

When she had gone he sat down at the table and wrote a note. It was quite short.

Dear Lucy,

Be at the theatre tomorrow for a dress rehearsal; I may have to press things forward. I am going up there tonight as I must have a place to practise in, and here it's impossible to do so. I have good hopes of success. Her friends still uncertain. But I don't think there are any troublesome ones.

Yours ever, Evan

Having washed his brushes in a businesslike way, and turned his canvas to the wall, first having examined it carefully, he left the house. In passing Mrs. Dukes' door he called out in his most bluff bohemian voice.

'I shan't be back till late, Mrs. Dukes. Don't trouble about keeping the fire in.'

3
A NEW ODDITY

Mrs. Dukes had dragged herself painfully downstairs after the sitting. To have her portrait painted was one of the few events that had occurred to her in the course of the last thirty years. Probably it was the most unusual thing that had happened since her husband disappeared abruptly into the intense inane. Had this portrait been extremely satisfying and answered to the vague excitement and curiosity she felt, all would have been well, but as it was it left her rather morally shaken.

She was always willing to affirm that she was 'an old fright' but she had never dreamt of anything so ugly as the portrait that her lodger had just made of her. It made her positively feel older — it was more difficult to get up and down stairs after having seen it. And it was to do a fright of a picture like that that he had made her sit for three days and taken up her time for nothing! Why? Here was another strange thing about him.

But then there was the question of his imitating her, aping her way of speaking. Her instinct told her that it was not to make fun of her. But there was no other conceivable reason why he should do it, unless he were mad, or a sort of man-parrot. She was confronted with a mystery. But being a hot-tempered and in a certain sense an energetic woman, she could not go on puzzling about that. So she became angry. She accepted, against her instinct, the theory that he was making fun of her. Then, in any case, if she were worried and puzzled by certain unaccountable things, they all had reference to him — it was he that was responsible for them. She got down to her room in a very bad temper.

But this convenient anger of hers did not entirely overcome her instinct. She was vaguely uneasy; her old room, each article of which was mixed, in a common element of personal dirt, with her life, seemed almost sinister. It seemed as though it were all about to change.

She had a dull and insistent presentiment of misfortune. With a feeling of sudden fear – feeling very old and helpless all of a sudden – she called out in an angry voice.

'Cole; whatever *are* yew doin' down there! I thought I ast you to clean the window before I went upstairs. The room looks mis'rble enough to give anyone the blues! – Well, aren't ye comin'?'

It was so humiliating to feel the need of her son Cole's company that she put more scolding into her voice even than usual.

Cole appeared and went straight to the window, and began rubbing it with his sleeve.

'Whatever *are* you doin', Cole?'

'Cleanin' the window,' answered Cole briefly.

'Well, just don't you do anything of the sort. You're sulky, as use-yal! Go and put the kettle on, and make *tea, do!* What a thing it is to have a sulky boy like you, to be sure!'

Mrs. Dukes always spoke of her son Cole as sulky – 'my sulky boy.' Indeed he was *extremely* sulky. But this did not account for the fact that in the course of the day it was rarely he uttered more than five or six words, and they very often anything but apposite – more often than not they were unintelligible.

Without being incapacitated for light work, and although quite well behaved, Cole had not all his wits; he was in fact a kind of cross between a sawney and a domestic animal. He had been queer, morose and delicate as a boy, and had grown into a man for whom all intercourse with his fellows was impossible, and who, besides, seemed in no way desirous to have any. He had always lived with his mother. He was busied with one thing and another from morning till night, having a marked preference for dark and dingy places. He would occasionally be seen to smile at the approach of night. He appeared to regard the darkness as rather a good joke.

He was short, stooping and usually unshaven, with cross-eyes, and a tuft of spraying hair at the crown of his head. His under-lip drooped, but with quite a normal droop – not the idiot's grimacing laxness. He walked very quickly, with his eyes always cast down.

Mrs. Dukes was fond of seeing Cole in positions of responsibility; insisted on his opening the door if there were a ring, although he created a very bad impression always on the caller. She once quarrelled with one of her lodgers because he had hesitated to pay Cole his rent, not finding her at home. Cole could go to market, could clean windows, do any domestic work confided to him. He was short-sighted, and whatever object occupied his attention for the moment, whether it were a window to clean, or nail to knock in the wall or what not, he kept his face riveted to it with a strange air of intensity.

Mrs. Dukes never spoke to him without scolding. This was of course to carry out the fiction of his sulkiness; she never appeared even to herself to own that he was different from other people – unless his colossal sulkiness could be termed being so.

Cole and his mother passed an animated evening. She relieved her feelings at great length on the subject of Mr. Nichols. Cole even deigned one or two more or less relevant remarks.

Mr. Nichols had made innumerable overtures to Cole. He had suggested, even, that he should have his portrait painted. But a dangerous light had come into Mrs. Dukes' eyes; she said shortly that Cole was always too busy, and her lodger had not pressed the point. But he lost no opportunity of speaking to him. Cole treated him with complete indifference; only once on seeing him approach he had retreated with obvious 'sulkiness' to the cellar.

The hours wore on, and Mrs. Dukes' anger and uneasiness somewhat subsided at the approach of sleep. Sleep and its approaches were with her like a drunkenness (even when it was not — as alas! sometimes was the case — actually so).

Ten o'clock arrived, she entered her bundle of night rags, and carelessly tied, buttoned and pinned herself up in them. Cole washed up the last dishes in the far corner of the room.

At the foot of the bed and a yard or so away from the door, was a high screen made of an old table-cloth, and a rickety wooden frame. This was fixed to the frame of the bedstead. It served to keep the draught from her at night, and prevent anyone from seeing into the room immediately, when the door was opened.

She was very sleepy, and giving her last incoherent injunctions to Cole, before he retired to his chamber at the top of the house, when her uneasiness of a few hours before possessed her again. But this time in a different way.

She felt suddenly that someone was in the room — someone besides her and Cole. Sensations of this sort are usually due to the fact that, without taking direct notice of them, we have been conscious of certain unusual sounds, and at last this uneasiness comes to a head in this startled feeling.

She stopped talking to Cole and moved restlessly about on her dilapidated couch. Then she suddenly sat up in bed, and getting stealthily on her knees and leaning forward, she dragged the table-cloth that served as a screen quickly aside. Close up to the half-open door, and a couple of feet away from her face, was that of Mr. Nichols, white and distinct, looking straight and quietly at her. But his body was twisted round, and he had evidently turned to move quickly away, but had done so a moment too late.

She let the curtain fall with a thick startled cry, and fell back on her pillow now thoroughly awake for the first time for many years at ten o'clock at night, and trying to collect her thoughts. There was a soft tapping at the door. She did not reply, nor did Cole go to the door as he usually did after nine in the evening if anyone knocked.

Then came the voice of the second-floor lodger, saying gravely and his usually noisy bohemian delivery toned down, 'I hope I didn't frighten you, Mrs. Dukes. I knocked a moment ago, but I suppose you didn't hear me. I wanted to ask you to be so good as to wake me up tomorrow morning at half past eight, as I have to meet somebody arriving by an early train. I can count on your doing so, can't I?'

'Yes.'

The answer came, but it came in a tone that had not yet been used by Mrs. Dukes to her artist lodger. The monosyllable was grim and heavy with things in reserve. The cup was full. On the following day Mrs. Dukes would not beat about the bush with Mr. Ernest Nichols. To find a reason why the latter should wish to eavesdrop on her at that hour of night she did not even think of doing. She did not actually go to the length of making up her mind to give him notice. But she was determined to do more than this. She would give him a piece of her mind about this last oddity of his.

But she was fated not to relieve her mind on the following morning as she proposed, and to be prevented from doing so in the most startling and unexpected manner.

As though with a grim will to make the morning and her settling with her lodger come all the quicker, she fell asleep almost at once, Cole leaving her the little night-light she never slept without.

4
A STARTLING DISCOVERY

Mrs. Dukes woke up earlier than usual. She combed her hair. The reader may consider this detail as superfluous; he may murmur impatiently 'of course!' He would be wrong however. The fact that Mrs. Dukes combed her hair was sign that no ordinary day had dawned. When Mrs. Dukes was clean it were wiser to keep out of her way, if she had a bone to pick with you.

When the hour arrived at which Mr. Nichols had asked to be called, his landlady in person mounted the stairs to carry out his injunction. She did not intend to beard him in his bed. She merely wished by the unpleasant sound of her voice to give him an unpleasant awakening, and also, as she was impatient, to get into touch with him, so to speak, as soon as possible. Then the trouble she gave herself in personally waking him, the honour conferred, her appalling punctuality — all this was meant to be a terrible and subtly ironical way of carrying out his orders. All these things went to swell the settlement pending between them. It was like offering a hearty breakfast to the condemned man before executing him — the last courtesy of life.

She took hold of the handle of the door, and pushed. It opened — she was slightly surprised at this fact at the time, for Mr. Nichols always had latched it up till then. When it was half open, without looking — her face turned discreetly and proudly away, although her lodger could not possibly see her from where he lay — she called out:

24

'You ast to be called, Mr. Nichols, at half past eight. You said you 'ad a train to catch. It is 'alf past eight *punchal.*'

But now, before closing the door again, she slightly turned her head. On the white cloth of the dressing table near the door, the light from which fell on it sharply, was something very odd. It was a horse-shoe shaped arrangement of hair. She only saw it for a moment, for the door was pushed against her, and the latch put down in a twinkling. But in this bare second she had time to make one more observation. The face that she half-saw springing at her, as it were, out of the bed, was clean shaven.

Her lodger's voice sounded immediately within the door.

'I'm sorry, Mrs. Dukes. I thought it was somebody else. Still, as you're shut out, perhaps the proprieties would be better served if you *remained* shut out now until I finished my toilet. I shall soon be down. Thank you very much for waking me.'

She stood and listened with an almost frightened face, as though that shaven man might open the door again and jump out upon her. Also he should at least have had another voice, and not Mr. Nichols'. She did not answer a word, but shuffled downstairs rapidly, so as not to have to think on the landing, and she felt thoughts crowding into her brain. Instead of holding her breath until she got to her room, she held her thought, so to speak. Her mind was an aching and portentous blank. But she would not think on the landing or staircase, she would wait till she got to her room.

Once there, she sank down in her chair, and said in a conclusive tone, 'Well!'

At last there was something palpable. She need be angry no more. She was as a matter of fact no longer angry. She was startled, and in an odd way pleased. To make a discovery always pleases us, and to be startled was vaguely pleasing also to this sensitive old woman.

There was no longer the shadow of a doubt that her lodger was a shady character – perhaps – who knows what? There was no longer any question of his making fun of her, or wasting her time with the portrait; the uncertainty and uneasiness of the last day or two was disposed of by this quite undeniable proof of there being something wrong. But she did not lose sight of the fact that her lodger's interest in her was extraordinary, to say the least of it; and in the light of this new discovery it seemed necessary to take some action at once. That he should leave the house within the hour she was fully determined. She had no more desire to 'give him a piece of her mind.' She would give him a simple and chilly order to leave at once. The desire to have a scene with him, and 'tell him what she thought of him,' was caused only by exasperation at the baffling nature of those phenomena that had lately accompanied Mr. Nichols' presence in the house. The last night's discovery of him behind the door was, it is true, conclusive also of *something* wrong. But the discovery was not explicit, it hardly showed in what direction to look for the key of the mystery. But a man who wore a false beard, who disguised himself, and who lurked in the passages at night, could only be one thing: a criminal.

She was at this point in her reflections when someone hurried past the door outside, and a moment later the front door banged noisily.

Mrs. Dukes got up from her chair and dragged herself rather quickly to the front door. Peering down the street, she saw Mr. Nichols already a good distance away, hurrying in the direction of Piccadilly, with a large brown paper parcel under one arm, a portfolio and the trumpet of the phonograph under the other. She came back discomfited and vexed to her den. What was to be done now? Perhaps he would not be back till late, and she was determined he should not sleep there that night. She would get Cole to bring his things down into the hall, so that when he returned he could be sent right about turn, and packed off expeditiously. But she could hardly pack his things up, as he had the keys of course.

What should be done? Should she tell the police? She liked the police as little as she liked doctors, not believing in and being afraid of both. She would wait. He would probably be back soon.

No doubt the asking to be woken up was merely a pretext to explain his presence in the passage the night before. It seemed odd to her that he should have left his door open, especially as he had asked to be woken up. It did not occur to her how easy it is for the most careful man, when very preoccupied, to forget something – the turning of a latch or what not.

The day wore on, and her lodger did not return. She ascended to his rooms again in the course of the morning, and found everything packed up. The painting and drawings had gone, the box was locked, and his few toilet things thrown pell-mell into his bag.

As night came on she grew extremely irritable and restless. What was to be done? He would come back when they were all in bed asleep. She would sit up for him.

But by half past eleven, as he had not put in an appearance, she locked herself in, and went to sleep. Nothing on earth could have kept her awake for another half hour.

The next morning by the first post came a letter addressed to her. It was from Mr. Nichols, and read as follows:

Dear Mrs. Dukes,

I met my friend at Victoria, and in consequence of a communication he made me, I am forced to go to the north on business *at once*. I have not even the time to come back and fetch my bag. Will you please keep my things for me for a week or so? I am sorry not to have given you a regular notice. I enclose P.O. for rent up to the end of the week.

Yours truly, Ernest Nichols.

There was nothing then to be done. She had to keep the things for the moment. But if they were not claimed in a week or so she would send for the police.

She put the letter down with a sigh of dissatisfaction. Her little slab of a face was almost startlingly white, due to her worry of the last day or two, and her unusual morning's ablutions. Then suddenly there was a volleying knock at the door – the sort of knock a postman, with his great professional skill, might give if he suddenly were possessed of the idea that he were President Roosevelt. Mrs. Dukes sat down as though she had been shot. Then she went towards the front door.

5
A VISIT FROM THE POLICE

On her doorstep Mrs. Dukes found a police constable and a man in civilian dress, who she at once divined was a detective.

They stepped quickly in, and the plain clothes man said sharply: 'Mrs. Dukes, I believe? One of your lodgers didn't come back last night, I believe, Mrs. Dukes? I am a detective, and have come to get certain information about the man in question, which you only, Mrs. Dukes, can afford us. I have a constable here with me, who will bear witness of our interview. I must impress upon you, Mrs. Dukes, that in dealing with the law or its representatives, to speak the truth and hide nothing is of the utmost importance. Will you please show us into a room where we shall not be disturbed? The room occupied by the young man about whom we've come would serve our purpose.'

Mrs. Dukes did not reply a word to this harangue. She led the way upstairs like a hypnotic patient. She had been hypnotized by the Law. She would rather have had Mr. Nichols back than these men come to catch him. She felt vaguely that the remedy was more dread than the disease.

Arrived in Mr. Nichols' room, the detective said, 'We shall have to examine the effects your late lodger has left here. It is very important that nothing that can clear up the extremely mysterious case with which he is connected should be overlooked. Let us begin with this box. Have you the pick, Constable?'

With a small steel instrument they prized the box open, and turned its contents out on the floor. There was nothing but a couple of suits of clothes, a considerable collection of books and art magazines and artist's materials. The bag, likewise, yielded nothing to the careful investigation of the two men. The policeman thrust the things back again, pushed the box into a corner of the room and placed the bag on top of it.

Then the plain clothes man turned to Mrs. Dukes.

He was a heavy dark man, just under six feet. He seemed to have an irresistible inclination to scowl, and at that moment was mastering it with an effort. He could not, however, help twirling his large, drooping black moustache. He looked at the old landlady most unpleasantly, and said suddenly, in a quiet voice, making her start slightly, 'Are you *sure*, Mrs. Dukes, you have nothing else belonging to the late occupant of these rooms?'

She quite forgot the letter she had just received – but later on she mentioned it, and the detective then scowled at her distrustfully as though to say she had been holding this back.

'Why should *I* 'ave any*thing* belongin' to 'im, I should like to know? Didn't 'e give me bother enough when 'e was 'ere, without my bein' worried about 'im now 'e's taken 'imself off? Why don't you take the things away with ye? *I* don't want them.'

'Very well, Mrs. Dukes,' replied the detective; 'You say you have nothing else belonging to him. You must keep these things here, without *touching* them, for a day or two, when they will be fetched. For the last week, Mrs. Dukes, your house has been watched. It has been reported that you were very thick with the man who here went under the name of Nichols; and although we bring *no* charges against you – mind *no* charge whatever as yet – still I recommend you seriously for the next day or two to be very careful. For instance, although, as I say, at present we have *no* charges against you, if you left your house you would be followed; we cannot be too careful in these cases. Although we might not construe your going out as an illegal act, we should still make sure that you do not communicate with our man.'

'Oh Lord, *I* don't want to com-municate with 'im, or anything else with 'im! All I ask you is to take 'is things away, and I never want to see or 'ear of 'im again, I'm sure!'

'Very well, Mrs. Dukes. But it is of the greatest importance that our man should not be apprised of the fact that we are on his track. So I must ask you not to chatter with your lodgers or neighbours – '

'I never talk to *my* neighbours! I haven't had any communication with them for thirty years, and I'm not likely to begin now!' the indignant old woman burst in. 'What 'ave I got to do with all this, *I* should like to know? To 'ear you talk one'd think – '

'Very well, Mrs. Dukes,' said the official heavily. 'I don't think we need take up any more of your time today. We'll go now, Hickman.'

In the hall, the detective stopped, and from under his black brows seemed to be examining Mrs. Dukes with a sudden interest, with a certain critical effort. The extreme dislike for her that had plainly shone out of his eyes during their interview upstairs, softened or changed rather into a cold interest. He scrutinized her for several minutes, pretexting one or two things he had omitted to say upstairs.

Just before leaving he said very impressively, 'We may at any moment now lay our hands on our man. You must hold yourself in readiness to identify him in case of need, although it is not likely we shall require your services.'

Mrs. Dukes, left alone, felt literally turned inside out. She was in some things as timid as a child. If she were the aggrieved party she felt strong. But she was confronted by a vast, all-powerful body, namely the Law, which might or might not be incompetent, but whose singularity was that it could never be *wrong;* she felt small, timid and at her wit's end.

Cole came out of some dark part of the house without being called. This seemed ominous. She watched him doubtfully, and then suddenly threw a wet duster at him. He did not move, but went on arranging the fire to boil the kettle.

'Oh Lord, Cole, you do make me wild! Let the fire alone, do! Go and chop the wood, as I ast you!'

There was a soft tap at the door, and a falsetto voice said, 'Mrs. Dukes, are there any letters for me this morning?'

It was the first-floor lodger, a young curate who had taken up his quarters there three weeks previously, having some work to do in the neighbourhood.

Mrs. Dukes went to the door, answering, 'No, Mr. 'igginbotham; there 'asn't been any letters for you this morning.'

'Have you lost your young artist lodger, Mrs. Dukes? I thought I heard some men carrying his box downstairs?'

The curate had made several overtures to Mr. Nichols; but Mr. Nichols had taken as much trouble to avoid him, and indeed everyone else in the house, as he had to foregather with his landlady and her son.

'Yes, Mr. 'igginbotham, and a good job too! He left this morning.'

'Oh!' said the curate, in an astonished voice, 'I thought you got on very well with him — I used to hear him reciting; was he an artist or what?'

'I don't know what 'e was. All I know is 'e's gone, and 'igh time too!' replied Mrs. Dukes sulkily. And the curate left her, astonished at such truculence.

That evening was a lull, a short period of comparative peace — the last that Mrs. Dukes was destined to get for many a long day. She passed it in their room at the back of the shop, almost as sulky as Cole himself.

6

MRS. DUKES WILL BE BACK IN A COUPLE OF HOURS

The next day in Marbury Street was spent by Mrs. Dukes, up till six o'clock, in attempting to resume her duties as though nothing had happened. She struggled with each one in turn. Things she had done for years mechanically cost her an effort of will. Nothing seemed quite the same; even the familiar and common element of personal dirt seemed estranged from her. She found herself going through with every little domestic detail of the day consciously; some little trick or habit of her life she would suddenly abandon, it seeming tiresome and useless.

The curate had smelt a mystery in his landlady's way of speaking of Mr. Nichols, and the latter's sudden departure, and his curiosity led him twice, once in going out and once on his way upstairs, to stop at Mrs. Dukes' door. The second time, approaching with his gentle noiseless step, he nearly frightened her out of her life, and in the flurry of this occurrence got into conversation easily.

'I'm afraid you've been rather upset lately, Mrs. Dukes, by something. You're really extremely nervous.'

'Yes, Mr 'igginbotham, I've not been feelin' myself all day; I 'ave such awful pains just 'ere, – cramp of the 'eart, yew know. That always comes when I'm worried. I can't get my breath; I gasp an' gasp; but no medicine's any good for that.'

'Dear me, Mrs. Dukes,' said the curate in a tone of realistic commiseration, as though it were no nonsense, and he were *really* concerned. 'You must really take care of yourself. Is there anything I can do for you? The great secret of keeping well, though, is not to worry.'

'Oh Lord! That's easier said than done,' laughed Mrs. Dukes. And the interview seemed at an end. His curiosity was not shameless enough to lead him to a direct prying into her affairs. Like many men sworn to a peaceful and saintly life, mysterious occurrences, scenes of violence, chapters of criminal life in which he could not participate, had a great fascination for him. And he was in the habit of relieving himself of his inclination for these forbidden things by entering very fervently into the lives of others for whom they were *not* forbidden, and who lived in them. At times he lived his parishioners' lives with far more gusto than they themselves. It was about half past six. Night had long drawn in, and the curate had a few moments before closed the door behind him with a little shiver, for the fog stood in almost every part of London in great clouds of blackness. Finding that Mrs. Dukes was not communicative, he was just going away, when there was a sharp knock at the front door. He went up the stairs slowly, looking back to see who it was, as Mrs. Dukes responded pessimistically to this summons.

A tall dark man entered the hallway hurriedly, saying to Mrs. Dukes in a deep authoritative voice, 'I'm afraid we shall require you after all.'

'Oh Lord! And must I go out on a night like this! Just *look* at it, ye know.' Mrs. Dukes' voice sounded very plaintive.

The curate stood on the stairs, looking back almost open-mouthed, with a slight flush at the same time at the consciousness of this unseemly display of curiosity.

The tall man, the detective who had come the day before in company with the constable, now caught sight of this black listening figure on the stairs. He stared for a moment almost as open-mouthed as the other, and then the most truly diabolical expression came into his face. His respect for the cloth was evidently a minus quantity.

'Let us come in here, if you please, Mrs. Dukes; we have some private business to settle.'

Then the curate found his voice, and coming down a step or two, said, 'Excuse me, Mrs. Dukes, but I could not help overhearing what was said, and I think, in your present state, it would be most unwise to venture out in this fog; most unwise.

Is there nothing, really, I can do for you? I shall be very happy
— '

The dark man threw back his coat with a gesture of such impatience, that the curate stopped dead short, and stammered a moment.

The detective now came between him and Mrs. Dukes, and spoke in a rasping decided voice.

'I have no time to lose, sir. I am doing my duty, and I hope I know what it is better than you. I would not ask Mrs. Dukes to come with me if her presence were not imperative in the interests of the Law. I have a few words first to say to Mrs. Dukes, and as it is a private matter, I must ask you to leave us alone.'

'I would not dream, sir, of thwarting the ends of justice, if there is question of that. But I must say that it is *most* dangerous for Mrs. Dukes to go out on a night like this in her present condition. But if it is necessary, as you say — '

And he retired up the stairs to ruminate in his room what all this might mean.

'Now, Mrs. Dukes, I'm very sorry to have to trouble you,' went on the detective, as soon as they were within the lugubrious sanctum at the back of the shop, 'but we have not a minute to lose. It is of the utmost importance that a man we are practically certain is your late lodger should be identified before he can get off again. And only you are able to do it. Will you come with me at once?'

'Oh Lord! At once?'

'Mrs. Dukes! Must I insist on the absolute necessity of our *not* wasting time?' The detective was very serious, and his voice sounded strained and harsh to her; she was now trembling with sheer indecision.

'Mrs. Dukes!' he began again.

'Oh Lord! All right, I s'pose I *must* come. How long shall we be?'

'You will be able to get back, probably, Mrs. Dukes, in a couple of hours. But must I again insist on the necessity of your preparing yourself at once? I will wait in the hall, while you get ready. But each moment gained is of the utmost importance, Mrs. Dukes.'

She hardly knew what she was doing. But in ten minutes she was more or less ready to accompany the dark man waiting in the hall. She had vaguely the idea that she was going to appear before an august assembly of judges and bewigged and awful men, and she made frantic efforts to conceal the disorder and slovenliness of her appearance beneath new layers of cloth and new disorder, and slightly more pretentious slovenliness. Her formlessness after these alterations was almost alarming. She had on an old ulster that thirty years before had been altered and re-altered, over a space of ten years, in a frantic attempt to keep pace with the fashions. But at last the alterations had become wilder and wilder, corresponding no longer to any known mode, and they had stopped for good some twenty-five years ago; her invention had given out. She appeared in the hall ready at last, and almost crying.

Cole was summoned. He came within hailing distance up the cellar stairs, but still seemed immeasurable leagues away; his voice sounded like a voice on the telephone. On being told that his mother would be gone for a couple of hours, he said indifferently, sulkily, 'All right,' and the gloom swallowed every vestige of him again.

Once outside, her conductor turned towards Oxford Street, threading the alleys and streets of half-lighted shops that form this district. Near Warings they took a bus to Orchard Street, and there changed to an auto bus, which disappeared in the fog with them in the direction of St. John's Wood, and Swiss Cottage.

Where they alighted Mrs. Dukes did not notice or care. She was inwardly moaning the whole time, and felt in the middle of this thick and dreary fog as though her last day had come, and she were being whirled through space to a doubtful doom.

They turned several times, walking between houses with little gardens in front of them, and each allotted two or three dirty trees. At last they stopped in front of a large, sombre, rambling house, deep set in a sort of cavity of a garden, lighted at one or two of its windows. A man, also well muffled up, who had apparently been hanging about and awaiting their arrival, came in with them.

Mrs. Dukes, on suddenly realising that they had arrived at their destination, and that this dark house contained a criminal that they were engaged in hunting down, stopped dead short, gazing blankly and with startled eyes in front of her. The one or two dull and steady lights within the windows looked so quiet. This large house was perhaps full of desperate characters, who were at the present moment quite peaceful, and whose peace they were going to disturb. She had been reading regularly for the past few months the accounts of 'famous crimes,' published in Reynolds' Sunday paper. This house looked to her like a house where a murder had been committed. She remained quite still gazing up at its windows. They wanted her to go in there, at that front door. But she felt that the whole house was full of evil and dangerous things, that no sooner would she have stepped inside the door than someone would fall upon her. She looked at the two men beside her. Would they be a protection? They seemed quite cool and collected, but were looking silently and attentively at

37

her. Then all of a sudden her fear of this big black house in front of them changed into a queer uneasiness about her companions – about the detective and this other man.

She had come there as though in a weary, uncomfortable dream, entirely wrapped up in her own thoughts. Now she seemed to have woken up, and experienced something of the unaccountable chill and terror of the sleep-walker who has suddenly come to himself.

What awaited her in that house? She looked wide-eyed and doubtingly at the detective. She had disliked this surly individual well enough, but it had never occurred to her to fear anything in him except his professional manners. She just then caught a quick glance that the two men gave each other. She had suddenly grown to fear them more than the gloomy house that they wished her to enter.

7
MRS. DUKES IDENTIFIES HER LODGER

Mrs. Dukes began in a hoarse voice. She was astonished at her own hoarseness.

'I suppose it's all right – that there isn't any mistake.'

'Of course not, Mrs. Dukes. Here we are. Our man's inside, and all you have to do is to say if he is or is not the man that lodged with you. Come along, please.' And the detective moved a step forward.

His companion had gone back and glanced rapidly down the road.

Steps were heard approaching from the direction they had come; Mrs. Dukes turned back quickly towards the gate. But the second man stood negligently in front of her. Just then a tall figure issued out of the fog, and turned in where they were standing. Mrs. Dukes recognised in him at once, although he was in plain clothes now, the constable, Hickman, who had accompanied the detective the day before. His face had that sternness and honesty mixed that one sees in some English faces preeminently, and that seems the best confirmation of the Englishman's belief that the English are better, more honest, than other people.

He greeted the detective. 'Good evenin', sir. Ah, there's the lady. We've got 'im this time all right.' Mrs. Dukes felt her nerves wonderfully steadied by the presence of Hickman. Her confidence restored, the four of them moved forward together. A moment later she found herself within the house. They were all standing silently together in a large, gloomy hall. A muffled sound of laughter and voices came from the top of the stairs. Mrs. Dukes tingled rather uncomfortably at these boisterous sounds. But she also wondered at her agitations of a few minutes before.

The old woman who had opened the door to them was very pale, and her eyes followed anxiously the movements of her guests.

She was about sixty, a subdued, respectable sort of woman, who, one divined, had various little social pretentions. Her accent was careful, well buttressed with heavy H's, impeccable in her solid prudence of utterance. One could guess that she had perhaps been a confidential servant in a good family. One felt that she did not aim to have the accent of her betters herself, but rather had set herself to make perfectly firm, grammatical, though perhaps rough, her own speech, that those coming after her would find good ground to build on, a solid foundation.

'I hope, detective, there will be no violence in arresting him. I feel so frightened. All this has come so unexpectedly. It's terrible, just to think of it, that I should have such a man under my roof!'

Mrs. Dukes was at once filled with aggressiveness at the sound of these measured syllables, but could not help feeling sympathetically towards this woman who was, it seemed, in the same difficulty as herself. And a feeling of relief came with this other landlady's presence and troubles.

The constable turned to Mrs. Dukes and said, by way of explanation, 'Yes, 'e took another studier 'ere, see, and's entertainin' 'is friends!'

'Oh Lord! Is 'is friends like 'im?' enquired Mrs. Dukes.

They conversed in whispers. The detective now said, 'If he hears anything that makes him suspicious, he'll bolt. So come up as quietly as possible.'

They all began moving up the stairs noiselessly. Mrs. Dukes, in the middle of them, felt once more the same odd feeling of sudden suspicion she had felt outside. The laughter from the door at the top of the stairs became clearer as they approached. They all drew up in front of it, and Mrs. Dukes opened her eyes wide, as though she could not understand the meaning of the words that reached them through the door. These words were quite simple and straightforward, however. 'Jane's looking like a fish tonight' – one of the phrases – certainly might have seemed unusual to Mrs. Dukes, but the rest was just chatter and mild jokes. Then a shrill and charming voice rose above the rest. 'Mr. Childe's trying to flirt with me, Mr. Nichols. Do stop him – call him off! It's taken me a half an hour to make out what he was doing!' At this unseen lady's appeal there was a good deal of laughter, and then a voice that Mrs. Dukes recognised with a shudder as her lodger's cried boisterously, 'Childe, you have no sense of perspective; you're much too far in the background – the middle distance, let's call it, the respectable distance of middle age, Childe – to flirt with Miss Mackenzie. She's years away from you! She occupies the centre of the picture, she's quite life size, you know. You'll soon be nothing more than a speck on the horizon. You have no sense of perspective! You're a primitive, Childe!' At this bluff hammering away at the unfortunate gentleman named Childe, the other members of the party in progress behind this door laughed heartily. Childe was evidently a source of great fun and solace to them.

Mrs. Dukes looked very alarmed at the end of Mr. Nichols' speech. She nodded towards the detective.

'I do hope there won't be nothing!' exclaimed the lady of the house, fervently and tremblingly. The detective silenced her with a diabolical glance. He turned the handle softly, and motioned Mrs. Dukes to enter; the others remained outside.

Mrs. Dukes found herself in a long narrow chamber, through the farther wall of which at a thousand little holes came soft, yellow light. This amazed Mrs. Dukes extremely, but she soon observed that this was not a wall, but a screen of some sort or other, reaching from floor to ceiling. A large and comfortable bed took up half the room. The voices now were heard quite plainly, and came apparently from underneath. The detective whispered to her to look through one of the holes, and see if she could recognise 'him.' Mrs. Dukes approached with her heart beating, and looked as he had directed her, then quickly drew her face away again. They were on a balcony, looking on to a very large and deep room, that Mrs. Dukes recognised as the sort of place 'artistes' used to paint pictures in. The wall through which the light came was made of fretted wood, and was the facade of some Eastern dwelling, fixed there to wall off the balcony, in which the painter slept.

Beneath her Mrs. Dukes saw a room softly lighted by two lamps, and a company of some eight or ten people, several of them ladies, very queerly dressed, with large rows of beads round their necks, and smoking cigarettes. All the party were extremely merry, and all eating nuts, which they cracked with their teeth – all except Mr. Childe. If Mrs. Dukes had only known it, she was witnessing a vegetarian feast, of which nuts were the most nourishing item in the menu, a plate of very large Brazil nuts taking the place of the homely joint of beef of most households. Mrs. Dukes would have noted, had she been better versed in these matters – I do not think it necessary here to send for the 'person of certain penetration' – two things. Firstly, that probably most of these young people had a vague notion that, in abstaining from animal food, they were behaving less like animals. And secondly, that they cracked the nuts with their teeth in an affected animal joy of having good and formidable teeth. Hence confusion.

In their midst Mrs. Dukes beheld that clean-shaven face that she had seen through the half-open door in Marbury Street, and which had caused her so much apprehension and trouble. It was undoubtedly Mr. Nichols.

'Have some coconut wine, Mrs. Peacey,' he was calling out. 'Palm wine – who wants palm wine?'

A moment later he was exclaiming to a lackadaisical long-haired individual who was gazing up at a portrait on the wall, 'Yes, that's a swashbuckling bit of brushwork, isn't it? He was with me at Julien's.'

'That's 'im!' said Mrs. Dukes.

The 'swashbuckling bit of brushwork' seemed to have loosened her tongue. She didn't know what these strange utterances of Mr. Nichols might signify, and certainly never guessed that they were in any degree for *her* benefit. But this phrase she recognised as peculiarly Nicholish, and her 'that's 'im' went off like a pop gun.

The detective signed to his subordinate, and moving towards a door in the fretwork screen, threw it open, and descended the stairs rapidly with the constable, calling in stentorian tones, 'In the name of the Law!'

One of the fretted lattices had come ajar with the wrench the detective gave at the door. Mrs. Dukes instinctively put her face to it and gazed down.

The women screamed; one of them fell over like a ninepin, while the gentlemen stood aghast.

'In the name of the Law, I arrest you, Charlie Keepsake, alias Ernest Nichols!' roared the detective. Another scream went up from the women. Mrs. Dukes saw Mr. Nichols, to her wonderment, burst out laughing, looking straight at the detective. She was more struck by the peculiarity of this laughter than by anything else. It was anything but his bohemian guffaw. It seemed genuine and sudden, but it at once stopped. The detective's hand closed down on his shoulder, and with the other he seized one of his hands.

Mr. Nichols suddenly wrenched himself free, with the exclamation, distinctly heard by Mrs. Dukes, 'You silly brute!' and the next moment the detective lay sprawling on the floor, landed there by a left-hander struck full in the eye.

Mrs. Dukes saw her former lodger take three steps to the right, and suddenly the lights went out. A vague hubbub rose from beneath, the detective's bellow sounding in the midst of it. A nut diet seemed to render the nerves unsteady, for in this unexpected crisis there was such a horrible sound of people fainting noisily, that it appeared the entire party would in another minute be stretched out unconscious on the floor. Then the balcony shook; somebody was rushing up the stairs in the dark from the studio beneath. Mrs. Dukes turned to run out at the door, but found it shut. At the same moment someone, apparently in full career, collided with her. She was conscious of some faint scent, of a blow on the face, and had a stifling feeling. Then she lost consciousness.

8

COLE MAKES AN AMAZING STATEMENT

An hour or so after the events in the last chapter, in which we left Mrs. Dukes in a state of unconsciousness in the painter's studio, there was a knocking at No. 21, Marbury Street. It was a quarter to nine, and Cole was in the room at the back of the shop. He opened the front door, his eyes fixed intently on the handle. He saw his mother's dress and the bottom of her ulster, and heard her panting a little, but did not raise his eyes to her face or show any signs of recognition. He went back and sat by the fire.

Mrs. Dukes on the contrary, the moment the door opened, exclaimed, 'Oh Lord, Cole, 'ow long you do take! Oh dear me! Those cramps 'ave been at me for the last 'alf hour somethin' awful. Fancy draggin' anybody out on a night like this! Does the kettle boil?' And so she went on in her usual way. But she did not seem communicative about her adventures. She abused the police, and she added that anyway they'd done their duty this time, and that they shouldn't be troubled any more with Mr. Nichols. And she added: 'All I 'ad to do was to point 'im out where 'e was with a lot of others.' A quarter of an hour afterwards Cole was in the same position by the fire, and Mrs. Dukes sipping her tea in silence. She was doing at the same time something that she had never done before. She was looking keenly and as it were questioningly at Cole. She would say something, or carry on her usual scolding dialogue, and watch him narrowly the while. And at last, a thing that Cole had never done before, he lost his indifference and immobility, and began to fidget.

Suddenly he looked up – not squarely but sidelong, with his almond-shaped squinting eyes – at his mother, and instantly cast them down in the fire again. His fidgetiness increased. Then he got up and walked out.

Mrs. Dukes called after him, 'Where are ye goin', Cole? I'm goin' to bed now, it's nearly ten and you 'aven't washed the dishes up yet.'

He paid no heed to this, but five minutes later he came back and took up his place at the fire again.

The room seemed more wretched than ever, and somehow its dirt and squalor seemed no longer to have a reason. The large table cumbered with things – at the back, against the wall, a deep layer of dusty objects that were never moved, some had been in the same place for years – and, nearer, a thinner collection of odds and ends not so permanent, and in the foreground a dirty plate, the morning paper, Mrs. Dukes' gloves; the bed that resembled Mrs. Dukes herself, formless, sometimes bulging up in one place, sometimes in another, apparently made in three parts, leaning against each other, adhering in one clinging mass of slovenliness; the old calendars and texts on the wall, and the grandfather's clock ticking lei-surely, as though time were a matter of no consequence to it – all these things, all the contents of the room, seemed to be withholding their peace and their customary gift of barrenness and blankness. They appeared to be sulky and brooding like Cole.

When Mrs. Dukes began to prepare for bed, Cole left

abruptly, going upstairs to his room. There were still several things to wash up, but Mrs. Dukes did not stop him. This was truly amazing. After waiting a short time she locked the door. About two hours after this, Mrs. Dukes was sound asleep, and snoring loudly, the faint flame of the night-light throwing a tragic and peaceful little light over the disordered room. Where the blind hung aslant, broken somewhere in its machinery of strings, against the window that gave on to the yard at the back, Cole's face was pressed, looking into the room, expressionless, deadly white like his mother's, his blinking eyes fixed on the bed. The face was no longer there a few minutes later, and a door shut noiselessly at the foot of the stairs.

The next morning the day, with its little round of duties, began as usual for Mrs. Dukes. But what had come over her? Each individual of us has a certain gusto in doing things proper to himself, especially in those trivial domestic things of which the animal life is composed. Mrs. Dukes seemed in some subtle way to have lost this. Cole silently reminded her, by his actions merely, of certain things she had forgotten. Several details she had omitted in the preparation of their mid-day meal, for instance.

About two o'clock, a young man speaking very little English, a Belgian, he said, asked to see the room to let.

'Are yew *sure* yew want it?' said Mrs. Dukes, in her semi-farcical manner. 'Because there was two young men 'ere last week that didn't know their own minds. *I* don't believe they wanted rooms at all. But they *thought* they did. They dragged me all up there for nothin'.'

The Belgian smiled, and it was evident he understood very little of what was said to him.

Mrs. Dukes preceded him up the stairs. Arrived at the third floor, she opened the door of a small room looking on the street, saying, 'This is the room; it 'asn't got a washstand in it yet. But I can get Cole to put one in by tonight, if yew really mean to take it.'

As soon as they were inside, the Belgian said in a low voice, and in perfect English, 'Did everything go off all right?'

Mrs. Dukes' expression did not alter in the least, and she was just opening her mouth to reply, when a door opened abruptly, and a lodger stepped out on to the landing to fill his jug from the tap.

'Well, can't ye make up ye mind?' said Mrs. Dukes, her head on one side.

'Oh yess, qui' well; I vill take him,' replied the young man.

'Very well, you shall 'ave the washstand there and everything ready by this evenin'. When do ye think yew'll come?'

They now began moving downstairs again, and in a moment's lull, Mrs. Dukes nodded her head quietly but emphatically; the Belgian seemed to understand.

He moved in that evening; he had only a small foreign valise.

The curate had gone out very early in the morning, but when he got back about four in the afternoon, he at once knocked at Mrs. Dukes' door.

'I hope you're none the worse, Mrs. Dukes, for your walk last night in the fog. I think, ill as you were, they might have chosen another time. I hope it was nothing that may cause you fresh trouble, Mrs. Dukes?'

'Oh no, nothin', thank you. I feel much better this mornin', only a little dazed, *yew* know!'

'You seem rather hoarse, Mrs. Dukes. You seem to have a cold. I should not neglect it, they are nasty things in this weather.'

47

He went upstairs with a sigh of resignation. Certainly Mrs. Dukes was very close.

As Mrs. Dukes and Cole sat over the fire that night, Cole began chuckling.

'Oo are you?' he said suddenly. 'You're not mother.'

'Oo am I, Cole? Whatever are ye talkin' about. What've ye got in ye 'ead now, I should like to know?'

'Where's mother?' Cole spoke again.

'What's come to ye, Cole! I do believe ye've gone off yer 'ead. Ye poor old mother leaves yew for an hour or two, and when she comes back yew've forgotten what she looks like.'

Cole did not stir, but went on gazing into the fire with an expression of complete indifference, his momentary gaiety gone. He did not open his lips again before going to bed, and left as Mrs. Dukes began to make her toilet, as he had done on the previous night, and she shut and bolted the door. He seemed to be getting into the new ways of the house.

Before getting into bed, Mrs. Dukes looked at herself from several different points of view in the glass. It was Mrs. Dukes' face, her mask, but not her eyes. She never had looked critically, coldly, *professionally* at herself as she now, to all appearance, was doing. A moment afterwards, although her swathing still remained on, it was no longer Mrs. Dukes' head on the body. With fair hair cut short, and death-white clean-shaven face stood Ernest Nichols, the second floor lodger. He had taken off the wig and false crown, and assumed in various other details his normal aspect. He seemed as calm and as much at home in Mrs. Dukes' den as though he had in truth passed all his days there. He got into bed, yawned, turned over, and in a few minutes was fast asleep.

9
A PRISONER

Mrs. Dukes remembered very little. She did not know how long she had been in a state of unconsciousness. She found herself in bed in a small whitewashed room, with two or three texts on the wall, a small crucifix at her bedside, and glasses and bottles on a table near at hand.

Steps occasionally passed along what, it seemed, was a stone gallery outside the door, and there was a murmur of voices now and then as a door opened and shut. She felt very weak indeed. She supposed that she was in a hospital; the appearance of the room led her to believe this. She had only opened her eyes a few minutes, when, from behind a screen at the foot of her bed rose a uniformed figure. It was a young woman about twenty-five, with the blue cotton frock and white cap of a nurse.

She came up to Mrs. Dukes' side, and asked her in a gentle voice how she felt.

'You must not on any account move, or try to get up. You have been in a very critical state for twenty-four hours, but we have managed to pull you through. You must stay quietly here for a week or so, and get your strength back again. Do you remember anything of the occurrence that led to this?'

'I remember seein' Mr. Nichols in the studio, and − ' she spoke weakly and with hesitation, and the nurse interrupted her.

'Yes, you had a fright. That was a most dangerous man, and you have done a great service in helping to arrest him. He knocked you over in trying to escape. Now try and get a little sleep. I shall be here if you want anything.' And she went back to her place behind the screen.

Mrs. Dukes lay trying to realise what had just been said to her, and what she had replied. 'You done a *great* service,' she repeated over to herself. 'You done a great service in tryin' to arrest 'im.' She tried to raise her hands to cross them on her breast. She could only do so with difficulty. She became suddenly afraid at finding herself so weak. She jerked her body convulsively, as though to sit up in bed. It was then she discovered that something tight, muffled with the clothes, held her where she was. She was tied down!

With a little cry of terror she wriggled weakly on the bed. She was mad, she thought. She had gone mad, and this was not a hospital but a mad house.

She lay quite still again. She stared in front of her at the wall, and her eyes fixed on a nail that had once held a text or calendar, doubtless. She gradually became conscious of an insane desire to get up and touch this nail with her finger – to pull it out.

As she became conscious of this feeling, her terror came back to her with a rush. She wished to cry out, but the cry seemed to stick in her throat.

Click, click, click went a needle behind the screen, and occasionally she heard what sounded to her like the swishing of silk.

There was a step in the passage and the door opened quietly. A small, very dark, clean-shaven man, dressed in a frock coat, and holding a top hat in his hand, entered, placing the hat on the table.

The nurse came quickly from behind the screen, and said, 'Good morning, doctor.'

'Good morning, nurse; has the patient had a quiet morning?' he replied.

'Yes. She woke up a few minutes ago for the first time. She

remembers quite clearly what preceded her attack. She seems very weak still.'

Mrs. Dukes fixed her eyes on the doctor, and a strange and insistent thought possessed her. Where had she seen him? She struggled with her memory, her eyes fixed all the while on his face, and her expression at that moment would have justified anyone in doubting of her sanity. He seemed uncomfortable under her scrutiny.

'Do you feel any pain here, my good woman?' he asked, laying his hand on her throat.

She did not reply but went on staring at him, the contact of his hand filling her with a new sensation that she was trying in vain to analyse.

He repeated his question.

'No,' she replied hoarsely. 'Do you? Because if ye don't, take yer hand off my neck!'

'I can't feel your pains, my good woman,' said he, taking his hand away, 'but it is for your own good I ask you, and so I expect a reasonable answer.'

'Well, ye won't get one,' replied still more hoarsely Mrs. Dukes. 'I'm mad, *yew* know that, so how can ye 'spect a reason'ble answer?'

The doctor looked astonished, and turned inquiringly towards the nurse. She shrugged her shoulders.

'You're not mad, Mrs. Dukes,' he said in a moment, 'and are quite capable of giving a reasonable answer if you wish to. But it is essential in your present condition that you should not excite yourself. As you seem determined to put difficulties in our way, I will leave you for the moment. You must ask nurse at once if you require anything, and get as much rest as you can.'

He seemed a very touchy little man indeed, and was flushed

and held himself very stiffly as he left the room.

The nurse followed him out, and closed the door behind her. In the passage outside, where they had taken a few steps, the doctor said to her in a low voice: 'If she seems to be getting too energetic, tighten the strap, and give her a dose out of the blue bottle. But if this doesn't seem necessary, just keep on with the other medicine.'

His business of healing did not seem to agree with his temper at all. Taking infinite trouble and pains to keep people alive seemed to go against the grain of this sullen and stiff-backed little doctor. He was one of those doctors whom, one feels, are willing to cure and do all the good you please to people, on condition they are allowed to hack them about and cut them up a bit first!

10
THE CURATE GIVES SOME TROUBLE

The next morning in Marbury Street the new Mrs. Dukes got up as she apparently resolved always to do, some half hour before Cole's appearance. After a wash and sponge down – being careful not to splash the water on the floor, for signs of so much water might cause the observant to question if this really were Mrs. Dukes or not some other – she, or rather Mr. Nichols, for he had not yet become Mrs. Dukes for the day, laid out several little boxes on the table, preparatory to 'making up.' By the time Cole was heard coming downstairs, Mrs. Dukes was up and dressed, and her scolding voice rang with a fresh and early gusto.

He came in, and they had breakfast together.

There were certain little differences to be noticed in Cole's manner. But they were all strongly in favour of the new Mrs. Dukes. A certain relief, expansiveness and even more frequent gaiety were to be noticed in him. Not in words, but in a hundred subtle little ways, instantly felt by Mrs. Dukes, who thoroughly appreciated them. He did not call Mrs. Dukes 'old cock,' and he was not capable, even in his own kind of silent speech, of such colloquialism. But one felt he would not have resented this interpretation being put on some of his glances and half-grins. His attitude seemed one of mildly gleeful complicity in the new state of things. There was not a shadow of doubt, to one who could read him, as the penetrating Mr. Nichols could, that Cole thoroughly approved of the change. When Mrs. Dukes was scolding at him at her best, it did not seem to render him 'sulky' as in the time of the first Mrs. Dukes, but he often stood, looking on the ground, it is true, but with an expression of vague whimsical enjoyment. So the first shock of recognition, or non-recognition, over, Cole and Mrs. Dukes, as we shall continue to call the young artist for the present, got on splendidly, in their respectively quiet and noisy ways.

The eight o'clock post brought an official looking letter addressed to Mrs. Dukes.

She opened it slowly and suspiciously.

It may here be remarked that in their strictest intimacy never did the second Mrs. Dukes depart from her role for an instant. She felt that any slackness or carelessness of this sort would be resented by Cole. Cole was delighted with her as she was — delighted to play up to her, and tickled at her skill. But she felt it would be an irretrievable mistake ever to drop the mask or give up the play, by which he was so strangely fascinated.

'Oh Lord, Cole!' exclaimed Mrs. Dukes. 'Who'd ever 'ave

thought of Cousin Anne remembering me after all these years. She's left us sixty pounds by her will. 'Messrs. Perkins, Hopkins & Bobbs, have the honour to inform Mrs. Dukes,' – sixty pounds, Cole! That ain't so bad. Now I'll do something that I've long been thinkin' about. I'll 'ave that first floor spring-cleaned and papered and done up nice, and I'll let it permanent like – not like with Mr. 'igginbotham, or that last one, Mrs. Grace, oo's in one month and out the next.'

And she went on to develop her plans to the motionless Cole.

The upshot of all this was that when the curate came home for tea, Mrs. Dukes, rather stiff and solemn, was at her door, and asked him if she might speak to him a moment.

'Certainly, Mrs. Dukes,' he replied, with a leisureliness that ill matched his curiosity.

'Well, I'm very sorry, Mr. 'igginbotham, but I shall want your room at the end of the week.'

His disappointment, combined with his annoyance at this piece of news, stirred some uncanny depth of choler in the young curate.

'Really, Mrs. Dukes, I'm afraid I shall not be able to let you have the room at such short notice. You let it me until the end of the month, and I have made my arrangements accordingly.'

Whether it was that the human being beneath the mask of Mrs. Dukes could not resist the temptation of seeing further into this choleric gulf that had suddenly, ever so mildly, of course, opened up in Mr. Higginbotham, or whether merely it seemed more true to his original, and more thoroughly Dukesesque manner, as he called it, to bridle and stiffen, become obstinate and combative, it is difficult to say.

The fact remains that Mrs. Dukes' voice grew a shade more unpleasant, as she said, 'I'm very sorry, Mr. 'igginbotham, but

I must 'ave the rooms at the end of the week. I'm not goin' to let them any more that way, but get someone permanent.'

'If you've suddenly made up your mind to do that, Mrs. Dukes, well and good; but I'm afraid you must wait till the end of the month, as it's not convenient for me to move just now.'

With this the curate 'passed' – yes, passed – up the staircase.

It was an excess of combativeness that had suddenly taken hold of him. His blood was boiling inside of his chilly frock. And indeed, with certain reason: for Mrs. Dukes' excuse was not adequate, and was in itself a provocation.

'Damn that beggar, he's going to give trouble!' was what Mrs. Dukes thought.

What she said was, 'Cole! What 'ave you been doin' to the bed? 'Ave you been burrowin', or what? It looks as though there'd bin an irupchin!'

A penny that Cole had found on the mantel-piece, and been handling, had rolled under the bed, and he had, as a matter of fact, been 'burrowing' – frantically. He was afraid of money. Going to market was an ordeal for him for this reason. His mother knew his touchiness and shrinking feeling on this point, and never questioned or counted before him the change he brought back.

That night, before getting into bed, Mrs. Dukes reflected in the following way. As Mr. Nichols, still very white from the paint, sat thinking on his bed, his head looked very extraordinary, and more marked and stamped with character than Mrs. Dukes' was with age.

'I must get rid of that parson now, anyhow. If it was necessary before, it is now doubly so, for he is certainly very angry. If he saw anything that puzzled him, got even vaguely suspicious, out of pure cussedness he would become almost intelligent, would watch, and perhaps see through it all one fine day. Before, if he'd fancied he saw anything odd about his landlady, he would have put the idea aside as absurd. His analytical powers are not very great, I should suppose. Then again, the animal's keen to know what was up — with detectives calling and all that. His observation is sharpened because of that. Of course, at any time he might have smelt a rat in any case, and that was one reason why he had to go. The other lodgers — my friend Hanz Schulz, the little French cook and the Swiss — they don't matter a bit. I don't suppose they ever noticed Mrs. Dukes, beyond the fact that she was old, and looked as though she'd be nasty if they didn't pay. I hope I wasn't too "realistic" though with Higginbotham. We must see whether we can smooth it down a bit and yet get rid of him, tomorrow.'

II

AN INFLAMMABLE YOUNG POET

About the same time as these things were happening in Marbury Street — to be exact, on the evening after Mrs. Dukes had notified the curate that she should want his rooms — something very remarkable occurred to a young man, who at this point enters into our story.

Hercules Fane was twenty-five years old and a poet. For the last year or so he had gained a precarious livelihood in 'walking on' in theatres. At that moment he was gaining thirty shillings a week at the Daphne Theatre.

Some quite ordinary people have such splendid 'presences' that the Stage Manager is torn between the desire to have them walking about his boards, and the fear that they will upset the equilibrium, the perspective of the piece. They dwarf the Stars, extinguish the Suns, look more immense, even more interesting often than anybody else on the stage; the Public rivets its eyes upon them, expecting them to begin speaking at every moment and reveal themselves; and yet through the whole piece, of course, they merely walk about, monuments of silence! If they have a word or two to say, when they utter their 'Hear, hear,' or 'This is from the Lady Elvira, my lord,' the Public is thrilled to the liveliest attention; but as they relapse immediately into their provoking silence again, a quick disappointment follows. The audience ends by getting angry with these dummies.

Hercules Fane, despite his Christian name, was not one of these people. He was short, not even of medium height. But still, short men as well as tall were always wanted — were *useful,* though not ornamental. He had managed to get fairly constant employment, thanks to the good offices of a friend of his, who had started him at a theatre the Manager of which he knew.

Still it was hard-commons, and the flesh-pots of Egypt that his poet's fancy cruelly conjured up before him so constantly seemed destined never to be tasted in the flesh by him.

In the piece then being given at the Daphne Theatre, he had some twenty words to say. He said them every night and twice a week at matinees to an accompaniment of roaring laughter beneath him — for they were twenty of the most facetious words in the piece. It seemed to him rather like firing off a cannon. Its great mouth bellowed infallibly each time he dropped his twenty words into it. He was terrified the first time it happened, but gradually got used to the noise. He would even sometimes strain his vocal powers to the utmost, and put all the quaintness he could into his little speech, for the fun of seeing it go off with a louder bang.

On the night in question he had kept his eyes fixed on a box, where sat, with an air of indulgent amusement, a very beautiful young woman. She was letting herself be amused.

He was fascinated by her beauty and her 'ennui,' almost luxuriously allowing itself to be slightly entertained, to be more conscious of itself. The heavy white shoulders, however, as he looked at them, and as they slowly moved, she turning to exchange a word with her companion, a large dark man — these puissant shoulders seemed made to shake in riotous laughter, and heave up like a heavy wave.

He determined to put laughter into them — to *make* her laugh, to put wild laughter into her body.

'A beautiful woman shall weep for me tonight,' said he to himself.

Flushed with this great idea, the young poet became extremely excited as the time for his speech came round. He entered wonderfully into the spirit of the piece, and became of an extraordinary vivacity.

At last his turn came. He said his words with such amazing spirit that one old gentleman in the stalls had an apoplectic fit, and several others most certainly hastened their deaths by their undue excesses of mirth, while all through the rest of the scene isolated individuals were going off like a cross between a paper bag and a syphon.

But the thing that interested him most was the beautiful young lady in the box. He had retired to his place again, his words said. He eagerly looked up in her direction, and, to his delight, saw every sign of the ravages of the tempest in her streaming eyes, and the subsiding convulsions of her person.

But at this sight — whether it were that his victory had rendered him capricious and proud, or that what he had admired in her was her indifference and her ennui, which he had destroyed – our poet no longer took so much interest in her.

But still, this was not the first time that beautiful ladies in the boxes had attracted his attention, and caused him to curse his fate as an impecunious 'walker-on,' and still more impecunious poet. The nearness of these boxes to the stage seemed almost appalling to him sometimes. There within a foot or two of him every night was the very elite of an idle and adorable world. He hardly saw the rest of the theatre – it was a vague roar, buzz or silence in a gaping greyness. But he was amongst these people in the boxes.

Then another thing that distressed him very much was that he nearly always had 'funny' parts, or rather the few words he had to say were ridiculous and laughter provoking. His spirit was a poet's, he was not a verse-writing poet, but a prose-writing poet – even after the slight disappointment of this revelation, which we kept back as long as possible, we shall still continue to refer to him as a poet – but the only thing he could express, or the thing he could express best in the flesh, by his body, was uproarious comedy.

That evening he took a particularly sombre view of life as he was dressing. The episode with the beautiful lady in the box had caused a good part of his depression. It was not the buffoon – who had moved her, it is true, but only to laughter – that the beautiful lady might dream about, but the tall, handsome stalking 'supers' that she watched with apparent cold indulgent ennui.

At the stage door he remembered that he only had four shillings in his pocket, and must keep them for his next two days living. He turned with a desperate swing of his body, as though he were swinging a horse round, in the direction of home – a small room on the third floor of a lodging house in further Bloomsbury, that part of it that is within sound of three great stations.

A man stepped quickly up, and after a moment's hesitation, looking hard at him, said civilly, 'Excuse me, sir, but was it you who played the second councillor's part?'

'Yes, it was I,' replied Fane.

'Then I have a note for you, sir.' With this he handed him an envelope.

Within, Fane found the following note hurriedly written:

Dear Sir.

I was much struck by your acting. If you have nothing to do would you favour me with your company at supper at the Cafe Firenze. My man will conduct you to the room I have reserved there.

H.S.

Fane turned immediately to the man, and said, 'You have orders to take me to the Cafe Firenze? Let's go at once.'

12

A HANDSOME OFFER

Who did Fane expect to meet in this private room of one of the most expensive restaurants in London? He purposely forbore to ask his conductor any questions. He could not help wondering, however, what anyone could have seen in any way attractive in the figure of a little bald old man, which had been his part that night. He knew himself to be a not ill-looking young man, and he was comforted at the thought that at least one of the disillusions that so often await those fallen beneath the charm of an actor would not await his correspondent. His collar was not over clean. He covered it carefully with his scarf. First impressions are everything.

They ascended the thick red plush carpet of the Firenze to the first floor, and the man now knocked at one of the three heavy gilt doors before them.

A deep voice said 'come in,' and with a feeling of disgust and mortification, the poet found himself in the presence of a very tall, black-bearded man, with the face and complexion of an Arab, and a dignity that only such handsomeness as was his can impart. He took Fane's hand and said very amiably, with the faintest trace of a foreign accent, 'Ah, it's so good of you to have come. I was so de-lided with your acting, and wanted to know you. You have real talent.' He turned to the table, saying, 'But let's have supper! I expect after your performance it will not be unwelcome. We will discuss your talent and what you are going to do with it afterwards.'

Fane had almost at once recognised him as the man who had been seated with the lady to whom his evening's homage had gone out. And he flushed rather when the other continued.

'My niece also was delided with your acting. I have *nev*-er seen her laugh so much! Did you not see us? We were in the first box, over the Royal box. I suppose, though, the audience is a non-existent quantity for you.'

His host's eyes were perfectly calm and expressed nothing but the reflection of his smile, a suavity without *arrière-pensé*. But in looking at him, Fane felt that he had been perfectly aware of the attention paid to his niece by the young actor. 'That beggar was watching me the whole time, I expect,' thought Fane. 'It's quite on the cards he saw the whole *manège* from the very first time I began looking up at them; he watched me, perhaps, work myself up for my part, and noticed my getting back to my place afterwards, and at once looking up in their direction. In that case, what on earth's he up to?'

The supper passed off in general talk about the Theatre. His host professed to love the Theatre as few people do.

'The whole thought of acting fascinates me,' said he. 'Even those people in life I'm fondest of are those that bring exaggeration into the life around them, *du théâtre* in short. I sometimes think my love of the theatre has spoilt my love of life. I was on the stage myself, but was forced to abandon it, as I took everything so much *au sérieux* in the pieces in which I played, entered so blindly into the spirit of the thing, that I couldn't stand the strain. It was literally as though I were ravaged by some event of actual living tragedy every night of the week. Then I used to conceive the most atrocious hatred for my enemies in the piece, and these sometimes continued even after the walls of the theatre were left behind. As these emotions had no connection or *rapport* with our relations in real life, or even with the personality of the man I hated, indescribable confusion ensued. And my love for the heroine was often so poignant that my days were spent in one long state of suffering, if she did not return my love in reality — and she could not *always,* of course. Nothing in life has ever been able to exasperate me so much as the reply some of those women with whom I played made to my declarations of love, outside the theatre — 'But it was only a part of *the play,* I haven't *really* those sentiments for you!' Only a part of the play! This shocked and stung the born actor in me. For I had loved these women with a strength more than I ever could have loved a woman in real life! All my greatest feelings, in fact, possessed me only when I was feigning.'

While he talked, and became animated in the course of this self- revelation, Fane was amazed at the subtlety of this man's face, that could suggest *in petto* – subdued and on a small scale, for the cabinet, so to speak, and hardly raising his voice – the 'fugue' and strength of great emotions, that needed a stage as wide as the world itself if they were to find scope for their gestures and their sound.

Fane as he watched this dark face, a light of unknown evil breaking through the suavity of its gaze, felt that, on the whole, he would not care to have this man's stage-passions pursuing *him* into the quiet of ordinary life. Also he felt that, in one of those stage scenes where daggers and swords are innocuously brandished, and plunged into the padded cloth beside the heart, that he would have felt very uncomfortable had it fallen to his lot to be this man's mock-antagonist.

Despite these reflections, Fane was perfectly attentive to his host's discourse, and indeed was more and more fascinated despite himself by the nature he divined beneath. The other, however, in the middle of a further disquisition, drew up short, as though suddenly feeling that perhaps these autobiographical details from a complete stranger would hardly interest the young man, and attempted to draw Fane out in his turn, asking him how he had come to be an actor, and what his particular ambitions were.

Fane made no secret of the poorness of his prospects and even of his desire to follow another profession. He liked the stage well enough, but all its magic for him was when he was off it. It was as draughty as a station platform, and, although it was true that it was the theatre of the human passions, he saw quite a different set of passions from those seen by the public; and although for the public it seemed every night the same piece, for the actor it was every night a different one, and much less heroic.

His new friend smiled at the story of his discomforts and

disgusts, and broke in at last, 'Yes, yes, but it would be a very different thing if you were one of the Stars. It would be just as different as life is to the rich and to the poor. Now, I am convinced of your talent; and although I cannot offer you a part in another theatre for the moment, I can offer you another and infinitely better part in *life,* which is not so circumscribed and where there is more scope for talent. May I ask you how much you get at the Daphne?'

'Thirty shillings a week,' Fane answered hesitatingly.

'Well, I will give you six guineas a week, and will engage you at once for two months, if you will join a private company that I have just got together. The work would be by no means irksome, and there would be free scope for your talent.'

Whether it were that the animation — and all animation with this man seemed to light up something evil within him, and to impart an almost sinister look to his superb bronzed face — whether it were that something of this remained over from his excitement while telling about himself, or whether it were a new sentiment, Fane recoiled and became suddenly almost afraid, as the other leant across the table to him in making this proposition. He leant across the table, in the attitude of a man bargaining. This was one thing that caused suddenly a chilly feeling in the young poet's susceptible spine. A bargain! A bargain was being struck! For what, about what? Dim memories of Faust came to him, and he plunged his eyes in these deep, black, luminous, watching eyes fixed on him — without fishing anything up! All his scrutiny did was to make him feel colder, as though he had taken a plunge in icy water. What did this man want with him? Why had he sent for him?

Suddenly the stranger rose, and walking quickly to the door, turned the key.

13

WHAT MANNER OF MAN?

Fane had half started up from his chair, as though to stop his disquieting host from doing what he had divined he was about to do. But the latter smiled on seeing his gesture, and went back to his place, leaving the key in the door.

'Don't be alarmed. I only do that so that we shan't be interrupted. I want to have a good talk with you, and I want us to understand each other perfectly. Remember, you're not obliged to do anything. If you don't think you would like what I am proposing to you, you only have to say so, and I shall not feel disappointed, except at losing the opportunity of utilising your talents. And I shall always have been charmed to have passed such an agreeable evening. But I think if you understand what I want, you will see how much more congenial and advantageous the place I offer you is than your present one at the Daphne Theatre. As it is, you will go on for some years — some years, think! five, six — getting staler and staler and more and more tired of existence, with no rise of salary, probably, and nothing at the end of it. The best of your time is taken up with new rehearsals and performances, and when you are out of work you cannot write your books as you want to, for the pinch of poverty takes all the heart out of you. I offer you at the present moment nothing but a temporary thing, it is true. But if we get on well together, and you would like to continue in my company, you can do so. All you would have to do just now would be to attend at a small theatre every day for two or three hours, and learn to imitate exactly and get into the way of talking, way of thinking, like an original, a model, I would give you. This is the prime difference between our theatre, which has the whole world for its stage, and the theatre that you are used to. We improvise. No pieces are written for us. The actors act the part as they go along. This is what I myself always wished to do when I was acting. Not only to 'gag,' but to go on with the play myself, develop the situation myself, without reference to the playwright. This is how the idea of my present theatre came to me, in fact. I wanted to see actors no longer bound by the 'piece' they had to play, but to *act* and *live* at the same time. You have no doubt seen the account in the papers of Maeterlink's experiment. Macbeth was played all over the grounds and house chosen for the occasion – one scene taking place on one room, another in the cellar, a third in the back yard. The audience followed these mysterious players about, and watched the scene from a corner, or from a gallery, as though it were really taking place. Well, we do not play Macbeth, but we enact tragedies and comedies of all sorts. Not in a house and its grounds, but all over the country. The play goes on sometimes in several places at the same time. One of the present players in my company is playing his part six thousand miles away from here, without audience, but none the worse for that. All my players are chosen because I feel them to be *born* actors. Then, you will ask, what sort of dramas do we play?'

He paused a moment, and his eyes were fixed so terribly on Fane's in this pause, that the young man remained without moving in his place, reminded vaguely of the Ancient Mariner, and wondering what curse had laid its hand on this dark and passionate man, that everything should assume such tragic proportions in his mind. The gaze he riveted on Fane seemed quite involuntary; he did not seem able to take his eyes off his listener, off any one that was listening to him – the contrary of what usually is found, namely, the listener that cannot take his eyes off the narrator.

'What dramas do we play?' He repeated in a minute or two, his voice deeper and harder for the pause, and its slight foreign accent stronger than before. 'You would not have us play nothing but light comedy? You would not, because we fear the dangers, the adventures of life, keep on playing nothing but farce, and tame comedies? No! In life as on the stage, the greatest spirits are attracted by another type of playing. Some of our playing is *tragic,* and we do not fear the dangers that this involves!'

Fane began to wonder if this were a madman; or rather he was quite convinced he was a madman, but he wondered if all the strange things suggested in his words were figments of his brain, or if they had a real existence. He felt suddenly startled at this thought, as though waking out of a dream. If they *had* a real existence, what did all this mean, who was this before him? The quaint thought came to him that it might be Jack the Ripper! The next word, pronounced suddenly and loudly, made him veritably jump.

'Crime! What is crime? The man that kills his sweetheart because she is unfaithful, the man that gains a fortune that necessitates the starving of many, Napoleon — all are criminals! It is only the sordid intention that makes the really despicable criminal.' Then, with one of the sudden changes of manner that characterised this extraordinary man, his face relaxed, and with some of his old suavity, with occasional bursts of tragic solemnity, that his musical foreign accent in some way saved from being ridiculous, he went on.

'But I am alarming you unnecessarily! I would of course ask nothing *criminal* of you. Your part would be quite well defined, and it would be purely to do with your profession, namely acting. It would be like an engagement in any other theatre. Nor am I a criminal,' and he smiled suddenly. Then his face became dark for a moment. 'I lie. I am a criminal. I am proud of it. I should be a coward to disown it. And I will not deny that people in my employ have committed criminal actions – but unwittingly. I take *all* on my shoulders! I hide nothing from you! I cannot be more explicit than I am. Then I was taken with you. I saw you looking at our box. I read your thoughts, I lived your life for that hour or so on the stage, I saw the gusto you put into your speech that set the house in a roar, I saw you look up at our lodge, I read afterwards your disillusion! Yes! I was moved by this quiet and secret little drama, so whimsical and passionate and lively, more than by the ranting of that absurd Almario, who gets a hundred pounds a week! And then you were the man, physically, that I was in search of. I am quite frank with you, and I hope my frankness at least will have its reward in gaining your confidence. When I tell you I need nothing of you but an innocent employment, that I should be employing you now as an actor, nothing more, I hope you will believe me, and if my proposal seems to show you a life more in conformity with your ambitions and tastes – no mere routine of a 'banal,' commonplace theatre, but good pay! time! freedom! – if so, I hope you will take up my offer for what it is worth. You could begin studying your part tomorrow, and you would be perfectly at liberty to dissolve your engagement at any time you thought fit. We would have an agreement drawn up in the customary form, etc. Well, do you take my offer?' he said brusquely, almost roughly.

A change had gradually come over Fane's feelings in the course of the latter part of this speech. He had been curiously won by his strange entertainer's account of his watching him on the stage, and an enormous sincerity seemed to possess this man's words at the same time as a mad vehemence, and the suggestion of all sorts of wild and unguessable things. His magnetism was enormous, and for a romantic young man like Hercules Fane the violence, the mystery, the physical beauty, and tremendous impression of power this stranger gave, each had its peculiar effect on him.

He was confronted on the one hand, if he continued at the Daphne Theatre, with just the mediocre, wearying, dreary life his new friend had pictured. His imagination told him he could not be worse off than he was – to go and rob a stage coach would be a thousand times better. And here was an offer that promised at least excitement, and his curiosity was thoroughly awoken. And the little prudence that was left to him by this time was finally soothed by his real conviction that what this man said could be relied on, and that he was at least not in immediate danger of getting into trouble, or being asked to do anything – what? – anything strange!

He accepted. He accepted quite quietly on the conditions his new employer had laid down. The latter wrote him out a cheque for six guineas, his first week's pay, then and there; and before he left the room all was arranged for the following morning, for his initiation. He was to be called for by the servant who had conducted him to the Firenze, and again personally conducted to his new place of work. He returned to his rooms, his head whirling. But the six guineas, his youth, curiosity, and the magic of adventure were stronger than his prudence or his scruples.

14
AT LAST!

Two mornings after Mrs. Dukes' difficulty with the curate, a strange scene might have been witnessed in the room at the back of the shop.

Cole was smoking a pipe by the fire!

He was doing so quite indifferently; but then Cole had an extraordinary dislike of showing his feelings, and from the steadiness and absorption with which he was puffing away at this brand new Meerschaum, it would have been surmised, by a penetrating observer, with a knowledge of Cole's psychology, that he was enjoying it in no small degree.

Mrs. Dukes was watching him with an air of grave satisfaction from her arm-chair.

'Oh Lord, Cole, what a *horrid* smell!' she was saying.

The room was rapidly filling with a dense blue smoke, for Cole was an energetic smoker, and puffed the smoke out again as soon as it had filled his mouth, being extremely careful not to swallow any of it. If Mrs. Dukes went out of the room for a moment, he would follow the clouds of smoke mournfully with his eye, and puff harder than ever.

She had presented him with a pipe and tobacco on the preceding day; he had recognised the gift only by a swift under glance at his benefactress, and had then disappeared into the cellar. But a few hours later, on coming downstairs from a visit she had paid to the Belgian, she found him enveloped in clouds of smoke. Some days later Mrs. Dukes came to the conclusion that this had been one of the obscure desires of Cole's life – that he had always wanted a pipe, but had always been too 'sulky' to ask his mother for one.

The reason for this gift was apparent when, Cole being sent out for something, or being engaged upstairs in making the beds, Mrs. Dukes herself drew out of a dusty corner a well used Meerschaum, and had a pipe or two with great relish. Also before going to bed, and in waking up in the morning, she indulged in another pipe or two. The new Mrs. Dukes was a great smoker! Evidently no one could accuse her of this unladylike habit if it were established that Cole had taken to smoking.

She was now in the midst of Cole's smoke, reflecting in the following manner.

'I wonder if that beggar of a curate is going to give trouble? He's sulking just at present – like Cole! – and hasn't come near me for a couple of days; when I wake him up in the morning, he says very politely, 'Thank you, Mrs. Dukes!' If he won't go, he *won't,* of course. But I think my plan is the best, and most likely will succeed. It'll be great fun, too!'

Just then the front door bell rang, and Mrs. Dukes said, 'Ah!' Cole answered it; he came back, saying, 'Somebody.'

Mrs. Dukes dragged herself out, and found in the hall a portly, eupeptic, rich-voiced, oleaginous clergyman, looking rather like the skipper of a passenger steamer, who spent most of the time with the ship's guests. He was very brick red, and very dark, and stepped forward in a kind of heavy mincing manner. Mrs. Dukes' eyes lighted up with what would have seemed real enjoyment at the sight of this individual – critical delight – only how on earth should Mrs. Dukes have a feeling of this sort for a complete stranger?

'I believe, madame, you have some rooms to let. May I see them?' he said with brief urbanity.

'Well, I shall 'ave some rooms soon; I 'ave the first floor rooms that I intend doing up new, as soon as the gentleman what 'as them now is gone. He's a gentleman of *your* cloth,' she continued with a snigger.

'Oh, really,' said the clergyman, as though feeling he had to show an interest in the presence of the cloth, 'oh, really.'

'Now, if you could *wait* a week or two – '

'Ah, I'm afraid I should want them at once,' he said decidedly. 'Have you none that could be occupied immediately? It would be for a year anyway, I expect — '

'Come up and see the first floor, will ye,' cried Mrs. Dukes, as though coming to a sudden decision.

It was now about eleven in the morning, and it being Thursday, Mr. Higginbotham was sure to be working in his room.

Knocking softly at his door, Mrs. Dukes, as soon as he appeared, said suavely, 'I 'ope, Mr. 'igginbotham, that you won't mind my showin' the rooms to a gentleman 'oo wants to take them for a year any'ow; 'e's a clergyman — '

There was no need to add this, as the clergyman himself was standing just behind her, smiling fraternally and apologetically at Mr. Higginbotham over her shoulder, whose face betrayed quite distinctly his discomfort at finding a member of his profession there, and extreme annoyance, all the keener since its own cause demanded its suppression. The least he could say was, 'Oh no, come in, come in,' and in came his hieratic superior smiling and apologising for disturbing him, speaking with profound insight and feeling of the weather, and saying afterwards that he was glad to find that a clergyman had already lived there, as he could not have a better assurance of the quietness of the house. He informed the young curate that he had just arrived in London from Australia, and was glad to have found a lodging place so soon. 'One often wanders round for days and doesn't find anything,' he said.

Mr. Higginbotham's discomfort was growing. He did not very well know how to make the announcement that he did not intend leaving for another three weeks at least.

'I suppose you are taking up your duties in some other district or the country?' the clergyman began tentatively.

'Well, to tell you the truth, I had intended to stay here until the end of the month,' replied the curate.

'Oh, in that case the rooms are out of the question, Mrs. Dukes,' said the clergyman, turning to her. 'This gentleman's not leaving for another three weeks. Have you no others? I'm so sorry we disturbed you, my dear sir. I understood Mrs. Dukes to say that they would be ready at once.'

'No, I didn't say *that*. What I said was that yew could see them. If I miss my let now, they may stay empty all the winter, and they are my best rooms, *yew* see. I was goin' to do them up a little – that'd only take a day or two – and let them for the winter. Mr. 'igginbotham 'ere isn't stayin' beyond the first of November any'ow, and then I shall 'ave them on my 'ands.'

The young curate was caught. If he insisted on staying here and losing the old woman 'her let,' he would be acting in much too brutal a way. But it was unqualifiable, evidently, to turn one lodger out in the middle of a month to make room for another, although this other were going to take the rooms for a year. He was so angry at this thought, and it seemed so preposterous, that he remained without speaking, for a minute or two, struggling with his bellicose feeling beneath the perplexed and questioning eye of his brother clergyman.

'But, Mrs. Dukes,' said the latter, 'I couldn't think of turning this gentleman out – of course not! Why, I shouldn't have dreamt of disturbing you, sir, had I known – '

'Don't mention it. I quite understand! Mrs. Dukes – ' And here the curate drew up short. His wounded feelings were vaguely mollified by the clergyman's apologies.

'Well, give me yer address,' broke in Mrs. Dukes. 'P'raps Mr. 'igginbotham may be called away sooner, one never knows.'

'Ah, in that case, of course! But really, Mrs. Dukes, you should have told me.'

And the clergyman withdrew, red, the colour of apology, since some confusion usually goes with apologies, deeply igniting the whole of his face.

As they were going downstairs, the clergyman saying he was sorry she had no rooms, etc., Mrs. Dukes made the following reflection, summing up the situation. 'That's done it, I think. He was trying to say as we went out that he would willingly give up the rooms and so on; he'll come down to-night and tell me he's going. I thought a clergyman would fire out a curate.

Meanwhile the clergyman had apparently been smitten with a tender feeling for Mrs. Dukes, a feeling hardly in keeping with his cloth. For at the door before leaving, he deliberately winked in the old lady's face.

A few minutes after the clergyman had left, a telegram arrived for Mrs. Dukes. She tore it open, and although her expression underwent no change, her voice sounded slightly different in dismissing the boy, and she seemed alerter all of a sudden.

It ran: 'He is dead. Be prepared.'

Telling Cole she would be back in a few minutes, she left the house and dragged herself down the road. Did she notice that as she started a man idling on the other side of the street began walking also in the direction she had taken?

15
A CHANGED WOMAN

[We are not, however, going to follow Mrs. Dukes as she drags herself off on her brief mission. We will leave this task to the mysterious idler, and return our attentions instead to the equally mysterious house in St. John's Wood, where – in a second-floor room – an odd assortment of gentlemen had gathered

74

together. One might ask for what purpose they had gathered, for they were at this moment linked by no common element of dress, manner, or even activity – unless, perhaps, one should consider a somewhat impatient quiescence an activity.

Had we the rather mixed pleasure of being in this room, the most familiar of these men would have been the tall, dark personage who on two occasions had presented himself to Mrs. Dukes – the first Mrs. Dukes, that is – as a police detective. Holding himself apart from the others, he half lounged, half stood against the far window, his black, deep-set eyes shifting restlessly back and forth along the view which it commanded of the street. His hands, long, gnarled, and distinctly sanguine, moved continually from the wood of the window-ledge to his pockets, his face, and back again. His lean body seemed tense, eager to erupt into some sudden brutality.

Of his four companions, the first would also have been familiar – although still lacking his constable's uniform. Hickman stood pensively at the near end of the room, gazing out a smaller window, occasionally pacing the few feet in front of it.

The second, like the ailing Mrs. Dukes, we might have only partly recognized. Neatly tailored in a dark-brown suit – a brown against which his already dark complexion shone benignly – the doctor sat in a small wicker chair near Hickman, his manicured hands folded in his lap; occasionally he tipped his chair to balance uncertainly on its rear legs. Like the others, he was silent – as indeed he had been on the previous night outside this house when Mrs. Dukes had hesitated, fatefully, before entering.

In fact, the only sound here came intermittently from the pen of a third man, whom we have not before seen, and who was seated at a large and ancient mahogany desk, the principal furnishing of the room. He alone had the assurance of action – hunched purposefully over two or three sheets of paper. His face, and shoulders, seemed poised as if contending with the rigours of a long journey] on horse-back. His hair seemed constantly retreating further back on his head, the skin on his forehead growing tighter, and his eyes becoming more fawn-like. He was very well dressed, very spruce, with long boots of continental shape, and a narrow tight-fitting collar.

The fourth was a sleepy looking man of about forty, with a heavy tow-coloured moustache, dressed in a tweed suit.

The detective turned back savagely from the window, and going to a phonograph that stood in the corner of the room, turned it on. Out of it proceeded a long sinister grating falsetto sound, and then a very faintly sounding high-pitched voice –

'Oh Lord, Cole – whatever are yew doin' of? Always sulkin' down there in the yard. I told you to bring them coals up two hours ago – '

He turned it off again with a desperate shrug of his shoulders. 'One of Royal's toys,' he said. He looked defiantly at the third man, who had looked up from his writing with a face full of meaning, and that meant he did not relish Mrs. Dukes' voice. The 'tec had evidently been getting on his companions' nerves for some time now.

'It's all right, Hillington, for you; you with your special privileges as overseer can get away from this hole at night anyway, if you want to. But here the rest of us are stuck for God knows how long. It's a one-man piece in any case. Royal has it all to himself. We may have to wait months for a dénouement. He may never die at all. He may get better!'

No one paid any more attention to him, and he went over to the window again.

'Ah, here's a telegram; let's see what that is,' he said suddenly and left the room just as a loud knock was heard downstairs. In a minute or two he came back waving a telegram in his hand, with an expression of gracious indulgent relenting, and no small excitement, mingled.

'There, read that; now we're coming to it at last. Things are warming up a bit.'

Hillington, obviously the most in authority of the party, snatched the telegram and read it at a glance. He dashed off the last few lines of the letter he was writing, and got up, taking his hat from a rack behind him.

'I must go,' he said shortly. 'As you say, this means we're in the thick of it now. You fellows must be ready to act at any moment.' Then addressing the doctor, 'see that the new 'un, Evan Royal's understudy, stays here the night if I'm not back. He won't mind that I expect. And don't scare him off by any silly talk. Above all don't let Luchars go near him.' Luchars was the name of the detective.

And he hurried out, the front door banging behind him. He evidently had some distant destination, for despite his nervous speed, he was already lost in thought, as a man having a long course before him often will be — just as a man going for a journey takes a book with him to while away the time. The front door slammed behind him, the gate too, and one felt that for some little time many things would go on slamming behind him, and the wind go on whistling past his ears, he plunged in thought the while.

Luchars' official companion of the other night, of the honest face so well befitting any uniform, took up the telegram, as Hillington was leaving the room, and read aloud.

'He died this morning. Omit nothing.'

'Clear for action! Yes, we're in for it now. It's a big game he's playing. I suppose nothing *can* go wrong?' said the fourth man, whom the others addressed as Charlie.

'No, it's as safe as anything with Evan Royal there. If anyone smelt a rat, he'd clear out in a twinkling. Royal is wonderful. They won't catch him napping!' replied the doctor.

'Bah! He's not such a wonder as all that. He nearly bungled that Eversham affair! That's the worst of this game where we all depend on him. If he makes a slip we'd be caught like rats in a trap! It gets on my nerves this waiting game. I'm jolly glad it's over.' And Luchars shouldered his way about the room, as though he were in the midst of a dense crowd of people.

'I must go up to my patient,' said the doctor.

His patient was none other than the original Mrs. Dukes. But she herself had begun to forget, it seemed, that she had ever been Mrs. Dukes. On the third floor, where the doctor now repaired, she still lay in the small whitewashed room got up to look like the room of a hospital, and where many before her had lain, and who, once they had entered in, never went out again to the life they had left, but went out changed people, transformed by some sinister magic subtly practised by this soft-voiced nurse, perpetually stitching at silk petticoats behind the screen, and this little doctor. Where had they all gone to? Some had gone out again into the world, but all with the stamp of that small whitewashed room upon them.

She still lay strapped down to the bed. The doctor and she were now on somewhat better terms. She derided his science, but no longer hurt his feelings by any approach to a personal slight. She treated him as an incompetent machine that entered the room twice a day and made boss-shots at curing her of her illness, which she had herself now given up diagnosing.

She slept the greater part of the time — a seemingly drunken sleep, as formerly, and its effects came on and lasted afterwards through the greater part of her waking moments, so that she gave the impression always now of having had a drop too much.

She was visibly weaker, and looked paler than ever. She often asked after Cole, and the thought of his being left alone seemed to prey on her mind a great deal. But she did not bother her attendants to fetch him, nor did this occur to her very often.

She was already a changed woman. She had been dragged up from life by the roots, and here in this little room was slowly bleeding to death.

16
AN AMAZING HAPPENING

Two days later, that part of Marbury Street where Mrs. Dukes' house was situated presented an unusual spectacle. During the entire morning a small knot of people stood outside, peering in at the door whenever it opened, and dozens of motors drew up in the course of the morning. What had happened, a new arrival would ask – a fire, a murder?

'No,' he would be answered, 'the old woman what lives there's 'ad a lot o' money left 'er.'

And the passer-by was referred to the newspapers.

If he looked through his halfpenny paper later on to find some mention of this, he would find the following account, more or less.

'Lodging-house keeper inherits vast fortune! over a million pounds!' he would find in large type, then:

One of the most amazing turns of the capricious wheel of Dame Fortune is to be found in the result of the will of the late Mr. Arthur

St. Giles Dukes, of Liverpool, merchant prince and lately elected Mayor of the great Mersey-side city. Also it includes one of the most romantic occurrences on record of a veritable return from the dead, but a return in the form of a vast sum of money, the living man being no more vouchsafed to these long abandoned eyes. But the best of him is there — his life's work, that life spent in piling up this prodigious wealth!

Thirty-three years ago Mrs. Dukes, then married for some seven years, was suddenly deserted by her husband; he disappeared from her side as though suddenly snatched away by a mysterious Fate from out the sky, suddenly ravished from her young side by some sinister destiny. The picric acid of the swarthy and anarchic vulture of reform could not, with his stealthy bomb, have more completely destroyed all trace of him, had it gone off under his chair and blown him to atoms.

But another Mr. Dukes appeared about this time in the City of Liverpool, a young and eager recruit in the offices of a great shipper of the illustrious northern port. Scamping not his work, stinting not his labour, quick as a lizard and sure as a die, he rapidly rose in his business. First he gained the confidence and admiration of his employers, soon became invaluable and indispensable. He climbed higher and higher; honours and riches began to shower upon his head, now turning grey, but still erect and still lighted by his tireless and indomitable eyes. And at last the miracle happened — the miracle that is always happening, but that never ceases to amaze us, and commands as freshly as ever our utter admiration. From being a young man in an office with hardly a penny to bless himself with, he became a millionaire, a man on whose words other men hung, as though for dear life — and this glorious mercantile career was crowned not a year ago by Mr. Arthur St. Giles Dukes, more than millionaire, receiving the highest civic honours in the City where he had won his laurels.

What was it caused Mr. Dukes, thirty-three years ago, to leave his young wife and her new born babe to shift for themselves, and go out into the world to seek his fortune — alone! without the helping hand of his wife and friend to soothe and sustain him through the trials, the weary hours that awaited him before Fortune definitely marked him out for her own? This secret will never be divulged. It is buried deeper than ever plummet sounded. It is buried in the heart of a man, but not only this, but that of a dead man! This we shall never know. The most intimate friends of this latter and glorious part of his life were never confided in — never knew even that he had been married.

And yet after all these years, when he comes to die, he remembers the little humble home he had left so strangely, so long ago, and thinks of his little wife still as a young woman — eternally fresh and young. Who should he leave all this wealth to? He had none near and dear to him, only those two far away in the little house in London, forgotten, lost, wiped out of his life, and yet ever present to his memory. To them he leaves the riches he has piled up far from them — he comes back to them in this form. Ah! who knows if the old heart, thirsting all those years for what it had so strangely and suddenly lost, would not rather than all this Croesus pile have back again the still remembered form — by her also not forgotten?'

Here the journalist had apparently ended abruptly, as though the tears were coming too quickly, and as though his emotion would not allow him to proceed. After a dash would follow a little paragraph explaining that Mrs. Dukes was a woman of fifty-five or sixty, with a son thirty-four years old, and had let lodgings in Marbury Street for the last thirty years, living behind a little bric-a-brac shop in one small dingy room.

The further information would be given that Mrs. Dukes, overcome by this sudden and so startling and overwhelming news of one she had long given up all hope of ever hearing of again, had taken to her bed, and could reply little to the many questions that callers of all sorts put to her, and stared wildly when congratulated on her good fortune.

So it was. Mrs. Dukes was indeed in bed, and it was no easy matter to get to see her. The greater number of the reporters got no further than the front door.

There was one innovation, at least, since the Thursday before when the clergyman had called. A large and languid and rather sluttish woman about forty-five, with some slatternly tow-coloured hair, had come to take some of the house work off Cole's hands, who spent most of his days now in smoking by the fire. Once or twice he had filled his pipe and disappeared in the cellar with it, to smoke in the gloom. This was no doubt the very summit of felicity for Cole.

Mrs. Dukes had taken to her bed on the previous morning, a few hours after receiving a letter, which, she assured Cole, made her doubtful whether 'she was standin' on 'er 'ead or 'er 'eels.'

The only people she saw were one or two of the most important and importunate reporters. She gave them little information, she seemed dazed, threw out exclamations, and seemed a little querulous.

The curate's position was more difficult than ever. He had not yet notified Mrs. Dukes of his willingness to give up his rooms in favour of his brother clergyman, but when he read of his landlady's good fortune, and the motors began arriving, he felt that it was impossible any longer to remain there, as it was now a millionairess whom he had to deal with. It was no good being obstinate with a millionairess. He felt quite timid and uncomfortable. He wrote a brief and very polite note, informing her that he would leave at the end of the week, or sooner if he could arrange it. 'He didn't suppose that she would let lodgings any more' − a flattering little way of referring to her inheritance − ended the communication.

Mrs. Dukes accepted his notice graciously enough. She sent word by Mrs. Beechamp, the middle-aged charwoman, to tell him to take his time − that she would not need the room before Monday. That she would be temporarily occupying it herself.

But it was at this point, as he was modestly stretching out his arm for his boots the next morning from his bedroom door, that he smelt a rat. He smelt a wrong rat, it is true, but he distinctly smelt one, and acted accordingly.

17
THE CURATE SMELLS A RAT

This is what the curate saw that set his sensation-loving brain whirling in an orgy of tragic surmises again.

He was by no means dressed, and yet required his boots, as he liked to complete all the difficult details of his toilet − get his boots laced up, and everything else finished − before slipping on his black clerical suit, and issuing forth for the day. He dreaded dressing in a vague undecided way − not a manly dread but a half conscious dread that did not dare to own it dreaded it. But he was a tenacious little man. Most people by the time they have got their trousers, jacket and waistcoat on, still have a score of little things to do − and have still got their boots to put on. This is the most wearying and disheartening part of dressing. It seems that it will never finish. The curate gave the finishing touches to absolutely everything to do with the underworld of his person, first, then, standing erect in these under garments, paused a moment. A minute later he was covered with his suit of professional black and issuing tranquilly from the room. This sudden crisp and clean finish lessened the terrors of dressing for him. Such was his method, especially adapted for his particular temperament.

On the third morning from the time of Mrs. Dukes receiving the announcement of her good fortune – that is the morning following that spoken of in our last chapter – the curate opened his door noiselessly and peered out to see if a bold dash for his boots would be likely to be witnessed by anybody. So quiet was he that he did not disturb two people who had apparently stopped a moment on the stairs, in passing each other, to exchange a word or two. One was the Belgian, the other the charwoman.

The curate who had several times heard the Belgian's attempts to make himself understood in English, and once had smilingly wished him good morning, was transfixed on hearing this youth remark in a low voice to the charwoman, 'Yes! But the difficult part's only just beginning. The great thing is to get hold of the old woman's money as soon as possible, and cut.'

The charwoman, with an idle feminine shrug of the shoulders, went on upstairs, and the Belgian continued on his way out.

The curate remained spell-bound, his mouth open and his hand on the door. He then seized his boots, and retreated once more into his bed-room with his 'booty,' locking the door behind him.

The rest of his dressing was very desultory. He would stop in the middle of doing up his ink-black tie, evidently following up some train of thought too hotly to permit of his finishing the knot for the moment.

Here, he told himself, by the purest chance he had discovered a deliberate plot to rob the poor old woman downstairs of the money she had just inherited. The money she had just inherited! But it was a million pounds and more! This was a tremendous plot, of enormous proportions. And perhaps, indeed more likely than not, her life was in imminent danger! These rascals would stick at nothing. Masquerading as lodgers and charwomen, a daring plot had been hatched to rob the old landlady. Or perhaps the charwoman had been won over, or perhaps the Belgian had been won over — and suddenly taught English! His head swam.

At last there was a genuine, indisputable excuse for interfering. Nay, it was his duty to do so. Duty had never seemed so delicious to him. He must at all cost save this old woman's life, frustrate these ruffians.

The last part of his dressing was done furiously, without any method — his trousers going on after his clerical coat, his comb snatched up to wash his teeth with, his collar put on the wrong way round. At last he was ready and, his heart thumping joyously, looking round with a delightful uneasiness, and feeling as though he had just heard that the house was unsafe, he descended to Mrs. Dukes' room.

He was by no means sorry to pay back Mrs. Dukes in true Christian manner, for the ill she had done, with such signal services. He was luxuriously conscious that he was about to save her life. Then he was not sorry, either, to be of such great service to the new millionairess. The thought of this sum had rather awed him when he had heard that his landlady possessed it. It awed him no longer, for he knew that it was in jeopardy, and that it was only through him that she would still have it in a week's time or less.

A new difficulty now presented itself. Mrs. Dukes was still

in bed. At his knock the very woman whom he had overheard in speech with the 'Belgian' a half hour before, came to the door.

'You can't see Mrs. Dukes this mornin', sir. She ain't well. She's still in bed,' drawled this large and sleepy slut.

The curate looked at her very severely − looked straight, and with an awful significance, into her eyes, and said, 'I *must* see Mrs. Dukes.'

''Fraid you can't,' she drawled, with the 'saucy' tone that often goes with just her degree of fatness and dirtiness.

He was just going to say something that would strike. her dumb, and reveal to her at the same time that her iniquity was known to him, when he drew himself up short. He must not give these malefactors the alarm. They must be punished for their offences against society. They must be caught. Also this might only serve to hurry on the crime he was bent on averting.

He assumed another tone − one of clerical dignity.

'That would not be the first bedside or the first sick room my duties had taken me to, my good woman. Inform Mrs. Dukes, if you please, that I am here, and should like to exchange a few words with her.' He raised his voice. 'I am sure Mrs. Dukes would not mind my coming in.'

'Ye can't just now, I'm afraid, Mr. 'igginbotham,' came the high-pitched voice of his landlady.

'It's very important, Mrs. Dukes. If I could see you for a minute or two!' pleaded the curate, in a voice equally high-pitched.

'Why didn't ye tell Mr. 'igginbotham that I couldn't see any one, Mrs. Beechamp? Yew know I can't now,' came Mrs. Dukes' voice again.

'Yew can't see 'er now, Mr. 'igginbotham, sir. This afternoon she'll be gettin' up, p'raps,' said the charwoman, and Mr. Higginbotham returned to his room to deliberate. There was evidently not a moment to lose. But those inevitable doubts as to whether he had not fancied something of the incriminating dialogue, as to the meaning of the words he had overheard, and so on, assailed him. He was timid of taking the responsibility of going to the police on his own shoulders, although thrilled with the thought.

He had some work waiting for him just then, however, and determined to do that first.

On the way back, about half past two, he passed a police station. On its steps stood a very imposing and self-possessed looking policeman. The temptation the young divine felt to suddenly become important in the eyes of this large, handsome, tranquil man of action, and also an infantile curiosity to penetrate that building which was the very home of sensations, was too strong for him. He mounted the steps, and asked to see someone in authority. He was soon shown into the presence of a cold-eyed and not very suave official.

18
HERCULES FANE AND THE SLEEPER

Hercules Fane would have continued his existence of 'super' to the end of the chapter, and certainly never have chosen as an alternative an adventurous and doubtful career, a career without a name, whose very remuneration witnessed to its doubtfulness. But now that one with more possibilities, although precarious, had been suggested to him, and the good gold guineas were in his hand, with the promise of freedom and time to go on with his literary work, he felt that it would be cowardly not to accept it, and his other employment of 'super' seemed hourly more detestable to him. Besides, he was not going to be asked to pick anybody's pocket. So far, all he had to do was merely theatrical work – this the strange man he had met the night before had assured him.

At twelve punctually his guide arrived, and they started together in the direction of Baker Street, getting a bus opposite Euston Station. In three quarters of an hour – they having taken from Baker Street onwards the same bus route as Mrs. Dukes and her conductor did on the night of the 'identification' – they were at the house in which that lady still lay, and which was apparently inhabited by the odd assortment of men who were presented to the reader in a former chapter.

An old woman, a *real* old woman, came to the door at his companion's imperious knock.

'Is Mr. Hillington here?'

'No, sir, he is gone,' answered she, with the same vague foreign accent that Fane had heard for the first time the night before. What this accent was he could not tell, although he was fairly familiar with the way of speaking of the principal neighbouring peoples. Also her bronzed and handsome face and the way she carried what there was left of her – for she was evidently only half the size that she used to be when younger, and steadily wearing away as though at the constant friction of something unseen – this carriage was in some way that of Fane's host of the preceding night. 'Mr. Hillington has said that the gentleman could wait his return in the library,' she added.

The library was a large comfortable room with a good many books in it, books of a description that suggested that once a very great lover of books had lived there. The house had, indeed, been bought as it was, furnished and stocked, by its present owner.

Before leaving him the man he had come with said to Fane, 'Mr. Hillington is the gentleman that acts for my master, and he will instruct you, as soon as he returns, as to your part and the studies that you are expected to make. Some luncheon will be brought to you immediately. I don't think Mr. Hillington will be long, but I expect, sir, that a literary gentleman like you will be able to pass your time here all right.' And the man glanced round at the books.

'How the devil does he know that I'm a "literary gentleman"?' said Fane to himself.

The deference that everyone showed this man was extraordinary. He went for a moment into the smoking room before leaving, to talk with Luchars, the detective, for a moment. Even this surly personage seemed subdued in his presence. Hillington had not half so much authority with his companions.

The old woman was waiting for him in the hall, and at once spoke to him a strange language, rapid, guttural and, as a man of any philological prowess would have divined, not of European stock, but certainly an Eastern tongue. They stood looking at each other silently for a moment. Then she grunted, as though thus inharmoniously terminating a train of thought, and he left quickly.

Fane made himself quite at home. After a good lunch that the old woman brought him, crouched over the fire with a volume of early French poetry he had found and long been looking for, he felt that really this was not so bad, and began to feel comfortably lucky.

As we have already indicated, Fane, though a poet, had never written a line of poetry in his life. This may astonish the reader. But we only call him a poet in the rough modern European sense, to indicate the lyrical character of his temperament. The terms Poet and Philosopher include daily a larger and larger number of people taken from all branches of life. Lloyd-George is a poet; an M.D.'s certificate, and the fact of having published a book on obstetrics, entitles a man to be called a philosopher. Napoleon now-a-days is seldom spoken of as a good general, but chiefly as a 'poet' and a 'dreamer'; and one would suppose from the writings of many people, if one were not acquainted with their music, that Beethoven was a brilliant general-of-division, and Wagner a War Minister famous for his organising genius.

After two hours of reading, Fane got up, and wondered when the 'Mr. Hillington' mentioned would put in an appearance. He was naturally curious as to the nature of the work he had so recklessly undertaken.

A certain feeling of creepiness he certainly did experience about this mysterious house he had come to, to receive some mysterious role in some fantastic 'life-piece' such as his new employer had hinted at. He pricked up his ears once or twice on hearing steps in the passages without. He determined to make himself at home, however, as though he were quite used to these sort of engagements. A little later, partly in bravado, he walked out into the passage-way, and continued along it to the farther end, staring about him nonchalantly. After passing several doors, it turned and led along the farther wing of the house. At the end of the passage a door was ajar. All his misgivings came back, and he felt already knee deep in adventure, on hearing weak groans proceeding from this open door. He was so near it, and his anxiety to solve any mysteries at once, if too uncanny mysteries there were in this mansion, and get rid of it without delay – induced him to gently push it open and warily put his head inside. He was gazing into a small whitewashed room. On turning his eyes to the side of the door, he discovered nothing more startling than an old woman in bed, apparently groaning in her sleep, for she was snoring slightly at the same time. She looked very white and ill, and several medicine bottles were on the table in front of him. There was something weird about this discovery, but, on the surface, he could not say what, except that he had been led to believe that this was a place of business — however unlike the business might be to other businesses — and here apparently was an invalid or sick woman of sixty or seventy years. This was the first inmate of this house, except the wizened but active old servant, he had yet seen. He got back to the library without meeting anybody, and began reading again, but with little concentration, his mind full of surmises as to what manner of work attended him, what house this was, who was his employer and a score more questions.

Hillington arrived shortly afterwards. He greeted Fane with frankness and informality.

'Ah, have you been here long? I'm sorry to have kept you waiting, but I didn't know you were coming round so early and I've been out all the morning. I'm afraid you will not be able to begin studying your part today, but tomorrow you can begin, I expect. It will not be difficult and you will be given every facility for doing so. I expect our employer told you more or less what you would have to do. This is an experiment of his — what he calls 'experiments in life.' You see our employer has a great belief in studying things from life, from an original who is a real person and not an actor. Your work for the next week or so will be to study the ways, the face, the voice of an old woman. She will not suspect what you are doing, and you will have no difficulties of any sort to contend with except those of your art. She is a very old friend of mine. Of course the advantages of this system of our employer's is enormous. If you are to play Othello or Shylock, for instance, you find the person that comes nearest by nature to either of these characters and study him. Your best way in the present case, will be to take up your quarters in the house of the old woman you are about to study. But we will see about that tomorrow. I expect it'll all seem very strange to you at first. You must look upon your employment as the whim of a tremendous practical joker, of a philanthropic turn; or as the dreams of a great economist, or as the experiments in life and human beings of a man of genius of colossal fortune, and in love with life. However, you will soon get into the way of things, and like everything else, in a week or so the strangeness will have worn off and you will have settled down to your work. The principal thing,' he added, smiling, 'is that the pay is excellent. And one has plenty of time on one's hands, and for you, who, I understand, are interested in literature, time will not hang heavy, as it does with some of us. I think, then, tomorrow, that we shall go together to the scene of your labours, your theatrical labours. Instead of going to a dusty stage in a theatre every day, you will merely go to a certain street or house, or as I suggest, take up your quarters there, and look upon that as your stage, and the people found there and incidents of real life as the piece you are playing. Would you care to stay here tonight, or would you prefer to go back to your lodgings? We can put you up all right, and members of the company often sleep here, some of them lodge here altogether.'

Fane did not know what to think of all this. Hillington impressed him as a capable and not dishonest man. But there was something strange about him. What he said was certainly more definite than their employer's hints about the nature of his new occupation. He was to study his part from a living model — an old woman. This was clear enough. But what part, in what piece? Then came the same vague talk about 'life-pieces' and so on that he had heard the night before. Hillington was not at all like a theatre manager. But he was a gentleman, seemed intelligent, and anyway, he was in for it now. He said nothing to Hillington about his discovery of the old woman lying sick at the end of the passage. He agreed to stay for the night.

19
FANE HAS A SHOCK

The whole of the following day was passed by Fane in the library, waiting for orders. He grew more and more restless at this delay, and it was only about four o'clock that he found a novel which at last relieved him from his boredom. The doctor had come in about mid-day, and had chatted with him about nothing in particular. Luchars had been strictly for-bidden to go near him. Luchars was the one element of disorder in this well-ordered house, and the one man his chiefs could not depend on. They retained him as a member of the company because they thought he would do less mischief amongst them than if he were dismissed.

He had met Luchars on the stairs, but the latter had given him a wide berth, sulkily and disdainfully stepping aside, as though to say to the absent spirit of Hillington, 'You tell me not to go near your precious new recruit, but I assure you I haven't the faintest desire to do so!'

On the following morning, when Fane came down to

breakfast, Hillington was waiting for him.

'I hope you didn't find the time too long yesterday. I did my best to get back, but was extraordinarily busy. I propose, as soon as we've had our breakfast, to take you round there, though.'

They had just sat down to an excellent meal of fish, eggs and bacon, when the old woman brought up a morning paper, and laid it down on the table between Fane and the 'manager.'

Fane took it up thoughtlessly, saying, 'Let's see what's happening. I haven't seen a paper for a couple of days.'

His eyes had just scanned the headlines of the middle page, when he felt it pulled out of his hand, and heard Hillington saying quickly, 'Excuse me, let me see it just for a moment, will you? There's something specially I want to see – but, by jove, what a boor I am – no, you keep it for a bit! – no, really, don't you want it? All right, I'll give it you back in a jiffy.'

He did not however, but for the rest of breakfast kept hunting through it, not finding, apparently, what he wanted.

This little incident startled Fane, rather. He was not deceived by Hillington's pretext for snatching the paper out of his hand, and saw for a moment a look in the other's face that he had not suspected it to wear so easily – of hardness and wariness, and that presence of mind that only comes of long practice of danger, not presence of mind that is the genius of courage and resource, but the talent that comes of practice. Why should this be used on him, Fane? Fane was now on his guard and estranged from this man immediately. An hour later they were knocking at No. 21, Marbury Street.

The heavy sluttish charwoman preceded them into the little room behind the shop, and Cole glided away before them down the back stairs. Fane heard a voice behind the screen as he was entering grumbling shrilly.

'Oh Lord — visitors? 'Ooever can it be?'

On arriving in front of the bed, however, he stopped abruptly, and gazed with sudden alarm at the old woman who lay there gazing wonderingly at him, evidently his surprise puzzling her as much as she puzzled him. Yes, it was the same old woman Fane had seen the day before in the little tour he had made in the mysterious house where he had passed the last two days, groaning in her sleep and evidently very ill. She still looked very ill, he thought, only much more vivacious. But how on earth did she get here? Of course, it was quite possible that she had come in a cab or even on her legs, or in any of a score of ways. But it was very odd and startling all the same.

Hillington was watching him, evidently disconcerted. Mrs. Dukes was watching him from her bed, and the charwoman from the door. And then they looked at each other and then back to him, and seemed as taken aback by his expression of alarm and astonishment as he was by finding this old woman before him. His nerves had naturally in the course of the last day or two been worked up into a state of unusual tension, and any mysterious or strange occurrence of this sort caused him actual fear.

Mrs. Dukes was the first person to find her tongue; as far as her composure went, she had never lost that.

'Oh, so yew're Mr. Fane, 'oo Mr. 'illington 'ere was talkin' about yesterday. Yew want a room, do ye? Sit down, Mr. 'illington, and yew too, Mr. Fane. I'm very poorly today, but Mrs. Beechamp 'ere will show you the only room I 'ave to let at present. It's up at the top, ye know. Yes, go up, will ye — Mrs. Beechamp will show it yew.'

They went up and examined the little room he was destined to sleep in. It was rather comfortable looking. Somebody had evidently been getting it ready for him, and some of the stock of the bric-a-brac shop that was not broken had been fetched to adorn it.

The charwoman left them, conveniently, for a few minutes, and Hillington then said to him hurriedly, 'You will be very comfortable here, Fane, and you can practise your part aloud without fear of being overheard. There is only one lodger, a young foreigner, on this landing. He can speak hardly any English and is as stupid as a brick. If you decide to stay here, rather than go back every day to your diggings, you can go round there this evening or tomorrow, and tell the people you will be away in the country for a week or two. Well, what do you think of the old woman? She's original, isn't she? You'll soon get hold of the part, and be able to imitate her to perfection. Well, will you stay?'

One consentment always leads to another, and Fane had been consenting to the most extravagant things for upwards of three days now. He said, 'I suppose so' rather gruffly, and Hillington left the house a few minutes later.

He spent a half hour talking to Mrs. Dukes. She was telling him how Mr. Hillington had lodged there some years ago, and what 'a nice man' he was. She never used the word 'gentleman,' and the respectful title 'sir' never sullied her lips.

In the course of the talk, Fane gathered that she had been 'in bed' — evidently meaning the bed in which she then lay — since the afternoon of the previous day. He puzzled no more about it, except lazily from time to time a conjecture would come into his mind, but unsupported by any proof, soon died again. When he had retired to his room, he reflected in the following way. He was in for it now, anyhow, and he had just as well do exactly what he was told, so long as he was not asked to do anything obviously dishonest. His reasoning was by no means loyal to his employers. He told himself: 'If there is anything shady, any rascality, at the bottom of all this, I at least know nothing about it as yet, and truth carries conviction. It is true that I entered into this agreement without knowing definitely enough what was expected of me. But then I could even, by changing things a little, if I had to answer to the police – for it's no use disguising it, this may be a matter for the police – I could probably find some excuse, making out that Hillington and his employer's proposals were more definite than they were, and more innocent looking. Any way, I shall consent to nothing more than what I have already consented to, and certainly will not do anything dishonest. I can always cut if necessary. Then it looks, in one way and another, as though it were going to be exciting. Anything is better than the 'Daphne!'

In this manner he quieted his apprehensions. But the presence of the old woman downstairs, and the obvious lie she had told him – namely, that she had been there in bed for over a day – continually puzzled and disquieted him. He carefully locked and bolted his door, and after a half hour of restless thought, went to sleep.

20
MRS. DUKES IS VISITED FOR A SECOND TIME BY THE POLICE

It was the next morning, in getting up, that the curate overheard the startling conversation on the stairs between the charwoman and the Belgian.

When Fane had had his breakfast, he went down to have a chat with Mrs. Dukes. He had to do something, and he thought he had better begin to earn his six guineas, as if he worked for them his conscience would be less troublesome, and it needed just now every prop available. There was no difficulty for him to get to see Mrs. Dukes. She welcomed him shrilly as soon as she heard his voice at the door. Naturally he could only pass a limited amount of time with her. He had no excuse for taking up much of her time. A quarter of an hour or so's chat, twice a day perhaps, was all he could reasonably expect. He determined to make the most of it, and studied her with great intentness.

It was she that facilitated his staying longer by her endless chatter about Mr. Hillington, for whom she apparently had the greatest affection. This was a link between them. To be introduced by Mr. Hillington meant at once to be taken into the landlady's good graces. Then she was ill, and sorely in need of a little distraction, and when Fane rose to go, she asked him to stop a little longer, if the 'talk of such a silly old woman did not tire him.'

He went up to his room after quite an hour's talk, and repeated aloud, imitating her tone, some phrases and parts of Mrs. Dukes' chatter that he remembered.

He had his lunch in a neighbouring French restaurant, and then went to his old lodgings to tell the people of his pretended visit to the country. He was there about an hour, putting his things together a little, and doing up a few books and papers to take with him to Marbury Street.

When he arrived there he saw one or two people gazing up at the door. He now had one of the severest shocks of his life, when, on knocking, a policeman came to open the door to him. All in a rush he regretted enormously his mad acceptance of his strange employer's offer. He was really frightened. But nevertheless, in alternate moments of lucidity, he felt that nothing could really happen to him, as he was completely ignorant of the doings of the men amongst whom he had come.

The policeman noticed no doubt the effect his presence produced on the young man, for he asked him sternly, 'Have you a room 'ere?'

'Yes, I only moved in yesterday,' replied Fane.

'Oh, yew only moved in yesterday.' Then the policeman called out at the door of Mrs. Dukes' den, from which several voices proceeded, ''Ere's somebody, Mr. Groves — another lodger.'

Fane was now quite near the door, and Mrs. Dukes' voice rose up shrilly.

'Is that you, Mr. Fane? Come 'ere a minute, will ye?'

Fane, pale and nervous, but still keeping his wits very well considering, entered the room, which was full of people. Mrs. Dukes was the centre of the group, upright in her bed, and dominating the whole company with her chatter. The curate stood near the foot of the bed, very red, and near him the charwoman. There was an Inspector of Police, a man who turned out to be a detective, the 'Belgian,' and then Fane and the constable.

'Now, you're not goin' to say, I 'ope, Mr. 'igginbotham, that Mr. Fane 'ere 'as been plottin' and plannin' against me? I wonder yew don't! Mrs. Beechamp 'ere, that I've known for thirty years, plottin' with a foreign feller to rob me, indeed! What next, I should like to know! Yew must 'a been dreamin' *I* think, Mr. 'igginbotham!'

The Inspector, and everybody else, was looking doubtfully and not too amiably in the direction of the unfortunate curate, who got redder and redder.

'Are you quite sure, Mr. Higginbotham, that what you alleged is exact?' asked the Inspector, angrily and dubiously.

'I cannot be quite sure of the exact words, but the sense of them I am sure of.'

Then the constable, who had been very struck with Fane's emotion on seeing him, drew his chief's attention to this new arrival again.

'So you only arrived yesterday?' said the Inspector to Fane. 'How did you come to take lodgings here; are you working in the neighbourhood? You're English, aren't you?'

'Yes, of course, I'm English. I was brought here – '

Mrs. Dukes broke in, 'Oh, what is the good of askin' 'im questions, when I tell ye 'e's a friend Mr. 'illington recommended, 'oo was the best lodger *I* ever 'ad by a long way. 'E's out of it,' she continued energetically. 'Mrs. Beechamp, as I tell ye, I knew as a little girl. And as to that young foreign feller there, 'e don't look up to doin' anythin' of that sort. *I* shouldn't think 'e was bright enough for that.'

'Yes, but Mr. Higginbotham is very positive in his assertions, Mrs. Dukes; and you see, Madam, we are anxious if there is anything criminal afoot of which you are the object, to protect you in every way in our power.'

One of the most noticeable things in this scene to Fane was the extreme amiability and deference that everybody paid to Mrs. Dukes. And Mrs. Dukes seemed to know her power; for she used her new authority freely to arrange things as she wanted them. Fane concluded that it was against this old woman that the plotting in which he was half innocently taking part was directed. But how was it that Hillington, her pet, should be betraying her? It was all very obscure as yet. In the meantime his nerves were strained to the uttermost as he awaited what would happen, what would be the upshot of the present scene.

Mrs. Dukes kept her eye almost constantly on the curate. She was very anxious about one thing. She was very afraid that Mr. Higginbotham would mention the visit of the police that had occurred a week previously. And she never let her attention wander from him; she was ready to catch him up if he showed signs of touching on that subject. If the worst came to the worst, and the curate blurted this out, she had resolved to accept the theory of a plot, and regard this former visit of the police — when it was discovered that no representatives of the police had in reality been there — as part of the plot. She would accept the theory that those men were thieves disguised. But all this was very tender walking; the police would be put very much on the 'qui vive,' and might even arrest everybody except her and Cole — would certainly establish a watch — they would probably do so as it was — and in short, increase enormously this second Mrs. Dukes' difficulties.

Evan Royal, formerly known to us as Mr. Nichols, wonderful actor as he was, and with a nerve that could be wrenched about in all directions and not give, needed all his resourcefulness in this moment. He routed the curate in a final magnificent burst, he convinced the policeman that it was quite absurd to suspect anyone there of any designs against her, unless it were the 'Belgian.' Mrs. Dukes had her own reasons for offering up the 'Belgian' as a sacrifice to the law, if absolutely necessary.

'Are you sure, Mr. Higginbotham, that you did not overhear this man attempting to secure the charwoman as an accomplice, merely?' asked the Inspector, persuasively.

'I did not hear Mrs. Beechamp say anything, it is true. But this man can speak English as well as you or I. How do you account for that?' Mr. Higginbotham asked desperately.

The Belgian who had been listening with great intentness, and apparently having great difficulty in following what was said, here broke out into incoherent expostulation. He had evidently understood the last sentence or two. It was the realest broken-English imaginable.

'That'll do, that'll do,' said the Inspector sternly to the foreigner. But he was evidently impressed by his accent, and his doubt shaken still more in Mr. Higginbotham.

'You don't think it might have been somebody else?' insisted the Inspector.

'No, I am certain on that head. This is the man I heard addressing Mrs. Beechamp on the stairs.'

The police, thoroughly puzzled, angry with the curate, disappointed at this unsatisfactory upshot to a thing that had promised so well, took the 'Belgian' away with them, as they could think of nothing better to do. Of the other three foreign lodgers, two, who happened to be in, had given a good account of themselves. Mrs. Dukes gave them all notice to quit within three days, as she said to the Inspector, 'Any'ow, I won't 'ave any of that foreign lot 'ere any longer. They may be all right, but one's never sure of them.'

'I expect, Mrs. Dukes, you won't have much to do with letting lodgings of any description before long,' said the Inspector, laughing obsequiously.

'I don't suppose I *shall*,' replied Mrs. Dukes, nodding her head at him, as though to say, 'you're just about right there.' Then she sank back on the pillow, as though, in her present state, this scene had exhausted her.

'Mr. 'igginbotham, I should like to speak to you a moment,' said Mrs. Dukes in a weak voice, just as the police were leaving. She did not want him to be left alone with them. He, for his part, had no further desire to awake interest in himself, and excitement in his discoveries in the broad breasts of blue-coated men of action. He stayed behind. Mrs. Dukes, in the complaining voice of a martyr, showing him in every tone that she considered him the cause of all these troubles that came clamouring around her poor old head, asked him when his room would be at her disposal. He said he would move on the following day, as he had heard of some rooms that afternoon.

The police carried off their prisoner without further incident.

21
A MYSTERIOUS RESCUE

Fane went straight up to his room, and sitting down before the fire determined to come to some decision one way or the other.

He had gathered from the preceding scene that the curate had asserted that some of the lodgers and the charwoman were leagued together to rob the old landlady of her money, of which she appeared, putting two and two together, to have a respectable and respect-inducing quantity. Then he was not the only one in the pay of his mysterious employer at present under that roof, and if the energies of the others were directed against their old landlady, he also no doubt was intended to play, unconsciously, some part in this rascally plot. But then came the puzzling attitude of Mrs. Dukes herself towards two of the plotters. Mr. Hillington and the charwoman were both, according to her, beyond all suspicion, as the latter she had known as a little girl, and Mr. Hillington had lodged there, and been a model lodger, for many years. This was of course not a definite reason, to Fane's imagination, that they should not be implicated in a plot to rob her. Behind all these questions was the obscurer enigma of Mrs. Dukes' falsehood of the day before, namely the assertion of hers that precluded the possibility of her having been asleep in that other house, where Fane was certain he had seen her two days before.

The Belgian, who might be an accomplice, had been arrested. Would that arrest lead to the police discovering the whole plot? In that case he himself might expect, at any moment, to be arrested and asked to give an account of himself. But if he deserted his new post, went back to his old diggings, and tried to get taken on again at the 'Daphne,' he might at any moment be tracked down. His leaving would be construed as a flight. The best thing for him to do, all things considered, was to go to the nearest police station, and tell them exactly what had happened, all he knew of the men amongst whom he now found himself, and ask to have his statements verified, and to be released from the possibility of suspicion.

But this course, of 'turning witness' — feeling, as he did, that he was, through his own will, even, somewhat implicated — appeared extremely repugnant to him. He did not want to do this if he possibly could help it. And after all it might lead to nothing, as his employers might be only jokers after all.

Fane, after a quarter of an hour's reflection, was as undecided as ever as to what course to take. Just at this point in his feverish cogitations, the front door rang and rang again beneath a furious knocking, and some minutes later several steps were heard on the stairs, and with sounds of considerable brusqueness and violence, the room next to Fane's, which had been occupied by the 'Belgian,' was entered.

Fane went to the door to see what was the matter, and found three policemen consulting angrily in the doorway.

They turned roughly to him, saying 'Yes, yew're another of 'em.' 'We must search the other rooms too,' said a second, and beginning with Fane's room, went through all the upper rooms, looking behind curtains, and stamping about as though to terrify a hidden fugitive. They all looked particularly sour.

But ten minutes later the house again was at peace. Fane then learnt from one of the foreign lodgers that on the way to the police station, in passing through a poor neighbourhood, the policemen had been tripped up from behind by the Belgian — who had stepped suddenly back to do so — and some other man, who, they supposed, was a friend of his. Both the policemen had been sent sprawling on the ground, and when they had recovered themselves the 'Belgian' was nowhere to be seen.

Two of the policemen still had dark marks on their knees, showing where they had collapsed on the damp pavement. For some reason or other, now that they were really angry, and each of them personally determined to lay hands on somebody and wipe out by their future zeal this humiliation, they did not scare Fane so much as before. On their first visit they were impersonal units, silent and chilly representatives of the law, but now they were angry, very noisy, and in their noise, rather impotent human beings.

The curate, despite his repeated rebuffs and mortifications, could not resist the temptation to sally out from his room on hearing all the hubbub. His attempt to good-naturedly triumph over everybody — as he looked upon this as a confirmation of his information — was received by everyone concerned very brutally. The police hinted that had he given a more exact account of what he had heard, they would have better known who they had to deal with, and would have taken greater precautions, as the 'Belgian' was evidently a 'most dangerous continental malefactor.' That was a notorious trick of foreign evil-doers — they referred here hurriedly and sullenly to the accident that had happened to them. He couldn't possibly have spoken English like an Englishman, as the curate asserted, and so on. They mouthed the words 'dangerous continental malefactor' with a mixture of awe and importance. Mrs. Dukes pressed the curate harder than ever, and he was soon driven back upstairs and into his own room again. Once there, the humour of the different situations, his love of adventure that his Viking blood, no doubt, had kept alive in him despite his calling, suddenly dawned upon him. That voice that intoned so melodiously in church thereupon broke out into peals of musical though polite laughter. Fane, who was just then lingering on the landing above, heard it, and this added another enigma to his already overstocked brain.

Out of a desire to please Mrs. Dukes, the chief policeman, as soon as the curate had beaten a retreat, made a contemptuous grimace, and therewith he and his evidence were dismissed together from the mind of all concerned. The Inspector and detective had gone straight back to headquarters, after leaving No. 21, Marbury Street a half hour before. The constables had little more to do, on their own initiative, than see if the 'Belgian,' for any reason, had returned there. After some minutes further talk with the old landlady, they left.

After all this new tumult and excitement had subsided, Fane went back to his room, and was naturally confronted with all the same questions over again, with just a little more certainty in his mind that he was in the hands of a gang, or a society, rather, of most dangerous and unscrupulous men. It almost seemed as though his headlong making up of his mind a week ago to accept this equivocal employment had used up all his capacity for final decisions for the moment, or made him shy of coming to new resolutions.

While he sat there before his fire, someone knocked at his door. His mind prefiguring no one in particular, he said 'come in.' The door opened, and he found his mind once more upset, so to speak, and splashing about in its attempt to regain its normal position.

There before him stood the charwoman, but wonderfully transformed. She was a large smiling and voluptuous young woman of some five and twenty years of age, with dark and scornful eyes, and in her movements at once rich, swift and calm, and quite overwhelming. And she was, among many other things, the identical girl he had seen in the box at the 'Daphne' with his present employer, and of whom he had spoken as his niece.

She apologised at once for intruding upon him, but in the half mocking tone of one who appreciates perfectly well that for her to *intrude* increased the honour that any visit paid by her constituted, until it was no longer a mere honour, but must be sought for in some other category.

She spoke with the vaguest foreign accent – that accent that Fane had only twice heard in his life, once in the 'Firenze,' and for the second time at the house to which he had been conducted on the day of his initiation. When disguised as the charwoman, she spoke the purest Cockney. She could speak cockney without a trace of anything but Cockney, or even affect a very thorough American accent, but in speaking English, the slight foreign accent was always noticeable.

Fane and she stood looking at each other for some minutes, and then both burst out into sudden and uncontrollable laughter.

22

FANE PUZZLED FURTHER BY THE ADVENT OF BEAUTY

Fane seemed to possess the inestimable gift of being able to provoke laughter in this woman, but laughter that never turned against him, but that sprang gladly so soon as she was in his presence. It may have been somewhat the recollection of her mirth at the scene that had caused her so much amusement in the piece at the 'Daphne.' But almost at once, when, under these strange conditions, they found themselves face to face with each other, a feeling of ease and bonhomie sprang up between them, and they felt an instant relief from their several cares. It was no doubt this detention and easeful feeling that, playing with their nerves, caused their merriment.

Her mirth this time, however, did not cause any disappointment or reaction in the young poet. He stood waiting for her to announce the reason of her visit, and to explain in some manner her late disguise.

'Well, it falls to my lot to do your room now, you know. But I did not come for that,' she laughed. 'I, as you have probably guessed, form one of the company in which you are now enrolled, and I am taking part in the same piece as yourself. I have come into you like this before I make up again, and in my natural colours, simply to relieve your mind, which is no doubt in a rather alarmed and perplexed state about all this fuss the police have made. That stupid-head of a parson overheard, certainly, a conversation that actually did occur between the 'Belgian' and myself, but he overheard it all wrong. The 'Belgian,' of course, is one of us, and it was quite true that when we met on the stairs this morning, he said something to me in the purest English. This is very natural, as he's an Englishman. Of course the curate couldn't be expected to know that, and at once became suspicious. I expect it was because he heard him speaking in English, and became consequently fanciful and alarmed, that his imagination made him hear a quite innocent remark as something dark and criminal! He's a fool, in any case, but his folly won't interfere any longer with our studies, as he's going tomorrow for certain. It was only through him that we had the policemen down here. You mustn't be alarmed at that, or suppose anything sinister. We shall not be bothered with them any more. If you were running any risk I would tell you. If in the future any unpleasantness awaited you, I will let you know in time. For of course in the most innocent pursuits there is danger!' She laughed strangely, and with mockery as Fane thought. 'But ours is a very well organised company,' she pursued. 'That chattering on the stairs between the pseudo-Belgian and myself was unpardonable. I'm the culprit! Will you forgive me for having given you such a fright, or having been instrumental in doing so?' And she laughed easily, looking calmly into Fane's face, with the perfect self-composure that he had remarked in her the first time he saw her.

'Well, it is rather alarming, when anyone is so much in the dark as I am about the nature of my employment, to find the real living police descending upon the stage of my activities a day or so after I begin work!' replied Fane.

'By the way, are you studying your part?' and she changed her tone as though turning now to a matter of business. 'I expect this little interruption today has hindered you a little. But if I can help you in any way, let me know. You can go and talk with Mrs. Dukes as often as you please. She's an old dear!' At this point the recollection of Mrs. Dukes' spirited defence of her charwoman came into Fane's mind. He remembered she had said that this same charwoman, who in the form of a beautiful young woman was now sitting before him, had been known to her as a child. How was one to account for this? His visitor seemed at once to notice his changed expression, and with a troubling divination, guessed its cause. 'Ah! I know what you're thinking. Why did Mrs. Dukes, in her defence of me, say she'd known me for forty years? As I said, Mrs. Dukes is a great old dear, and she knew that if the police found people masquerading in the house after what the parson had said, that their suspicions would be confirmed, and that we should all be marched off to the police station. To avoid us all this inconvenience, she played a part herself – for Mrs. Dukes also acts sometimes – and by her extraordinary intelligence and tact – she is an old woman in a hundred – she saved us no end of trouble and endless explanatory dialogues with thick-headed officials. She herself enjoyed the scene enormously! I think you'll get to like Mrs. Dukes very much; in the meantime, fellow-player, study her, get up your part. We have such scope that it's difficult to know where to begin, it's true. But note her phrases and learn them as though they were the words of a part in an ordinary theatrical piece. I studied this old charwoman, that I shall become again in a few minutes, from the life, for days and days. Let me hear you do Mrs. Dukes!' she said suddenly.

'No, I'm shy. Besides, I haven't studied her closely enough yet. I'm afraid on this new theatre of the world I shall be dreadfully subject to stage-fright! I should so much like to know of what use my studies will be. Can't you give me an inkling?'

'To what use am I putting my studies of the charwoman?' she replied, rising. 'You see I have almost become, body and soul, the charwoman, Mrs. Beechamp; Mrs. Beechamp's own mother wouldn't know me from her daughter! Well, I'm let out as a charwoman, you see, and do Mrs. Dukes' work for a week or two, and incidentally have to make my fellow-actors' beds, answer the bells, hunt Cole up from the cellar, and so on. It goes without saying that I get an excessively handsome salary for a charwoman – far in excess of my deserts. But that's the affair of the 'Management.' You will no doubt have a much easier time than I do; you will be an invalid old lady, who spends part of her time in bed. For Mrs. Dukes will in future pass a good deal of her time in bed! You will be let out as Mrs. Dukes, no doubt! There will be two Mrs. Dukes; or they may even multiply ad infinitum!'

'Yes, I know; but why should you be paid a heavy salary for charring here? Wouldn't an ordinary charwoman be good enough? I don't see, I confess, the eventual use the 'Management' are going to put me to, once I am as like Mrs. Dukes as two peas!'

'But the pea simile is by no means applicable to you as yet. If you are curious to know the meaning of this enigma, you must hasten and grow as like her as the proverbial sister-pea, and then perhaps suddenly the veil will drop! But now I must go back to my "dressing-room." We are still theatrical people, so my dropping in upon you, although unconventional, may perhaps be excused, especially as our rooms are so close together!'

He had had it several times on the tip of his tongue to ask after her 'uncle,' but a sort of shyness had prevented him.

With a gay 'so-long,' the girl left him, a vague scent that he had certainly never noticed in the charwoman still perfuming his room, and the image of this splendid and enigmatical young woman, following such a strange calling, remaining with him for a time, vaguely and yet poignantly, like the perfume she had abandoned in going away.

'Well! what now?' thought Fane.

But he knew that all his prudent impulses had been routed, and that the only thing he wanted to do now was to stay on and enjoy the companionship of this girl. He knew that his wish to do this would find adequate reasons enough against the perils and uncertainties it involved. He hardly took the trouble to think about it. He knew from the start it would be useless to struggle. And then – oh, of course, and then, she had put things anyway in a better light, and it was deucedly difficult to know *what* to think about all this affair. Then once more throwing a sop to his prudence in the grave promise that the moment anything definitely illegal was demanded of him he would withdraw from his engagement, or the moment he had irrefutable proof of the dishonesty of his associates, he let his mind take the bit in its teeth, and pursued his late visitor's image through an intricate reverie.

The girl for her part, once in her room, throwing herself on her bed, burst into tears. Laughter and tears were evidently her domain, and even mockery; but from the change that came over her once her door was closed, it would be guessed that her elaborate languor, indifference and self-possession was only another part played by her, more often than, and as completely as, the charwoman. She was evidently of an extremely nervous nature, and the scene in appearance so simple and easy that she had just passed through with Fane, and the earlier brushes with the police, had taken all the strength out of her.

'I *hate* this life, I *hate* this life,' she muttered.

23
EVAN ROYAL TAKES COUNSEL WITH HIMSELF

At this point we have determined to penetrate somewhat beneath the pale and slab-like mask of Mrs. Dukes – that is, the incarnation of Mrs. Dukes to be found at that moment at No. 21, Marbury Street, in the place of that suddenly and mysteriously uprooted old woman now lying weak and ailing at the other end of London – and beneath this appearance become more familiar with Evan Royal, alias Mr. Nichols.

At this stage of our story this young man's task becomes, through two happenings — one of which we are about to relate — so difficult, and such repeated calls are made upon his resourcefulness, that it is essential to become better acquainted with the temper of our enigmatical hero. It is on Evan Royal that the success of the mysterious enterprise we are progressively relating depends — on his genius as an actor, on his courage and resourcefulness in moments of danger. Up till now he has appeared vaguely, first behind the disfiguring mask of Mr. Nichols, the noisy and vulgar bohemian, and secondly still more effectually buried and disguised beneath the eccentric personality of Mrs. Dukes.

We find him, on the morning following the visit of the police, sitting up in bed, his wig lying on the chair beside him, his eyes fixed on the morning sky — it is very early, no one is as yet astir, and the full daylight has only just come — he is smoking his Meerschaum pipe, and is evidently holding counsel with himself.

Evan Royal had fawn-like, expressionless eyes, that yet always seemed filled with light, and a mouth at once suave and energetic, that, eyes and mouth, usually go in one's fancy with the pointed beards and long hair of the Cavaliers. But the general expression of his face, more in its lines than in the occasional intensity of his eyes or mouth, is one of great energy. He managed to get up wonderfully like Mrs. Dukes, thanks to a certain resemblance in the thinness of their faces, the almond shape of their eyes and the length of the nose. And his mimicry was amazing. But just this point, at that particular moment, was causing him very grave misgivings.

'It seems to me,' he thought, 'that I am losing the trick. I have had to do so *much* talking, that I'm afraid I have substituted a tone of my own for Mrs. Dukes'. I can't say for certain, anyway. But I don't think the imitation is as good as it was. Anyhow, to make sure, and to freshen myself up, I must make a little journey to "the theatre," and have another look at the old lady, and get someone to make her talk, while I watch her from behind the screen. But the worst of it is, the only time I can possibly be spared here is at night. That's awkward. If that new fellow could only take my place. But I don't suppose he's good enough yet. I must get Lucy to buck him up again.' He went on looking at the sky, and another reflection came to him; in words it would have formed itself thus: 'dismal hole!'

'This is the most complicated affair we've had on hand since I came into the company two years ago, although my part's simple enough. There are too many people in it though! What the deuce does he want to send Lucy and Thompson, masquerading as a Belgian, to spy on me for? It's surely security enough having three of his men day and night watching both the doors here. Although, if I wanted to cut with the money, it isn't they who would stop me! Well, all's plain sailing as yet; the tussle'll come when we try and get all the money in our hands; and although it wouldn't enter anybody's head by any chance that I were *not* Mrs. Dukes, still the old man's solicitors are very wide-awake, according to all accounts.'

In this way he turned over in his mind the various chances for and against success in this tremendous enterprise of his employers, in which more than a million pounds were at stake.

His mind going back to the question of the charwoman and the Belgian, sent there to watch him, and his conviction that this multiplying of the actors in this drama imperilled the scheme, he drew a deep breath and puffed the smoke in clouds towards the open window and the hazy sky. 'Yes! of course

114

they haven't the ghost of a reason to trust me with a large sum of money. What amazes me is that they should consider Lucy, and the other people hanging round here sufficient to outwit me, to stop me, if I wanted to get away with it. But I don't want to get away with their money. I am a perfectly honest person, although I've done nothing for the last two years but dishonest and disreputable things. I only did it to earn a wage; I don't suppose I should ever do anything of this sort on my own account. And I was hoodwinked into doing it, as that young chap upstairs is. But the thought of this million pounds has made me restless — it's no good denying it. It isn't that the idea has even entered my head to make off with it, but it seems insane my working here — and they couldn't possibly bring this thing off without me — for a few hundred pounds, while they are putting over a million in their pockets. It makes one feel rather a fool, and however pleased they may be with me for carrying it through all right, certainly the feeling will be left in their minds that I'm rather a soft 'un. I hate haggling and paying these gentlemen in their own coin. But what I *ought* to do — not only out of justice to myself, but to keep their respect, which I need, as it means at present my living — what I should do is this: just when the critical moment comes, and all depends on my action, I should turn round and say, 'Gentlemen, I'm your willing slave and all that sort of thing, but I'm not going to be imposed on. This is no ordinary venture; and the success of it, all the danger and work, falls on my shoulders. If you wish me to carry this through for you, give me twenty thousand pounds down. Otherwise — well, you can whistle for your million!' Of course, that little chap upstairs is sent here to understudy me in case I should cut up rough, at the last moment. But a precious lot of good he'd be in my place! But they know, practically, that I shan't do anything of that sort. They don't seem even to be taking very much trouble to train their substitute. No, I shan't do anything of that sort. But what I will do is, when this is once finished, I'll get out of the damned gang, and go off somewhere – France, Germany – and try some other sort of life. Life would be amusing anywhere, and dangerous too. I used to think the excitement I got this way couldn't be found in a more regular existence. Delusion! There's only the same old tiresome police-scare each time – always the same interest, always the same element of danger! I'm sick of the sight and thought of the police – they don't stir my pulses any longer, but only come and fuss round and worry one. I know they can't find anything out if one takes sufficient trouble to hide it from them. I yawn now when I see them. This is the element of adventure in my life! This police force, these organised squads of duffers, are supposed to supply me with the pepper and salt of existence, with the element of danger my nature needs! No! this is by no means "life," as my charming employer is so fond of asserting.' So reasoned this arrogant young scoundrel, puffed up with the scandalous successes he had scored over that noble body of men that stand between us and such sharks as he and his employers.

'Being brought up as I was, quite conventionally,' he continued to himself, 'taught to consider dishonesty in any form not only as abhorrent, but very far away from such respectable young men as me – I could have sworn, for example, that whatever else happened to me, I should never become a thief – the plunge I took when I found out, on joining this company of mysterious villains, that I was indeed no longer honest, was stimulating for the moment. To be a thing that in my farthest dreams it had never occurred to me I could be, and also taking the leap, as it were, without the pale of society, excited me. But it is duller outside the pale than inside it. It is like the romance of the ring: we are told that a prize fighter is the most cold and scientific of mortals, and considers the ring as the safest place in the world. I am quite sick of the commonplace dishonesty of my employers. With such a man as I to serve them, they run very little risk of being found out, even in a big 'coup' like the present. No, my connection ends with them once this business is finished. But what I will do is this. I will insist, before going further, on being paid four thousand pounds down, for my share in this transaction – not twenty, but only four. That, with the thousand I have already put away, will assure me against starvation anywhere in Europe.'

He went on gazing out of the window, at the chilly sky overhead, and listened to the first sharp early sounds of the moving city.

'To lie here smoking in this chilly dingy room, supposed to be an old woman, considering my plans for the day, twenty minutes after sunrise, few people awake for a mile round, except the poor dull boring old policemen – the feeling of loneliness and strangeness – there is *stimung* in it, as the Germans say, a certain swagger. But how much finer if there were real human interests in it, and significant dangers – not the old clock-work menace of the police – clock-work that seldom works, or is always too slow! And then instead of living interest, always this same cold, mechanical scheme of robbery – always this blight of sordidness! I believe my employer to be a remarkable man, he has somewhat the same feelings as myself. But like many artists he is unfortunately poor, and is compelled always to do only the things that pay, and alas! also, only in the *way* that pays. What we are doing now need not be a pot-boiler, but it is. What a terrible thing poverty is! He needs about a hundred thousand a year to carry on his company, to keep it up properly, and go on with his fantastic projects. The result is that he has to be thinking constantly of money, money. This preoccupation enters into all our schemes, and spoils them. Of course, if he did not always conceive things on such a gorgeous scale! That's the Oriental in him. Where I could carry a thing out with the simplest means, and would prefer it for that very reason, he must always have a host of retainers, and every detail planned in the most sumptuous fashion. He's a failure, there's no doubt about it, simply because he wasn't born a multi-millionaire. For his particular temperament he needed to be that. As it is, something sordid always enters into his schemes — namely, the humiliating necessity to make them pay!'

He emptied out the ashes of his pipe, and getting out of bed, sat down at the table and began to write a letter. He had to get all his *private* correspondence over, all Evan Royal's correspondence — before Cole appeared.

24

MRS. DUKES' FAMILY PUT IN AN APPEARANCE

Mrs. Dukes, for Evan Royal had now become Mrs. Dukes again, sat in front of the fire watching Cole smoking with meditative eyes, when Mrs. Beechamp announced 'two gentlemen to see the Missis.' Mrs. Dukes, at this unexpected announcement, at once pulled herself together, and a look of great keenness came into her eyes.

There is no moment more propitious for revelations, not only of breeding, but of character and intent, than the moment a man enters a strange room for the first time. Its aspect, its strangeness, the furniture, all seem like a watchful guardian to intimidate him and unmask him. In these cases the unaccustomed chair he sits on, or slides on to, is more efficacious than any watch-dog. And Mrs. Dukes, like every true observer, did not lose this opportunity to examine the newcomers closely in this first moment of embarrassment.

Her comment made to herself while her eyes rested blandly on them, ran somewhat in this way. 'So here they are at last! I might have known that that big treacle pot of honeyed millions advertised in all the papers, would attract *some* little flies! Here are the first comers, then! A dubious pair.'

The first man looked rather like a German; he was short, with ugly blonde moustaches sticking stoutly up, hard blue eyes, and high, level cheek bones, and had a very self-possessed and energetic air. He was that type of Englishman that an echo of German trenchant business methods have produced here. But England ten years before when it first made its appearance, along with a kindred Yankee type, was not ripe for its advent, and despite all its smartness and go — even for that very reason — it often met with considerable difficulties, and was driven into dishonest paths and methods to keep its personality intact. The second was an insignificant little man, who always had a far-away look in his eyes, and who had constantly to be recalled to the realisation of his present situation, geographically and temporally. His absent-mindedness did not, though, give him an air of innocence, unworldliness and honesty, but only that of a strange and peculiarly irritating hypocrisy. Because of this characteristic of his, he had rather the air of following the other. They seemed both from forty to forty-five years old.

Mrs. Dukes only said 'Well?' She had determined to let them say all they had to say before committing herself.

The first man began, in seating himself, 'We — my brother

Jim 'ere, and I — saw in the papers what good fortune you'd 'ad, and we said, as we were up this way, "Let's go in and see Auntie Dolly." It's so long since we've seen any one of our kin, we felt quite funny like at the thought of seein' anyone again, well — yew know — what's near to us like. I hope you won't think, Mrs. Dukes, that we've come 'ere because we 'eard you was rich now. That made us 'esitate. Jim 'ere says, "P'raps she's proud now, and don't want to see any of *us!*" Well, *yew* know — there are some feels like that when circumstances is altered. I don't mean any offence, Mrs. Dukes. Besides, I says to Jim, "No," I says, "what father always used to say was, 'My sister Dolly ain't got no nonsense about *'er,* and if she'd only married another man!'" — but there, we won't say nothin' about them what's dead,' he added, at a certain severity that had come into Mrs. Dukes' face at the reference to her dead husband. 'Bygones is bygones, and 'e did be'ave 'andsome at the last. "No," says I to Jim, "Auntie Dolly ain't that sort." And so 'ere we are.'

The second man changed suddenly the position of his legs, became unabsent-minded for a moment, and swallowed huskily, as though in confirmation of all that had been said by his more loquacious companion.

'Oh, so you're my nephews, are you,' said Mrs. Dukes, very coolly at last. 'I thought you were younger. 'Ow old *are* ye?'

She had apparently been fortunate in her guess, as the slightly more alert expression of the first man showed, and his answer.

'Well, we've gone through a lot, ye know, my brother Jim and I. It's that what ages a man. We've been in South Africa workin' now for upwards of fifteen year, and we didn't 'ave no luck. 'Ard times, 'ard times, it often *was.* Jim 'ere, 'e isn't exactly *weak,* but, well — yew know — 'e ain't so strong as I am, and many's the time I've 'ad to work for two. I'm thirty-seven, and Jim 'ere, 'e's thirty-five. Everyone takes us for more'n that. Well, Auntie, ye don't look over pleased to see us,' continued he, attempting to be a little brusque and cheery, and put things on a more sentimental footing at the same time. He seemed to feel if he were going to find his way to 'Auntie Dolly's' heart, he must put an end to this one-sided dialogue and draw her out a little. 'Well, Auntie Dolly, you're lookin' very well, ain't she, Jim?' he said, turning to his mooney brother.

'Yes, just what I was thinkin',' said Jim, with a strange jerky utterance.

Mrs. Dukes was still silent. She was enjoying all this very much, but was not unalive to the fact that she was in a very ticklish position, which required the most delicate handling. She was forced, despite the fact that she was quite convinced that these were bogus brothers, bogus nephews, and in short, bogus individuals in every way — she was compelled to respect and consider the bare possibility of them being quite bonafide relations come to see her. And so she had to be doubly careful and doubly armed. For she had two pairs of individuals to defend herself against — the possible relations, and the possible sharpers or what-not, claiming to be her relations.

Her thought, parallel with their dialogue, ran as follows. 'That fellow that does all the talking has hitched himself down a bit for the occasion, drops more aitches than he usually does, and talks somewhat more roughly. That — since his own speech cannot be very much finer, but only a little — argues a certain exactness in his information. I suppose the nephews do exist somewhere or other — they may turn up at any moment — and he appears to know that they are very rough people, and not just *rather* rough and ready, as he is, no doubt, in reality. If he has this precise information, I must be doubly careful not to make a slip. He looks a rather cute chap, the talking one, and he hasn't done it badly, after all. A nuisance we couldn't get more information about her friends and relatives.'

The first man seemed rather surprised at his reception. What he had expected it is difficult to say. But he now remained silent for some minutes, looking intently at the fire-place, momentarily as absent-minded as his brother Jim.

He was startled out of his minute-long reverie by receiving a smart rap on his head, from a small crust of bread thrown by Mrs. Dukes, and looked up wonderingly at the sound of sudden laughter.

'Ah, Auntie, as gamey as ever!' laughed the obsequious nephew in return.

'Yes, up to all sorts a' little tricks, bless ye! So yew thought ye'd come round and see your rich auntie, did ye? None of ye would a' come near me for love or money a month ago, and now money brings the lot of ye round me ears. Oh, yew pretty grovellin' time-servin' lot, yew!'

Mrs. Dukes said this with a great show of sneering bitterness.

'That's just what my brother Jim said, you'd go on like that. Can't one 'ave the desire to see one of the only relatives as one 'as in the world, without 'avin' it thought sordid motives 'as prompt ye? I didn't expect that of you, Auntie Dolly. We're poor, but we 'ave our pride. It ain't because yew're rich, Auntie Dolly, that we come 'ere.'

He made a movement as though he were going to get up, in a dignified manner, and take his departure, and Jim began moving his legs, twirling his hat and swallowing, in responsive activity. But he seemed to reconsider his decision, and leant forward in his chair.

'Now, Auntie Dolly, don't let's quarrel like; there ain't no need for us to quarrel. We shall be goin' in a minute or two;

'aven't yew a word 'a kindness to say to two poor devils what 'as no 'ome to come back to, when they do come back, after fifteen years down there at the Cape? Jim 'ere 'e don't say much, but 'e feels, that man does! It was Jim said 'Let's go in and see Auntie Dolly,' before I did. Yew mustn't think because the world i' mer-cen-ary, and grabbin', and now that yew've got the shillin's shews itself brazen like, that all's like that. Blood is stronger than water, ay, an' stronger than gold! You're our kin! Remember that, Auntie Dolly!'

That Mrs. Dukes remained unmoved at this last speech seemed to nonplus him considerably. All she said was, 'Well, I suppose yew an' Jim'll be goin' back down there to the Cape again soon?'

'Not for a month or two. We 'ave some business to see to up North, near Liverpool, next week. Was you at the fun'ral, Auntie Dolly?' he asked abruptly.

Just then the charwoman appeared, and announced with a voice of dull awe and importance mixed, 'The Inspector a' Police to see yew, Mrs. Dukes!'

The change in the countenance of the two men could not have escaped anybody. The man who was on the point of speaking again shut his mouth up with a snap, and sat up stiff in his chair, then with a spasmodic jerk rose to his feet. 'Jim' also rose, his eyes grown very active and wandering towards the door continually.

'Well, Auntie Dolly, as you 'av visitors, I will say good-*bye* to yew for now. If I and Jim are passin' your way again, we'll nip in. So-long, Auntie!'

'Ain't yew goin' to give me your address − or ain't ye got none?' cried Mrs. Dukes after them. They crossed the Inspector at the door, who looked at them narrowly. They got out as quickly as they could.

The Inspector had come about some details on the 'Belgian,' and to overhaul his rooms again. This was done, and after twenty minutes' futile bustle, the police left too, and Mrs. Dukes was once more alone. But not for long.

25

MRS. DUKES PREPARES FOR THE SOLICITORS

As soon as the Inspector had taken his departure, Mrs. Beechamp came in and stood, arms akimbo, leaning against the door. Mrs. Dukes had settled herself meditatively near the fire. She looked up slowly at Mrs. Beechamp, and they exchanged a glance, the intimacy of which showed that this was not the first campaign that they had been on together.

Mrs. Beechamp approached the fire, and began warming her hands.

'Did you see those gentry, Lucy?' asked Mrs. Dukes in a moment, in a low voice – the voice of Evan Royal. 'It was very lucky the old policeman turning up just then. That definitely settled from what walk of life *they* hailed. You should have seen them scoot. I thought they were going to knock over the bobby in their flight. They are two charming young relatives of mine, they tell me: my nephews. Now, whether I have any nephews or not – other than these agreeable young fellows who have constituted themselves my nephews temporarily – whether there really are two unfortunate beings anywhere about who bear such a close relationship to me – that, Lucy, I cannot tell you. The gentleman who gave the Boss the tip about this – through whom we know that my late husband was preparing to die and leave me that enormous, absurd, white elephant of a fortune – that gentleman gave no information of this nature. I did my best to get it out of my double while I was painting her portrait, but she insisted on joking about her relations: 'Lord, yes — uncles and nephews and cousins any number,' she told me she had. The Duchess of Bentland was a cousin of hers, she informed me. In that case I may expect a visit from her ladyship at any moment. But my respected double, Mrs. Dukes, treated her as though she were the dirt under her feet. I shall be compelled to do the same if she comes here, of course, much as it goes against the grain. But these nephews of mine may turn out troublesome, Lucy. The brighter of the two looked like a three-card-trick man, the other like a journeyman burglar. The three-card-trick man is capable, Lucy, of giving me a knock on the head, if he thinks I have a hundred pounds in the house, and if he despairs of bamboozling me out of any money. Now, I should be too quick for him, no doubt. But if I began scuffling about in here, I'm afraid my wig would come off, and then all the fat would be in the fire. So the next time these gentlemen put in an appearance, Lucy, you keep coming in and out; also, get Fane to come down, and I'll introduce him to them. You see, an old woman like me must be protected.' Mrs. Dukes stopped a moment at a sign from her companion. They both listened, but it seemed Mrs. Beechamp had given a false alarm.

'I wonder where they got this information from, since we, who wanted just that sort of information, couldn't get any. They evidently wouldn't come here claiming to be my nephews, unless they knew that I or my husband had had a brother or sister. This affair has been *recklessly* started! Think of the slimness of the material we have to go on. Of course that was due to the devilish hurry we were in — we had to do it all at a moment's notice. But the Boss really does put too much trust in my sagacity. I wouldn't trust any man so much as he trusts me. Of course in a sense it's as safe as anything. No one would ever dream of supposing I were not Mrs. Dukes. The only way we might be caught out would be if some long-lost relation turned up – some *real* one.'

'You'd manage them all right, Evan,' said Mrs. Beechamp with conviction.

'I expect I should,' replied the old lady sleepily.

Mr. Higginbotham had moved out that morning with all his belongings, and Mrs. Dukes had arranged to move up there as soon as the rooms were ready. Now, assuming the peevish tones that had echoed beneath that roof for the last forty years, she asked Mrs. Beechamp if 'them rooms wasn't ready yet?'

'I'm not feelin' *nearly* so well, Mrs. Beechamp. And then I feel all of a tremble; Mr. 'atchett will be 'ere at three – Oh dear me!'

Mrs. Beechamp went upstairs to complete the preparation of the first floor rooms for Mrs. Dukes' reception.

The Liverpool solicitors, Truman and Hatchett, in whose hands all the affairs of the late Mr. Arthur St. Giles Dukes remained, were sending one of their chiefs to London to interview Mrs. Dukes personally, and get fuller instructions than could be received by letter. They had written two very long letters to her, as there were several details connected with the winding up of the late millionaire's estate which demanded immediate attention. But the present millionairess from her residence in Marbury Street had replied to these epistles so incoherently, with such mingled ambiguity and sententiousness – she had, in several passages evidently been attempting a forensic turn of phrase, and had copied directly out of their letters several legal expressions and catch words – that they determined no progress could be made in this way. Yet she would have to be constantly referred to during the legal business incident upon the abnormal decease of a millionaire. It was evident, then, to the council called in the offices of Truman and Hatchett, to consider these two terrific epistles emanating from Marbury Street, that before anything could be done, before the estate of their late client could be put in order, it was essential to first of all introduce a little order into the head of this chaotically worded and minded old woman. This was a difficult and not very grateful duty that devolved upon this respectable firm. Order in Mrs. Dukes' head! Mrs. Dukes' head to be put in order! This, after deliberation, the four rather bald but energetic middle-aged gentlemen sitting seriously round the table in Judd Street, Liverpool, resolved was the next step to take, the thing that must be brought about somehow. The smartest of these four gentlemen was despatched, with a clerk, to attack this problem — to see how ingrained the incoherence was, to inspect the new client and millionairess, and, generally, to see what could be done. The thing that seemed most desirable to Messrs. Truman and Hatchett was to get the old woman up to Liverpool. If they had her under their eyes they would feel more secure — they could clear up and arrange her very eccentric and disordered brain bit by bit, as they needed it. They could go on working in parallel fashion at her and at the business in hand together. They could relieve one another and take her in hand by turns. But what certainly would paralyse them would be to feel at the other end of England this vague anarchical menace, threatening their proceedings at every step; and then to have those strange letters arriving twice a week to fill their minds with bewilderment, discouragement and dismay.

So Mr. Hatchett on his way to London, rehearsing what he should say to Mrs. Dukes, for the first time in his professional career saw himself forced to dispense with the rhetoric and phraseology of the law, and sought to prepare as simple explanations as possible on the various most important points that he had first of all to discuss with her. In a sense he had also to clear up his own mind. He cursed the late Mr. Dukes heartily for leaving his money to this old woman, and foresaw that there would be as much trouble, first and last, as though three millionaires had died instead of one.

To teach this old woman to be a millionairess, was, he felt, hardly the business of the most illustrious solicitor in Liverpool. Yet he was evidently let in for it, now; he would have to give her, anyhow, a few elementary lessons. As he drew nearer in the London express to this dark, chaotic, antiquated mass that was the brain of Mrs. Dukes, he became more and more gloomy at the thought of what lay before him.

It was for the reception of this gentleman that the first floor rooms were being prepared, and whose far approach had put Mrs. Dukes 'all in a tremble.'

26

THE ARRIVAL OF MR. HATCHETT

Evan Royal was going to receive Messrs. Truman and Hatchett's representative in the sumptuous saloons of the first floor for a reason other than respect for those gentlemen. He had, in thinking it out, considered it most likely that the original Mrs. Dukes — who had so utterly, and apparently forever, given place to him — would have received the solicitor behind the shop. Especially if she had not been well, she would not have wished to be transplanted in that state to any new surroundings, even so far as the first floor. And he felt that to behave exactly as his model would have behaved was the surest guarantee of success in his difficult part. But then also he reflected that the lawyer would be too much shocked to find a millionairess still immersed in such utter squalor. And he did not think it advisable to *disgust* the solicitor with his new client. It would be preferable that he should merely look upon her as a joke. As far as removing permanently to the first floor went, this seemed inadvisable because of Cole. Cole was a question that had to be treated with great delicacy. There was at present a kind of spell over Cole. Cole had been under a spell of silence and 'sulkiness' all of his life; for that reason it had been easier for him to be put under this new spell, a spell of double silence, so to speak – a conniving, wilful silence as well. But Royal was afraid that if his habits were changed too brusquely, or those of the new Mrs. Dukes, that Cole would get restless and moping, and might suddenly begin giving trouble. Until they moved to a new and more aristocratic house – as they would have to do before long, as a millionairess could not go on living in Marbury Street without attracting too much attention – he determined that the greater part of his time must still be spent in the room behind the shop.

At three o'clock that afternoon, Mrs. Dukes, looking rather white and ill, was installed beside the fire in the room from which she had driven Mr. Higginbotham. It was the largest, best papered, most sumptuously furnished room in her house. As we have already indicated, everything in this room reminded one of the flight of time: if one sat down on practically any of its chairs, one was reminded of the flight of time by a sensation that that chair's legs were not either so strong or steady as they doubtless once had been. If one glanced at oneself in the glass from a certain angle, one would discover with surprise that one's right eye had suddenly been removed to within a quarter of an inch of one's scalp. But everywhere, in the cracked or defective glasses, the battered fire-irons, the chipped picture frames, Time's flight was evident. The overflowing of the curiosity shop into the rest of the house was here witnessed as in no other room. Vast, heavy and dilapidated cabinets, too immense to climb up to the third floor, had found their way up here. Had they attempted another flight of stairs, one felt they would have collapsed altogether, and fallen into dusty fragments. In the middle of the mantel-piece stood a burly porcelain boy, disembowelled, the left half of his stomach having disappeared in the struggle for existence that he had no doubt carried on for many years in the shop beneath. Two dark figures, in yellow and black clay, exhibited their terrible mutilations – one with the stump of an arm, the other with part of her face bashed in – like horrible beggars in the streets of southern towns. The table had not been moved an eighth of an inch for many a long day. It was covered with a heavy cloth, and this hid its many legs and rather complicated machinery; but if anyone attempted to move it, it literally put up its back like an angry cat; at one of its principal junctures with one of its principal wings, it humped itself up.

Mr. Hillington was standing warming himself at the fire, and looked nervously at his watch from time to time.

There was a ring at the bell. But it turned out to be merely one of the many callers on behalf of business houses of one sort and another, that the news that a defenceless old woman was in possession of a vast fortune all of a sudden, and doubtless itching to spend it, had brought post haste to Marbury Street.

Royal continued where they had stopped a moment on hearing the bell. 'That he should suspect you of being an unscrupulous and wily businessman, attempting or already possessing an ascendancy over me, and intending to have the control of my money, or of as much of it as you could lay your hands on – all this diverts suspicion from me. Not that he would be likely to suspect me of anything. There is only one thing he could suspect, and that is the bare and awful truth – namely, that I am not I. And this, evidently, is the very last thing in the world that it would occur to anyone to suspect. My make-up is as good as it could be. – Yes, I agree that you should play for that suspicion. But not too much! It mustn't be overdone, for the very good reason that suspicion is infectious: once a man is suspicious of one thing, he rapidly becomes suspicious, without reason, of others. I shouldn't stir him up too much in that direction. Just make him dislike you a little – you need do practically nothing to effect this – and get him to look askance at you a little. In your capacity of stock-broker – by the way, it was a stroke of luck our keeping that office on – I think the Boss ought always to have a stock-broker in the company, it's of no end of use – in your capacity of broker, you must hint that you will be able a little later on to advise me about the placing of some of my money. Also you will say, as you are one of the only people who have known me for a long time and in whom I can trust, that you have consented for the present to help me with the business details that taking over the property involves. That tone, I think, is the best. I shouldn't give him any digs. I shouldn't suggest that you intended to do *him* out of anything. But there he is, I expect,' broke off Royal, at the sound of a motor, and a sharp ring and rap below.

A moment later the solicitor, followed by a young man who was evidently his clerk, entered the room.

There was nothing trenchant in the appearance of Mr. Hatchett, as his name suggested. He was large, loose and extremely carefully dressed. He had one of those English faces that when one first sees them at once suggest a *sound,* namely the lowing of a cow. But as a matter of fact his speech was rather quick than slow, and behind his glasses his eyes were very immobile and alert. Of the four rather bald men that were 'Truman and Hatchett, Solicitors,' he was, as we have said, the smartest and most practical.

The presence of Hillington evidently made him rather reserved at first. 'Who the devil's this?' was the form his querying glance took in his own mind. He hastened, by various means, the moment when he should know all there was to know about Mr. Hillington. He gave both Mrs. Dukes and Hillington, in the first five minutes, every opportunity for disclosing the identity, occupation, and business there at that particular moment of Mr. Hillington. Mr. Hillington gradually disclosed himself, like a flower − disclosed his name, his profession, his connection with Mrs. Dukes. And then Mr. Hatchett said − but still inaudibly, in the depths of his large professional person − 'Humph.' Evidently, he thought, he must go on with his business for the moment without paying any further attention to this interloper. He would ascertain, by the amount of interference he permitted himself, and Mrs. Dukes permitted him, the status of Mr. Hillington.

The solicitor considered his present job as having many analogies to a dentist's. What he first of all had to do, as with a decayed tooth, was to thoroughly clean out Mrs. Dukes' mind, before putting the gold − the million pounds, − into it. She evidently did not realise that she was a millionairess − this was palpable. Her fingernails alone were proof. He would go about his business as though Mr. Hillington were not there. It seemed to him that one of the simplest ways of getting her into shape would be to advance her a very large sum of money, and turn her loose in London for a week or so. He felt the spending of large quantities of money was essential to her if she were going to become rapidly a presentable old plutocrat. So he at once offered her the use of five thousand pounds. He then tried to 'draw her out.' He began the examination of the contents of her mind, that is to say. But no dentist ever found a wisdom tooth so far back in the mouth and so difficult to get at as he found Mrs. Dukes' perverse old mind.

27
THE INTERVIEW

On entering the room Mr. Hatchett had exclaimed, with a sort of condescending deference, 'I am very happy, Mrs. Dukes, to make our new client's acquaintance, and I hope that we shall be of equal service to you as to your late husband. Are you feeling better now, my dear madam? We were concerned to hear that you had been forced to take to your bed the other day. Of course the events of the last week or so must have been very trying for you. This is one of my clerks, Mr. Woodcock; I have brought him as we have a certain amount of business to transact, if you feel equal to it? Yes? That's right.'

'I'm 'fraid I didn't understand all the things you wanted in your letters,' said Mrs. Dukes. 'If I'd 'ad Mr. 'illington 'ere, I should 'a been better able to answer you. Oh Lord! What am I goin' to do with all that money? I don't know, I'm *sure*. *Fancy* bein' left money like that, ye know! I never thought 'e could make a 'apenny. And now I've become a curiosity. Yew should just see the people that comes 'ere to 'ave a look at me. I feels like a Barnum's freak. Oh! Lord!' And Mrs. Dukes screwed all her face up, threw up her hands and let them subside on her knees, and swayed her body forward, and then let it fall back again.

Mr. Hatchett and his clerk, Mr. Woodcock, sat down beside the large table. Mr. Woodcock, who had chosen a receptacle for his person that turned out to be a basket chair submerged in faded cushions and velvety cloths, became at once conscious of the most subtle and gradual downward movement imaginable – as though the floor were a kind of springy mud, and his chair were slowly sinking into it. He discovered, however, on nearer inspection, that it was not the floor that was giving beneath him, but that the hidden basket-work within the seat he had chosen was closing up like a concertina. But while his clerk was going through these successive experiences, Mr. Hatchett, for his part, was also momentarily absorbed in the Windsor chair he had carelessly mounted. A jerky and plaintive noise rose from one of its metal feet. He had no sooner fixed his eyes and his attention on this foot when suddenly, from its opposite side, came an alarming cracking sound, accompanied by a slight tilting over in that direction. At this point the clerk and the principal's eyes met, and simultaneously they rose to their feet, their respective chairs subsiding and reeling away behind them. They gingerly chose others, and, after a few minutes, found, each of them, a chair that, if manipulated with great caution, permitted them to maintain that human attitude that is exactly half way between standing up and lying on the floor.

These little adventures, with much clearing of throats, rustling of papers, remarks about the weather, etc. having been got through, Mr. Hatchett came to the business of the day.

He spent the next five minutes in finding out who Mrs. Dukes' visitor was. And then, as we have said, he settled down to the examination of her mind. Subsequently, he gave her exhaustive details on the size, shape, character, potentialities, etc. of her husband's fortune. He introduced her to this as though it had been a living organism, as indeed it was. It had certain peculiarities, little eccentricities, quite like Mrs. Dukes herself. It had a history, just as a patient has a pathological history in a doctor's voluminous note-book. Its robustness had been chequered by certain periods of indisposition. It still felt at times the after results of these indispositions. It had a very large frame — indeed it was a giant, measuring exactly one million, eleven thousand, three hundred and thirty-six pounds, five and two pence three farthings. But for this very reason it was rather delicate, and needed great care.

Mr. Arthur St. Giles Dukes had made his money principally in importing beet sugar into the country. He had done other lucrative things as well; the commerce of bananas, for instance, had brought him in very large sums of money. But it was out of beet sugar that he had made the bulk of his fortune. A year or so before his decease he had definitely retired from business, and since then had still done a certain amount of varyingly successful speculation; but his fortune had remained nearly stationary. It included a certain amount of house property in Lancashire and Glasgow.

One of the things that Mr. Hatchett urged upon Mrs. Dukes was the advisability of her coming up to Liverpool to inspect the house that Mr. Dukes had left her in that city — the one he had died in, and in which some of the servants still remained. And then the house in the country, near Liverpool — they would like to know whether she intended to keep it on or not. In short, in this and other ways he showed her how necessary it was for her to bestir herself, and first of all in the direction of Liverpool.

For the whole of her life Mrs. Dukes had shown a distinct predilection for words that she could not pronounce properly, and that she only half understood. But it seemed that now, and especially in the presence of the lawyer, she often hesitated to use any ordinary word at all. Her speech in parts was quite incomprehensible, sounding not unlike Esperanto, and causing awful pauses in the course of their three-cornered discussion. 'Wherehunder I should – er – hemphatically interpret this, as – er – emanuating from the hunder-signed.' Such sentences as this caused a deep hush for several minutes after their utterance, only broken by Mr. Hatchett's loud and chilly cough. It seemed that no other words or phrases dare appear immediately after such a one as that.

Mrs. Dukes' attitude was first of all that of a rather ailing and bewildered old woman, hardly grasping the situation, and regarding this enormous sum of money she was being so much bothered about as quite unreal and impossible, and therefore all the trouble and worrying she was being subjected to as mad and unnecessary. Then would come ten minutes or so in which she pulled herself together, felt important, and entered into the discussion, asking the solicitor what she evidently considered as very shrewd questions. It was during these phases of the interview that she became so obscure, and the terrific sentences to which we have referred put in their appearance. Then at other times she would sit grinning at first one person and then the other, as though to say that *she* was not going to trouble herself about it all – let them settle it – and seemed determined to treat this absurd sum of money that had so unceremoniously entered into her life as it deserved – as a joke. A million of money, indeed! What was that to her?

The solicitor felt that he had really made some headway. Towards the end, where her discourse became involved, he did his best to break it up at once; he charged it and scattered it, he interrupted it, put it in simpler language, etc. It was her relapses into this Volapuk of speech and mind that he principally dreaded, and that he was come to London about, in truth. If it had not been for this, a subordinate would have served the purpose for the moment.

He made her sign a good many papers, more than was necessary. He felt this would increase her sense of her own importance, and also make her strive to understand the business in hand better. For he knew the enormous importance that illiterate and obscure people attach to their signature. He hoped even that all these signatures that she had given would weigh a little on her mind. He hoped to make her a little afraid, a little suspicious that perhaps she was being done. This might sharpen her wits.

Every morning before Cole put in an appearance Evan Royal spent a half hour or so in forging Mrs. Dukes' signature, and studying her handwriting. He had done so systematically. He had made a typical alphabet of 'Duke letters,' as he called them: a typical Duke A, a typical B, etc. For this was a very important part of his role — that he should be able to write as Mrs. Dukes wrote. He never lost an opportunity during the day of writing a note, or doing up a lodger's book — of practising. And he had become very proficient.

Mr. Hatchett treated Hillington with courtesy but reserve. He concluded that he was a man to reckon with, and one who might have a great influence with Mrs. Dukes. On learning that he was a stock broker, he said to himself, 'hum, hum!' There was only one other profession that Hillington could have declared himself a member of that would have caused an even more emphatic mental ejaculation on Mr. Hatchett's part: namely that of solicitor. He foresaw an enemy in this sleek, nervous, keen looking member of the Stock Exchange, but that would be in the future he felt. He treated him as one would treat a man whom one had learnt, from some divine and prophetic source, would in five years time give one a black eye. He felt that the future enmity of his firm for Mr. Hillington was inevitable, and therefore was quite calm about it, and treated him accordingly. They were in Fate's hands. Mr. Hillington couldn't help being their adversary later on even if he tried. This was quite understood, therefore it would be superfluous to take any more notice of it now. It was just as churlish to bear a grudge in expectation, and let a future thing rankle and affect one's manners, as it was to go on ruminating a past injury. Let by-gones be by-gones, but let the Future remain the Future, also. For the present Mr. Hillington might be useful, if he were going to attach himself to Mrs. Dukes, in putting some order in her affairs, and launching her as a millionairess.

He stayed for three hours and a half, and resolved then to return to Liverpool that evening, as everything essential for the moment had been arranged between them. And besides, Mrs. Dukes had definitely promised to come to Liverpool in the course of a day or two.

When the solicitor, with many amiable courtesies, had withdrawn, Hillington and Royal looked at each other very seriously for a few minutes in silence, until they heard the front door bang.

Everything had gone off very well, and they had very little to say to each other. Hillington soon left too, to give a report in a distant part of London of this interview.

28
A STRUGGLE AT THE DEAD OF NIGHT

At one o'clock in the morning, seven or eight hours after Mr.

Hatchett's visit to Marbury Street, the door leading from the large out-house, that took up half the wall-like yard at the back of the premises, opened, and a silent figure stepped out into the moonlight. It was a short and sturdy figure of a man, with a large motor cap drawn tight down on his head. He closed the door gently again behind him. He then stood for several minutes quite still and apparently listening. He shivered slightly; for it was freezing hard.

Leaving the personality, the wig, the garments and the odour, of the landlady behind him — leaving, in fact, their envelope, for the first time for many days — this figure was Evan Royal's. He was dressed more or less like a respectable chauffeur. He held himself a little stiffly, as the hours and days spent in the cramped and hunched-up position his impersonation of Mrs. Dukes necessitated were beginning to tell on him.

He heard a cab in Marbury Street, in the front, clattering off, and when that sound had died away, everything seemed quite still, and he crossed softly over to the gate, opened it and stood in the little side street, that ran up, between blackened walls and the backs of houses, towards the ghettos to the north of Golden Square. He had no sooner closed the gate, still with great precision and being careful to make as little noise as possible, than it seemed to him that the wall at his side — all deeply in shadow, — moved with a jerk. His head was turned away from the Marbury Street end and towards the far end of this alley. The next moment he found himself face to face with a policeman, who had been leaning in the shadow of the wall as soundless as a mountain pool on a summer night, or as the wall itself. What it was that had inspired this policeman to remain so quiet it was difficult to say. But it is a fact that policemen seem to enjoy very much playing ghosts at night. It is the effect of the silent shoes, most probably. To suddenly find themselves perambulating silent streets at the dead of night, practically as silent as the streets themselves, awakens in them the desire to be *still more* silent, even more mysterious. In these lonely, soundless walks, they become romantic about their calling; romantic about their shoes! They have vague notions of being silent, invisible, mysterious agents of Justice. They enjoy passing you at night, with their great bulk of black clothes and helmet, without making a sound, the face set and impassive. One not infrequently sees them lurking in dark corners, or gliding down the shadowy side of a street.

Whatever had induced this particular policeman to lurk just where he was lurking, there he was in front of Royal, and had apparently given up simulating a statue, for he stepped forward towards the young man.

After a second of hesitation, Royal stepped over to the farther pavement, and started walking away from Marbury Street and in the direction of Oxford Circus – which lay northwards through a half dozen gloomy little streets.

The policeman stepped forward as though to intercept him, but as Evan Royal was too quick for him, he merely followed, trying to get level with him. For quite ten yards neither of them said a word. Then the policeman called out in a strained and hollow voice.

'Stop! Where are *yew* off to? What 'a yew been doin' in there?'

Royal made no reply, but walked on. The policeman again broke silence, still walking quickly, and taking one or two running steps.

'Stop! I says stop! What 'a yew bin doin' there? Stop, will ye?'

Royal stopped, and said in the sort of oily conciliatory voice of the London rough, 'Nothin', guv'ner; yew kind o' frightened me like. Nothin'. That's where my missis works. I come out quiet like, 'cause I ain't s'posed to see 'er there, see? There's nothin' wrong, guv'ner.'

'Yew come up 'ere with me to the light,' replied the policeman, looking towards Marbury Street, and placing himself on the farther side of Royal, as though to prevent his going further in that direction.

Evan Royal stood quite still for a moment; then, stepping suddenly back, he hit the policeman between the eyes, and dashed straight ahead as though intending to spring over him. The latter went down cleanly enough, but in his spring forward, Royal's foot slipped on a little frozen pool in the gutter, and in a moment he was on top of the policeman. Before he could scramble to his feet again, the man had caught him round the waist, and his whistle was sending out its strident alarm. Royal wrenched it from his mouth, and seizing him by the collar and throat, dashed his head up and down upon the pavement, in the same moment trying to jerk himself out of the other man's grasp. But the policeman hung on stoically, attempting the whole time to roll over and swing Royal underneath.

'Confound you! What are you hanging on like that for?' cried Royal forgetfully in the heat of the struggle. He saw the other's eyes fixed on his in a wide expressionless sort of stare — like a drowning man's, he thought. He showed none of the conscious effort and resolution that made him cling so tightly. It seemed a long time since he had blown his whistle, and yet no one had come into sight. Royal kept looking to left and right, dashing his antagonist's head with furious blows against the curb stone, but still without effect. He felt he could not drag himself free, and a change of tactic might result in a change of position, and to a less favourable one, as the policeman was a much heavier man than he. If no one came, he

141

was sure that this brutal battering process would have its effect, namely that of knocking the other man silly. Then suddenly he saw that a black figure, running quickly, had entered the lane at the farther end. As it came on, by the light of the farthest of the four lamps in this narrow alley, he saw it was a policeman coming to the rescue of his colleague.

He was caught in this man's embrace as though in a man trap. He relinquished his grip on the other's collar, and put his arms behind his back, wrenching at the hands that held him so obstinately. The policeman, finding his throat freed, began to shout hoarsely.

The other man was slowly approaching — slowly as it seemed to Royal, although he was running as fast as his legs would carry him. But he seemed to be creeping forward only. Royal was furious at this fancied slowness, although it was naturally what he desired. But all the same he was getting much nearer, and his antagonist had discovered that help was coming, and seemed waking up from his passive role of vice or man-trap. His hug was becoming more energetic.

Royal could now hear the new arrival calling to his comrade, and the man within whose arms he was struggling, answering.

''Urry up; I've got 'im!'

His breath blew strongly in Royal's face as he shouted out this, and it smelt very strongly of beer. Royal wondered if he had been a little drunk, and if that was why he had come down there to repose in that dark corner.

But not a moment was to be lost. He knew that he need not be caught. The idea of being caught had never entered his head for a moment. He now had his hands on the policeman's throat again; he took one quickly away, and seemed feeling for something at the back of his trousers. But, the way the policeman was holding him, his jacket was drawn round him at the bottom as tightly as a glove. Suddenly he broke out in a sweat all over. What if he shouldn't be able to get at it after all? He tugged frantically at the cloth, and a second later, with a hoarse cry of satisfaction, seemed to loose something behind. At the same moment the policeman relinquished his hold, and rolled over and away from him, holding his hands up to his face, and emitting a sound between a bellow and a scream.

29
A WATCHER AT THE WINDOW

Evan Royal sprang up, and darted back towards the gate of the house, thrusting something bright into his pocket. It was only then that he saw that a second man was coming straight at him from the direction of Marbury Street, cutting off his retreat, as he was already level with the gate.

He stopped a moment, looking back towards his late assailant and the first man he had sighted, arriving from the other end of the lane. This man was only fifteen yards away, and nearly up to his fallen comrade.

Drawing his knife from his pocket again, he ran at headlong speed up the road towards Marbury Street and towards his new antagonist, who seemed to hesitate as he saw him coming. Royal bounded along, in great leaps, and just before he reached his mark, he lowered his head, and the next moment the individual who had barred his way to the back gate of the house in Marbury Street, lay rolling breathless on the ground, having received Royal's head like a battering ram in the pit of his stomach. This trick, so favoured by the Paris Apaches, had succeeded admirably. He slipped his knife back in his pocket again, and had entered the gate and turned the key on the inside in a flash.

He now for an instant cast his eyes up the side of the house, and saw, at his third-storey window, Fane leaning contemplatively, to all appearance an interested but by no means perturbed spectator of all these goings on in the alley-way beneath. He had leant out a little and was gazing down at Royal, as though to follow the further movements of this interesting party to the fight. Royal was delighted with this attitude, and from that moment, in his capricious way, took a great fancy to Fane.

The young poet had become remarkably philosophical about the various dubious aspects of the enterprise on which he had embarked. He studied his part carefully, and found all the rest of his time taken up with his growing admiration for the charming charwoman.

Also, he was becoming convinced, in an extraordinary way, of the assurances of safety that were lavished upon him. He felt quite secure. He felt that he was in powerful and resourceful hands, at least, even if they were not honest ones.

When, a few minutes later, the police entered the house, he took it quite as a matter of course. He was getting used to their visits. He was also growing accustomed to this house, and the mysterious vortex of excitement of which it appeared the centre. As the most inveterate landsman will at last get used to the plunging of a boat, and become as unconcerned as the seamen themselves, so he was getting over his first alarms and anxieties, and regarded these multiplying visits of the police as the nervous landsman would at length come to regard a particularly heavy and giddy dipping of the boat.

Meanwhile the new arrival in the lane below, standing over his fallen comrade, was blowing his whistle furiously. A more fanciful and timid malefactor than the intrepid Royal would have imagined hundreds of constables rising up out of the ground, springing over the walls, flooding the neighbouring streets. But that young man acted with a clearness of purpose and coolheadedness that argued little of that sort of impressionability. His feelings, as a matter of fact, at that particular moment, were rather of extreme anger than anything else – a kind of cold, reasoning, terrible anger of his own.

His glance up the side of the house, his rapid impression of the observant Fane, and a quick smile this evoked, was the matter of an instant only. Fastening everything behind him as he entered, he unlocked Mrs. Dukes' bedroom, went in and turned the key behind him, whilst above him he could hear Mrs. Beechamp's steps descending slowly the stairs, as though hurriedly putting herself in order as she came.

He tore his clothes off breathlessly, and holding them up to the moonlight, saw that there were patches of fresh blood on the side and back of the jacket, and on the sleeve. Holding them at arm's length, with one hand he raised the conglomeration of mattresses and boards and other articles of which Mrs. Dukes' bed was composed, and then thrust them in the slot-like aperture thus made, pressing them down flatly.

He then sprang to the window, and pulled down the blind.

Someone was shaking at the gate without, and then, evidently from the sound, flinging himself against it. There were several new voices in the street, and a moment later the front door bell began ringing shrilly, just outside the bedroom door.

'You can knock every article of the house down, and make as much uproar as ever you please in doing so, so long as you leave me this room intact for four minutes longer. And that I'm sure you'll do, for if you begin pulling the house down, you'll have to begin at the top. And you're only policemen after all!' During this bantering soliloquy, Royal lighted a candle, placed it near the looking-glass, and taking a box from a corner, proceeded with his make-up, while the bell still rang madly in the passage outside. Mrs. Dukes' face — for it was rapidly becoming Mrs. Dukes' pallid mask again — wore a more unpleasant expression than in the whole course of her life that extremely ill-tempered and crotchety old woman's had ever done before. With extraordinary rapidity and deftness he was transforming it, and yet with perfect presence of mind, and thoroughness.

'Shall I let 'em in, Mrs. Dukes?' screamed a voice, Mrs. Beechamp's, at the door.

'Oh yes, let 'em in. Oh Lord! What *is* the matter now?' Mrs. Dukes answered immediately. The wig was now fixed on, and Royal had instinctively assumed the stooping attitude of the old woman. He presented the grotesque sight of a bent old woman, standing in a man's shirt, pants and socks, and flying round the room with the rapidity of a monkey.

Just then there was a scrambling and scratching outside in the yard, and suddenly the window behind the blind was pulled noisily down, and part of a policeman's helmet thrust forward from the edge of the blind.

30
'THE HOUSE OF MYSTERY'

In a twinkling Royal had blown the candle out, and started forward towards the window with a torrent of Dukesesque invective.

'Lord! yer enough to frighten the wits out of anyone; what hever are yew doin' up there; what *is* the matter, with all this ringin' and whistlin' and breakin' into my 'ouse? There, yew made me knock the candle over and I can't see nothin'! Get down from there, do, and don't come gallivantin' in at my window! What next, I should like to know!'

While Royal was pouring out this and a lot more at the retreating policeman, he was rapidly assuming the right costume of Mrs. Dukes in all its elaborate dinginess, and was adding to this one or two other garments, destined to hide the night attire somewhat.

A few minutes later it was Mrs. Dukes in all her vehemence, personal disorder and characteristic odour who opened the door to the police-sergeant without.

'Well, Mrs. Dukes, I'm sorry to disturb you, ma'am, but a party what's wounded one of our men ran in 'ere, into your 'ouse, and we was obliged to come 'ere to look for 'im. 'E said your charwoman was 'is missis.'

''Oo ever 'eard of such a thing! Mrs. Beechamp 'is missis, indeed! And Beechamp's been dead and gone this three years. You're always comin 'ere disturbin' people with your silly sayin's.'

'You see, what we fears, ma'am, is that, well, it bein' known that you're *wealthy* now, that in this neighb'rood you might attract the attention of some people we know. And such funny things do 'appen round this 'ouse. 'Ere's one of our men just bin stabbed, when he was tryin' to stop someone what came out of 'ere — '

The sergeant and Mrs. Dukes argued a few minutes longer, the former very respectfully, and pulling himself up if he thought he were about to say anything that would be too disagreeable to the new millionairess. Certainly the appurtenances of rank were not there to aid his imagination, but the thought struck him dully every minute or so, that this vociferous and bedraggled old woman was possessed of a million of money.

The history of this police raid was more or less that of the last one, when the curate had brought the law down about Mrs. Dukes' ears. They found nothing, were thoroughly baffled, and anything they might have done if left to themselves, they were prevented from doing by Mrs. Dukes' imperious assurances. They left, discontented, in a quarter of an hour or so, the sergeant muttering that if she lost all her money it would serve her right. But a watch was left at the street-corner.

Royal, left to himself, cursed heartily under his breath.

'It seems there's no way of getting out of this place. They'll all be waiting there for me, and they'll get a scare when I don't turn up.'

The next evening Royal found the following notice of his exploit in the paper that Mrs. Beechamp brought him. Several reporters had been to Marbury Street in the course of the day, so he knew to whom certain dabs of local colour should be traced, and attributed.

'Sequel of a legacy. House becomes suddenly the centre of mysterious aggressions.'

'Confound them!' thought Royal on reading this, 'Now they'll be coming down here every day to squeeze new mystery out of this poor old house. They'll give it no rest. Once a house becomes a "mysterious house" no more peace for the inhabitants.' The report began:

It will be fresh in everybody's memory how an old lady who had spent her life in letting lodgings to foreign waiters and barbers, was suddenly left over a million pounds, under the will of the late Arthur St. Giles Dukes, of Liverpool, her husband who had deserted her thirty-five years ago, and only remembered her on his death-bed. This old lady, despite her sudden affluence, still resides temporarily in the strange old house in that dingy quarter of London in the neighbourhood of Golden Square, where she has lived so long. But since the news of her good fortune has been so widely advertised, this house has been the scene of a series of the most baffling and extraordinary occurrences, and a midnight man-hunt.

It went on to fancifully describe how a man 'burst out of the rear premises' of this 'mysterious mansion,' and fell upon a policeman who happened to be passing and who had called out to him to stop. He 'fell on him with such fury that, had not some other members of the Force fortunately arrived on the scene, he would no doubt have finished the work he so desperately began.' The policeman, it was further affirmed, was terribly slashed about the arms and head with knife or dagger, and one of his thumbs 'seemed only hanging by a skin from his nerveless hand.' The report continued:

Two things are to be specially noted here. First of all, the injured officer affirms that the man when first addressed replied with the coarse accent of a working man; but that in the heat of the struggle he let several words escape him in what was apparently his natural tone of voice, and the officer is certain that his aggressor was a gentleman, that is, a cultivated and well educated man. Next to this comes another curious fact connected with this amazing affair, a detail much insisted on by the police. When, having wounded the man who was holding him, he started to run away, he found a civilian, Mr. Timothy Long of No. 8, Goodge Row, barring his passage. He disposed of this obstacle in a moment, by running at him head down, and butting him in the stomach. This is a trick particularly characteristic of Parisian malefactors, we are told – of those strange bands of foot-pads that infest the French Capital at night, known as Apaches. Also, it is seldom that an English criminal uses a knife. But only a few days ago, a young Belgian, arrested in this very same house, and in connection also with a supposed plot directed against Mrs. Dukes, escaped from his captors on the way to the station, with the aid from accomplices who had been lying in wait for the police at a convenient spot. But, the authorities affirm, the trick used to render the officers powerless for the moment, thanks to which the prisoner got away, was also one employed almost exclusively by continental criminals.

But now comes the most mysterious part of this amazing affair. The courageous officer's aggressor, frightened off by the arrival of other constables, rushed back into the house from which he had made his bloody 'sortie,' fastening all the doors behind him. And yet, when the police surrounded the house, and penetrated simultaneously from the back and front, nowhere was there a trace of the unfortunate P.C. 56's mysterious assailant to be found. The inhabitants of the house, including Mrs. Dukes herself, roused from their beds, assured the officers that it was impossible for anyone to have entered, as it was carefully locked up, and none of the doors had been forced. It was as though this were a man risen from the bowels of the earth, issuing from some nether regions of murderous fire within this peaceful house, and, his crime accomplished, descending into the earth again, the way he had come. Some suppose the house to be haunted. But as these things have only occurred since Mrs. Dukes came in to her fortune, it seems only too likely that this old lady, whose circumstances have so wonderfully changed, but who has not yet changed her residence, is the object of a deep laid and mysterious plot to rob her of some of her wealth, that the thieves apparently imagine to be on the premises! But this hypothesis again does not stand the test of reason. What malefactor would be stupid enough to suppose that any appreciable part of her newly inherited fortune had been 'sent on,' so to speak, to her present home — in a big bag, full of gold, for instance? No. It seems rather that we must look deeper and for more subtle and perhaps formidable motives than this. What can these men — for men and not one man the police are firmly convinced are at the bottom of these strange occurrences — what can these mysterious miscreants want with this old woman. How do they hope to profit by these mad and reckless proceedings? However this may be, this old woman, so late in life suddenly smiled on by Fortune, is now, in that dingy and sinister house, to which she still clings for a moment, the centre of a wild, strange, hidden and malignant activity, that may at any moment close round her — and what then? and why? Perhaps it is not for money these mysterious beings are come. What secrets in the life of that man who died the other day, and to do with his mysterious bequest, lurk in these strange doings? Perhaps we shall never know. But a strict watch is being kept by the authorities, and means are being taken to prevent any further or more deadly outbreak on the part of these nameless evil doers.

But this troublesome adventure of Royal's had a still more troublesome sequel.

While Royal was reading the reporter's version of his brief and dramatic sortie, and attempt to become himself again — he being so speedily driven back into the old lady's clothes that he had temporarily forsaken — in another part of London this same account was being read with awakening interest. And the strange things we are about to relate were the direct outcome of this interest so suddenly awakened.

31

MR. ARTHUR O. PASSION CALLS

The next morning numbers of people stared at No. 21, Marbury Street, as though it had completely changed in the course
of the night, or as though it really were 'the sinister-looking
house,' 'the house of mystery' that so many reporters affirmed
that it was. It wasn't a 'sinister-looking' house at all. It was
only a very dirty-looking house, but dirt does not constitute
tragedy or mystery. If that had been the case, Marbury Street
would have been a most creepy street to walk down, for all the
houses in Marbury Street were very dirty indeed. Still, people
passed it and gazed up at it, and peeped in at the door, and
passed down the walled lane at the side, as though it were the
most blood-curdling looking edifice imaginable.

The day before, from an early hour, the stream of tweed-
suited reporters had been incessant: Harris tweeds, Irish
tweeds, shepherd plaid suits. A constant stream of imported
Scotch cloth had been launched against Mrs. Dukes' front
door.

From the upper windows Fane watched this uncouth tide
break on the steps of the strange house, which had suddenly
become so prominent, and tried to place each of them as he
came. 'Ah, you collect scraps of news for the Morning
Looking-glass!' he thought, as a young man whose face betrayed amazing capacities for indelicate behaviour, and whose
suit of Irish tweed was of an especially repulsive green,
mounted the steps.

About seven in the evening, Fane returned from a short
walk with one of the last editions of an evening paper, and
went back into his own room to read with great attention the
account of the affray in the back street of which he had been a

witness, and the fanciful conclusions drawn by the reporter on the many puzzling elements in the various things that happened round this suddenly made millionairess. He was bound to confess that he himself was no nearer the truth of the matter, however, than the papers were. It was more difficult for him to give a guess, for the very reason that he knew more about it, was in possession of more facts.

'Well, if there is a plot of any sort, I'm hanged if I don't believe that Mrs. Dukes is in it too.' So he wound up his reflections. He was rather inclined now to accept the suggestion that Hillington had made him — that he should regard all this as a big practical joke.

But the most vital thing for him for the moment was his relations with Lucy. They had progressed considerably in this short time, and they were now on very good terms. They seldom talked 'shop,' as this always seemed to cause a constraint between them, and the girl especially seemed to wish to avoid that subject. And yet as his interest in her grew, he realised that this subject, their 'shop,' was a very important question, as if she were a knowing accomplice of criminals, and a criminal herself, his interest in her might lead him into strange paths. For a moment he would want to know passionately, with a sudden and great impatience, *the truth,* what was at the bottom of all this, and what part she was playing. But he was always reassured by her presence. And then, bit by bit his disinclination to know anything about all these secrets became acute — his fear of what might result from the mystery being cleared up, and its effects on their relations to each other, grew, and he got as far away from the subject as he could.

She came up as he was sitting and meditating there in the twilight, and looking into his room laughing, with her face still that of Mrs. Beechamp, with the lines and dirt and sallowness. He looked at her gravely, at this squalid and careworn face, and a melancholy fancy possessed him. What if she were *really* like this, and if the charming girl she appeared to him, when her make-up was discarded, was the untrue and unreal aspect of her? And he recognised that he had felt this before, though he only was conscious of this impression now for the first time. For he realised that his dislike of seeing her in this state had been steadily growing.

'We're not going to answer the bell to any more of them. Mrs. Dukes has just been telling a blood-curdling story of vendetta in her family to a stange young man, who got purple in the face with excitement, as he realised that he had the material for a whole-column article. He pressed her with questions, and she contradicted herself so much — on purpose, of course — and gave such unlikely explanations, that the reaction set in strong, he became more and more crestfallen, and at last determined — one could see — that he would have to make it a mere paragraph of ten lines, with a parenthesis "we give it for what it's worth." She asked a sixpence entrance fee of some of them to see the "mysterious mansion and its 'orribly menaced old hoccupant." They most of them seemed at bottom very shocked at her levity, although they pretended to be delighted at her droll ways. They seemed to wish to convince themselves that they were in a cut-throat house in the presence of a trebly-doomed old woman. Her wealth impressed them enormously, too; their manner was a strange mixture of condescension and servility.'

'Oh well; I suppose the poor beggars must make their livings.' And he at once reflected that it was because he had to make his living, that he was where he was.

'Yes, apropos of your earning your living, are you earning it? How are you getting on with your part?' asked Lucy. She had noticed the grave expression that had come into his face at the mention of the manner in which livings were made, and she always made a point of not avoiding this subject, but rather, whenever he mentioned it, to take it up. But she always spoke of it in an off-hand way, or in an ordinary matter of fact manner.

'Oh fairly well,' Fane replied. 'I've got a kind of system now for studying Mrs. Dukes, and can reel off Duke-like sayings by the score. Her conversation is quite original, always extravagant and whimsical, and therefore, like all strong mannerisms, is more or less easy to imitate. All her quaint sayings and ways of putting things follow one or two very simple rules, once you've observed them closely and compared a certain number with each and all of the others. As far as that goes, I flatter myself I have the secret, and am master of the part. As to the tone of the voice. *That* I think I've got also, but haven't yet practised enough working them together – the tone and the matter – *what* she says, that is, and the way she says it. That will soon come. As to her attitudes. I can't say that I have penetrated the secrets of her physical structure. That would be a feat indeed. And of course the peculiarity of anyone's attitudes depends a good deal on the peculiarity of their physique. But I think by twisting my spine into such a curve as to form a sort of platform of the top part of my back, and then by resting the back of my head on this platform – by keeping my knees slightly bent, and moving my arms as though they were made of wood, as she always does, that I could impersonate her very well.'

It will be seen from this that Fane was going about his work scientifically, just as Royal had done before him.

Lucy went away laughing to her room.

That evening, amongst other people, came a dark, quietly

dressed young man with whom Mrs. Dukes remained closeted for only a short time, but whom she received very differently from the young reporters. Mrs. Dukes related to him in a few words the unsuccessful sally of the night before, and promised to try again as soon as possible. This was an emissary from headquarters, in touch with his mysterious chief.

The following morning, as we have said, saw the house in Marbury Street the object of universal attention, and one or two belated reporters arrived at an early hour.

About eleven a loud and emphatic voice was heard in the hall way, and Mrs. Beechamp brought in a large card, whereon was printed

MR. JOSEPH J. PASSION
Chief Office, Boston, Mass.
The Millionaire's friend.

and then, in pencil was written underneath

MR. ARTHUR O. PASSION, London Agent.

A loud voice preceded this card, with a strong United States accent.

'Take it *right* in. She needs Joe Passion, and that's a fact − needs him bad. Get a hustle on, or Passion might cool down, and he wants to serve. No-o. I guess she don't know me, but it's time she did.'

Evan Royal had a weakness for Americans, and told Mrs. Beechamp to show the gentleman in.

Mr. Passion was about six feet high, very dark and very lean, his blue shirt cuffs lying among a growth of long black hair. His dark eyes rolled melodramatically in his head, and two deep, premature lines ran down from the nostrils to the extremities of his mouth. His mouth had a twisted appearance, a droop, and a little expression that seemed to have come through a combination of excessive habits of expectoration, and the continual spitting out of words of contempt.

He strode in to the first floor room in which Mrs. Dukes sat awaiting him, his eyes rolling around in all directions, taking in, in their rotary course, ceiling, wallpaper, carpet, windows, and at last alighting on Mrs. Dukes. He at once assumed an expression of extreme consideration his countenance became very grave, his eyes fixed themselves solemnly on Mrs. Dukes' face, and he held out his hand deliberately.

'I am glad, Mrs. Dookes, to make your acquaintance,' said he. 'Yes, ma'am, I shall be happy to serve you.'

Mrs. Dukes had watched with an interior gleam of satisfaction the entrance of this gentleman, and his pretence of not seeing her for the moment, and the various expressions of his face had caused Mr. Royal, hidden in the depths of Mrs. Dukes, a delight that the dull and dogged reporters had not awoken.

'Well, Mr. Passion, what brings *yew* 'ere?' asked Mrs. Dukes.

Mr. Passion looked behind him, espied a chair, stretched his arm out and drew it slowly towards him and slid it underneath his bent and waiting figure.

'Mrs. Dookes, listen to me attentively,' he began impressively. 'When the other day you came into that little bit of property, you became a public character. This you don't seem to have entirely realised. To remain as you are, madam, exposes you to mysterious dangers, that the ordinary man could scarcely conceive of. You became the possessor of the mystic sum the other day! A million! If it had been a farthing less, madam, you would never have received my visit. You would have been able to get on without Arthur O. Passion. I only become necessary when the million's reached. Do you realise, Mrs. Dookes, that no almighty king, perched upon his gorgeous throne, is so exposed as the millionaire? Allow me to di-gress; I will re-count a little story before going further. There was once upon a time a man named Hosiah B. Angelman. At the age of eighteen he launched himself into the seething waters of fi-nance, with only a half dollar in his pocket as life-buoy. He was possessed with the inordinate ambition of twirling round his thumb a million dollar cheque. Within four years he was possessed of nine hundred and eighty thousand dollars; it needed but a turn of the wrist to make him a millionaire. But two days afterwards, owing to an un-fructuous operation in Wall Street, he was left with nothing but a few cents jumping about at the bottom of his capacious but otherwise empty pocket. Angelman just whipped his tongue inside his mouth, snapped his teeth down in front of it, and then stuck his two lips together in front of that, jerked his jaw forward, took a reef in his back muscles, and tightened up all over. Then he started in again, just grim. For ten years Angelman worked slowly ahead. Everything that had seemed easy before, seemed difficult now. But, by gosh, he hung on, and ran round like a madman, and in ten years' time he reck-oned his fortune at nine hundred and ninety-eight thousand dollars. He put off countin' up as long as he blarmed well could, but at last he just *had* to figure it up. But he couldn't no way make it come to more than that. Waal, two thousand dollars ain't so hard as all that to make, in New York City. But that night his clerk scooted with nearly all his money, and Angelman was left half daft, his million missed again. But that man wanted some beating. He started right in again, and before three years was over, there he stood, spry as ever, within twenty dollars of his million again. He was as careful as a thief tip-toeing past a sleeping man. He held his breath. He crept up towards that million as quiet as a little boy with a pinch of salt creeps up to a little bird to powder its tail. He added cent to cent. He refused to go faster. He'd have sooner drowned than make half a dollar. He would take in nothing but a cent at a time. Sudden somethin' went wrong. He lost in a lump while he wasn't lookin' two hundred thousand of his dollars. He plunged for all he could, and lost all again within the week. He didn't try again. But he got to hate that number as no man's ever hated anything before, and everything to do with it — specially those who'd climbed in where he was thrown back. And, by golly! he's made it pretty warm for anyone who wants to sit where he tried and couldn't. That's the story people tell, Mrs. Dookes, of the chief of a famous society on our side of the water, whose operations are entirely confined to millionaires. It may not be *troo,* Mrs. Dookes; but I guess it about figures up the dislike that Angelman had for people with the pertickler sum of money that welters in your coffers. But a million, madam, is a mystic number. Thirteen is nothing compared to it. This fact has to be faced. A man who has that number of dollars at his bank can't go about without a gun. It's more dangerous to have that sum at your bank than to have your mouth full of gold-mended teeth when you're in poor company. And here we may consider the first reason why you need Arthur O. Passion round just now. I grant that there *are* people, Mrs. Dookes, whom their million don't trouble much. But you, ma'am, are evidently marked out to have a rough time. You have been made to feel the change of atmosphere at once. I read this morning in the newspapers that things, without any reason, had begun to boil round you right away. Mystery, mystery! I told you about Angelman. Waal, that's only one example of the sort of energies that this ill-fated number, this mystic number, set in motion. You don't know what it is to be a millionaire, Mrs. Dookes.'

He said this in an almost tearful, appealing tone.

'There was Ekhart. One day, after a bit of clever buying, he found he'd passed the fatal number twice over. Two million were scored up against his name. He hadn't been a millionaire twenty minutes when he was shot right down, no one knew who did it, on Twenty-first Street.'

He cleared his throat brutally, his eyes fixed on Mrs. Dukes. 'I guess we could clear this street of what's worryin' you in twenty-four hours. We guarantee, absolutely guarantee the person of any millionaire for periods of five years, from the day of contract. We've never had but one die on our hands — that was Joe P. Banks of Milwaukee, 27 millions, and that was under pertickler circumstances. He wanted to back out of the contract. Not the money part. He wanted to get rid of our special watch. Waal, he was tryin' to escape from one of our men one night, and he got himself run over.'

He told this as though it pointed to the angry intervention of Providence.

'Of course, ma'am, if we get that five years' contract signed, the understanding would be mutual, that you consent to live with certain restrictions. Our duties are not easy at the best, and you would agree not to make them more arduous by unnecessarily exposing your high-priced person. Strategically, a theatre is not a good place to be confronted with danger in — we should recommend you to fight shy of theatres! A theatre has too many entrances and exits, and places where mysterious enemies, beings who hate the number 'million' can glide and ambush themselves. I might affirm, ma'am, that a theatre is a trap specially built for millionaires. Yes, we should consider goin' to a theatre as a wanton act of bad faith on the part of our protégée, a deliberate attempt to defeat our ends, and equivalent to an attempt to spurn our contract. I speak energetically, ma'am, because in the past we have had some little trouble with the more illogical of our clients. One ruffianly Westerner insisted on coming home at midnight, whereas one of our strictest rules is that every millionaire under our care should be in bed by eleven. I think, Mrs. Dookes, that you will subscribe to the reasonableness of this request?'

It was by this time quite evident to Evan Royal that this eloquent American was 'up to something.' That is, it was plain that his story of a society for the protection of millionaires was a pretext only for an interview. For he was making the service he offered so hedged round with inconvenient conditions that even a stupid old woman would not have listened to him. This amused him all the more, as it would be a pastime to find out what was his particular little game.

But a few minutes afterwards Royal was destined to feel much less amused with his visitor, and feel also for the first time since he had undertaken his present role, extremely uneasy and doubtful as to the result.

The American now slid nearer to his interlocutor on his chair; he began in an awful, hushed and emphatic whisper to detail to her some of the mysteries of secret service work that only millionaires were entitled to know. His face came nearer and nearer to that of Mrs. Dukes', and she looked at him still with amused interest, when suddenly the watchful spirit of Royal beneath her mask noticed the American's eyes travelling, for a second only, but constantly, time after time, to Mrs. Dukes' half real, half manufactured brow, where they fixed themselves intently for that moment, although his exposition of the advantages of his company's services was not interrupted for a moment. Suddenly Evan Royal grew suspicious; the smile did not at once pass from Mrs. Dukes' face, but it passed from Evan Royal's spirit within. He was no longer amused. This man was examining that part of his head where the real flesh joined the paler top of the head with its spare white meshes of hair, with a keen purpose, while he rattled on. It was very important to show no change of manner, however.

'What brought you over 'ere, Mr. Pashun?' Mrs. Dukes asked, and continued apparently attentive to him.

'Why, Mrs. Dookes, I could tell you something that would astound you,' he said, a little later, and bent forward as though to whisper in her ear. Royal felt his eyes in this moment fixed on that part of his make-up that was likeliest to betray him to an initiated observer.

He drew away from the American, saying, 'Oh! Mr. Pashun, you reg'lar frighten me with your stories,' and putting out her hand to the bell by the side of the fire, rang sharply. 'I'm afraid I shall 'ave to ask yer to leave me, as I 'ave several letters to write, business letters, yew know?'

Mrs. Beechamp came in answer to the bell, and Mr. Arthur O. Passion rose to take his leave, his card remaining as a witness of his having passed that way, however. He pointed significantly to the address, and wound up by saying, 'Consider, Mrs. Dookes, all I've said to you on the desirability of having the resourceful cooperation of my firm in squeezin' all the honey out of your million, and keepin' undesirables from hanging round. No,' he continued slowly and meditatively, as though seeking some other solution of the difficulty and finding none, 'No; I don't see how you can go along without us. In your position I reckon you can't do without us nohow. Just say the word, and I come right round with the papers, and we fix it all up in no time. Waal, I'm glad to have made your acquaintance, Ma'am. I wish you could know our Boss; he and you'd hit it off fine. Good-day, Mrs. Dookes.'

When Mrs. Beechamp had come back from letting him out, beneath Mrs. Dukes' mask Evan Royal's face was very grave, and he almost glared at Lucy.

33
ROYAL DETERMINES TO WAIT

'Lucy, shut the door and come here,' he said, as soon as she had entered. 'Can you see — no, with your face close to mine — where the false crown joins?' Evan Royal was staring at himself in the glass, with his forehead nearly touching it. He turned round to her as he said this.

She came up and looked hard at the place indicated for a minute or two.

'Yes,' she said, 'I think I could tell it was false. But one would have to look pretty closely, and not only that, but look on purpose.'

'Well, that Yankee — I'm sure he was a Yankee, but that's all I am sure about as regards *him* — he's been staring at this part of my head for the last quarter of an hour, or for the last half hour, I expect, confound him. This is the worst that's happened yet. What can have put him on the scent, what the devil can he want, who does he come from? How's our secret leaked out? It can only be through one of the company. What the devil is that man going to do with his information, now he's got it, and now he's assured himself that I'm *not* Mrs. Dukes? He put his nose near enough to stick it in my paint!'

'I suppose you're sure?'

'Well, I don't usually make my jump to a conclusion, until I'm sure it's a safe one. Yes, that's sure enough. He was looking at my head to see if I were made up or not, and if I wore a wig.'

'If so, it looks as though the game were up,' Lucy remarked indifferently.

Evan Royal had regarded his unsuccessful sortie two nights previously as one of the first humiliations of his professional career. It had been rankling ever since. He now was blaming himself in no measured terms for letting the American get the better of him – that is, by not seeing through him at once. He was so pleased with him – his accent, his appearance, the quaintness of his calling – that he had omitted to be suspicious. He had been thrown off his guard. But in any case, he could never have guessed that this man was possessed of his secret, or that he suspected his impersonation. Royal's whole conduct, and the attitude of his mind, was based on the assumption that whatever else happened, whatever other ideas might enter people's heads, the fact that he was not Mrs. Dukes, that he was someone, a man, impersonating Mrs. Dukes, would never occur to anyone for a moment. And indeed he was quite justified in this assumption. His perfect make-up, his genius as an actor, and his wonderful presence of mind on all occasions in themselves justified it. His way of regarding the enterprise, in fact, had been not unlike Fane's. There might be many complications; he had felt the ship of their adventure might be rolled about, bend beneath squall after squall, but the essential seaworthiness of his employer's idea (based, as said above, on the fact that the real truth was the last thing people would think of) — its soundness he never thought of doubting. This visit of the American was like a sudden and ominous swishing of water in the hold. His fine confidence was suddenly at an end. What was to be done now? He must either, along with his two companions, vanish that very moment, leave the house empty and to be the prey of the reporters — leaving behind them a deeper mystery than had ever been known before — or he must stay where he was and await events. But although Mrs. Dukes' million was not destined for his pocket, he recognised the magnitude of their present undertaking, and he did not feel inclined to throw such a sum away — as leaving his post would be doing. The company so far had worked like clockwork. It had never left a trace behind it. It had almost always succeeded. But one of two things struck him principally apropos of the American. Either he was to do with the police or was not. In the latter case he was probably a gentleman of fortune himself. And again, if this were so, Royal need not fear being denounced to the police at once, as his game would evidently rather be to share the spoil of Mrs. Dukes' inheritance. They could expect to be blackmailed at once. But if the blackmailing negotiations the Yankee would probably institute on the morrow did not succeed then and there, he would still not denounce the fraud he had discovered to the police at once — not until he were finally convinced that Royal and his accomplices would not share.

Now Royal was tremendously piqued in his *amour-propre*. He had never felt so baffled and helpless. He was sure for many reasons that his late visitor was not on the side of the police, but rather belonged to those who defy that body. In the course of the negotiations that would doubtless ensue, Royal would probably see the American again, and all sorts of things might happen. And he swore to himself that he would get even with that American gentleman somehow, and make up for his present humiliation, as he considered it. He felt confident that he would find some opportunity of doing so, and felt competent to outwit these new enemies. They were without doubt worth his steel, for Mr. Passion struck him as no fool. Then again the society to which Royal belonged was at least as powerful as a Neapolitan *Camorra*.

The thing that troubled him most was the question of how Mr. Passion had got possessed of his secret. It must have come through one of the company, he thought. This was the first instance he had heard of treachery. He was frankly alarmed at that thought. The whole safety of the organisation had depended so far on the absolute faithfulness of its members – this a good deal due to the wholesome fear with which their mysterious chief and his inner circle inspired them. Lucy was one of this dread inner circle. What relation she actually bore to he whom they knew as Raza Khan, Royal did not know. But in adventures of the highest importance, such as the one on which they were now engaged, she often bore a part. He felt all he said – that could be of interest to his employers – would be repeated to them by her. He nevertheless, with his customary carelessness and defiance, began to abuse the way the society was being managed, and prophesy its speedy fall.

'Things are in a pretty bad way when things begin to leak out like this. I for one am not going on risking my skin if that's the turn things are taking. So long as one could rely on one's chiefs to manage *their* part of the business properly, one could go ahead with one's work with confidence and in comparative tranquility. But one doesn't want to be at the mercy of fools. I confess that my confidence in the inner workings of the august society to which we belong, is rudely shaken. There's not the ghost of a doubt that something's gone wrong with the working of it. Something's leaked out. That's the only thing that could account for the purpose of that fellow's visit today. He can have got his information in no other way. If I didn't want to pay him out, I'm hanged if I wouldn't chuck up the whole thing – million or no million – and clear out of this house within the hour.'

Lucy's indifference had disappeared. While Royal was speaking she listened eagerly and, it seemed, thoughtfully, and now she said, to his considerable astonishment, 'Yes, it's true, once the smallest little thing went wrong with the workings of the company, we could undertake nothing more. It would be simply better to get out while there was time. I can't think what Raza Khan was doing in taking on Fane – the boy upstairs. I think that was a mistake.'

Royal looked at her in astonishment for a moment, then he concluded that this was merely duplicity on her part, and said on purpose to lead him on, and make him speak even more fully what he thought. Contempt at the obviousness of the trick, and anger with his companion, made him turn gruffly away, and he left Lucy where she was. He thought he'd go to the lower regions and have a look at Cole.

Royal now asked himself whether he ought not to communicate at once with headquarters. But his disgust with his employers was now complete, and he felt little inclined to trust them in this crisis. Letting them know could do little good, until the new enemies had taken their next step, and showed their intentions a little more clearly. He determined, then, not to complicate matters by a communication at once. Also he resolved not to attempt another sortie that night, as he had promised the messenger sent by his employer. He would see what move Passion and Company made on the morrow, and if he thought it advisable, attempt to get past the watch the police had set on the following evening.

34
THE RENDEZVOUS AT THE WHARF

The next morning a messenger boy brought Evan Royal a note signed Raza K., asking him to come to a certain rendezvous, if he could possibly manage it. It was curt and mysterious as were all messages from that source, but this time Royal saw in it a special significance. Something had happened, he thought; perhaps the treachery had been discovered.

Royal waited all day long in expectation of some new development in the brand new situation created by the visit of the American. But the hours went by, and no sign came from that quarter. If the American's plans needed so much maturing, what on earth could they be? He felt that Mr. Arthur O. Passion was not a man to hesitate.

The winter evening had already settled dirtily and dismally over the town, and Mrs. Dukes was sipping her third cup of tea. The knocker, which, in collusion with the bell, had been so rowdy lately, seeming both to have acquired a sudden maturity of sound from being so much used, sent an alarm through the house.

'Ah,' thought Royal, 'our American friend!'

It was not, however; but a messenger boy, with the following communication:

Treachery feared. Immediate action necessary. Come at once if possible Tilder's Wharf. Do not attempt to 'changer de sexe.' Raza K.

Royal's comment on this missive was, 'Ah, so they've neglected me, my American friends, and started their attack in another quarter. I suppose they wrote to Raza. I wonder what he wants the launch for?' This last reflection was caused by the change of place of rendezvous. Tilder's Wharf was a frequent meeting place for members of the company; utilized in many of their enterprises was a small steam launch, often to be seen scudding about amongst the shipping on the Lower Thames, bound on mysterious errands. The rendezvous given at Tilder's wharf evidently meant that a voyage was to be made somewhere or other.

Evan Royal's impatience had been considerable during the whole of that day. The non-appearance of the Yankee or of any sign of him had certainly worked on his nerves. He was relieved at least at the thought that now he was going to learn the meaning of this day of silence, and possibly even was going to see his yesterday's visitor again. He had never sped to an interview with his chief with so much alacrity. That is to say in will, if not in fact; for in the first place he would be forced to go in the guise of Mrs. Dukes, and Mrs. Dukes didn't move quickly; and then he was compelled to outwit, in some way or another, the vigilant individual who was promenading outside, despite the cold and damp, and who would no doubt follow him. For the police had given their watcher orders, doubtless, not to let Mrs. Dukes expose herself to any unnecessary danger. Cole was not in the room just at that moment, and Royal scrutinized his make-up very closely in the glass. Satisfied with this, he adjusted his bonnet, and then called shrilly to Cole, summoning him from the depths to receive some parting injunctions. He also called to Lucy, and told her of his summons, showing her the last message received. She looked at it, and handed it back to him without saying anything.

As to the delegate of the police-force waiting outside in the cold and fog, he had his eyes fixed suspiciously, not on Mrs. Dukes' door, but on another man lounging on the other side of the street. This second man did not seem in the least concerned with his scrutiny, which he had supported now for a couple of days. But he seemed extremely preoccupied in his turn with the person of a long, boney, red-headed individual, who had been standing in an archway some twenty yards up the road the whole day long. This third man appeared perfectly cool and collected, and he had the tail of his eye, if not the full frank front of that orb, fixed on Mrs. Dukes' front door.

Like three rivals hanging round the house of a peerless young lady, quite unacquainted with each other, or as yet with the object of their respective passions, these three man looked at each other askance, and seemed to be summing each other up.

The police officer was so occupied with the second man that he might not even have noticed Mrs. Dukes' appearance at her door, and her subsequent slow and painful progress up the street in the direction of Oxford Street, had it not been for the sudden animation of the second man, on whom his eyes were fixed, whose excitement, in turn, was not caused by the appearance of the old lady, but by the rapid movements of the *third* man, who had issued out of his stable archway, and was gazing after Mrs. Dukes with evident interest.

Now while the first two men stood irresolutely looking after Mrs. Dukes and then back again to the respective objects of their former interest, — like a dog divided between its duty, that of following its master, and the claims of friendship or enmity with some fellow — the third man began slowly moving in the direction Mrs. Dukes had taken. This determined a general movement. All three began drifting down the street in the wake of the old lady. The plain-clothes policeman glared at the second man, as he saw him drawn onward as though by some sort of magnet attached to Mrs. Dukes' bustle; and the second man looked before him and behind him alternately as though attempting to keep exactly half way between the old lady and the tall red-headed fellow. Mrs. Dukes turned a corner. And now came another moment of hesitation on the part of the three pursuers. None of the three seemed to wish to lose sight of the other — none wished to 'take the corner.' They closed up, and all negotiated the corner about the same time, one in the middle of the road and one on either pavement. There was Mrs. Dukes ploughing along still in front of them. In this order the pursuit continued as far as the Baker-Loo Tube. Mrs. Dukes made her way towards the ticket office, got her ticket and passed through the gates, and disappeared in the lift just as the three men were hustling each other in their attempt to get through the gate in time to go down in the lift with her. This they did not succeed in doing.

When, a few minutes later, they arrived on the platform, Mrs. Dukes was nowhere to be found. After wandering about the passages and stairs for a short time, constantly coming face to face with each other, they all three repaired to the outer air again. Here the third man hailed a taxi-cab, and disappeared in the direction of Holborn, the second man gazing wonderingly and indignantly after him. The member of the police, feeling that Mrs. Dukes, in a sense his protégée, had at least escaped from the pursuit of that ruffian — as he designated the second man — as well as himself, made his way back to his post before the house in Marbury Street.

Evan Royal, having tricked the trio in the Baker-Loo Tube, ascended rapidly again the way he had come, crossed over to the Oxford Circus Bank Tube, and took a ticket to the City. A little more than half an hour afterwards he was approaching Tilder's Wharf.

As he got to the head of the narrow lane leading down to the wharfside, he was surprised not to find a man there, for invariably one of the two or three members of the party lounged there on the look-out, for their use of this landing place was not quite 'regular.'

As his predecessor in Marbury Street, on the night of the 'identification' of Mr. Nichols, had hesitated in the garden of the St. John's Wood house, and the first shade of suspicion had crossed her mind, so Evan Royal, that monstrously resourceful, acute-minded and experienced young man, felt for the first time a doubt as to whether the message sent him should not have been more narrowly scrutinized by him.

He stopped, and looked back a moment down the street, a street of high grimy warehouses, nearly all of which were closed by then. He saw a policeman slowly making his way along towards him, and as the sight of an old woman walking down towards the river would no doubt cause this good man groundless suspicions, he started down the lane towards the wharfside.

But he was astonished at himself for his unquestioning acceptance of the message, and, although it seemed impossible that it were not from whom it purported to be, his uneasiness deepened as he advanced, and he kept a sharp look out to right and left, and glared into the shadows before him.

Arrived at the bottom of the lane, he felt along the edge of the brick wall that faced him, and getting his toe in a familiar crevice, had soon hoisted himself up on to the wall. There he sat gazing at the dark, wet, misty wharf, and could see no launch waiting where he had expected to see one.

35

ROYAL FOLLOWS IN THE STEPS OF HIS PREDECESSOR

From where he sat, still perched on the wall, he saw two heads moving farther along the wharf than the place at which he had been gazing, and heard a low familiar whistle. He slid down, and walked over to the waterside. There beneath him was the launch right enough, and the engineer – known to him for two years now – just getting back to his engine, which started churning and thumping beneath his busy hands. He looked up and wished Royal good evening, and asked him to step down, as they'd been told to waste no time. There was a tall, clean-shaven man with a heavy coat thrown round his shoulders, already seated in the stern, and this seemed the entire party as far as Royal could see. He let himself down into the boat, still in the costume of the Marbury Street landlady, and took his place in the stern beside the silent stranger.

Not over-impressionable in that way, his reception, the aspect of the launch, the wet and misty night, the splashing of the water, all seemed particularly eerie to him. As he was getting down he suddenly looked beneath him uneasily, as though to see whether his defenceless position were going to be taken advantage of. He was accustomed to find three or four men seated in the stern, all known to him. This solitary and silent stranger seemed somehow unaccountable.

There was something even more odd in the engineer. He did not seem quite the same. Without being able to say in what, and although there was no striking difference, his dress, his way of dressing, seemed different. And his voice had a brief, constrained sound. Looking down from the wharf, Royal had promised himself, the moment he was down there beside him, to get the silent stranger to give an account of himself.

And now, after having jumped aboard, he had installed himself in the stern, his back to the wharf, and facing the stranger, he looked hard at him, trying to make out the lines of his face. He could see a pair of cold, quiet eyes fixed on him, but still this strange man did not utter a word.

And suddenly and definitely Royal became uneasy. He must act at once. As a beginning he said to the man in front of him, 'Are we going far tonight, do you know?'

'I guess *so*.' At last the stranger spoke, and at the sound of this American accent, a chill went down Royal's back, all the bleakness and sharpness of the river-night seemed to strike him. This American accent was like a sudden and lurid light for him, a sudden danger signal seen too late, a shock. In the same instant he started up. He did not doubt for a moment. He *knew* at once that he had been trapped. He sprang to his feet as though the man in front, instead of merely answering his question with a strong American accent, had threatened his life, or brimstone had come out of his mouth.

As he sprang up something flashed before his eyes, and the next moment he felt his arms pinned to his side. A rope had been flung over his head from behind, and the knot drawn tight, and at the same moment, he was flung forward on to the seat of the boat. He struggled madly, but in a few minutes was firmly secured, both arms and legs. It was of course out of the question shouting for help, as his profession was not such as entitled him to the protection of the police. Nevertheless his assailants gagged him after they had run the rope several times round his body and legs. Then they put him in a long sack, with just his head left free of it to breathe.

There were only two men there — he had been taken by these two. The one who had attacked him from behind — he had been hidden in the shadow of one of the piles of the wharf — he suddenly recognized. It was Arthur O. Passion. His mortification on this discovery was immense, although from the moment that fatal American accent had fallen on his ears, he might have expected something of the sort.

Arthur O. Passion nodded his head towards the stranger and said briefly, 'May I introduce you, Mrs. Dookes, Mr. Joseph J. Passion. Now you know the whole firm I guess.'

The engineer thrust his head over the partition at this moment, and asked if they had not better start. Royal saw with renewed mortification, that this was merely a man, a stranger to him, roughly got up as the engineer of the launch. He had now abandoned his disguise, and had rubbed his face more or less clean. Royal thought he recognised him as a man he had once seen in the company in a subordinate position. But he was not sure. Yes, he had been taken with the same acts and tricks that he himself professed. He had made a pretty mess of things this time! He probably passed the most miserable half hour of his life in the bottom of that launch.

They got under way almost at once, and scurried out into the middle of the stream, and headed down the river. They went on and on, passing under bridges, shooting past great ships, running in and out of drifting barges.

The cool way in which they had reckoned on his falling into the trap was one of the things that rankled most in the breast of the unfortunate Royal. He supposed that Mr. Arthur O. had sized him up the day before, and had reported accordingly to Joseph J., the head of the firm. No doubt Arthur O. had conceived a considerable contempt for him because of his accessibility, because he had allowed himself to be examined so carefully, and because he had not at once seen through his, Arthur O's, pretence of an eccentric calling. Alas! Americans do not know how charming and amusing they are, merely as Americans, he thought. It was the perverse pleasure he felt at the sound of the American accent that had lost him. Still, bound there, and as securely trapped as a man could be, Royal still swore to himself to be even with these gentlemen. When Arthur O. bent down to him and asked him if he felt 'too blamed uncomfortable,' and if so to let him know, he merely shrugged his shoulders and went on staring up into the sky above him.

Messrs. Passion did not waste many words, apparently, in private life, their wordiness being reserved for their business transactions. Their self-sufficient silence, their complete coolness and air almost of tired indifference irritated Royal all the more. He reckoned that they must be somewhere near Greenwich, when they at last turned sharp shorewards, and his head was thrust unceremoniously into the sack, and the end loosely tied together. There was still enough air for him to breathe, however. They remained for about five minutes quite still, except for the gentle bumping of the launch against what Royal supposed was a landing stage. Then one of them, who had left the boat, jumped back into her again. He was taken by the head and heels, and hoisted up a little distance, and then slowly carried along what was, it appeared from the sound, a cinder track. They bumped through a gate, up some steps, and the next minute were in the warmth of a house.

A growling near his ear and a quick pattering step, and several blows from a vigorous tail brandished in welcome, apprised him of the presence of a dog. There was a good deal of energetic sniffing. Then there was a faint bang and the pores of his sack were flooded with a faint light. The gas had been lighted.

He heard the stranger's voice, Joseph J.'s, say,

'Waal, there's our packet, let's undo it and have a look at the contents. Jumbo seems to think it's a toy for him.' This referred to the dog, no doubt.

And here the sack was untied, and Royal was dragged out of it. It was Arthur O. who did this, and he did it very tenderly, smiling encouragingly at Royal the while.

'I'm sorry, old chap, to have to treat you so darned unceremonious, but in our profession, you know' — and he laughed easily. 'Tight round the legs?' he asked, and proceeded to remove the lower fastenings, also the gag.

'I'm real sorry, mister, we can't undo your hands; but of course you're indignant-like for the moment, and we want to get all the indignation out of you before we cut all the strings.'

Arthur O. forced Royal good-humouredly into a chair, and then and there Joseph J., the head of the house of Passion, revealed in a few words the reason for their late violent proceedings, and the amazing plan that had a day or two before matured in the brain of the firm.

36
AN ADVANTAGEOUS PROPOSAL

Evan Royal found himself in a particularly large and lofty room, with four large shuttered windows at one side, and two heavy carved doors at the further end. He had been placed in an old leather-covered arm chair near a blazing fire. The rest of the room was quite unfurnished, but there was a kind of encampment round the fire-place – a litter of papers, a book or two, several chairs, and an umbrella stand. Furniture seemed suddenly to have sprung up, like plants, in the immediate neighbourhood of this genial warmth. Beyond this small inch of civilization stretched a dreary waste of empty floor, until near the third of the windows, suddenly another little settlement was discovered; it consisted of a large bureau, like a cave, that was chock full of little drawers, sliding panels, little cupboards and piles of papers. There were also two chairs, a waste paper basket and a few feet of litter. These articles of furniture seemed to have sprung up just in that place, not through the glowing heat of any fire, but because of the light. It was evidently the clear bright stream of daylight that had attracted this gaping bureau, squatting there like a heavy and clumsy animal with its mouth open. Beyond this oasis the desert stretched out again, and one encountered no further sign of human habitation until one reached the remote corner of the room, where suddenly a camp bed, a deal box and a basin on it, and a few old garments hung on nails drew the eye in the surrounding desolation.

When Royal had been lasooed in the launch, his artificial headgear had been carefully put on one side, along with Mrs. Dukes' bonnet. He now sat, with his intent face, still white with the paint of his get-up, and his look of a handsome young priest, fronting the self-possessed countenances of his two captors. Of these two, Arthur O. Passion's appearance is already familiar to the reader. Joseph J. was evidently his elder by some years, being perhaps forty-five or six. He was a little taller than Arthur O.; he was dressed like most Americans, in clothes several sizes too large for him. Even a man of sixty in America still leaves room for growth. It is symbolical of the youth of the race, one must suppose: although no amount of growth would fill up an average pair of American trousers; they would be baggy even for a Fat Man in a show. So Joseph J.'s clothes were voluminous and expensive looking affairs, of a non-committal slate-grey colour. His face was very much like Arthur O.'s; he had the same deep folds of flesh running up from the corner of his mouth, but his cheeks were rather more wasted, and his flesh was very sallow. The same bitter and strained expression strangely stamped his face. His eyes, blue and rather washed out, were extraordinarily cold and self-possessed. There seemed to be a bravado and wager almost in their coldness. They seemed sitting there like intrepid riders, with all the passions surging beneath them — wild, raw, impetuous passions, and cold, too, like themselves. He had an ash-coloured spray growing out over his forehead from the rest of his hair, on the left hand side. There he sat enormously cool and collected, and with such an air of taking it for granted that he should be master of the situation, that it seemed almost comical to Royal. He seemed to affirm that there was no need on Royal's part to apologise for being captured so easily, no need to 'feel bad about it,' since it was inevitable he had been captured by him. Or he seemed rather to be ignoring this side of the question altogether, taking it quite as a matter of course that Royal should sit there, bound, before him, and a slightly preoccupied expression on his face suggested that he was working at a point or two — as though he had several equally infallible and unerring ways of proceeding now, and was considering, in the calm of logical thought, which to choose. He was biting the second fingernail of his right hand. When on a holiday, a real holiday, Joseph J.'s nails would grow quite long; after a week of great business activity they would almost entirely disappear.

'Waal, here we are!' he began after a minute or two of silence.

'Now I don't see why we shouldn't make straight for the point without any talking, as I guess we shall understand each other pretty well, and you won't like me any better for leadin' you round a long way. I must apologise to you, Mr. Royal, for the way I've gone about gettin' into communication with you, but it seemed the only way. I guess we won't quarrel over that, once we've got to business. I may tell you, sir, at once, that I know Raza Khan and the whole gang as though we'd knocked about in the same cradle; Raza and I were like blamed twins at one time. Waal, we're not any longer!' He said this rather grimly, and very drawlingly.

'I've known of course what the game was in Marbury Street all along, and by gosh! it ain't a thing to sneeze at, five million dollars — that's your fortune ain't it ma'am? But I know Razy well enough, and I bet my bottom dollar that, though he depends on you to see things through, he don't give you so much as five per cent by a long way. Waal, it just struck me that for this time Razy might go and take a back seat. From what I read in the papers he's mismanaging things bad! So I thought I'd just step in and buy Razy out. Now, see here; you're a cute chap, and if it weren't for you and your play actin' Razy wouldn't see a durned dollar of Mrs. Dukes' money. Of course, he got the tip, and he put you on to it. But I won't mind bettin' somethin' handsome that you don't get five per cent, by a long sight, out of this transaction.'

This affirmation seemed to wait for an answer, for Mr. Joseph J. Passion stopped speaking for fully a minute, and fixed his eye encouragingly on Royal.

'Waal, see here; if the show were taken over one fine day by another man, who offered you thirty per cent — thirty per cent — of the total gained, wouldn't you go on working spry enough, without pinin' too much after Razy? See? I guess I put it plain enough.'

Royal shrugged his shoulders slightly and contemptuously, and answered after a moment.

'Is it a childish donkey of that sort, then, who has made my capture? Is that the silly idea you have in your head? You ought to go into light comedy, my friend, and leave the more serious walks of your profession severely alone!'

There was a silence of a few minutes after this. The American, and in any case the elder, had expected nothing of this sort.

He changed colour sharply, from his customary jaded sallowness, to a kind of dirty pale colour, which was the result of a flush attempting to struggle through. His eyes narrowed on the young man for a moment, but the latter was looking indifferently away, with an expression of irritation and boredom on his face.

At last Joseph J. spoke again.

'Will you kindly favour me, Mr. Royal, with the exact signification of your remark? That's irony, I understand, Mr. Royal — durned irony, that's what it is!' and at the sound of the word irony in his own mouth he suddenly flared up into a cold rage, and smote the arm of his chair with force. 'Irony' was the thing he could stomach least in the world, and at the thought that 'irony' had just been directed at him, his indignation got the better of him. But he drew himself up sharply, and went on evenly.

'You seem, sir, to consider our plan with contempt; in what way does it strike you, Mr. Royal, as not practical?'

'It's no good wasting breath upon you, apparently, as you seem a fool — a very queer kind of fool, of course.'

'Thank you, Mr. Royal,' drawled the American.

'But since I'm here stupidly tied up and in your hands, and shall be compelled to listen to any nonsense you like to talk to me, I suppose I'd better answer you at once, and have done with it, in the hope that you will then let me alone. You say you know Raza Khan; I suppose you're not fatuous enough to suppose that you can do what he can do? Or, in the second place, that he'd ever give you the chance of trying?'

'Oh, that's your difficulty, Mr. Royal?' said the American at once, pleasantly. 'Waal, I guess you credit old Razy with a little bit too much pen-e-tration, and also that he's taken you in a bit, like all the rest of them. I know all the company, because he hides a bit and don't show his ugly face too often, got a sort of idea there's somethin' mysterious, terrible and all that sort of thing about Razy. Razy ain't a fool — all that goes down very well. Bluff, Mr. Royal, *that's* only bluff! Razy wouldn't hurt a fly! Have you ever heard of Razy doin' anythin' desp'rate? I guess not. Razy knows too much. He might threaten and look black enough up to the last moment, then he'd just clear out, and say nothin' more. If anyone stood up to Razy, they'd soon find out how far *Razy* cared to go! And that's not far, you bet! Oh ye-es, you've heard about Maclean, who was found with his neck wrung in a drain pipe! But it wasn't Maclean at all, I b'lieve. Some crazy people will just identify any old corpse that's shown to them — they can't help it, seems like, they just must! "Is that your missing brother, ma'am?" And they stare a bit, and see an ugly thing there, and holler "Yes, that's him!" They like to think their brother was murdered, see? No, Mr. Royal, if I take this affair off Razy's hands I ain't goin' to say he won't cut up rough about it. But he'll just clear out, and pocket his share in the end, and glad to get it, like a little lamb. You mark me!'

'I wonder to what exent you know Raza Khan? Hillington

and I are the only two people in the company, at least in our section of it, that have ever heard his name, much less seen him. I speak so openly with you because there doesn't seem the least doubt that you *do* know him, or of him, anyhow. You profess to be great chums with him,' Royal continued. 'So much the better for you. But I advise you to mind your eye for all that. I should think that America would be the safest place for you for a bit. But still, whether you take my advice in that or not, I suppose now I must answer your ridiculous proposal. I wouldn't "change hands" in that way, for one thing, for the simple reason that I care very little about making considerable sums of money, and am quite content to work, just for the fun of the thing, for a reasonable wage, as though I were working for a theatre manager. In the second place, if I installed myself in Marbury Street 'under new management,' although I'm not at all afraid of Raza Khan, I know that I should not remain there twenty-four hours. And as far as you're concerned, all I can say is what I have already said – that you are running risks which it grieves me to see such charming, though misguided, men as yourselves doing. You will suffer for your naïveté.'

Just then the dog sprang up from Joseph J.'s feet, and started barking angrily, walking threateningly towards the door. They all looked up a little taken aback. A vague idea that Raza Khan might appear at the door seemed to have possessed all three.

37
THE QUESTION OF RAZA KHAN'S NATIONALITY

In place of the redoubtable chief of the 'Actor-Gang,' a tall red-headed young man entered, respectfully kicking his boots against the wall in a rude attempt to dispose of the mud that encrusted them, before advancing farther. This young man was none other than the third of the trio that had followed Mrs. Dukes to the Baker-Loo Tube and lost her there. His face would probably become in time like that of his two compatriots — for there was no doubt as to his nationality. Just now it was rather sensitive and ingenuous, although it wore a superficial look of supercilious indifference. He grinned on seeing Evan Royal, as though to say that they had met before. He was evidently on terms of equality with the other two, subject to a certain natural respect to seniority and a maturer rascality. He sat down and stretched his legs out, thrusting his hands and forearms if not also a portion of his biceps in his trousers pockets. He gazed amiably at Royal as though considering with pride and interest their capture.

No one had said anything. Suddenly the new-comer withdrew his left arm from his trousers' pocket and slapped his thigh resoundingly, bursting into a rather hysterical, high-pitched guffaw.

'Have you been to the office, Win?' asked Arthur O.

'Yep. It's all locked up,' replied the third tall American.

'The baby of the firm — Winter P. Passion,' said Arthur O. to Royal in an explanatory way.

Joseph J. did not move, and it was evident that he still had something to say.

'Have you ever ascertained, Mr. Royal, where Razy comes from?' he asked abruptly.

'Your mind still running on that gentleman?' said Royal. 'Yes, he's a Median prince, a Parsee, and some of his family live in India, in the north. His family anyway is of Hindu origin. He has one peculiarity, I believe, and that is that he has no name. All his names, and he has about a dozen, are titles. Khan, for instance. Or Raza, which means Excellency, or something of the sort. That's no secret. Any more information about your chum I can give you, Mr. Passion?'

'Waal, my b'lief is that Razy's a dago, nothin' more nor less. Median prince and all the rest of it's all my eye. He's just a dago,' announced Joseph J.

'An Italian, you mean? And Lucy too?'

'Who's that?'

'Oh, you don't know Lucy? Well, she's a very nice young lady that lends us a hand sometimes, and she's from his country – or partly so, part of her's from his country. Well, they speak together a very funny language. I know most of the European languages, at least the sound of them And it seems to me very likely that the language they speak is Persian.'

Royal was getting over his disgust and indifference, and was determined to be nice to Mr. Passion, and get all he could out of him – find out who Mr. Passion was and how much he knew.

'Yes, that's all right, they may jabber a bit to make you think they're talkin' some infernal outlandish sort of a tongue; but you mark me, Razy's just a durned dago.' And Joseph J.'s bitter and scornful expression deepened, making all the lines of his face harder and heavier.

'Do you know Bellamy Street?' asked Royal.

'No – Bellamy Street? Hwhere's th-at?' drawled Joseph J. with a sulky and suspicious glance at Royal. It was quite certain that he was not simulating an ignorance, and that Bellamy Street signified nothing to him.

'You don't know much, mon vieux,' Royal thought to himself.

'What I say is, that Razy's an infernal dago, and he just kids you fellers he's a prince and all that sort of thing,' repeated Joseph J. with a dogged stupidity.

Although Joseph J. had passed over the insulting manner in which Royal had addressed him at the beginning of the interview, he had not forgotten it, and whenever his eyes rested on this young man's person now they narrowed slightly, and a disagreeable coldness crept into them. His new feelings were manifested when a few minutes later he got up, and said to Arthur O. that they'd better be on the move again. He had not renewed his proposal to Royal. He said something in a low voice to his partner, and added rather loudly and in a decided manner, 'I guess so.' Going to where the cords lay on the floor, he bound several ends together, and then spoke to Royal.

'Now, sir, we're goin' out, and we can't leave you your legs to walk away with. We won't cut them off, but if you don't mind we'll just slip this string over 'em.'

Royal did not move, and allowed him to lift his feet, and slip the knot round his legs. Joseph J. drew it tight, and pulled it several times around, pulling equally tight further knots. Royal did not say anything, but his face underneath grew as white as the paste of his make-up. Winter was left, evidently with particular instructions about the prisoner. He sat down near the fire, and pulled out an evening paper. He had evidently realised from the manner of his superior that their captive had not been giving satisfaction, and so he did not show himself socially disposed towards him.

Evan Royal, left to his own thoughts, took little time to review his situation. This needed no reviewing. All his mind was taken up with the problem of his escape. A less promising prospect could hardly have presented itself. Tied tightly hand and foot, and in the presence of one of his captors, told to mount guard over him, who would, at any repeated movement on his part, take measures to make him keep quiet — there was little chance of his having the opportunity even barely to try to do so. And anyway he was bound too securely to be able to free himself of the cords.

So there was the second Mrs. Dukes, as much out of the way and as definitely disposed of as the first! 'No. 21 is an unlucky house,' thought Royal whimsically to himself. What were his American friends up to now? Probably they had seen that it would be useless to press him with their absurd proposal of transferring his services to them, and to go on securing the million for their pockets instead of Raza Khan's. They had, no doubt, determined to make another use of him. He supposed that they would now treat him as a hostage, and demand a very considerable sum from his employer for the use of him again. 'For the genial actor Evan Royal, in his famous part "Mrs. Dukes" of Marbury Street, the life and soul of the company, a hundred thousand pounds down.' He knew what Raza Khan would do. He would strain every nerve to discover the retreat of the three Americans; and Evan Royal knew something of the means that he had at his disposal. Still, whatever Joseph J. Passion might say derogatory to the awfulness of the subtle and very powerful Oriental, in whose employ he worked as an actor-criminal, he thought that Joseph J. would probably have respect enough for him to induce him to take the greatest care not to be tracked home. And, furthermore, if Messrs. Passion *did* take very much care, that it would be doubtful whether Raza's agents would rescue him in time.

If Raza Khan gave way, paid the money, and he were handed back, a still more difficult situation would confront him. He had been made a fool of, treated like a mere object, and he would not then want to go on with his work again. He had worked in a very proud and independent way for Raza Khan —

he had said and done what he liked and had always been successful. This was all over. He felt that he would never be able to make his own terms again, and would no longer be treated with the same consideration. He resolved, quite definitely, that if he were released, he would refuse to go on with the great Marbury Street mystification, and that, with the little money he had saved, he would go abroad, disappear in one direction or another.

But his sporting instinct urged him naturally to go through with the wonderful game he had successfully kept up so far, and to collar the million. *If* he could escape! Ah! he said to himself, if he could do *that,* he might perhaps go on with the Mrs. Dukes affair. Escaping from the Americans would wipe out more or less the humiliation of being so stupidly captured – kidnapped just like an old woman, like Mrs. Dukes! It was, in this sense, an ironical happening, this capture of him.

To escape, to escape! He *must* escape! He banished all other thoughts and centred his mind on this problem alone. But it seemed hopeless. For three days he thought feverishly and without result, getting more and more desperate and impatient. And then, all of a sudden, he thought of a way.

38
A RECEPTION AT AN EASTERN EMBASSY

In the meantime, consternation reigned elsewhere. We shall have to penetrate, in one case, to a very exclusive sphere, to feel the full effect of this second kidnapping of a Mrs. Dukes.

In one of the most dignified squares of the West End stood the Embassy of an Eastern Power, a near neighbour of Persia, with a history equally great. This was one of those squares that lie out of the way of life and are inhabited by enormously wealthy, or prodigiously distinguished people, and seem ominously silent and uninhabited, as though it were not decent that one should know that such extremely illustrious people do such a thing as *inhabit* at all. One knows, nevertheless, that these cold and impassable buildings swarm with servants and bulge with riches. Still, this part of the town is neither a thoroughfare, nor is there the merest hint of commerce of any form; no one comes there except occasionally enormous motor vans groaning with the weight of boxes and cases full of eatables for these extremely rich and distinguished people, and their extremely distinguished, if not precisely rich, servants. But on the evening of the kidnapping of the second Mrs. Dukes, before the Ambassadorial mansion mentioned above, was a long line of carriages, and from them stepped large and small men and women in various advanced stages of prosperity.

Within, the splendid reception rooms of the Embassy showed every sign of having been expressly prepared to receive them. Shortly after ten a barbaric profusion of human beings thronged them decorously. They were everywhere − with one exception − furnished in European fashion, but the most superb carpets, in which people sank almost ankle-deep, and every here and there a gorgeous ornament of Oriental cast, suggested that the owners had special access to the treasures of the East.

The one exception to this was a long peculiar shaped room, with several alcoves, and a trellised window at the end, got up in a fashion that one associates with the palaces of Indian Rajahs. Still there were numerous chairs, besides a prodigality of divans, and on this occasion the lower half of it had been curtained off.

Two late arrivals, two young and charming looking men who had met in an adjoining room, passed into this, and its aspect evidently impressed them.

'Sarandur Khan is rather weird, isn't he?' asked the first of the second. 'Some people say he's got an extensive harem next door, and kills off his wives systematically once they pass thirty or thereabouts.'

'Yes, but he only shows one wife, you know. She's always the same one. So I don't expect he keeps up his harem very publicly.'

'He's very well off, isn't he?'

'Well, it appears he's very rich in a funny Eastern way, but which doesn't count much in Europe. He has very expensive wives, several mountain ranges, millions of quite penniless people, and so on, but all that he has in the way of actual cash, in our sense, doesn't amount to much. He's quite European-ised, though, and a very clever man, people say.'

Just then a tall, very dark, bearded man passed them, and the second young man, who had all the information, nudged his friend, and said, 'That's our host.'

He was a very striking man indeed. In fact he was the eccen-tric individual who had so impressed Fane in the private room of the Firenze, and who was now that young gentleman's employer.

Near the foot of the stairs down below, these two inquisitive young men a short while afterwards hid a little behind a large palm to gaze at an astonishing looking woman, whom the second of the two explained to his companion was the wife of Sarandur Khan.

She was an enormous woman, a giantess indeed, measuring about six feet two, and monstrous otherwise in build, and like an extremely ugly, but clearly chiselled sphinx. Her face expressed absolutely nothing. Her eyes never closed for a moment, and she stood, dressed completely in deep red, massively graceful, receiving the people that poured in, like a Sphinx three thousand years old receiving a crowd of vulgar tourists with a handshake. Her dark, almost green-coloured skin and dark red dress looked almost more sombre than black would have done. The people arriving too seemed struck silent at this salute, and passed up in a hushed stream from this monument of silence, who never opened her mouth, or smiled. Some had the same sensation that one proves in taking the hand of some freak in a circus, or of feeling, at her invitation, the biceps of the Fat Woman in a show.

The young men wandered off again — but let me hasten to explain that we are not following these young men round because they interest us in the least. On the contrary, they are very tiresome — although charming — young men. We are merely using them as a convenience. As we have not been invited ourselves to this reception, and there is no one that we know, except the host, we are using the eyes of these young gentlemen — and even we have condescended to make use of their voices — in the imparting of a little information. For this reception is of great interest and of importance in the progress of our story. This is merely said in case the reader should imagine he was expected to pay any attention to them — glance at them, give a smile. No, he can be as rude as ever he pleases with them. They are people of no interest or consideration. Mere conveniences.

Some three quarters of an hour later these young fellows had come together again, and were suddenly surprised and flattered by the sound of a soft and exotic music proceeding from the room rather strangely decorated and arranged, that we have described above. They entered, along with a great many other people, and took up their position against the wall near one of the alcoves. It was a large room and accommodated a considerable number of people. When everyone who could crowd in had done so, the host himself sitting beside two handsome ladies in the centre of the piece, the heavy silk curtain that had concealed the lower end of the room was drawn aside, and a group of strangely dressed people was discovered standing, as though to attention, facing the audience, whilst one in the centre played on a large wooden instrument, that looked somewhat like a flat wooden bagpipes, and had a mouthpiece like that of a mouth-organ. A sweet, profound and very simple melody was rising from this fantastic instrument.

When they had stood at attention a moment, the group sat down, forming a circle round three or four musicians, two of them with drums. There were four men and two women, besides the musicians. They all were very dark, and very like a certain type of Hindu, with black hair falling on their shoulders. They were dressed not unlike Caucasians. One of them, a very handsome young man, with a face of a kind of intense proud gaiety, and a curious way of holding his head up, was dressed in a tight fitting long black silk garment. It was very wide at the shoulders, and his brown neck rose out of a dark red shirt. His legs, very muscular, were swathed also in a dark red silk, and he had embroidered shoes, turned up at the toes, and a long sword.

The music shortly became fuller and more impassioned and one of the men got up and began dancing slowly. Then a girl joined him. They danced in mincing little steps, their hands on their hips, then they began flying round and crouching down while they went, as the Russians do. The others joined the dance, first one then another, and last the handsome young man sprang in amongst them with a cry. He took a dagger from his belt, and threw it up and caught it, held it at arm's length, looking whimsically at it, and shrugging his shoulders, and singing a kind of dirge. His movements then became wilder and wilder, and he finished by planting it quivering in the ground, and dancing round it. The others had gone back to their places.

The music was the strangest and wildest imaginable. While the young man's frenzy was at its height, and he was whirling round his dagger like a dervish, suddenly, to the amazement of the guests, from the side appeared their hostess, the giant-like woman the two young men had seen on the stairs, dressed in a tight-fitting dark red dress, and with innumerable shawls, jackets, trinkets and things covering her otherwise, and a low crown of jewels on her hair. Thereupon she performed the most savage dance, with the young man at first, and then alone, to the wailing and screaming and thudding of the instruments. Her strength must have been enormous, and her grace and amazing activity, for a woman of her prodigious size, left everyone dumbfounded. Her expression did not change for an instant. Her eyes only seemed to light up, like coals blown up, and towards the end blazed in her face. Her immense arms were constantly thrown up with a wild involuntary gesture, and then came falling down to her side again despairingly, with struggling and reluctant hands.

When she disappeared again at the door at the side from which she had come, there was a burst of applause, and the curtains were then slowly drawn to again.

But during the early part of the performance, before she had appeared, something unusual had happened amongst the audience, that had attracted at the time as much attention as the dancers themselves.

39

HOW TWO KNAVES FIRST MET

While the first two dancers were going through their vivid mimicries, a servant had entered at the further end of the room, with a silver platter, and made his way through the throngs of guests up to the place where Sarandur Khan was sitting. Arrived there, he went down on one knee, and held out the platter to his master.

Sarandur Khan took a letter from it, and turning apologetically to the ladies at his side, tore open the envelope and glanced inside. He at once put it down, and waving the servant away, sat quite still watching the dancers. He then slipped the letter into his pocket. A moment later, as though remembering the ladies at his side, and wishing to show them that they were not forgotten, he turned towards them smiling. But his smile was such a terrible grimace that they half started away from him in fear. He seemed to realise that his smile was not what he had intended it to be, for he at once turned his head away again, and riveted his eyes on the dancers. For the rest of the performance he hardly moved, apparently absorbed in the dancing, his face having something of the impassivity and intensity, at the same time, of the performers. But when the tremendous figure of the woman who presided over his receptions appeared, she had hardly danced a couple of minutes when he appeared extraordinarily moved. At the burst of applause following upon her exit he rose brusquely, almost violently, and without noticing the ladies with whom he had been sitting, or anybody else, made his way rapidly out of the room, and was not seen again for fully half an hour. Then he returned smiling and self-possessed as usual, found out the two ladies he had treated so strangely and made them the most elaborate of apologies for his rudeness, and for the rest of the reception was tireless in the pursuit of his duty as a host. He explained that the woman he always referred to as 'the Ambassadress' was too fatigued by her exploits to again enter the 'salons' that evening.

When the last guest had gone he mounted the stairs three at a time to the top of the house and burst into a room at the end of a long passage, with a strange impatient cry. There, outlined against the night sky, leaning out of the window, was the enormous bulk of the Ambassadress and dancer. This woman was not his wife, but their relationship, without love contributing to it, was yet of a very close and peculiar nature. She drew herself up and away from the window, and confronted him in silence for some time. Then Sarandur Khan began talking quickly in the language of his country, and the woman answered him in short precipitate sentences. The name of Lucy occurred frequently.

The note he had received during the performance was from Lucy, written in their language, and saying simply that Evan Royal had left at six o'clock to go to the rendezvous he (Sarandur Khan) had given him at the wharf, and was not yet back. It was then eleven o'clock. She asked what she should do in the event of Royal's not returning. The Khan knew it was not the police, and at once guessed who had sent a false message, if a message had been sent. Evan Royal had told Lucy that he had a rendezvous at the wharf. He soon dismissed also the idea of Royal having lied, and as he rejected first one hypothesis and then another, his reasoning narrowed in more and more upon those to whom he alone could attribute this trickery.

A year or so previously the individual known to Royal as Joseph J. Passion had suddenly left the company, after a slight disagreement with Sarandur Khan himself. The Khan had got to know him under rather curious circumstances. Joseph J. Passion, whose specialty was blackmail, had tried to blackmail him in an odd manner. It would never be very difficult to convince an Englishman that a foreign potentate was a klepto-maniac, especially an Oriental notable. On returning from the East some years before, he had remained at a London hotel for several days, as some alterations which he had ordered at the Embassy were not quite completed. There was a fire at that hotel, and in hurrying out he had first gone into an adjoining room to see if his secretary had noticed the alarm. He went into the wrong room by mistake, and found Mr. Joseph J. Passion forcing an escritoire. There was no mistake about it. He retired at once, as he did not object on principle to any form of activity, and discriminated very little between the criminal and non-criminal. Also Passion (as we shall continue to call him, though Sarandur Khan knew him under another name) seemed very cool and business-like. It was evidently his trade, or a branch of his trade, and his regular means of subsistence. He had probably set the hotel on fire, thought our Oriental, and frightened the occupant of the room out into the street by clamouring fire at her door. He smiled at the thought. Also he had smiled on leaving the American to his work, at the exquisite indifference with which his advent on the scene of Passion's naughty activities had been received.

A short time afterwards, in the crowd, he met Mr. Passion again — this time a cool and leisurely spectator. Passion saw him too. He had been extremely cool when he had been suddenly surprised in that way, but he had been nevertheless extremely astonished at the immediate withdrawal and amused smile of his interrupter. He at once concluded, and quite rightly, that Sarandur Khan himself was a dishonest person. Into the bargain he was a 'dago,' some sort of Southern or Eastern foreigner. So, when he found him in the crowd, he tried, quite regarding it as in the day's work and a matter of routine, to blackmail him. He would pretend of course that he had detected Sarandur pillaging during the panic in the hotel, thus skilfully reversing matters. But Sarandur Khan was a very fascinating person, and Joseph J. Passion came under his fascination. He liked his wit, they understood one another. But also it did not take him long to see that he was in the presence of no ordinary man. The Khan, at the least, was always extraordinarily distinguished. They had become quite friendly, and the Khan had given him rendezvous in a large restaurant near Piccadilly. There they had met, and undertaken one or two dishonest financial operations together, mostly consisting of blackmail, which was really Joseph J.'s strongest point. He had on one occasion acted in concert with the company, just before Royal had joined. He had never, however, discovered that the Raza Khan of his acquaintance was one and the same with the famous Ambassador, Sarandur Khan, whom he knew well by name. He had come, indeed, latterly, to believe that Raza Khan was rather a fraud, and not such an exalted person as he was made out to be, but some Eastern adventurer, with a plausible way 'those niggers' have. And last of all he'd put him down as a dago. *Quite* last of all he tried to rob him, and the Khan had protested so energetically that Joseph J. had indignantly left him forever. But just before the Khan had undertaken the kidnapping of Mrs. Dukes, he had received a blackmailing letter, at a house the company had looked upon as headquarters before they had moved into the house they at present occupied in St. John's Wood – where Mrs. Dukes still lay awaiting events. Several letters had followed in rapid succession, and Sarandur Khan had at last concluded that the only thing to do was to change quarters, without leaving any trace behind him. This Yankee was the only man who had once taken part in his nefarious enterprises, and who had quitted his service, and was also the only man who was not apparently afraid of him. He was an American, and his imagination was of a severely practical type — a practical imagination alone he possessed — and he had grossly underestimated this energetic Oriental's capacity for mischief, and had never appreciated his charm and his gifts, as Royal had at once. He also had had a fundamental contempt for him as a 'nigger'; when he had shown himself more energetic and redoubtable than he had anticipated, he had promoted him to a 'dago'; he had then less contempt for him, but still he was a 'dago.' Farther he could not go, of course, as he was evidently not of a northern race. This was the history of these two men's relations. Sarandur Khan had at once thought of the American when he heard of the faked letter, and the rendezvous at the wharf. And, further, in beating out the question afterwards, he came to the conclusion, which was the right one, that Joseph J. Passion had got on his tracks again through the accounts in the newspapers of the Marbury Street mystery.

He had been angry enough when it had seemed necessary to move his headquarters for this cursed American. He had thought then, and thought carefully, whether it would not be better to suppress once and for all the source of this vexation at once, but had decided not. But from the moment he had come to the conclusion that the American's hand was here again, thwarting him — he had already become certain of this while watching the dancers — he had but one thought. He knew *now* what must be done with this man. While he was taking passionate counsel with the woman who had been awaiting him upstairs, after the guests had left, through all this talk this idea was uppermost. But it was now regarded by them as almost an accomplished thing — it was a thing that was fated, that had to happen. They were quite calm about it. They discussed no more the point as to whether this American must be made to disappear very finally or not. He had not been the first that these two had known to disappear.

40
THE THIRD MRS. DUKES

Fane for the last few days had been really very badly in love. To ease this fever he had taken long cold draughts of reflection — he had allowed his mind to dwell on the very uncongenial mystery that surrounded his present mode of life, and had faced all the possibilities, nay probabilities, of his getting into a very bad scrape indeed. But on this evening of the second Mrs. Dukes' disappearance his temperature, amorously speaking, was very high indeed. Being of a very romantic disposition — so much so, indeed, that we have been compelled often to refer to him as a poet, as the only means of conveying an idea of the excess of these romantic tendencies in him — he was extremely alive to the exotic charms of his colleague, the beautiful Lucy. Her impenetrability — her face was in a sense as hidden as though the heavy veil that Turkish women wear had hidden it — her voluptuous forms, that seemed to have grown like the rich silk cushions they must for long have lain amongst, her delightful intelligence, that seemed so admirably to pair with his own — all worked upon him irresistibly. And then the strangeness of their position, that threw them so much to-gether and gave them so much privacy. They had turned a little bedroom in the front into a kind of sitting-room. There they read or conversed in the evening, and he recited his part to her — that is, played at being Mrs. Dukes.

After an hour or so spent downstairs — on the look-out for the returning Mrs. Dukes — Lucy came up to him about half past ten and asked him if he would take a letter she had just written and find a messenger of some description to bear it to the address indicated. He did so, and on re-entering their common room at the top of the house, found Lucy evidently in a state of great depression.

'What's become of Mrs. Dukes, do you think?' he asked.

'She'll be back soon, I hope,' she answered.

They were silent for a few minutes, both standing by the grate, then Fane did what he had wanted to do for several days past. He put his arm round Lucy's waist, and drew her to him. She threw her arms round his neck and buried her face on his shoulder. Then she began shaking all over, and Fane discovered to his extreme discomfort that she was crying. He attempted to soothe her by one of the simple masculine recipes for soothing on these occasions. That was by kisses. He could think of nothing better for the moment. Then she put her tear-stained cheek to his, and their kisses mingled so sweetly that Fane felt that he was tasting a happiness that would henceforth be tyrannical — he would do anything to secure it. Then suddenly Lucy broke away from him and poured out quickly the following enigmatical and bitter words:

'No, I won't kiss you, I won't,' and her slight foreign accent became more pronounced. 'I mustn't. Tomorrow I may have to ask you to do something, and then you'll think that I accepted your love tonight out of calculation and to make you more docile. No! I do *not* accept your love, do you hear? I have *not* kissed you. You owe me nothing. I am a dangerous woman. I *am* a traitress. I *have* kissed you to deceive you, and lead you to your ruin. When I ask you to do something that seems dangerous to you, you must refuse! Do you hear? You must refuse! Oh! Hercules,' (and the ridiculous effect of his name, like an oath or an invocation, passed quite unnoticed with the rest of her quaint speech), 'Oh Hercules, I'm a bad poor girl!' And with this she rushed out of the room sobbing and waving him off.

Fane did not follow her beyond the door. He returned to the most comfortable of two armchairs and sat down to consider the meaning of her words, and to luxuriously reflect on the happiness that had just been his, prior to the words. Of course she was very thick with 'the management,' and knew certainly the inner secret of the mystery of this house and its immeasurably wealthy old landlady. But she was evidently quite sincere with him; that is, if she did not reveal to him the real nature of his employment, at least her attitude towards him was frank and loyal. That part disposed of, he began ruminating on the more exclusively delightful portion of the foregoing interview with Lucy.

Then he began to think of the future. He wanted these moments he had just passed to be repeated, to become a fixed thing, in fact. He wanted to have Lucy all to himself, to marry her, to get her away from these people. But he had not the vaguest notion what the difficulties might be; in the next few days he would sound her and try to discover how permanent was her connection with these mysterious people who employed him.

His thoughts wandering back again to less practical reflections, he fell asleep in the large armchair before the fire. He was woken by a chill feeling in his lower limbs, and rose, put out the gas, and turned to go into his bedroom. On the landing he heard the sound of voices downstairs, and noticed that Lucy's door was ajar. It was two in the morning, and he went quietly downstairs to see what was the matter.

Peering over from the first floor landing, he saw beneath the gas-jet in the hall a fierce excited face, bound with a small rose-coloured turban. It was a man — an Indian, he thought — with enormous black eyes and white teeth, and he was talking vehemently to Lucy, who stood like a statue before him. Then Lucy moved towards the back door, the man following her and still talking hoarsely, and let him out and locked and bolted the door.

She stared a little at first when she saw Fane, then she answered his questions softly, and in a caressing voice.

'It's one of our people who comes with a message from another of our people. They are very excitable.'

She had told him that her father was Persian, but had always lived in a neighbouring state, and that her mother was an English woman.

She wished good-night so quietly and simply and with such a softness that he went to his room wondering at and blessing her.

The next morning she brought him his breakfast as usual in the adjoining room. She had, of course, turned herself into Mrs. Beechamp for the day. The get-up was so perfect that as he looked at her he could not believe that she was the same woman. She sat down and looked at him steadily for a few minutes. Then she spoke in a voice that seemed somehow sulky and dogged.

'Fane, it's now time for you to make use of your studies. If I help to make you up, will you play at being Mrs. Dukes for a day or two? You will only have to lie on her bed and pretend to be ill. You need say very little.'

He remembered what she had said the night before about

the 'thing that she would ask him to do' on the morrow. Here it was, evidently. He accepted at once. He quite saw how this might be a very foolhardy and ill-advised proceeding. He accepted at once like this chiefly to show that he trusted her absolutely – this was the chief reason.

'There is no danger for you,' she said, and he noticed that whilst she said this her mouth was screwed to one side a little, as though tears were coming.

It evidently cost her a great deal to make this request, and seeing this, he hastened to comply with it.

'All right,' he said, 'get me some of her rags. I'll make up here.'

In a half hour he was installed in Mrs. Dukes' bed, and saying in a wheezy voice, 'Oh Lord! my 'eart's thumpin' fit to knock a 'ole in the bed!' The third Mrs. Dukes had entered upon her existence – the chequered existence that seemed the lot of each successive Mrs. Dukes. Cole was sitting by the fire and smoking. He had come up, apparently, to have a look, out of the tail of his eye, at the new Mrs. Dukes. He made no comment, and did not show, by any look or sign, that he was aware that there was a new aspirant to the role of his mother.

Fane had not by any means Royal's power of mimicry, and had not got the timbre of the voice with very great exactitude. But his invention was good – he strung together 'Dukes phrases' nearly as well as his predecessor, and his make-up, like all the make-ups of the Actor-Gang, was marvellous.

When Lucy and he were alone an hour or so later, Cole having retreated to his beloved shades beneath, Fane asked her suddenly, 'I suppose I am here in Mrs. Dukes' place, and am meant to get hold of the money. What happened to Mrs. Dukes last night, have you any idea? Did that Indian chap tell you any thing about it? It's only natural that I should like to know where I am. If her throat's cut, it would of course be more regular that I, her successor, should be informed.'

'No, no, that I can promise you — no violence has been done to her. As to last night, it was not us who were the criminals. We have enemies, it seems, and there has been some trouble. But it was not us. And she is safe, you can be quite sure, and will be back here in a day or two.'

Fane was more puzzled than ever. For she was evidently sincere in what she said. He gave it up, but determined to remain Mrs. Dukes no longer than was absolutely necessary.

41
THE ENEMY AT LAST IS HEARD OF

For two days the Americans gave no sign of life. The second Mrs. Dukes seemed to have disappeared utterly off the face of the earth. As hour followed hour, the waiting household in Marbury Street — where Hillington had come to establish himself permanently until the crisis was over for good or for bad — and the other more potent parties interested, became more and more uneasy. Something was brewing.

But on the third morning the first raindrop of the storm, so to speak, fell on the house in Marbury Street — the first indication of hidden activities. It came in the form of a wire from the Liverpool solicitors, asking if all were well with their client, and begging her to inform them by wire at once.

What might this mean? Hillington and Lucy held a council of war upstairs. Hillington had been rather alarmed on observing that the detective watching the house had been joined by a comrade that morning. What did this wire mean? Had any rumours been put about, that Mrs. Dukes had been injured, was ill – or had her death been announced, perhaps? On the other hand this wire might be from their enemies, and merely sent in the hope of getting some information or other. The address was not that of the solicitors' offices. A simple reply in the affirmative, however, could do no harm. So Hillington sent off at once a wire, simply containing the words, 'In excellent health – Dukes.' Then they waited.

An hour or so later another wire arrived. 'Did you wire me yesterday from Cavendish Street?' This brought them up short. Hillington was very excited. 'Ah, that's it,' he exclaimed, and he was for answering 'no' at once, and asking for further explanations. But Lucy suggested that someone or other – Raza Khan – might have wired. 'But Cavendish Street? – he hasn't a house in Cavendish Street, Pimlico.' However, it was necessary to move with the greatest prudence. All the responsibility was on their shoulders now. They had been the first attacked – and the attack was sharp. They were the firing-line, the first engaged with the enemy. Hillington at once telephoned to headquarters, and was instructed to answer 'no,' and to keep his chief informed of the result and all subsequent developments. The 'no' was sent, at the same time with a request for particulars as to how the mistake had arisen.

Another hour or so passed, and a wire arrived informing Mrs. Dukes that a representative was being immediately despatched from Liverpool to investigate matters, and to give an explanation of what had occurred. So now they had to wait until the evening to hear further details.

The third Mrs. Dukes had already begun to suffer the usual ill-fortune that attended the occupying of that role. The sheets that had been provided for him by Lucy had not been properly aired – presumably Lucy's perturbation was accountable for this – and Fane had been sneezing and snuffling the whole morning, and was now rather hoarse. He was one of those young men who have ordinarily a young and rather high-pitched voice, but when attacked by a cold or cough, can speak in nothing but the most harsh and burly bass. The volume of rude and masculine sound that now proceeded from his chest whenever he opened his mouth, had even had an effect on Cole, when he had attempted a little conversation with the latter. Cole had said, 'Oh, I say' – exactly what Cole meant by this it was difficult to understand. But he had at once retired to the cellar for the rest of the day with his pipe. It was quite out of the question for Fane to attempt to impersonate Mrs. Dukes for the moment. Hillington had got him all sorts of medicines, and the room stank of eucalyptus, menthol, peppermint, camphor and various other things exhaling from bottles and boxes of quack medicines. He must be left in Mrs. Dukes' bed, and his make-up carefully renewed, however, as he might, as a last resource, be *shown* to people, although he could not speak to them.

About six o'clock a very blond and decided looking man, about thirty years old, arrived in a hansom cab. He was confidential clerk – a very astute and energetic young gentleman – of Messrs. Truman and Hatchett.

He was one of those people who live up to the description so frequently given of the hero in books – 'he looked keenly' at people, at everyone. He pierced Cole through and through, and turned away brusquely and guardedly, as though reserving his opinion on Cole – though one guessed that Cole had seemed to him a very stealthy and malignant looking person.

His first inquiry was for Mr. Hillington. On being told by that gentleman himself that he was in the presence of Mr. Hillington, he looked at him with razor-like keenness, and then followed him upstairs. Hillington informed him that Mrs. Dukes was not at all well, and that he was acting for her – had promised to represent her to the best of his ability.

'You do not know Cavendish Street, I presume?' asked the clerk.

'Yes, I know it; but – '

'What I mean is that you have not lived there lately, or are not – ah – very familiar with it.'

'No,' said Hillington, wondering what this cross-questioning might be leading to.

The clerk then told him, rather guardedly and as though wondering whether he were not going too far, that Truman and Hatchett had received a telegram the previous afternoon, purporting to come from Mrs. Dukes, from an address in Cavendish Street, asking for an immediate advance of a few thousand pounds. What the clerk did not inform Hillington, but what actually happened, was that on receipt of this telegram, the Mr. Hatchett who had visited Mrs. Dukes rubbed his hands with satisfaction, and said conceitedly, 'I thought I would put everything in order. And there you are. She feels herself a millionairess at last, and will be perfectly easy to deal with now. Several thousands? She must be going it!' They had wired back and said she could draw on their bankers for two thousand pounds, and that Mr. Hatchett would come down again in a day or two. But early on the following morning, Mr. Truman, the gouty member of the firm, had had misgivings. He happened just then to be reading some detective stories in a new sixpenny magazine, and he determined to do a little investigation on his own account. So he sent a wire to Marbury Street – this was the first wire received.

Later in the morning they had telephoned to the bank in

London, telling them not to cash a cheque if offered. But it was too late. The two thousand pounds had already been paid out.

In the meantime a letter had arrived, apparently in Mrs. Dukes' handwriting — the clerk showed this to Hillington, who pronounced it the clumsiest of forgeries — which was apparently meant to be the first step in a demand on Mrs. Dukes' part for a much more considerable advance.

When all this was told — or the outline of it, at least — the clerk was silent and looked keenly at Hillington.

When the firm had discovered that they had been tricked, they had at once all suspected Hillington. Hillington's name was familiar to all of them, and he was already execrated by all of them. Each had formed, from Hatchett's account of Mrs. Dukes and her 'adviser,' a different picture of Hillington, but in each separate brain-portrait made for himself by each partner in the firm, Hillington was a scoundrelly adventurer — for the moment, however, to be accepted as Mrs. Dukes' man of business. The clerk now added that the police had been communicated with, and that if the thieves were still in Cavendish Street, they might yet be caught.

While Hillington was considering what next was to be done, the clerk proposed something, very energetically, which put Hillington out extremely.

42

AN EXPLOSION, AND HOW IT AFFECTS THE CLERK

Truman and Hatchett's clerk looked very blond and very resolute. He said, 'I have been asked especially by my employers to see Mrs. Dukes personally before returning. I have, indeed, a message for her. It would be desirable to ask her permission before communicating it to you, as of course, sir, we do not know how far you are in her confidence, and there are certain things that perhaps only the party supremely interested should know. Would it be possible, do you think, Mr. Hillington, for me to see Mrs. Dukes for a moment?'

'I'm afraid — ' began Hillington slowly, looking very grave and doubtful.

'Oh, but it is the simplest matter in the world; it would not cause her any undue excitement.'

'Couldn't Messrs. Truman and Hatchett write her what they have entrusted you with?' asked Hillington.

The clerk's eye stabbed Hillington in a hundred places; his glance became alarmingly 'keen.' He was becoming suspicious. Why did not this gentleman, whom his employers had given him special instructions about, want to admit him to the bed-side of Mrs. Dukes? Now, we may as well reveal it at once — the *entire* firm of Truman and Hatchett, including *almost* all of them, 'looked keenly' at one another, and all, to a man, transfixed their client, with piercing glances, each in his own way.

The most horrible mystery at once began to suggest itself to the clerk. He had read in the newspapers all about the 'Mystery of 21, Marbury Street,' the strange occurrences, the series of crimes, etc.

His manner became extremely cold and extremely determined. Hillington was positively alarmed. He wondered if this good fellow could possibly know anything. He concluded that he did not, however, and determined to show him, just show him, Mrs. Dukes in her bed.

He found Fane in the midst of a fit of coughing. He waited a minute or two until it was over, and then went to fetch Messrs. Truman and Hatchett's representative.

This gentleman bowed respectfully to Mrs. Dukes, and having announced the nature of his errand and told her his position in the firm, he waited for some recognition on her part. Hillington then told him hastily that Mrs. Dukes had a very bad cold and could hardly speak above a whisper.

She appeared to him in the last stage of some terrible disease. He could not be expected to know of her usual pallor, which was extreme, and she certainly was at present ghastly. And then to keep up the pretence of being very ill and speechless, Fane rolled his head a little, and let his mouth hang a little open.

'You have a doctor, of course, Mrs. Dukes?' said the clerk, addressing himself directly to her.

'Oh, it's nothing so *very* serious,' smiled Mr. Hillington.

The clerk shot at him an indignant and penetrating glance.

'But I think really you should see a doctor, Mrs. Dukes. Allow me to fetch one for you.'

Mrs. Dukes smiled faintly, tapped her chest, and then said in a husky whisper, the clerk respectfully approaching his head, 'It's all right, mister — er; it ain't anything *very* hawful, as Mr. 'illington says. 'E knows.'

But here something very tragic happened. The effort to speak in a whisper, and with a voice that was not his own, caused a considerable tickling in Fane's throat, with the result that all of a sudden a terrible and cyclonic fit of coughing seized him. He snapped his mouth down, and became purple in the face, his eyes watered, his veins stood out. Something of all this appeared through his make-up, and positively terrified the watching clerk. 'She must at once see a doctor!' he exclaimed to Hillington.

But the attack of coughing, up till now silent, was reaching a climax, and if Fane was not to break a blood vessel, he must allow nature to have its way. He waved the clerk frantically out of the room.

The clerk not understanding what was meant, approached Mrs. Dukes rapidly. Fane was at his last gasp.

Everything hung in the balance; this was the most critical moment in the whole of this elaborate plot up till that time.

The success of this nefarious enterprise depended on this young man's capacity, by tightening to bursting point nearly all the muscles in his body, by deadening with sheer force of will the sensitiveness of his mucous membrane, or whatever it was, to resist this fiendish, this tremendous tickling all the way up his throat. If a single little muscle gave way, and demoralised the others, the cough would be let loose within an inch or two of the clerk's face — a raucous, bass, unmistakably masculine uproar.

Fane thought he should go mad. His eyes glared into the clerk's face, they implored, they protruded from his head big as walnuts. In his enormous attempt at silence the other two people present seemed to join. One could have heard a pin drop for a moment.

The clerk, still thinking his client had beckoned to him, bent attentively forward. The thought flashed through Fane's brain of assuming sudden madness, of seizing him by the hair, of startling him so much that he would not notice the accompanying sound, that he could intersperse with words screamed out at the same time. It was just a flash of thought, he dared not even think, all his mind was centred on preventing the eruption. It was rejected as too risky — it was put aside as a last resource.

Hillington realised what was happening, and was standing white and anguished behind the clerk, whom he was regarding with the liveliest hatred. Hardly a minute could have elapsed in this state of tense agony, although it seemed a fortnight to Fane. Then Hillington seized the clerk by the arm, and, in desperation, dragged him away, the latter indignantly resisting. Hillington, feeling it was only a matter of seconds, pushed him frantically towards the door. Probably the clerk would not have gone, had it not been that when Hillington first seized him in this manner he had been very much frightened. In that first moment the first wild thought that occurred to him was that Hillington was going to attack him, throttle him, just as he was poisoning this poor old woman. He was a very nervous man, and the detective stories had only made him more so. By the time he had recovered his senses, and discovered that he was merely being put outside the door, it was too late to stand his ground. Hillington apologised hurriedly the while; the clerk heard something about 'Mrs. Dukes ... sudden attack' – 'frequent vomiting' – 'do you mind ... a moment?' And he thrust him frantically through the door, and came out in the passage with him.

As the door shut on their backs, a most terrific explosion, a wonderful and composite sound, was heard within. It had rapidly grown not only in dimension, but in character, by being so hugely suppressed, and was no longer a simple explosion of coughing. It seemed to combine every sound a human being can make – and one of the largest too. It might have been a giant from the sound. It was a bellowing, a spluttering, a reaching, a coughing, a spitting, a roaring, and – stranger than all – laughing. For the strain had been so great that Fane had become positively hysterical. Hillington and the clerk remained with their eyes fixed on each other's faces – distended and round. The clerk was rooted to the spot. We should say that his hair stood stiffly on end, but we do not believe that people's hair ever does stand on end, having frequently been extremely terrified ourselves, but never having remarked any commotion on the scalp.

He did not think. This was not a case for thinking but acting. What this terrible noise might signify he could not say. But one thing was certain. In the interest of his client a doctor must at once be fetched. His worst suspicions of Hillington were confirmed. He would be able to tell his employers — how sensational! — that *they* had told him that Hillington was a slippery customer, a crafty little adventurer; but that *he* had discovered him to be something worse — a criminal of the most blood-curdling type.

He did not listen to Hillington's apologies and amenities. He informed him curtly he was going to fetch the doctor, and left the house, leaving consternation behind him. For Hillington could only *show* his Mrs. Dukes to the doctor, as he had to the clerk. The doctor could not be allowed to touch her — even to feel her pulse. And Hillington had a superstitious dread of the practised scientific eye. The doctor would not be deceived, perhaps, by the make-up. And Fane might have a similar attack to that that had already endangered them. Hillington rapidly, and with much mental imprecation, laid his plans to resist the doctor.

43
THE DOCTOR'S STARTLING OBSERVATION

Once the clerk was out in the street, he turned with unflinching eyes to the *right*. He did not hesitate. He would go straight to a doctor's, and he would seek for one to the right. Why not to the left? Because at the bottom of the steps he found himself turned slightly towards the right, and he must not swerve or hesitate so much as a hair's breadth.

But now that he was in the open air again a certain uneasiness overtook him. The scene he had just participated in seemed unreal. Especially the noise he had heard through the closed door. This was more unreal than anything else. He began thinking and putting two and two together. Whatever was it? What was the matter with the eccentric old woman? What disease was it made noises like that, he asked himself, as though a disease were a wild beast. What deadly poison induced such outbursts of sound as that? He gave it up. But it was clear that that fellow Hillington was keeping the poor old woman locked up there and was doing her to death. His familiarity with cases of this sort — everyday occurrences in the literature that he most affected — made it very easy for him to divine this. And it was a place of no small danger he occupied; he had already had a narrow shave! He would have a doctor see that old woman, if he had to break open the door himself. And if the doctor thought things looked shady, he'd have Hillington arrested, in the interests of his client.

He was very blond and very determined, and rang the bell of a house marked with a doctor's brass plate, and shone on by a red lamp (for the night had long since come) as though he would have brought the blasé doctor himself to his feet. Unfortunately the doctor was not at home. He 'gave a keen glance' at the maid, and continued his search further along the street. At last he espied a large, formal and important looking building, like a private hospital. It was a doctor's house, however — two doctors'. To the servant's query 'Which doctor?' he felt inclined to answer 'Both' — to take both along with him. He glanced at the plate, however, and decided on Doctor Door, rather than Doctor Bunting.

Doctor Door was a large, heavy man, with a very grave and

rather vexed face, a large nose, black side whiskers, glasses, and large, dark, peevish eyes.

The clerk explained the case. The doctor frowned a little, and then asked him briefly, 'You, then, are acting for a firm of solicitors. You wish me, against the will of a certain lady's friends, to attend her, because you suspect foul play, and because she makes a very peculiar noise? That sounds rather awkward. I naturally don't care about going to a patient in that way, unless I were sure that your suspicions were – er – well grounded. You say she makes an astonishing amount of noise – has a noisy illness. I have known old people make the most disconcerting sounds that one could trace to no organ, and that were apparently without cause. But you suspect this gentleman of poisoning her? But no poison in its action causes outbursts of peculiar sound in the patient. What do you suggest he's poisoned her with?'

'I don't say he's poisoned her at all. I say only that there seems to be something fishy about the way he keeps her concealed, and about her state. I felt it my duty as she is now one of our principal clients, to make quite sure – '

'Exactly. What is her name?'

'Mrs. Dukes; she lives in Marbury Street; it is not very far.'

'Oh yes, I remember having read something about Mrs. Dukes in the papers. Yes, hum! Yes, well, I will come round with you anyhow.'

It was not curiosity on Dr. Door's part; but if there were going to be an inquest or a scandal, it would not be amiss to get his name in the papers a little. And it might be remunerative, as she was rich.

The clerk, accompanied by the doctor, shortly afterwards knocked at the door of No. 21, Marbury Street. Mrs. Beechamp let them in, and they stood in the hall while she announced them in the room at the back of the shop. Dr. Door coughed in a short and mechanical manner. This small pretended ill — that of a slight dry cough — is, or was, almost inseparable from the art of healing. Doctors seemed to have no medicine for this tiresome little cough.

In a few minutes Hillington issued out of the sick room, carefully closing the door.

'I have brought a doctor to see Mrs. Dukes, Mr. Hillington. I am convinced she is in need of it.'

'It's extremely thoughtful of you,' replied Hillington, 'but we already have called in one. He was here this morning and pronounced Mrs. Dukes' state as in no way alarming.'

'Yes, Mr. Hillington, but it was this evening, only a half an hour ago, that I myself saw Mrs. Dukes in what seemed to me a very bad way. Since the doctor's here, there can be no harm in his having a look at her.'

'I of course don't mind in the least. I'm an old friend of Mrs. Dukes, and I'm sure no one could be more eager to do anything for her than me. I have, as I tell you, done everything that was necessary. She is professionally attended already. I know how scrupulous you gentlemen are,' he said, turning smilingly to the doctor, 'about each other's patients, and I expect you would not care to visit anyone who was already being attended by a colleague.'

'I don't mind in the least. I'll have a look at her, if she's not well. I don't think as I have been called that that would be a breach of professional etiquette.'

He said this in a ready, determined voice, and had been prompted to do so by a certain dislike Hillington had inspired him with — Dr. Door was, in fact, in presence of Dr. Fell, as we all are at some time or other of our lives — and then he did not like coming so far for nothing. But, most of all, Dr. Door had taken an infection, the disinfectants with which his person was perfumed were powerless against. He had become suspicious of Mr. Hillington. Suspicion was in the air. And Hillington, although perfectly smooth and self-possessed, felt himself cornered, and the other two men knew this instinctively, telepathically, perhaps. The doctor was not a very amiable man; this instinct he had that the man in front of him was in a hole induced him to be rather brusque and uncompromising. And then his time was being wasted.

'Well, Mr. Hillington, if you will allow us, we will go to Mrs. Dukes,' said the clerk impatiently.

'But I assure you, Mrs. Dukes has no need of his services. If that had been the case — '

The doctor drew out his watch, and said brusquely, 'I must do one thing or the other, as I have other patients to see. If you will not let us see Mrs. Dukes, I shall have to go.'

Hillington did not reply for a moment, and just then the front door bell rang. Mrs. Beechamp, who had been standing just inside the door of the bric-a-brac shop, went to see who was there. Hillington did not move from his position in front of Mrs. Dukes' door. The doctor noticed this, and afterwards, when it would have been natural to move forward, he still remained in this strategic position. It was as though he were waiting to repel a rush of the doctor and the lawyer upon the old woman's door.

Now appeared in the doorway two men asking to see Mrs. Dukes, one saying in a loud voice, 'Say it's 'er nephews, Tim and Arthur; *she*'ll know.'

Mrs. Beechamp answered that her mistress was not well and could see no one, when the clerk, who had heard the men's announcement with interest, came quickly towards them, saying to the charwoman, 'What! Not let her nephews see her!

Why, surely — ' Then he called back to Mr. Hillington, 'Two nephews of Mrs. Dukes want to see her. Shall I tell them to come in?'

'I don't think Mrs. Dukes — ' began Hillington, still not moving an inch from the position he had taken up, but visibly nonplussed by this new difficulty, that had arisen so extremely inopportunely. The doctor was looking at him with his black, professional eyes seeming sourer than ever.

'Perhaps there are other nephews who would not quite like these nephews to visit the same aunt as themselves; or perhaps only some *friend* would not like it,' said the doctor pointedly.

'Sir!' said Hillington at once, taking a step forward, and his irritation against these people aided him in his assumed resentment — it was very realistic. 'I don't permit people to address me in that manner! You came here in a professional capacity. I have told you that you are not wanted. You evidently are disappointed, but that does not excuse you; you have just addressed me in words that I very much resent!'

Hillington was glad of the opportunity. He had been waiting for one or the other to go too far; he knew this would be a way of ending the interview.

In the meantime the two men — it was the two who had visited the second Mrs. Dukes a week or so before this — were in the hall, and no one showed any signs of moving.

The doctor replied at once.

'I have not come here with the intention of breaking into that room. So why do you stand so carefully in front of it?'

'But I have!' exclaimed the clerk suddenly, and advanced towards Hillington.

Just then a burst of uncontrollable coughing — stifled under bed-clothes, for Fane even rammed the sheets in his mouth — proceeded from within.

'There!' said the clerk, turning towards the doctor.

'But that's a man coughing,' said the doctor simply, with a rather puzzled expression.

At the silence that followed these words of the doctor's, we will leave this group as it is for a moment, and go back to Evan Royal dreaming desperately of escape in the house of the three tall Americans.

44
IN THE HOUSE OF THE THREE TALL AMERICANS AGAIN

When the two Misters Passion returned from one of their mysterious expeditions, Evan Royal was partially unbound. But his hands always remained tied. They would tie up his feet and legs and take off the rope that bound his arm sometimes for half an hour or so, 'to let the blood circulate a bit.' But after half an hour they thought it appeared that the blood had circulated enough, and they tied him up again. This little relaxation usually happened at meal times, and Evan Royal was given something of whatever was 'going.' They spoke in this off-hand way of the gruesome meals that Winter prepared for them when they were at home.

Joseph J. always addressed Royal with careful consideration, and hoped, Royal thought, that – living like a mummy all day long – the painful thongs and Winter's cooking might subdue him. If he were subdued, he might become suddenly communicative, or put his services at Joseph J.'s disposal. He might be of great use to them, anyway, if he chose. This was how Royal accounted for the pleasant way in which the elder Passion addressed him. He was infuriated by this honeyed tone, and all it inferred. But he was determined to insult Mr.

Passion no more. He must at all costs escape, and the more things that happened — conversation was a happening, something in it might give him a hint — the more likely was he to find a way. Passion regarded this comparative amiability of Royal's as a good sign, but was puzzled that it went no further.

In the meantime, Royal got no nearer to a solution of his difficulty. He could see no chance of escaping as things were. He had been waiting and waiting and expecting at every moment that the American's rigour would relax, and that he would be allowed to walk about. Then he would soon find a way. But their good temper and suavity was perfectly uninterrupted and monotonous, and also their system of securing their prisoner showed the same placid continuity. He now felt sure that so long as he stayed there he would remain bound hand and foot. And he would stay there, no doubt, until he was of no further use to anyone — until the question of Mrs. Dukes' million and who was to have it had been settled between these individuals and his employer.

On the morning of the third day, he woke up with a slight fever, and his impatience at bursting point. But it could not, alas, burst his cords for him. Winter was always there with him — they never left him alone. Winter was his constant companion. The third tall American had, since he found that his superiors were so pleasant with Royal, concluded that he also might be. And as he was a sociable fellow, he often pressed Royal into conversation when the latter did not feel inclined for it. This third day was a dark and dismal one, and Royal, his deck chair drawn towards the fire by Winter, warmed his corded feet before its blaze, staring into the coals. Winter, on the other side of the hearth, lolled back in his chair, read and talked alternately. Royal was established on the inner side, Winter nearer the window. If Winter had only left him for a moment, he could, Royal thought, by putting his feet actually into the flames, burn the rope away without injuring his legs too much – or scrape the cords on the hot bars of the grate, like a file.

After hours of fruitless thought he concluded that Winter himself was his only hope. And he now turned towards this thin, languid-looking young American, to see if there were any weak point in his guardian. He saw an easy temper, laziness and various other things that would, in themselves, serve his purpose, but the man, as a whole, seemed sound, and seemed to realise the importance for his employers that this prisoner should not escape. It was only towards dusk that suddenly, in a flash, Royal saw how he could escape. A bright flush came to his face, and in a moment he felt new life in his locked-up body. The blood that had moved sluggishly in the various compartments marked out by the cords, seemed to squeeze tumultuously through these barriers. He was afraid he was going to break a blood vessel.

He now set about arranging in his mind his order of procedure. First of all he determined to make use of the particular kind of sentimentality that he had always remarked in Americans. Royal began to talk about his home in Wales, the mountains rising above the waters at Port Madoc, Snowdon in the distance, the valley road to Festiniog, etc. He assumed an almost chanting tone, with that slight strange accent of the Welsh so suited to inspired speaking. Winter's jaw dropped, and he evidently was getting into the mood that Royal had wished to imbue him with. The twilight, the chill of this foreign land and so on, soon worked on him as Royal had wished. His prisoner, with great subtlety, led him to speak of his own native country, and half in imitation of Royal – for he was a very impressionable young man – he dropped into a kind of sing-song voice.

If he had not been so lost in the luxuries of this sentimental colloquy, he would have been rather startled by the brightness of the other's eyes, and the new expression that had come into Royal's face. It was slightly frowning – severe and rigid.

It was still the hour of long dusk before the evening actually sets in, a premature London twilight. There was practically no sound in this vast room, except an occasional distant splash of oars. Occasionally the tip of a sail passed along the bottom of the window; Royal had also observed, in one of his 'walking' intervals, that the house to which he had been brought, probably a very large one, lay in the midst of a piece of charred and weedy waste land, with a cinder path down to the river.

'"Go west, young man," they say. Waal, I went west, and that's where I met this crowd. Guess I'd 'a done better to stay where I was!'

And Winter, lost in meditations, gazed into the fire. After this bitter reflection – the last he uttered aloud – the last, in fact, he ever uttered! – he fell into a soft and regretful train of thought, and saw again in fancy the far side of the Rockies, and a chance he once had had in life, if he had only taken it. And here his mind became confused. He thought he was living in that time again, and had that chance again. And *this* time he was going to take it! You bet! The satisfaction he felt at vistas of the renewed existence was so great that he felt a moment of exultation, and would have liked to shout Hurrah! But at this juncture his mind became a blank.

Winter's head ducked suddenly towards the fire, then he righted himself, and seemed struggling for a moment; he gasped once or twice, and his eyes opened wide, staring in front of him. Then he was still. Suddenly he got up with a long disciplined movement, and stood with his head high, and then slowly turned towards the bound man on the other side of the fire.

Evan Royal was leaning out of his chair, with his head strained towards him, and his face fixed and grave. Then Winter took a step towards him, his hands at his side. Then he took another. His face in the dusk looked very young and unformed. Royal had hypnotised him! If the spell were strong enough, he was doubtless in the other's hands to do what he liked with.

45
THE CUTTING OF THE CORDS

Winter took three more steps, and stood silently over Royal, looking down at him. He stood there for several minutes immovable, the firelight playing on these two intent faces staring on each other, the one, Winter's, with a vaguely startled expression, but a blank placidity smoothing it away, and Royal's with its customary intentness increased ten-fold, till it was almost hideous with the will with which it was imbued. Then Winter mechanically put his hand in his pocket, fumbled a moment, and drew out a knife. This he unclasped and held loosely in his hand. Now Royal shifted slowly his position, working his hands out from underneath his body, and turning his back slightly to Winter, his head all the time strained over his left shoulder and gazing up in the other's face.

Winter bent down and stared hard at Royal for some minutes, their faces now so close together that Royal could see a little vein pulsing at the side of his forehead. He looked like a man remaining motionless in the effort to remember something that has escaped his memory. Then he seemed to sigh. The next moment he commenced sawing at the cord with his knife, cutting Royal's arm in several places in his clumsiness. Then he began sawing harder and harder, and then cutting jerkily. Then all of a sudden all the cords slackened the whole way up Royal's arm, and Winter stood up again.

The pain was very great for a moment, and Royal thought, with a quick tremor of apprehension, that he might faint. But in a few minutes he could move his hands a little, and then he took the knife from Winter's hand. He had to wait some five or ten minutes longer before he was able to grasp the knife with sufficient strength to cut the cords that bound his legs.

While he was bending down to do this he suddenly felt Winter's hand on his neck. He sprang back and nearly knocked the American over on the floor. He had merely collapsed on top of him, from fatigue probably. He fixed him again with his eyes, this time making passes with his hands, and soon Winter was sitting quietly in his chair, on the other side of the fire.

Evan Royal now sat up, and waited there, the knife still in his hand, until the numbness should have left him.

He smiled with glee at the slickness of the result of this forlorn hope of his. Some years earlier he had known a prestidigitateur and professional hypnotist in France, who had taught him the very simple rules of this act. He had hypnotised various people, including the conjuror himself, who, although he knew the rules, had never really hypnotised anyone in his life. He was very angry with Royal on waking up, and they had parted company. Since those days it had never again occurred to our young adventurer to hypnotise anybody. But in looking at the third of the tall Americans and wondering how on earth he could make this man the agent of his escape, it had struck him, among other things, that Winter would make a good medium. From this thought it was the matter of a second to the complete plan of his escape, which flashed into his mind with the rush of hope and confidence. As he was not quite sure about his man, the conditions must be extremely favourable before he began his attempt. The twilight, the somnolence of the hour, and the memories he had evoked in the spirit of the impressionable Winter, all contributed to his success. He thought if he could get Winter to tell some of his own reminiscences, that his own voice, even, would, with its emotional monotony, help to hypnotise him, or rather to put him in a favourable state. All had turned out better than he could have hoped. There he sat, free, and his guardian sat in a state of coma, in front of him.

He got up and walked stiffly about a little. When he felt his limbs more or less under control again, he picked up the severed cord, and got a supplementary piece that he had noticed on the table, and laying Winter out on the floor at his full length, began to bind him securely. He began with the hands and arms.

While he was doing this he thought he heard a soft step outside in the passage. A cold sweat broke out all over him. If it were the two Americans! He swore that he would not be stopped now that he had got so far, and seizing the knife, he sprang towards the door. He listened for a considerable time, but no new sound came from without. But, within the room itself, the dog began growling, low and continuously. Perhaps it was a stranger! He opened the door very slightly, slipped his hand on to the outside, and secured the key. Then he closed the door again, and locked it on the inside.

He now approached Winter, and by the dog's fiercer growling realised that it was *he* that had upset it – that the good beast was taking exception to his binding hand and foot one of his three tall masters. He tried the rope and found it firm, and began fixing the knot round Winter's legs, the dog still keeping up a steady and uncompromising growl. Then all of a sudden Winter woke up. Royal found the American's eyes fixed on his with a very startled expression. Then he began rolling about and struggling. Royal had nearly finished the leg-fastening, but the dog had now got up, was barking violently at his back, and at each new movement of his bound master became more infuriated. He was a large retriever and by no means to be despised as an enemy. Winter noticed the dog's excitement, and began kicking about violently. At the same moment, with a murderous snarl, the dog rushed at Royal, knocking him across Winter's body, and the three of them tumbled about in a frantic mass, like live fish in the bottom of a boat. Royal managed to hold the dog at arm's length for a moment, while he got ready to spring to his feet. He then leapt up, the dog, freed, dashing him against the wall, going straight for his throat. His hand was covered with blood where Winter had hacked at the ropes, and this no doubt rendered the dog more furious. The next few minutes were like a nightmare to Royal. At one moment he was rolling on the ground, with the dog furiously shaking him — the next he was on his knees, trying to protect his throat, the dog for the moment satisfying itself with a piece of his arm. Then he had hold of the knife, and while he held the dog's head upon the floor with his two knees on its throat, he was doing his best to destroy it with Winter's jack-knife. He had apparently blundered on some vital place in the canine anatomy, for the dog stopped struggling. But at this point he himself fell back in a dead faint.

When he came to himself everything was quite still, and he felt his cheek lying in something wet and chill. Quite near him was a black mass, and another a little further away. He got up, feeling very weak indeed, staggered to the table, and lighted the gas. The dog lay dead not far from its third master – third in order of importance, but, still, for whom it had fought as well as though Winter had been the first.

Royal felt more compunction and regret on seeing the poor animal stretched out there than if it had been a man he had killed. He changed the old trousers and coat they had lent him for a suit of Winter's hanging on the furthest corner – the bed-room corner. It was many sizes too big for him. But a hat that he also found there fitted him pretty well. He turned the trousers up and tucked the sleeves in, fastening them with pins in the inside. He looked nearly as broad as he was high – he formed indeed, almost a perfect square, looked at from in front or behind. He did up those of Mrs. Dukes' clothes that he could not replace in a packet. Then he went over to Winter, and bent over him – for the latter's immobility was puzzling. His face was flushed, and his body was disturbed with little restless movements. But he was asleep! Royal was so surprised at this that he thought at first that his late warder was shamming. Then Royal wondered how long he himself had been uncon-scious.

But it had not been long as a matter of fact. Only Winter had no great incitement to struggle any more – he knew it was useless, and he was prodigiously tired. So he had fallen asleep.

Royal turned out the gas and, leaving this large dark room with the dead dog and the bound and sleeping man lying side by side on the floor, made his way out of the house of the three tall Americans by a back entrance.

THE PURGING OF MRS. DUKES' HALL

We left the people grouped in the hallway of No. 21 Marbury Street in a moment of silence, following upon the doctor's words, 'But that is a man's cough.' One or two were silent in the effort to grasp, *not* the meaning of these words, but what they might imply, what they might portend.

For all felt that they were momentous words. One or two, on the other hand, were silent to see what would happen next, and one or two were silent because they seldom were anything else — among the latter that nephew of Mrs. Dukes known as Jim. Then rose a voice suddenly from the door saying, 'Well, that don't surprise me, that don't. If you expected that to be Mrs. Dukes a coughin', you're mistaken. That couldn't be Mrs. Dukes because she ain't 'ere. She ain't been 'ere, what's more, for three days now!'

All turned towards the speaker with amazement. A short, indignant looking little man, with heavy fair moustaches, and a very erect carriage of the shoulders — his chest was puffed out like a pigeon — surveyed them with undisguised delight. He had made a profound impression. It was what he had intended to do.

Mrs. Beechamp had been ineffectually struggling with this little man at the door for some minutes past, but she'd given way at last before his authoritative pushing. It was the little detective who had followed Mrs. Dukes the other day to the Tube station, and who paraded up and down outside continually, only disappearing periodically for meals and sleep.

'But I saw Mrs. Dukes with my own eyes a half hour ago. She is in there right enough, but this gentleman objects to the doctor visiting her,' said the clerk, after he had regarded the new-comer in amazement for several minutes.

'I can't 'elp what *yew* saw. I tell ye she ain't there,' replied the detective emphatically.

The doctor then addressed Mr.Hillington angrily. 'Then this is all a hoax, sir? You have been playing the fool with us!'

Hillington smiled grimly. He did not know how things were going to turn out. But it looked as though he were going to get rid of the big black doctor, who, for him, also, was Doctor Fell, with this difference only – and with this modification of the popular saying – that *he* knew very well indeed why he did not like him.

'It's a fool's trick, wasting people's time!' continued the doctor, shooting a last lurid glance at Hillington's smiling face.

'I confess that I cannot make head or tail of your proceeding, sir,' he went on, turning to the clerk, 'and all that rigmarole of an old lady ill, suspicious circumstances – I am quite unable to make head or tail of it! You hadn't even seen Mrs. Dukes. And you distinctly led me to believe that you *had*. You took me away from a very important case on your representations – '

'But, Doctor, I assure you I saw Mrs. Dukes a half an hour ago – at least.' And here the clerk was interrupted by a guffaw from the direction of the detective.

The clerk now approached the doctor and began explaining excitedly that he had in no way deceived him, that he was convinced that Mrs. Dukes *was* in there, etc.

The detective had become silent for the moment, all his attention being fixed, with a ferocious scowl, on a new arrival. It was the second of the two watchers who had followed Mrs. Dukes to the station, and the detective's particular bugbear.

He eyed him for several minutes. The other took no notice of his portentous and wrathful glances, and at last the detective spoke. It was the first time he had addressed him, though they had circled round each other for the last week or so perpetually.

'What do yew think *yew*'re doin' 'ere, eh? Oo ask yew to come pokin' *your* nose in 'ere? This is a private 'ouse.'

'What are you doin' in it then?' interrupted the other contemptuously.

'What am I doin' 'ere? I'll tell yew what I'm doin' 'ere! I'm 'ere to keep gen'lemen like *yew* outside! See? That's what I'm 'ere for!' He stepped quickly forward, and drew something out of his pocket, thrusting it beneath the other's nose. 'See that? That's what I am. What are *yew,* that's what I should like to know!'

Jim was conversing in undertones with Mrs. Beechamp, and the other nephew was arguing plaintively about something with Hillington. It was an extremely busy scene.

Then came yet another person to join this petulant throng. A voice resounded from the doorstep, quavering, but still imperious, and with a most bitterly scolding tone.

'Oh Lord, what *is* all this about, I should like to know? Get out of the way, do; what are ye doin' blockin' up the 'all like this? Did ye think it was an auction, all of ye? Anyone'd think I was sold up, by the look of it. What's the matter, Mr. 'illington?'

And there stood Mrs. Dukes, indubitably Mrs. Dukes, in the doorway, her face looking startlingly white against the darkness of the street.

This time the silence was deeper, although it didn't last so long, than at the last shock this little company had been given. Each of them was affected differently.

Hillington dared not leave his place, but his face had cleared up as though by magic once he had grasped that this was Evan Royal returned.

'What did I tell ye?' shouted the detective, triumphantly. The doctor contented himself with a shrug of his shoulders, and made his way through the little crowd, and took his departure.

'Ah, I thought you wouldn't go far, Mrs. Dukes,' exclaimed Hillington.

Mrs. Dukes answered after a moment, 'No, you was quite right, Mr. 'illington.'

'I hope the chemist gave you something that will not affect your eyes like that last medicine. You've quite got your voice back.'

Evan Royal took all this in, and soon saw where he was, and although he could not guess exactly what had happened, he saw it had been something very unusual, and that he had come in the nick of time. Also that he had to carry out Hillington in some story or other.

'Yes, I just took something, and it came back sudden like. I'm still a little 'oarse,' and Mrs. Dukes tapped her breast-bone, which resounded in a muffled way beneath her old ulster. 'Oo's this?' she asked, pointing to the clerk.

This was a slip that Hillington had not foreseen and that was quite unavoidable on Royal's part. He could not be expected to guess that he already knew this gentleman.

The clerk's bewildered face shewed him that he had made a slip, but Hillington at the same time was saying to him hurriedly, 'That's Truman and Hatchett's representative, don't you remember him? I daresay you were right, sir, after all,' he went on, turning to the clerk. 'Mrs. Dukes was certainly very indisposed an hour or so ago, although of course it was nothing serious. You must excuse me for having played you this little trick,' he said, laughing. 'You see I thought I would pay you out for mistrusting me and fetching a doctor. Mrs. Dukes, you know, is a very eccentric old lady — aren't you, Mrs.

231

Dukes? — and she insisted when you had gone on getting dressed and going alone to the chemists — his shop's quite near by as a matter of fact — and I could not, with all my eloquence, dissuade her.'

'Yes,' thought the clerk. 'She probably saw that if she didn't do something soon she would never leave her bed alive.'

'She has become more headstrong than ever since she has become one of the great ones of the world,' said Hillington. A certain amount of tender banter evidently went on between Mrs. Dukes and her business adviser.

The detective still stood there, although the man he'd just been apostrophizing had slipped away. Mrs. Dukes next turned her attention to him, and, with irresistible sarcasm drove him forth into the night again. Then she confronted her nephews. These good fellows she covered with tender raillery and, telling them to come in the morning, she dismissed them too.

On learning that the clerk had wished to confer with her a little, and deliver her a message entrusted to him by his employers, she sent him upstairs to wait for her in the large first-floor room, now reserved for such occasions.

So in a very short time after Mrs. Dukes had arrived, the genuine and only Mrs. Dukes — except the old lady still lying dazed in the house in St. John's Wood, and who had ceased to feel herself anybody in particular — so this brusque arrival had speedily dissolved the noisy and eccentric meeting. It had sent each man about his business again — each one very puzzled, and almost dazed with the rapid succession of contradictory statements and phenomena. The nephews slipped away, and each of them was 'blowed if he knew what to make of it.' The doctor was not interested in mysteries, but he could not help acknowledging that there *was* one here, at all events. The detective was in a state of concentrated indignation and suspicion that rendered it impossible to remain stationary or do sentry-duty any more just then. He went home and unburdened his mind to his wife.

The clerk upstairs was the most completely mystified of anybody. Two things, however, it never occurred to him to doubt: first, that the old lady who had entered the front door *was* not actually Mrs. Dukes; and secondly, that the old lady in bed was not one and the same with the one who had just broken up their gathering. Yet he did not accept Hillington's account of things. The wildest solutions occurred to him — Hillington had tried to kill Mrs. Dukes and she had fled from the house; or it was all a joke played on him (he did not know why), or Mrs. Dukes was mad. These were three of the solutions that occurred to him, with their numerous corollaries. In the meantime he sat, rather crushed and mystified, awaiting this eccentric client of his firm.

47
A DOUBTFUL ERRAND

When Mrs. Dukes and Hillington passed into the room behind the shop Fane was at once very much astonished and very much delighted to see her — also a little embarrassed at being discovered in her bed made up to represent her.

Mrs. Dukes feigned great surprise, but Hillington explained it was only a joke, and Fane was bundled upstairs, and assumed his own clothes again.

When Hillington and Royal were alone the former began congratulating him on his escape. Royal cut him short by asking almost savagely where the Khan was to be found at that very moment.

'I have not a minute to lose. We must catch those fellows who carried me off. I have one of them gagged and bound down there. I don't expect the others will be back before midnight, but we mustn't risk missing them.'

Royal's whole attitude towards him was brusque and imperious, and he brushed aside all congratulations on his escape impatiently. Royal felt that, in a sense, and although he had made his escape in the nick of time, that he returned amongst his companions shamed, and that they would never have the same confidence in his astuteness and resourcefulness again. He was determined to demand an even higher measure of respect from them now than before; where he had been independent, aloof and going his own way before, to be cold, contemptuous and imperious now. He knew that they could not do without him, although he had for once endangered their plans by his imprudence. And more and more he was making up his mind to part company with them before long.

He now asked coldly, in an off-hand way, a thing that he had been very anxious to know but had purposely refrained from asking.

'How much has the Khan lost through my capture? Did he let himself be blackmailed?'

'Oh no, nothing's happened at all. They got to work in another way. They got two thousand out of Truman and Hatchett's, and were trying to get more.' And he described the proceedings of the Americans and the result.

Royal then went upstairs and had ten minutes' conversation, in his best Duke-like manner, with the clerk. The latter only had one or two papers that their client was to sign — papers referring, as far as Royal could see, to wheelbarrows and spades or something equally insignificant.

Mrs. Dukes did not strike the clerk as the sort of woman to allow herself to be poisoned, or robbed, or got the better of in any way by anybody. He went back to his chiefs sadly perplexed, his keen glance quite blunted on all these mysteries, and not knowing what to say if asked for impressions. He determined however not to say very much – not to mention the doctor, among other things. He would send the doctor his fee privately, out of his own pocket.

The Mrs. Dukes that this young man had to deal with was a very different one to the quiescent old lady that Mr. Hatchett had known a week earlier. For an extraordinary thing happened. The change in Evan Royal, and his new attitude towards his comrades and employers, had a great influence on his manner of playing the part of Mrs. Dukes. Mrs. Dukes became trenchant, more sarcastic than ever, overbearing, and recklessly energetic. It was a new Mrs. Dukes, verily; yet another! Although outwardly the same and played by the same actor, we might speak of her as the fourth Mrs. Dukes. And she was disposed to comport herself for the rest of the piece in a very different manner from any of her predecessors.

The clerk had intended, as he was to stay in London overnight, and visit the bank in the morning, to do a little private detective work on his own account in Cavendish Street, Pimlico. But he felt no inclination to do so any more, and spent his evening in a music hall, drowning his trouble in the humour of George Robey, and forgetting his late mystifications in the astounding deceptions of the polite French conjurer.

Three-quarters of an hour later, Royal, now dressed in his own clothes, Mrs. Dukes' outfit hanging on the wall near by, was sitting over the fire in a large sparely furnished room in a side street off St. Martin's Lane. It was a room for which three or four members of the company had keys, and that could be used for purposes of flight, for change of clothing or what not.

He got up as a tall, erect figure entered, muffled up in a heavy fur-coat. It was Sarandur Khan, or Raza Khan as he was known to his criminal followers.

He came forward quickly, his hand outstretched, and the most flattering of smiles on his dark face.

'Ah Royal, how spendid, how perfectly splendid of you! I knew you'd do it! You only let yourself be captured to show us how much we needed you, and how easily you could escape. I am glad to see you. Of course' – he pronounced it 'off corze' with his trailing accent – 'you've dined? You are all right – not hurt?' he asked with concern.

Royal was very reserved and answered shortly that, save a cut or two and a bite or two, he was quite sound.

Sarandur Khan noticed at once his change of manner. Although he did not in any way abate in his own effusiveness, he remained sharply on the look-out for further manifestations on the other's part that would enable him to judge of the cause of the change.

But Royal at once went into the details of his capture and escape. 'I thought you would like to know at once about what happened, and also to know where you could find these gentlemen within the next few hours.'

'Yes, I am very glad to know where I can find them,' the Khan answered softly. 'What do you think, Royal, that we ought to do with these troublesome people?' he asked dreamily.

Royal remembered the conversation that he had had with the elder of the three tall Americans, who had scoffed at the idea of 'Razy,' as he called him, being dangerous. Royal thought that he had never seen a man look more dangerous than this Central Asian noble did in this moment – luxuriously reclining in his furs, a sort of voluptuous gloating look in his eyes, his jet black beard parted deeply down the middle, his fawn-like eyes fixed on the fire.

'This is not the first time they have troubled me. I have been very patient with these Americans. I gave them the chance of discovering what sort of man I was. They only understand their own people. One cannot treat them reasonably. I'm afraid, Royal, we shall have to do something very' – and he rolled the r slowly and guturally – 'very disagreeable to them.'

Royal did not answer him. He had a strange boyish feeling of satisfaction that his warning, received with contempt by Joseph J. Passion, was going to be confirmed.

Royal was back again, and Mrs. Dukes' fortune would be his yet. The Khan was mollified. But of course these men were in on the secret, and his enemies. There was only one course open to him. And there was no time to be lost.

'Royal, you need not get back to Marbury Street for an hour or two. Will you go first of all to Bellamy Street? I want you to point out the position of this house, the house where you were detained, to someone you will find there.'

The Khan was now standing before the fire, and he had assumed quite a matter-of-fact tone, looking at Royal seriously but as though giving him quite simple instructions.

Bellamy Street was that locality that Royal had asked the Americans if they knew. And they had answered no.

He looked at the Khan doubtfully for a moment. He was hesitating in himself as to how he should reply. The Oriental was looking at him curiously, with a strange amusement in his eyes and lips. He seemed to be weighing Royal in his mind – not the whole of him, but someting in his nature that he had never, until now, had occasion to measure. The process evidently amused him. Royal interested him extremely. He was quite impersonally interested in this young man, whom he really admired. He seemed watching this play of hesitation in Royal with keen appreciation, as a man will make acquaintance with a new work by a master he admires.

'No, he never goes so far as that. This was what Royal's measuring of his employer, on his side, came to.

'Bellamy Street, yes. Am I expected?' Royal asked.

'Yes, I've just wired.' The Khan accompanied the young Englishman as far as Charing Cross, talking of some music he had heard the night before, and then of music more generally. He showed himself, as he often did to Royal, for as we have said he liked him – the exquisite companion that he was.

Royal took the underground at Charing Cross. Bellamy Street was in the East End, and he had several times made this journey before.

48
THE AMBASSADRESS AGAIN

Royal walked along the Whitechapel Road looking with pleasure along its thronged pavements, lighted by spasmodic and lurid electric globes at the top of lofty pillars, and by the belching flame of the huckster's stalls, and by the languid eyes of the thick, undulating tide of houris that at that time of evening rolls along these Eastern thoroughfares.

He observed with interest a savage crowd fighting their way in a large building, to witness other men fight more professionally inside. He saw a small show of some sort emitting a thick and silent stream of people, by which he was somewhat swept out of his course. He observed people trickling in and out of an Electric Palace, where a perpetual performance was advertised. One went in and kept on looking at the sheet above the stage until one had a feeling that one had seen one of the items before; one waited a moment to make sure, and if one were confirmed in this idea by feeling somehow that one had also seen the next, one hastily took one's hat and left. Royal wondered for the hundredth time how it was that Yiddish writing came in the window of a sausage-shop. Could this be a Yiddish shop? Or was it merely a fanatical pork-butcher who stuck up a printed defiance in his window, directly at passing Jews?

The road Royal was following became less peopled, the great and lustrous flux of houris was left behind. Instead of shops he was passing between rows of dingy private houses, and an occasional chapel or hospital. Then he crossed the road, and disappeared down a dark and narrow street. This was Bellamy Street. There were little shops here and there, that sold gingerbeer, newspapers and sweets. About half-way down this street were two shop windows together, both dimly lighted, and both with cards in the window covered with a strange writing that was not, however, Yiddish. He opened the door of the second, and entered a long room with tables and chairs disposed along the whole of its length, as far as a counter, which was covered with glass dishes. Behind this was a curtain. The room had a general perfume specifically Eastern, a kind of sweet musty smell. There were large archaic pictures of turbaned men and palaces with minarets around the walls, and a strong immediate smell of curry in the air. Two or three swarthy individuals were eating silently near the door, and near the counter in a high-pitched uneven voice a man was talking to a person who was evidently the owner of the restaurant. The man in talking opened his mouth as wide as he could, showing all his teeth, as though his words were so big that not otherwise could he have got them out. And yet his voice was thin, and his words seemed attenuated and all run together.

The man behind the counter, a short bearded man in a pale orange-coloured turban, advanced smilingly to meet Royal. He was quite leisurely and greeted him as though Royal were a regular customer, and he had seen him that morning already. As a matter of fact Royal had not been there for several months.

If Sarandur Khan's urbanity was that of an aristocratic Oriental, this little man's was hardly less striking or less perfect. One was forced to suppose that there were subtleties that the European could not grasp, and that he was really very inferior in manners to his illustrious countryman. It is true that his presence was in no way so commanding, and perhaps, if one looked very carefully, his gestures were not so expressive.

'Ah, good morning, sir; you have come to see Harran? Yes, he's upstairs. Will you come this way? And he led Royal under the folds of the curtain onto a sombre stairway, and up to the second floor of the house. He knocked at the door and then, without making any remark, descended again. The door opened, and a very handsome young man drew Royal inside in a friendly way. It was he who had been the principal dancer at the Embassy a few evenings before.

He enquired after Royal's health and, still holding him by the hand, he drew him towards the fireplace. Two other men had risen from chairs; they had been sitting round the fire. They inclined themselves slightly to Royal, and one at once left the room on a word from the young man. Royal had answered the latter with a courtesy equal to his own, and the

three of them now stood silently by the fire; they were evidently waiting for something, or somebody, although Royal
did not in the least know who or what. The young man
offered him a cigarette, smiling agreeably. He seemed to have
no care in the world, this handsome, bronze-coloured young
man, and his passionate dance around his dagger the other
night would seem to have been a pure piece of acting, and
having no part in his life.

They had not waited long when the door opened, and,
muffled in a huge ulster with a sort of hood over the head, the
point of which touched the ceiling, the lady who had received
the guests at the Ambassador's reception entered, followed by
the man who had gone to fetch her.

Royal had never seen her before, and was naturally very
much impressed at her prodigious size. But this was as nothing to the impression her face made upon him. The penetrating young man saw more in this huge and impossible looking
woman than the guests of Sarandur Khan had done. The
errand on which he had come, besides, gave a direct colour to
impressions that otherwise might have remained vague. She
seemed to him like the figure of some implacable Eastern
goddess, that, from its seat in the gloom of the temple, had
gazed over generations of men who had sacrificed to her. Or
she seemed the embodiment in human form of the coldness
and cruelty of some stone figure of a god, as though some man
or woman, from intense brooding over the image of their
deity, had given birth to a child that had grown up like it. From
the moment this woman appeared at the door, Royal felt the
strongest misgivings, and all the time he remained with these
people, he felt that he was being carried along inevitably
towards *something,* he did not know what, by this woman, as
though a fate had personally made himself of the party.

She gave him her hand as she had given it to the guests at Sarandur Khan's reception, and looked at him without the least alteration of her features, which remained perfectly composed and grave. The young man at the entrance stopped smiling, and remained silent and without any signs of his customary insouciance for the next half hour. This was the most strange and ominous sign of all for Royal. Our young adventurer still felt in his hand the touch of the woman's palm, he thought. The hand was enormously muscular, with long tapering powerful fingers, and he had felt the coldness of several rings.

They all went out together, and contrary to his expectation, he was not appealed to to lead the way, but the woman silently took the direction of the farther high road, to the south. After a short tram ride, and a good deal of walking, they emerged on the river-side, and found, in the shadows of a landing place he had once been to before, the company's launch. He noticed by various details, that he had not noticed before, that this launch was not one and the same with that that the Americans had decoyed him with. They all got in and headed downstream.

When they had gone a certain distance, the woman said something in low sonorous tones to the man sitting next to Royal, who then asked him, in rather broken English, to let him know when they came to the place where he had been taken.

Royal was debating with himself the whole time as to what he should do. This party that he was conducting seemed to him a most uncanny band. He felt as though he were some mortal, chosen by the immortal gods to personally conduct four very ill-omened looking fates to the house of some transgressor of divine law, since the fates were not quite at home on the earth, and would have some difficulty in finding it. Royal was not squeamish in any conceivable way. and perhaps at another time he would have quieted any uneasy questioning he might have had, and simply shown those people the house they wanted as though it were a man who had asked him the way to a certain street, and trusted in Raza Khan's prudence to have ordered what was best for the good of the company. But that evening when he had met the Khan he had felt, despite the extraordinary self-possession of the man, and his incredibly soft voice, something that he had never felt before. He felt that he was not acting impassionately and calmly as usual, and that he had been very much moved, that beneath that glossy surface, he was raving mad for the moment. He had said to Lucy before his adventure with the Americans that Raza Khan was no longer so circumspect and infallible as he used to be — that in several things lately he had made a false step, that there had been a hitch. And he had meant this. He did really feel that the company had been so wonderfully organized when he first entered it that failure in any scheme seemed impossible — or at least that things were so arranged that it would be impossible to trace them. But an irritability had entered in somewhere, he felt, and things were no longer quite safe in the company. Then, he had almost made up his mind that this would be his last adventure, that when the million had been secured to the Khan, and he had got his share, that he would chuck up his job. These things influenced him considerably in his attitude towards this expedition, which, it seemed to him, could only have one purpose. Still, he felt there was nothing to be done, and perhaps Raza Khan was right. And he still had that boyish feeling of exultation that the American's sneering estimate of Raza Khan would cost him dear.

Royal had carefully noted several landmarks on either bank

before leaving the place a few hours before, and at last the special chimney and the special building he had been looking for came into view.

They grounded a little farther down from the landing-stage used by the Americans, and, scrambling ashore, walked slowly across the waste ground towards the house, bearing round to the back, Royal making for the side door by which he had left the house that evening.

The American's launch was not at the landing-stage they had seen in passing, and Royal thought it improbable, from his knowledge of their present habits, that they had returned yet.

The door was ajar, as he had left it, and he let his four companions in noiselessly. The woman in the hooded ulster looked like some enormous capucin; she stood quite motionless just within the door while Royal and one of the men crept forward towards the hall. Royal indicated to him the door of the front room where he had lain for three days. Then they went back to the others again.

Royal saw the woman's eyes turn towards the young man, and the other, with his strange prettiness of manner, took Royal by the hand, and led him outside.

Then he said, speaking for the first time since they had left his room, 'Thanks, you need not wait. I think all will be well.' The smile and manner were quite empty of any significance except the polite acknowledgment of a service.

Royal walked quickly away, his mind full of the dark inhabitants of that dark empty house — the bound man on the floor and the two men who would walk up to the door in a few hours' time unsuspectingly. He thought how, when they were inside, they would see the shadows moving and how they would find their comrade bound. Or perhaps they would never get as far.

Or perhaps the Khan was only preparing some pleasant trick for them after all. Perhaps they would be kept prisoners there as he had been. But the figure of the immense woman haunted him like some ill-omen.

49
TWO OF MRS. DUKES' BRAVE COMRADES

The next morning Royal — who had taken up Mrs. Dukes' life where he had left it off — examined the papers with a more than habitual curiosity. When he had found nothing in the four or five great columns on the middle page — the four or five big events of the last twenty-four hours, that had often a dozen minor telegrams, beside the long journalistic outpouring — he searched carefully amongst the small fry — the little half dozen lines under some heading in small type — that filled the lower halves of the two or three principal pages. Often a great sensational event did not come with a burst — did not at once find its place in big black type at the top of the page. Often an event of the greatest magnitude first crept into the papers as a little three-line notice. Royal had often observed storms of this sort brewing for days, getting from a three-line notice to a ten liner — made up of a couple of telegrams — and so on till at last it squeezed everything else into the background, and triumphed in type half an inch thick.

What did he expect to find? He knew what he expected to find, and yet he had assured himself on the previous evening, before going to Bellamy Street, that there was nothing sensational to fear in carrying out the Khan's orders.

On Royal's return from captivity it would have been natural to give Hillington, personally, some account of what had happened to him. But he did not allow his colleague to remain a moment alone with him. He made great use of Cole; whenever Hillington showed an inclination to speak privately to him he called Cole; and Cole came and smoked his pipe obediently by the fire. He seemed to have taken a great fancy to his new mother, and liked the second Mrs. Dukes far better than he had ever liked the first. He was evidently quite aware that yet a third Mrs. Dukes had reigned there for a short time. He had odd ways of showing what he thought and knew; it was rather like divining the thoughts of a dog — a very sulky dog. But he gave Royal an ovation, positively an ovation, on his return. He flowered into speech several times in succession. He said, 'It's rather warm in the cellar.' This was the longest and most important of his remarks. To anyone who knew Cole it would have proved, as it proved to Royal himself who understood Cole, that the second Mrs. Dukes had moved him as no other human being had ever done. This gratuitous piece of information about the temperature of the cellar was the nearest Cole had come to getting in touch with his fellows. He had never mentioned to anyone else the part of the house where he spent the greater portion of his time. It was a triumph for Royal, a last proof of his extraordinary capacity for getting on with his fellows. That day this gift of his was going to be illustrated again, and almost as strikingly, and in a case which, in its results, has more influence on this story.

In the meantime, as though he were determined to drive Hillington out of the house, he nagged at him in their respective capacities of Mrs. Dukes and his adviser, till the company's secretary, who was a very nervous man, could stand it no longer. He left, wondering what on earth had come to Royal.

Then Mrs. Dukes went to market that morning. She found

herself followed, as usual, by the second of the two watchers, not the plain-clothes policeman. He knew this man to be a spy of Raza Khan's, placed there quite openly, just as Lucy was placed in the house quite openly. He knew that there were probably others that he could not see – perhaps men watching his door morning and night behind that gauze curtain opposite. He did not know. But this avowed watcher exasperated him. On his way to the market he chose a rather circuitous route, and when he was in a small empty street he turned sharply back, walked up to the following man, and stopping in front of him spoke in his natural voice, and very low.

'Go to your master and say to him that I don't need curs like you to watch me. If I see you around here again I shall see if I can get rid of you myself. Turn round and walk back the way you came. Quick march!'

The man, without answering a word, turned back and was seen no more in that neighbourhood.

Hercules Fane, the third Mrs. Dukes, was back in his room upstairs again. But a strange light had suddenly flashed into Fane's mind. On being Mrs. Dukes himself, it occurred to him all of a sudden that other people could be Mrs. Dukes also without necessarily being the very Mrs. Dukes of very Mrs. Dukeses. And the more he thought of it, and the enigma of the whole situation, the more it seemed to him that the old lady he knew as Mrs. Dukes was probably some member of the company to which he belonged. And so he was at last in possession of the truth.

He had a long conversation with Lucy – they had become avowedly lovers now, Lucy no more rushing away denying that she loved him at the end of their interviews. The upshot of this was that Lucy came downstairs in the course of the morning, and telling Royal that his understudy had guessed

247

the truth, asked him if he would come up to make his acquaintance.

As soon as Cole was in bed, Royal slipped on a pair of Cole's trousers, and having otherwise removed his makeup, he went upstairs to Fane and Lucy's little parlour.

Lucy soon left them alone, and her lover, from being astonished at finding Royal such a nice fellow, came to think, by the time Royal got up to leave him, that he was the nicest fellow that he had ever met.

Royal, on his side, was not altogether merely diplomatic in his amiability. He thought Fane 'a nice little chap,' and the only decent member the company had ever secured, except himself. He did not admit Hillington into this category. Royal was not unsociable, and living the strange life he did, it was a welcome thought to him that he had a comrade whom he could talk to for the rest of this adventure, which might last some time. He did not regard himself as a criminal, but as a disinterested adventurer. He had come into the company just as Fane had – he had been drawn in by ruse, and stayed for the love of adventure. Fane stayed for love of Lucy and a *respect* for adventure combined. He also had been 'discovered' by the Khan in a theatre. He was a very different man to Fane, but they had a good many things in common. Fane was very much more inclined to go through with this adventure now that he had seen the sort of man his colleague was. Yet more so as Royal assured him he, personally, was going to retire once this enterprise was brought to a happy conclusion. Then he confirmed Lucy's assertion that there was very little risk, although the prize was so enormous. So, Fane said to himself, he would spend the next month or so in seeing through this adventure, and in trying to induce Lucy to withdraw herself from this disreputable company. There was something exhilarating in the thought of the danger, and something equaly comforting in the thought that the risks he ran were really slight. For Royal convinced him, by many arguments, that it was almost impossible that the hoax could be found out.

Fane went to bed rather doubtful about his mad decision, but entirely charmed with his new comrade.

50
THE FATE OF THE THREE TALL AMERICANS

We have had occasion on one or two occasions already to quote passages from the eloquent pen of a certain journalist. We will no longer hide the name of the paper from which those extracts have been taken. It is the *Morning Looking Glass*. We shall once again have recourse to this means of information, for it was this paper that Royal opened on the following morning, and it was on its central sheet that he read the following headlines.

TERRIBLE TRIPLE TRAGEDY.
MYSTERY OF A LONELY HOUSE.
SUPPOSED WORK OF EXOTIC ASSASSINS.
VICTIMS OF AMERICAN NATIONALITY.

Royal sat quite still for a moment in reading these lines, and a deep flush mounted to his face. He was very angry with Raza Khan — quite illogically so, for he really knew quite well what his employer's manner and the party he had conducted to the house of the three tall Americans meant. Still he felt he should not have been mixed up with murder without being told about it; this was not in his agreement. And he had felt the whole while that the fact that Raza Khan had made use of him so directly in this affair was a guarantee that nothing very desperate was intended.

The report of the murder began by announcing that an errand boy, coming to the house with some provisions ordered the day before, had discovered, on looking through a window, the shutter of which had swung open, in the stream of light along the floor a man bound and gagged. He had told a policeman, and shortly afterwards the house had been entered. They had found two dead bodies in the hall, and a third, that of the bound man, in the inner room. In addition a retriever dog, killed with a knife, it seemed, lay near the bound man.

The doors, both back and front, were locked, but locked from the outside, and the keys had been taken away. There were no papers to identify the victims by, but from their clothes, unmistakably of American cut, and from their faces, also unmistakably of American cut, there was little doubt as to their nationality. A pile of ashes in the grate suggested that a good many papers had been burnt.

What, then, was the occupation of these three strange men found murdered altogether in this lonely house, apparently, from the medical evidence, not more than two days ago?

In many ways it was one of the most mysterious murders of modern times. Three men, each of them strongly built, and well able to defend himself, were found murdered in a house that one of them had rented six months previously — giving the evidently fictitious name of Brown — of which he had never furnished more than one room, and that only 'in parts.' Then the room where Royal had been imprisoned was described. There were a couple of beds in an adjoining room, it appeared, but nothing else.

From the footmarks in the dust of the hall the assassins must have numbered at least six, and one of the prints is so big that it can have belonged only to a man of great size. The two most important indications of the identity of the murderers are the following. One of the two men in the hall had been simply throttled by a pair of human hands. But the print left by these fingers is very distinct, and is of a hand of unusual dimensions. But, strangest detail in the whole of this enigmatic and lugubrious affair, it is evident from the marks on the neck of the murdered man that the hands were covered with rings! Passing this detail without comment — for this justifies the wildest suppositions and where there is nothing more definite to go upon it is idle to speculate — we come to the second clue. It is incontestable, from the medical evidence, the second man was strangled in a manner only know to and only practised by the peoples of the East, a method akin to the Thug. And this belief is carried out by the fact that some very fine particles of silk were found clinging on the rough edge of the collar. But, as a startling confirmation of this, the bound man within the room had been stabbed several times with a long dagger such as the Hindus use.

The reporter up till now had been observing an admirable restraint. The material was so rich, the opportunity so magnificent, that almost incredulously he had remained calm for the moment. The splendour of his opportunity seemed too good to be true. His case was rather that of a man who has just been prodigiously insulted, and because of the very unbelievable grimness of the affront remains calm and almost good humoured for the moment. We have of course been the gainers by this. At this point he suddenly loses all self-control, however, and breaks out into the most fulsome jargon of his trade. We have resolved, however, to give one or two further extracts although they must be culled from this swamp of malarial eloquence.

The police, turning over the heap of ashes in the grate, discovered a small and dingy piece of paper, on which appeared the one word 'Passion'! Passion, that had blackened these set and horrified faces as though it were a reflection of the faces of black hate that their dying eyes had last gazed upon – black faces? – ay, faces, perhaps, black not only with hate, but from the torrid effulgence of some eastern sun – passion that had swept down with its devastating wing on this lonely mansion – passion is the only human word that is found, left behind by the destroyers, as a clue to this terrible mystery. As though in some ruined city in the desert, only one word, in hieroglyph had been found – Love, Hate, or, more simply, Passion!

It was affirmed a little further on that some small change had been found in the pockets of the murdered men: 'Ah, what did he who killed with crowds of flashing rings on his fingers care about the slight sums of money that might be found on those poor corpses?'

Some rings however had gone from the fingers of the dead men, and it did not apparently occur to the reporter that they might have been taken to baffle police attempts at identification.

That evening Royal received an invitation to dinner from the Khan. He at once wired a refusal, saying that he had his business to attend to in Marbury Street.

Fane had also read the *Morning Looking Glass*. Since he had become temporarily a criminal he read everything striking in the criminal line in the papers with a sort of half thought that it might be the doings of the organization to which he had the honour of belonging. Now this account of supposed Oriental assassins, and Americans, and especially the word 'Passion,' set his memory to work. But he could not connect them in his mind. He knew that the word 'Passion' had some connection with some experience of his lately, but *which* he could not tell. As a matter of fact he had heard Arthur O. Passion announce himself in the hall a week ago.

Nevertheless he asked Royal that evening what had happened to him during his three days' absence. Royal evaded his question; he said he had been having a rest.

In the course of the next few days no further clue appeared to 'dissolve the cloud of mystery that hung over the mysterious house on the riverside.'

In a day or two Mrs. Dukes moved in state to Liverpool.

51
THE CAUSE OF THE GUARD'S PERTURBATION

Three days later in a second-class carriage in the Liverpool express sat Mrs. Dukes and Hillington, surrounded by parcels and funny looking bags and sacks. This was the sum of Mrs. Dukes' movable belongings. A sinister looking sack lurching about over her head contained outer rags, an oblong canvas box contained inner or under rags, a brown paper parcel and a brand new and very expensive looking leather bag contained articles of Mrs. Dukes' toilet. A sheaf of umbrellas, the most elegant from the stock in the shop, reposed side by side with a bonnet box. But beside these things were many nameless packets and parcels, not to speak of Hillington's hand baggage.

Mrs. Dukes, or rather Royal, as, once the train had started he resumed his ordinary voice again, did not waste many words on his companion. Hillington tried to draw him into conversation several times, but he continued obstinately to read one of the many papers and magazines they had purchased.

They had tipped the guard liberally and he had locked them in in consequence.

At last Rugby was reached, and at the end of four or five minutes of door banging – the bangs to the left growing fainter, the bangs to the right growing louder – an official presented himself to examine their tickets. When, however, his eyes fell on Mrs. Dukes, he hesitated, and took her ticket as though she had been a ghost and he had half expected the ticket to fade between his fingers. Both Hillington and his companion noticed the inspector's startled and doubtful manner. Hillington called out, as he thought, gaily – but Hillington could not be gay, and the effect that resulted from his effort only seemed to startle the man more.

'Why, what is there so funny about us? Anyone would think from the expression of your face that we were your long lost brother and sister.'

The inspector was one of those men who become sullen when mystified or startled or when experiencing any unusual emotion. He did not answer Hillington but looked grumpy and quickly went to the next carriage.

'That's funny, isn't it?' asked Hillington. 'I suppose the game's not up, by any chance!'

Royal only went on with his reading, shrugging his shoulders at Hillington's observations. But when a few minutes later, several faces, some openly and some with an air of casually glancing in, were seen scrutinizing Royal from the platform, he acknowledged that something was amiss. He even put down his paper and gazed up at the watching faces outside, and then began angrily protesting, in Mrs. Dukes' voice, to

Hillington. The window was open, and one of the men on hearing these quaint and emphatic tones, turned to another with increased interest, and began talking in undertones.

Hillington by this time was seriously alarmed. But before he had decided to do something or other with a view to penetrating the mystery, whistles sounded here and there, and the train moved out of the station.

Hillington now racked his brain aloud and attempted to rack Royal's for him also, as to what this could portend. He even suggested that as it might mean that they were going to be arrested at Liverpool, they had better wait till the train was going slower, as it did at some point they would soon be reaching now, and then jump out and make off across country.

Royal told him shortly that he for one was not going to jump out of the train, although no one would prevent Hillington from breaking his neck, if he felt that it was wise to do so. He said, further, that he could give no explanation for the excitement they had caused at the station, and that he was going to wait till they got to Liverpool, and see what happened there. Perhaps they had seemed funny to the inhabitants of one town, but would appear quite ordinary folk to the inhabitants of another. The rest of the journey passed practically in silence.

At last Liverpool was reached, and as their train threaded its way through the converging lines leading to the great Lime-Street station, Royal as well as Hillington wondered what awaited them at their destination.

When they had drawn up at the platform, both of them gazed out sharply to left and right, and secured a porter who brought a truck for the reception of all Mrs. Dukes' paraphernalia. They followed at a distance. No one seemed to notice them here. Both were very much mystified. Suddenly just in front of them a springly and portly gentleman sprang to earth from the door of a second-class compartment, from which a guard with his key, such a key as one winds clocks with, had just released him. Royal stopped a moment, and turned half round, but it was too late – and Hillington had not apparently noticed this man. The springy and portly gentleman was no other than the rubicund clergyman who had called at Marbury Street and successfully fired out the curate. But he was no longer dressed as a clergyman, nor was his face so rubicund, nor his moustache so grey. He wore ash-coloured side whiskers and moustache, and a dark morning suit of a distinctly American cut. And indeed his whole appearance had now distinctly something transatlantic about it, down to the very way he held his head and arm in assisting the old lady to alight.

This old lady was very weak and white, and stared out on the world with eyes that seemed to be viewing everything round her as a mere phantasmagoria; but for the most part she kept her eyes fixed on a vague point some twenty yards ahead of her, on the ground, or on any intervening object. But from her rather elevated position, namely from the railway carriage, her eyes were now fixed suddenly on Mrs. Dukes' face. Their vagueness seemed at the same moment to clear up, and a terrified expression to come into her face, something the same expression the guard's face had worn on first seeing Mrs. Dukes, but a hundred times more intense. And then, instead of feebly feeling her way down to the platform, she fell there in a mass, nearly knocking over the gentleman who was offering her his support.

Mrs. Dukes and Hillington, who had witnessed this, hurried on, and were soon driving off in a cab, partially submerged in their packets and papers. As soon as they were alone Royal turned angrily to his companion, and said shortly, 'There's bungling, if you like! It's time all men who respect their skins get out of this concern! Besides, it's fiendish the state they've brought that old woman to.'

In the meantime the old gentleman at the carriage door helped the old lady to her feet. She had not fainted. She had, it seemed, merely lost all power for the moment, and just fallen down. The normal state appeared so pitifully weak that it was not very far from fainting. This was not improved by her half fall — broken, happily, by the robust form of her companion. The walk she now had to take from the carriage door to a four-wheeler was as much as she could manage. She kept muttering to herself, but clung to her protector like a little child. In their wake came a young woman in the uniform of a nurse, carrying a shawl and bag, and then a porter with more light luggage.

Many people had witnessed the scene, but none had realized the cause of the old woman's sudden collapse. The reason was that her eyes had suddenly fallen upon an old woman, in all ways exactly like herself — with the same walk and manner of carrying her head, and dressed in clothes, even, that she recognized as hers. But this old woman was far more active than herself — as active as she used to be.

The proximity of this ghost, as she vaguely felt it to be, had startled her so much that she had suddenly been deprived of all her strength, and had tumbled down in the manner we have described.

Then she felt that it was probably *she* who was the ghost, and this other woman the reality. The feeling she had had for some weeks back of being out of life altogether, quite dead to the world she knew, supplied her with this whimsical reasoning. Yes, she thought, that other old woman was the *real* Mrs. Dukes. She was Mrs. Dukes no longer.

But as a matter of fact this old lady was no other than the

Marbury Street landlady, who at this point emerges once more on the scene of our story. But before going further it would be well to explain how she came to be travelling in the same train as Royal and Hillington, and what *she,* in her turn, had come to do in Liverpool.

52
HOW THE PLOTTERS CAME TO BLUNDER

While her successor was bravely playing his, or her, part in Marbury Street, wrestling with the lawyers, with soi-disant nephews, being kidnapped and escaping, the first and original Mrs. Dukes was passing blank weeks of debility and suffering in the house in St. John's Wood. A day or two after her first awakening in the whitewashed room at the end of the corridor she had been told by the nurse that she had broken a blood-vessel in her effort to escape from her lodger, Mr. Nichols. In his flight this desperate criminal had collided with her, and, believing that it was somebody placed there to cut off his retreat, had struggled with her, and she with him. She was warned that her internal injuries were of a very grave order, and that she was to keep very quiet; indeed, said the nurse, they had been forced to strap her down as a precautionary measure, in case, being light-headed, she might attempt to rise. So for weeks she had remained there, getting weaker and weaker, and caring less and less about life. The medicines they gave her, alone, were sufficient to produce a depressed and strengthless condition of body and mind.

A couple of weeks after the beginning of her confinement, she had heard several voices in the passage outside, and noticed the nurse bustling about and arranging things. Then the doctor and two strange men had entered, the sight of one of whom affected her strangely, and to all appearance she affected him no less. His eyes remained fixed on her in a long and mournful gaze, and after a few minutes of embarrassed silence they were left alone together.

He sat down on her bed, and said after a while, 'Don't you know me, Wobbles?'

Her eyes grew rounder, her heart began to beat softly against her side, and at last she spoke in a hoarse and croaking voice.

'Oh, *yew've* come back, 'ave ye?'

And she went on staring at him. This was her only way of greeting the man she firmly believed to be her husband. Allowing for the thirty-five years that had elapsed, his appearance, his voice, his manner with her was just what she would have imagined his to be. During her long widowhood, since he had left her, she had occasionally kept his image in her mind up to date, so to speak. She would, in remembering him, say to herself, 'I 'spect 'e's grown fat,' and she would promptly, in her mind, invest him with a certain corpulence. Then she gradually sowed with grey hairs his once brown head. And in her mind he had really grown very much like this man who now presented himself to her. Then she had always thought that he would turn up in this way sooner or later. There he was. But in one thing her prophetic fancies were not confirmed. She had expected that she would be much more harsh with him. As a matter of fact, although her reception of him was quite cool and matter of fact, she felt, she was compelled to acknowledge it to herself, glad that he had come, and she had very little bitterness in her mind towards him. She had felt so helpless and isolated here in this hospital, and now he had come from the outer world to her.

He came to see her the next day and the next, and on the third she pressed him to take her back to Marbury Street. And she spoke about Cole. He looked grave and very sorrowful at this. On the following day the nurse broke to her as gently as possible the news of Cole's death, and she was made to sign some papers necessary, she said, for the formalities of the funeral. This news had upset her so much that very little medicine was needed on the following days to depress her. She supplied the depression herself.

Since that time she had not felt so kindly towards the returned Mr. Dukes again. She would have preferred Cole to him, if the choice had had to be made; and she connected vaguely in her mind the arrival of the one with the withdrawal, in death, of the other. But still she was civil with the one that remained, and was glad to see him each day.

He told her all his doings since his desertion of her. He had gone to America, and made a considerable fortune. Then at last, when she was saying one day that she would never get well in that place, and that she wished she could get out with or without the doctor's permission, he said that she must come with him to America and share his fortune.

She scoffed at the idea — scoffed faintly, for she had little strength left for superfluous vehemence in any form. But he repeated the suggestion. Then she got angry — very feebly — and told him not to be a 'fathead.' Shortly afterwards, however, she began to discuss it: what should such an old woman as she do in a new country and so on. How could she, in her present state, make a journey like that?

'But that's just what the doctor recommends for you, a sea-voyage. It's the only thing that will pull you round, he thinks.'

She was silent, and the subject was not again touched upon

until the next morning, when he came again.

While following the fortunes of the second Mrs. Dukes we have treated the old lady herself as though she had no further history, and had been definitely entombed in the house in St. John's Wood. This was more or less indeed the case. Her existence there was a series of lifeless monotonous days, only broken by the arrival of this man announcing himself as her 'long-lost husband,' and since that event, the slow persuasion of the terribly weakened and almost light-headed old woman to make the voyage to America for her health.

Eventually, a little to get out of the hospital, and chiefly from sheer inability to resist the pressing of this obstinate man, she consented to go on this voyage, that the doctor recommended with so much conviction.

And thus it was that Mrs. Dukes found herself in the Liverpool express. How it was that she had taken the same train as Evan Royal — which fact our young adventurer had stigmatized as a gross blunder on the part of the 'direction' — was the purest chance.

The doctor, nurse and pretended husband had been watching her, and awaiting not merely physically a fitting moment to make the start, but had also been waiting until her state of mind should be favourable to the enterprise. This was a very grave step for these three to take, for they were accountable to the Khan — the mysterious chief that none of the three had ever seen — for their actions, and they wished this journey to the ship at Liverpool to pass off without a hitch. Never had an aviator waited for suitable weather with more impatience, and, at the same time, attention, than these three people as they observed Mrs. Dukes' moods and physical condition.

At last, on the day that Evan Royal suddenly decided to go to Liverpool — without announcing his arrival at the other end, although he had let the Khan know of his intention – it had seemed to the three plotters in the St. John's Wood house that their patient's condition was most favourable for making a start. They hurried her clothes on, accordingly, and sending for a cab were soon on their way to Liverpool. The doctor had not gone further than the station. The self-styled Mr. Dukes and the nurse alone accompanied her to Liverpool.

The old woman, after her collapse on the station platform, seemed for some time incapable of connected thought, and in an extremely weak condition physically. As a matter of fact this turned out to be very favourable for their plans. They had not anticipated any difficulty, but naturally the actual embarking of the old lady was a ticklish business. One could never be sure that at the last moment she would not have a sudden excess of energy and obstinacy and refuse to pass the gangway. The sight of the ship, the crowds of passengers, the gangway leading her off terra-firma into a ship going to the other side of the earth, might have shaken her from her apathy. She had consented to all this hardly realizing what it meant. All had seemed unreal to her – she was no longer in touch with life in the sick room at the St. John's Wood house. The effect of the sight of the reality on her was what the plotters feared. But her extreme weakness, both mental and physical, consequent upon the shock of her fright and her fall, obviated all this. She was practically carried on to the boat, and only revived somewhat when they were already half-way across the Atlantic. The sea-air did not revive her very alarmingly. She reached America still in a more or less dazed state. A week after her arrival they were all three installed in a comfortable house in one of the minor cities of New York State, and she accepted the new life they had thrust upon her without giving much trouble.

A few weeks after their arrival, she, being able by that time to drag herself about a little, entered Mr. Dukes' room rather unexpectedly one day. He had not heard her outside in the passage, nor had he in any way anticipated this visit. He was packing his bag. At sight of her he sprang up, and was visibly vexed and abashed at her sudden appearance.

She stood there in the doorway looking stupidly at him, taking in slowly his occupation and evident annoyance at being surprised in it. Then she spoke without any show of feeling.

'Ah, so yew're orf again, are ye?'

She was getting accustomed to being abandoned! She was getting to know his little ways! She turned and left him to his packing.

He changed his mind, however, and told her when he came down to supper that evening that he had contemplated a little trip to New York, but had resolved after all not to go just yet. But a week later he left all the same, and Mrs. Dukes remained alone with the nurse and a servant.

There we will leave her for the time being, and return to the astounding adventures that awaited the second Mrs. Dukes in Liverpool.

53
THE GOUTY MEMBER HAS A TERRIBLE EXPERIENCE

Mrs. Dukes — the second of that name — arrived unannounced, as we have said, in Liverpool. The night had already fallen when she and her friend and adviser, Hillington, arrived before the substantial mansion in Inchbeck Road that was hers from chimney to cellar, with all it contained. It was of an old build — how old Royal's familiarity with architectural styles did not permit Mrs. Dukes to fix. But it was a house that did not look so big as it in fact was — like many comparatively narrow-chested men who are, as a compensation, excessively thick from front to back. In another way, also, it deceived the stranger. With its sleek light-coloured plaster work one anticipated that it must be rather a light and cheerful house within. On the contrary, furnished on a darkish scheme of colour, and because of the formation of its rooms, it was rather a dark house within.

The new owner and Hillington gazed at it from the window of the cab. There were indications of light and warmth from the direction of the basement, and an upper window was illuminated.

Mrs. Dukes left the cab, and mounting the steps rang and knocked loudly. The door was shortly opened by a tall, dark, inscrutable looking man, who was evidently the butler. As Mrs. Dukes' eyes met his the watchful spirit of Royal, within, was at once put on alert. This man must be considered before one went any further. A note of warning was struck deep in his being. This man looked too inscrutable even for a butler. Even a serving man had no right to be so impassable. There were limits even to *that*. This dark, smooth and waiting, watching face did not even show surprise at Mrs. Dukes' appearance, as she stood there announcing herself as his future mistress. It is true that the lawyers might have told this man to expect something very peculiar to come and reign over the lately bereaved household. Everything about this man as he stood there struck the new owner as ominous. His way of appearing to hang on the handle of the door somewhat as he opened it, slightly swaying with it, a little trick no doubt of his, even seemed sinister. However at last Mrs. Dukes managed to drag herself and her questioning scrutiny away from him, and entered her house.

One or two other servants were also on the premises, and fires were soon lighted and things rapidly took on a more cheerful aspect.

In the choosing of her bedroom Mrs. Dukes shewed a little perversity and obstinacy. The butler seemed determined that she should have a certain large and sombre first-floor room. He brought everything a domestic can to bear upon his eccentric mistress. But when all his efforts seemed of no avail to decide her to remain in that one, he led her to another on the same side of the house. His attitude was very strange now. He seemed determined that, if she would not have the other, she then must have this. The wakeful spirit of Royal then became more than usually wakeful in presence of this quiet undemonstrative obstinacy of the servant. Royal felt that somehow it was not merely for a domestic's reason — that of fitness — that the mistress should occupy the best rooms, that this servant with a face so intensely mask-like was pressing these rooms upon her. Eventually a room at the back of the house was chosen, opposite to those insisted upon by the butler.

Very much on his guard, Royal sternly rebuffed Hillington's attempts at intimate conversation. Shortly after dinner Royal went to bed, heaving the packets and boxes, large and small, brought up to his bedroom.

Then Mrs. Dukes' voice rang shrilly over the house already, in no way respecting the sedate silence it had found.

'Oh Lord, Mr. 'illington, these stairs ain't so easy as them at Marb'ry Street! I feels like lyin' down 'arf way up, and they're broad enough and soft enough too.'

Cries of 'Mr. 'illington!' and 'Mr. Clarke' (as Mrs. Dukes called the butler, thus bringing them together in a common designation of Mr.) echoed on the stairs for some time before the new proprietress' door shut for the night. Mrs. Dukes took possession noisily.

The good Hillington wasn't very touchy, but he did not like being made to run about with a domestic, and like one. And Royal had given him a great deal of unnecessary running about to do lately – he grossly overdid the part (Mrs. Dukes' imperiousness) just for the pleasure, Hillington thought, of overwhelming him with all sorts of tiresome little services and injunctions.

The next morning Hillington was up and out very early. He only returned at ten o'clock, when he found Royal finishing his breakfast. The latter looked at him sharply, and returned his good morning deliberately, and in a tone that signified many things. Mrs. Dukes' man of business chattered a little, said he'd taken a turn in the town as Royal wasn't down yet, and then a silence ensued, Royal's head – or rather Mrs. Dukes' head, for he was of course now constantly in that part, except while in his bed with his door locked – buried in the morning paper. He did not in any way relinquish his precaution, and spoke with Mrs. Dukes' clear Cockney drawl all the time. One could never be sure that a servant might not linger at the door to listen before coming in. One could not indeed be sure that one of the servants, the inscrutable butler for instance, was not in touch with Truman and Hatchett.

Mrs. Dukes, sitting in front of her business man, suddenly broke the silence by laying her paper down, and addressing him directly in a rather long speech. 'Mr. 'illington, I've been thinkin',' it began. She had been thinking that there were not enough servants in the house. She wanted to have eight, at least, and to have the use of a carriage. Hillington was very embarrassed, for although they were both speaking in their respective roles, he knew that this was not what Khan's direction would be, for the direction was strictly economical in some ways, as it was absurdly lavish in others. On the other hand it was of the first importance that Royal, on whom the chance of securing the million certainly depended, should not be ruffled up. Even in a thing of this sort, it was better not to demur, he thought. And then he was rather afraid of Royal, at bottom. Still, he remained rather taken aback and embarrassed. Of course Royal was given carte blanche to act his part as he liked, as realistically as possible. Yes, he must carry out his orders. But, he promised himself, with a certain reservation; he would first communicate with his chief, as he had done once already that morning.

The solicitors, informed of Mrs. Dukes' arrival, came in the person of the gouty member, this time, to see her. Mrs. Dukes seemed very taken with him, and invited him to dinner for the following evening.

That day was a busy one for everybody. Hillington kept turning up at Palm Lodge – the name of Mrs. Dukes' house – and disappearing again, darting out in this way, according to him, in his negotiations for the four or five additional domestics desired. Mrs. Dukes herself took in state – in a large loose and gilded hired carriage – to the nearest dressmaker one of her old dresses, and with a shrill haughtiness commanded the gaping woman to cut her out a dress like that in black and dark green satin. The dressmaker made various tentative motions to bring about a measuring of Mrs. Dukes' body; she did not consider that an exact imitation of the ragged garment presented her would be a credit to her establishment. She at last became particularly pressing – 'just to take a simple measurement or two.' Mrs. Dukes had the air of a little hunchback whom a tailor has just asked if he may measure her hump. She drew her extraordinarily shaped mantle and shirts round her, as though in scorn, and silently looked the dressmaker up and down. Then she said, 'If you think you can make anything better than *that*,' pointing to the dilapidated costume she had brought as a model, *'yew're* vastly mistaken. I never 'ad anythin' fit me better than that frock.' The dressmaker took it up in despair; however, she resolved to do what she could to make as good a dress as was possible on those lines, trusting to subsequent alterations to pull it into shape. Mrs. Dukes told her that she was going to fetch her the satin. The satin was duly chosen at a neighbouring emporium, and Mrs. Dukes then informed her that she wanted the dress for the next evening – at six o'clock. How the dressmaker got over these repeated shocks it is difficult to say. But that she did, and that Mrs. Dukes had her black and green satin dress in time to don it for next evening's dinner with the gouty member of Truman and Hatchett's, is an established fact. Also, for that occasion, her shoulders were enveloped in a black Indian shawl; in addition she wielded a very unwieldy fan. Her manoeuvres with this heavy article so disconcerted her guest at certain moments that he felt distinct and premonitory twinges in all the centres most given over to the gout, as he did whenever very much worried. The dinner passed off very well nevertheless, but in a strong current of air.

After dinner, in the midst of a violent swirl of air, the startled old gentleman was carried off to the drawing room *on Mrs. Dukes' arm!* On rising, his hostess had come round the table to where he was standing, and, grasping his hand, drew it under her arm. She had then, working vigorously her fan the while, ascended with him in tow to the drawing room. He had escaped as soon as possible. Thrice he had attempted to get to the door, but had been flung back in his chair by his imperious and barbarous hostess. But the fourth time Hillington had laughingly come to his rescue, and his last glimpse of the drawing room he was flying from was of Hillington and Mrs. Dukes engaged in a half-playful, half-angry wrestling bout on the hearthrug.

When they were left alone, Hillington smilingly said to his gifted colleague, 'I say, don't you overdo it a bit, Royal?'

Royal who was in a very good temper after his buffooneries of the evening, deigned to reply: 'My dear Hillington, one can't overdo it. To draw people's attention, to play the eccentric old woman, to get talked about and be much in evidence, all this takes people further away from finding out the *real* person I am, and the fraud that is being practised on them. The more I impose myself on them as a tiresome, whimsical old woman, the less they would ever guess I was anything else.'

The gouty member of the firm appeared amongst his partners the following morning with a long and woeful tale of his tribulations at the house of their client. He depicted the horror of the situation he had found himself placed in in glowing colours, and added that had not that fellow Hillington turned up after dinner, that he might never have escaped from the terrible old woman's clutches.

For two or three days Truman and Hatchett's heard vague and disquieting rumours of Mrs. Dukes; how Mrs. Dukes had gone to the theatre, how Mrs. Dukes had made a descent on the principal shop of the town, etc. Her movements were reported to them, swollen by rumour, and the firm at every moment were expecting to have to go and bail her out; for it was popularly said that on most occasions she appeared distinctly the worse for drink; this was the matter-of-fact way the Liverpudlians seemed inclined to take her eccentricities.

Then two or three mornings later the entire firm received a

command to repair to her house to discuss some important business matters.

54
HILLINGTON DISMISSED

Only two members of the firm of Truman and Hatchett responded to Mrs. Dukes' invitation to a grand council. That was Mr. Hatchett and an old and trusted clerk. They had sent their strongest man again, namely the acute and penetrating Mr. Hatchett. The firm had felt that the situation demanded a strong head. There was no knowing what line their client might take up. She had bloomed out so remarkably.

But Mr. Hatchett found her very grave and sober and evidently prepared to go into her affairs in the most serious and responsible spirit. Mr. Hatchett again went over for her the list of her possessions, her investments, etc. Hillington was present, and several times, wishing to carry out the part he had originally played before the lawyer, interrupted the latter to explain things to her. She looked at him with heavy, steady eyes while he was doing this and said nothing, but suddenly, at the third or fouth interruption, she spoke abruptly.

'Mr. 'illington, will yew please leave Mr. 'atchett an' me alone; we 'ave somethin' private to hin-vestigate.'

Hillington remained wide-eyed for a moment. Then he rose, and saying 'Very well, Mrs. Dukes, I shall be at hand if you require me,' retired in good order.

''E's goin', 'e is!' commented Mrs. Dukes when he had left the room. ''E thinks 'e knows everything; I've 'ad just about enough of 'is interferin'. When I'm talkin' to my legal adviser pokin' 'is nose in like that!'

Mr. Hatchett was delighted at Hillington's discomfiture, but naturally concealed it from his client.

Mrs. Dukes then got up and went to the door, which she opened sharply. There was no one there however, as she had, it seemed, expected. She then returned, and after a moment of reflection, said to Mr. Hatchett that she would keep him no longer that day, but would come to the office the morning after the next. She had been the whole time very quiet and well-behaved with Mr. Hatchett, and listened repectfully to what he had to say, and this gentleman consequently augured favourably of their relations together in the future, and thought that perhaps her more violent eccentricities would not interfere with their business relations, but be confined to unimportant escapades among her fellow townsmen in general, and in the prosecution of her pleasure — in her theatre-going and so on. He reported to the anxiously waiting firm that he believed she would always conduct herself soberly in her business interviews with them, and was, moreover, getting quite a good grasp of business principles, and becoming amazingly independent; he told them with satisfaction of Hillington's dismissal.

Mrs. Dukes spent the rest of her day in the cellar and on the road to it. She was preparing part of the cellar for Cole's reception. His bedroom upstairs in one of the attics had already been arranged. Now part of the Palm Lodge cellar had to be arranged like the cellar in Marbury Street; an unlimited supply of wood and a chopper placed there, several pots of blacking and other things, so that Cole should feel perfectly at home. A separate entrance was arranged for him so that he should not be forced to pass through the servants' quarters to get upstairs. A flight of stone steps at the back of the house, and a door leading into the cellar, solved this difficulty. A kind of housekeeper's room near the door giving on to these steps Mrs. Dukes appropriated for herself and made it sufficiently grimy and sordid so that Cole could slip in there and smoke his pipe beside his mother without feeling oppressed at their changed circumstances.

The butler watched all this grimly; the other servants kept out of sight, except the one ordered forth to help her eccentric mistress.

That evening Royal had a conversation with Hillington after dinner, an interview that Hillington had been seeking all day, ever since his dismissal in the morning. They were seated at the further end of the drawing-room, and it was Royal who came to the point first – a point his companion had not been expecting.

'I don't think, Hillington, there's very much object in your staying on here and depriving the Khan of your valuable services in London. He must surely be missing you. I propose that we should go back together tomorrow – that you should stay there and that I should bring Cole, Lucy and that young chap who is understudying me back here at once. You see, now that I've taken this free line with the solicitors, and in everything, in fact, which is after all the best way to get our hands on the money, there's not very much for you to do. You see, this *is* the best way – the best line to take. By making Mrs. Dukes' eccentricity *active,* so to speak, anything I do will not awake surprise – even getting the larger part of "my" fortune into my own hands. To do that my eccentricity *had* to become active – I had to develop initiation all of a sudden – had to appear to want to manage my own affairs. And my dismissing *you,* my business man, will be a very good and plausible move. It will please the solicitors, too. This is the best way of managing things, I'm convinced. If all her fortune is to be turned into gold, and we are to disappear with it, then the gathering of it together must create as little stir and surprise as possible. They must get into such a state, you see, that they would not be astonished at anything I did. When you make your report to the Khan, tell him how I've conducted things so far, and give him my reasons for this change, or development, rather, of tactic. So I dismiss you,' Royal said, smiling.

When Royal had first touched on the 'gathering in of the money,' Hillington's eyes had suddenly narrowed oddly, and his face had become quite formal and expressionless. Every word of this conversation would be reported to the Chief, but Hillington was listening intently to detect, if he could, any intention beneath the young man's words. 'Could he be up to that?' he kept repeating mentally to himself.

'Besides,' Royal added after a pause, 'if the boss is afraid, there's Lucy to mount guard always. And I expect the street is bristling with his spies as it is.'

'It's just as you think,' Hillington said, after another pause. 'You know of course that I don't want to stay here particularly. The Khan's so keen on keeping several of us together in a case of this magnitude to help each other if anything should happen. But then nothing can happen to you,' he added, smiling; then he added quickly, 'if you *were* taken and locked up in Newgate, you'd be out and away within twenty-four hours. It was fine the way you got away from the Americans. The Khan told me all about it. He was delighted with you!' This was the first reference that had occurred between them to Royal's escape. The latter so far had not condescended to recount his adventures, except to the Khan. Hillington was sincerely enthusiastic, although he no doubt said this to Royal with a conciliatory intention.

'Well,' said Royal, getting up, 'I must go to bed; and since you appear to agree to my plan, you had better do so too. For we must be up betimes.'

The next morning with one or two little packets and Mrs. Dukes' new, handsome bag, Royal started – Hillington, with all his luggage, accompanying him. As he got into the carriage, the butler's very enigmatic face gazing at him without expression suddenly caused him the same uneasiness and preoccupation as on his arrival – seemed to sound the same note of warning within him. He remained thoughtful and moody for some time, as though wrestling with a problem.

55
A DRIVE IN THE COUNTRY

That same evening there were three new inmates at Palm Lodge, Inchbeck Road, Liverpool, and Mrs. Dukes was dragging herself about, attempting to get them all settled down properly.

The journey had come off without a hitch. Cole had been abnormally 'sulky,' but otherwise had behaved himself properly. He had evidently enjoyed the darkness of the tunnel very much, and had been seen in the faint light thrown by the lamp overhead to smile slightly. The new experience so suddenly overtaking him – the railway train, cabs, etc., had left him quite unmoved. He seemed at first very shy of the cellar so artfully prepared for him. But next day he was heard there chopping wood, quite as though he had been in Marbury Street.

Mrs. Beechamp, no longer quite so slatternly, took up her residence as, more or less, Mrs. Dukes' maid. The charming young lady underneath this unprepossessing exterior had quite wonderfully disguised her charms. With various cunning pads and ill-fitting clothes she had been as successful in making herself look uncouth as most women are in making themselves look couth. Her charming plumpness came to look like an ungainly fatness, her wealth of hair like a gigantic and rebellious mop, and so on.

Fane, for his part, had come to take Hillington's place: not, of course, as business adviser — that department Mrs. Dukes had taken over herself — but rather as private secretary. He wrote Mrs. Dukes' letters for her, and she signed them, merely. In this way in a day or two everything was going smoothly and the new order of things was established.

Evan Royal was without doubt an extremely observant young man; there were few things that escaped his notice. So it was that, in examining the new servants Hillington had at length secured for him, he came to the conclusion that they were not servants at all, but people, like himself, in the pay of the Khan. Royal did not know, any more than the rest of his colleagues, how extensive the company was. But he believed that the Khan had a good many irons in the fire and had people 'working' for him all over the place. One of the servants seemed to him genuine, but the other three he was willing to bet his bottom dollar were there to watch him.

Now Royal, in speaking as he had done to Hillington the night before, was quite aware that he would be putting the Khan and his satellites more than ever on the qui vive; and he had noticed Hillington's change of manner when he had spoken of 'getting the money into his hands.' But Royal had reckoned on all this. This new attitude in his role, his new way of playing the part of Mrs. Dukes, was not altogether the result of a reckless and defiant mood consequent upon his humiliation at the hands of the defunct tall Americans. There was another reason, and a more serious one. To become acquainted once more with the workings of Royal's mind, and to see what was beneath all this eccentric behaviour, we cannot do better than relate a conversation that took place between Fane and him on the following day. This conversation had a determining influence on their lives, and with it the reader will be confronted with a new and startling element in the development of the story.

Mrs. Dukes returned from the lawyers the next morning just before lunch, and ordered her carriage for two in the after-noon.

Lunch over, she invited Fane to go for a drive with her. He at once prepared himself, and a half hour later they were passing through the last blocks of houses of the town, and the more or less open country lay before them. Once amongst the fields, they left the carriage, Mrs. Dukes telling the coachman to wait for them, and they struck out across country. They had about an hour more of winter sunlight before them, and when out of sight of the carriage Mrs. Dukes looked for a place where they could sit down. The charred remains of a cottage in a field near by offered what she sought. As they approached it Royal took Fane by the arm, and began what he had to say in the following words:

'You see, Fane, if anything *did* happen to go wrong, you could now say that you had simply engaged yourself to me as secretary, and did not know I was *not* Mrs. Dukes, the mil-lionairess, any more than Truman and Hatchett's know it. So you're quite "out of danger." If the police came to arrest me tomorrow you would not be troubled in any way. I should say that what you said was quite true – that you were totally un-aware that there was anything wrong, and had come to me merely as secretary. But then I shan't be caught,' he added, smiling.

'I hope you won't,' said Fane simply.

'Now what I want to know is this,' continued Royal. 'Do you intend to throw in your lot with the Actor-Gang as I have done, and become in the course of time, doubtless, an amazingly accomplished sharper, or do you look upon this adventure as the last of this order?'

He looked straight at Fane while he was saying this, and watching his face cloud, was sure that he had not been wrong in his estimate of his new companion.

They now had arrived at the broken wall for which they had been making, and sat down.

Royal was quite convinced of Fane's honesty, and was sure that *he* at least was not a spy set to watch him. His intimacy with Lucy had puzzled him. But he had determined that this was entirely Lucy's doing – that Lucy had been interested in the breaking in of this novice. It was characteristic of Royal that it never occurred to him that there could be any question of love between them. He had never been very attracted by the fair sex himself, and seldom recognized this motive in others.

Fane, on his side, was very anxious to get Lucy out of this gang of scoundrels into which he had been drawn, and was determined to leave it himself at the earliest opportunity. But he was very worried about Lucy. Would she come with him? Could he induce her to leave these companions of hers and give up this life? She had promised to. But could he trust to this? He was particularly drawn to Royal. He felt that although this man was, in a sense, the most accomplished rascal of all, that he was quite apart – that there was something different in him. He had a real feeling of friendship for him already, and was glad to be able to speak freely with him. He felt, besides, that he would not be betrayed.

The thing of course that most worried him was that, if he went back to his theatrical work, he would not get *more* than before, and probably *less*. And how could he ask Lucy to marry him if that were the case. And he supposed that Lucy got as good pay as himself, if not better, at her present extraordinary occupation. He was grateful for Royal's assurance of his safety; but he knew that if Royal were arrested, Lucy also would probably be arrested, and in that case he had just as well be arrested himself. His remark to Royal — 'I hope you won't be' — that the latter took as applying to himself, rose as a matter of fact with such feeling to his lips because of his reflection that Royal's arrest was synomomous with his losing Lucy.

But the next moment Royal was making him an astonishing proposal, that left him speechless for some time, such great possibilities of happiness it held out to him, such a solution of all his difficulties, and yet such dangers for him and his love.

56
AN OVERWHELMING PROPOSAL

But first of all Fane answered his question.

He turned frankly to Royal and said at once, 'I feel I can trust in you. I have rather the feeling at present of being the member of some desperate secret society from which it is dangerous, even impossible, to escape — '

'You are,' interrupted Royal.

'Well,' Fane went on impetuously, 'danger or no danger, I don't intend to stay any longer than I can help, and I would clear out this minute – danger or no danger – if it wasn't that something keeps me.'

'What?' asked Royal.

'Well, I see no harm in telling you – I suppose you are being sincere with me?'

'My dear fellow, although I'm their principal scamp, so to speak, I assure you that I have very little in common with them; and when I solicit your confidence, it is not to betray it.'

'I was sure of that,' said Fane quickly. 'Well, I'm very much in love with Lucy, and want if possible to get her out of this business. There's my secret.'

Royal sat staring at him sunk in amazement. He had probably never been so taken aback by anything in his life. But immediately afterwards he was asking Lucy's admirer, in an eager voice, 'And does she – how does one say – return your affection?'

'Yes. I can guarantee she's sincere enough in that. And she says that she'll clear out with me if I can only find somewhere to go to and something to do. But that's the difficulty. And besides, I don't know whether I can reckon upon her to give up her present occupation, although she promises to, and means it, no doubt, when she says it, right enough. But – of course I've been getting six guineas a week ever since I've been at this unholy job, and have *them* carefully put away.'

Royal was looking at him with eagerness and satisfaction in his eyes. Then he said, 'Yes, what you say surprises me. Everything about women always does, and especially that one. I don't mean I'm surprised at her liking you,' he added, laughing. Then he cast an eye, cautious from long habit, into the little ruined house at his back.

'I have something to propose to you, Fane. It will solve all your difficulties, and some of mine. You have already run some risks, and therefore, since you've been under fire, no doubt will not shrink at those that my plan undoubtedly involves.' He stopped a moment and bit his lip thoughtfully.

'I am no better pleased with my work than you are with yours. Lately these confounded people that boss this disreputable business, have been getting very careless, and unnecessarily endangering my skin. Also they've been going rather far − farther than I care to go. Now look here,' and he suddenly sat straight up, and fixed Fane with his eyes. 'I have a million of money in my hands, almost as entirely as though I *were* Mrs. Dukes in truth. I could go on being Mrs. Dukes for the rest of my life if I liked. Well, my scamp of an employer is going to get all of it. I don't do this for money, as I have told you already, but for fun − not innocent fun, because I am not a particularly honest man, anyway, but fun all the same; a funny sort of fun of my own. But I did not take up this job for life. I am at the present moment very much inclined to put a large portion of this money in my pocket, enough to live grandly on for the rest of my life, and go and see life overseas somewhere. I was born for adventure. The only way of getting a sufficient amount of adventure, and always on tap, for my very big appetite in this country is being a criminal. I don't particularly mind being a criminal, but it naturally hampers one, and cuts one off from all decent people. But in certain parts of the world I could secure as much adventure as was necessary for my health − for it is a case positively of *health* with me; if I don't get my daily portion of adventure, I get a headache and my stomach gets out of order; well, I say there are distant and glamorous countries where I should get this without going out of my way. I should get it as an ordinary citizen. I should not have to become a sharper and outcast to get it. I shouldn't at all mind being president of a South American republic, for instance. If I went there with a hundred thousand pounds in my pocket, I've no doubt I could become so in a couple of years. But this is beside the point. The point is that I must get out of this — I'm sick of it. Yet if I threw up this disreputable job of mine tomorrow, what would become of me? I imagine that I have the best gifts — a good deal of energy. But all that I have got of that sort would be wasted for want of a little money to back it. Now, I expect you are somewhat in my boat. You are not up till now a criminal — I don't think that you're as yet even liable to be "had up." Still, you're worse off than you were a month or so ago as a "super" in a theatre, and that's about as dreary and unpromising a thing as one can be. You're unsettled. And, worse than all, you're in love. You're in love with a young lady for whom I have the greatest admiration, but I'm sure that she, like all clever women, would fret at the tiresome needs and mediocre life that a marriage such as you propose to her would entail. Now, your being in love with Lucy simplifies things very much for me. It was she I mostly feared in my plan of absconding with some of this money. For you've fallen in love with a most amazingly clever and energetic young person, you know.' Royal laughed. He drew breath a moment, as though arranging his thoughts for the clinching of his 'proposal,' then he went on.

'I was struck particularly when you came on the scene by the similarity of our cases. They fished you in in the same way, and the things that induced you to stay were somewhat the same. When my idea of doing a little business on my own account, doing it once and for all, occurred to me, I thought of you, and determined to ask you to throw in your fortunes with me, and to suggest that we should get out of this senseless life of rather mean hoaxing together. Now to put it clearly. If I can get three hundred thousand pounds in my pocket, will you take half, and bring Lucy with you, make a run for it? We would leave eight hundred thousand pounds in that way for Mrs. Dukes — quite enough for an old woman seventy years old. That a vulgar old woman and her idiot son should be left all that money, is a waste if ever there was one. We, with our youth and gifts, merely take a quarter of it, and leave her more than enough. This does not seem very immoral to me. But if it is, that makes no difference. It's the chance of our lives, of your life and mine. It is not for a word, 'moral' or 'immoral,' that we are going to lose it! No! Let us once and for all have done with poverty and all it involves. You and Lucy coming with me makes it, in one way, a little more dangerous. But I like it all the better for that.'

Fane had remained spellbound during this discourse. A thousand ideas and impulses rioted in his mind; he had found no words, when Royal paused, to answer him with. The latter then continued.

'You have a famous guide and leader in me. I think I know pretty well my capacities for intrigue and adventure, and I think I can guarantee absolutely our getting safe away. You see, our great pull is that we all three — you, Lucy and I — are comedians, and have the secret of very perfect disguises. We can make up, thanks to the Khan's science, which he has imparted to all of us, so perfectly that practically we become different persons at once. We would have to arrange the escape with as much method, and precision of detail, as the Khan employs in one of his fraudulent enterprises. Everything, I'm sure, would go smoothly. Ask Lucy, for that matter! She knows all about the way our impersonations work! But that's a difficulty. Are you so sure as all that that she really means what she says, that she really feels like you — is in love?'

Fane at last spoke, as though waking out of a dream; he

merely answered the last question – but this was in any case a good sign.

'Oh yes, I'm quite sure that Lucy is all right. I'm not a fool, and I know she means what she says; I'm quite sure she's not deceiving me.'

'Well, what do you say to my proposal?' asked Royal abruptly.

'I don't know what to say,' answered Fane, staring at him fixedly.

'I'll leave things as they are, then, until tomorrow. But no time's to be lost. Tomorrow you'll let me know what you've decided. Of course, it's no joking matter to get away from Raza Khan. I must, in all honesty, warn you, that there is a risk. It would be a great risk if I were not sure of being able to get the better of them. As to the police, we have nothing to fear from them. But we'd have to be at every moment on our guard, have our wits constantly about us, use every bit of energy, resource and intelligence we have in our bodies to get past Raza Khan's people, once they got wind of anything. And I'm afraid they're moving already, closing in. But never fear, we'll outwit them, if you'll join me.' Royal got up, and then facing Fane, before turning back to where they had left the carriage, he said, 'I've spoken to you rashly perhaps. I've spoken to you as to a good comrade, and a man, if you'll allow me to say so, more of my own stamp than I should find among the other members of this precious Actor-Gang. I am enormously vain. My speaking to you is a proof of it. I am so sure of the infallibility of my judgment of other people's characters, that I did not hesitate to make this proposition to you. I was sure that if you did not accept, at least you'd not betray me. It is such a chance, remember, as you will never have again.'

Then he turned back and added, before they had gone many

yards, 'If you talk to Lucy of this be sure that it is where no one could possibly overhear you. Remember that any of the servants may be the Khan's spies, for all we know!'

Then they went back to where the carriage was waiting for them. Royal's excuse for this little excursion was to see some land that Mrs. Dukes had been left somewhere about there.

They returned to the house very noisily, that is, that Royal, in the role of Mrs. Dukes, of course, kept up a perpetual rattle of whimsical talk.

57
THE BUTLER AGAIN

The greater part of that night Fane was awake, considering Royal's proposal. By the way Royal had put it to him, and also because of the frankness of Royal's own personality — he did not look upon this new adventure as a criminal act at all, somehow. It seemed too much an adventure to be a mean theft. Then the sum offered him was so enormous that it seemed all a sort of fairy story, something unreal — although he knew that Mrs. Dukes' fortune was a solid enough reality. The question chiefly with him was whether he should launch forth into this new, and avowedly perilous, adventure. One thing, among others, that made him hesitate was a paragraph he had seen in that morning's paper. It was about the murder of the three Americans. And while reading it he had suddenly remarked why the word 'Passion' was connected so strangely in his mind with Americans. He had heard it in the hall at Marbury Street pronounced in tones of confidence by a man who apparently owned it as a name. 'Arthur O. Passion, she needs him bad. Take it right in!' He had remembered these words, uttered by one of Mrs. Dukes' numerous visitors. And about that time Royal had disappeared.

He was a lover, and love made him prudent and desirous of living. Had Royal had any hand in this murder? He put this thought aside at once. He was sure of Royal's sincerity, and was sure that Royal would not for 'fun,' as he described his present occupation, take the life of three men. Then he wondered if their mysterious employers could have anything to do with it. Then all of a sudden Royal's words that afternoon — 'They have gone lately further than I care to go' — came back to him.

The upshot of all his reflections was that he would have another talk with Royal, and then speak to Lucy about it.

The next morning when he went up to the room that the late Mr. Dukes had used as a study — to write any letters his 'mistress' might have to dictate, to prosecute his secretarial duties, in short — he told Royal in a low tone that he would like to speak to him for a few minutes.

The study was a large front room, next to the drawing room, part of a large lump of masonry added at that side of the house at some remote epoch. Royal drew him to the farther end of it, first turning the key in the door, and in a large embrasure of the windows, sat down. He was just going to speak when suddenly he got up and walked back softly into the room. He had heard a dull sound, but one that he could not mistake as proceeding from anywhere but in their immediate vicinity. He was certain of this. The sound had been made in the room itself — muffled by something, no doubt, such as a curtain or piece of furniture. He pulled aside all four heavy curtains at the windows, looked behind each table and in every corner in which someone could be hidden.

He then stood silent in the middle of the room, his eyes

fixed on the wall. Saying in Mrs. Dukes' voice to Fane that he would be back in a moment, he quickly left the room. Finding a servant on the landing, he told her to fetch the butler at once.

After several minutes in the depths of the house, she returned saying he was not there, and then went upstairs to look for him. Royal still stood waiting for him; he stood in one of Mrs. Dukes' most characteristic, huddled-up poses.

Suddenly the door of one of the principal bedrooms, the one the butler had specially wished him to take, near which he was standing, opened. The butler appeared in the doorway, came slowly out, and closed the door behind him. He fixed his eyes on Royal's, and with his same look of cold impassibility was moving past Royal, when the latter arrested him by saying sharply, 'Where've *yew* bin, I should like to know?'

'In the master's bedroom, madam. I told Mary to dust it well yesterday, and I went to see if she'd carried out my orders.'

He waited a few minutes, in case his mistress should think good to address him any other remarks, and then slowly and with a kind of cat-like stateliness, passed down the stairs.

The servant returned from her search upstairs for the missing butler. Mrs. Dukes informed her he had been found.

'Now what on earth's he up to?' reflected Royal. 'He was here in Mr. Dukes' time, so he isn't one of the Khan's spies. But I swear he was behind that wall in the study, listening to what we were saying. There's a passage along there as sure as fate. These old houses are often honeycombed in that way. Then why on earth did he want me to sleep in this room here so much? Did he mean to murder me?'

Royal walked back to the study reflectively. 'The immediate thing is whether or not he heard my change of voice when I spoke to Fane just now without the Dukes' voice.' Royal concluded that he had not. First, because he had spoken too low, and secondly, because he thought probably the listener in the wall, if there had been such a thing, had only just arrived when he heard the dull sound that put him on the alert.

He told Fane of his suspicions, commenting that that only showed how careful they must be. He thought it very unlikely that they would be spied on any more just then, and asked Fane what he had wanted to say to him.

Their talk was not long. Fane asked him point blank if he knew anything about the murder of the three Americans. Royal looked on the floor silently for a few minutes, then answered.

'Yes, that's the sort of thing I meant yesterday when I said to you that it is by no means *safe* what I propose to you, that is, that it would not be safe, unless we were very careful and very cunning. The Americans paid the penalty of crossing the path of the Khan once too often.'

Then Fane asked him when he proposed carrying out his plan of escape or of absconsion.

'It depends,' Royal answered him. 'In three or four days, I hope.'

The definite nearness of the time for action startled Fane for the moment. Then he concluded their talk by saying, 'If Lucy and I agree to do it, I expect you and she could settle the details better than I.' Royal nodded, and they went back to their secretarial work.

Late that afternoon Mrs. Dukes went out for a drive, taking Mrs. Beechamp with her instead of Fane.

58
ROYAL'S PROPOSAL ACCEPTED

This time Mrs. Dukes told the coachman to drive into the

heart of the town. Before a large draper's store in Bold Street, Mrs. Dukes and her attendant got down and passed in at the swing doors together, the carriage waiting for them. Five minutes later they passed out of a door that led on to a side street, and, walking slowly, were soon descending a silent and empty street behind the draper's extensive premises. Leaning on Mrs. Beechamp's arm, Mrs. Dukes was talking in a low harsh voice, that, had anyone been there to listen, they would simply have taken for an old woman's hoarse mutterings in the ear of her attendant or friend.

'That wall in the study is hollow, and I believe a secret passage runs all along the walls of these front rooms. Do you know anything about it?' Royal was saying.

'No,' came Lucy's monosyllabic reply.

'I know quite well what *you're* here in Liverpool for, or rather why you were sent to Marbury Street. But I wonder how many more there are to spy on me?'

Lucy did not reply.

'Has Fane spoken to you?' muttered Royal, dragging heavily on her arm. Lucy walked on a little, her eyes fixed on the distant street they were approaching. Then suddenly she began speaking.

'Fane told me what you had proposed to him. How can one be sure that you would give him half?'

'Because I should actually have the money in my hand before we started, and I would give him half of it at once. If I didn't, you would give me away to the Khan's spies.'

'A hundred and fifty thousand?'

'Yes.'

Then after a moment Royal added, 'It's quite enough. I am sending fifty thousand to the Khan. He won't put the police on our track if he would have to give up fifty thousand pounds to

288

do so, however angry he may be. But he wouldn't dare to in any case.'

'Very well, then, Fane and I have decided to go with you.'

They now turned back again towards the shop.

'Which of the servants are the Khan's spies?' asked Royal.

Lucy said she didn't know. Then she added, 'You can guess pretty well. You only have to look at them. It would not do for me to *ask*. You see if the Khan got suspicious about *me*, that would be very bad for our scheme. I'm afraid that one of the spies may guess that I am doing more than breaking Fane in, or that I am having interviews with you. What do you think of the coachman?'

'He's one of them, right enough,' said Royal. 'But so long as we are with him, other spies do not follow. So that's an advantage, in a way.'

'What is your plan, once you get the money?' Lucy asked.

'I don't know yet. What do you say to drawing all their attention suddenly upon me? You might give the alarm, for instance. Then you two could get away, with your share of the money. As far as I'm concerned, I'm sure I should find a way of getting past them.'

'I'll manage to have another talk tomorrow,' said Royal as they were entering the shop again by the side door. They made one or two purchases, things calculated to make very large and important looking bundles, and then went back to the carriage.

From here Mrs. Dukes drove to a large shop in a neighbouring street, where many impregnable looking safes were exhibited in the window.

She examined all of them in turn, having each lock explained to her. This lock, the Ex Voto, had been attacked by Zigomar, the most expert safe-breaker on the Continent, and it had successfully resisted him. This lock, the latest American patent, was used by Mr. Harryman, the Billi-millionaire. This other one, as abstruse looking to the uninitiated as an aeroplane's machinery, was guaranteed against thieves by the American firm that sold it up to the sum of a hundred thousand pounds: if you deposited any sum up to a hundred thousand in this safe, and it allowed itself to be burgled, the Chicago firm would refund you the money.

Mrs. Dukes ended by buying the largest and ugliest looking safe in the place. It was an old-fashioned one that was kept there among the others to show what progress had been made. Mrs. Dukes appeared delighted with it, and told them to send it at once.

In two or three hours time, with much puffing and hoisting, and staggering, and stumbling, the enormous safe was introduced into Palm Lodge, and eventually placed in the centre of the study.

On issuing out of the safe shop, Mrs. Dukes told her coachman to wait there for her, and, on the arm of her attendant, dragged herself into a neighbouring street.

'So long as you're with me, Lucy, they trust you to spy on me,' Royal murmured.

Mrs. Dukes entered a large building given over to offices, and disappeared with Lucy through the baize door that led to the bureau of a stockbroker, recommended to her by Truman and Hatchett. Between the outer and inner doors Mrs. Dukes drew out a portfolio she had been nursing from under her clothes. In this were piles of papers representing very important sums — American railway debentures, South American silver mines, and a score more of the late Mr. Dukes' investments.

Royal was now playing to Truman and Hatchett's the old

woman who had suddenly realised her wealth, and who wanted to see it palpably before her — who would be capable, indeed, of sleeping with a million pounds in gold and notes under her bed. She had got from the solicitors almost all the papers representing her fortune that had been deposited in the Bold Street safe deposit. She had wanted to go through them, she said. Her visit to the stockbroker was to sell out a sheaf of shares in various quarters to the sum of two hundred and fifty thousand pounds. She had told the solicitors that she was going to deposit all this in the Bank of England for the present, where already a hundred thousand pounds of her fortune reposed. After she had been to the stockbroker, she went back to her carriage and before driving home, dropped in upon her legal advisers. It was then that she explained her reasons for selling out, and her determination to deposit what money came to her from this selling out process, in the Bank of England. She said she had examined the papers, and that all those shares she had just given to the stockbroker seemed to her unsafe. She wasn't going to risk *her* money in that way. Royal played very well the old woman who, obstinate, vain and ignorant, was determined to show these lawyers that she 'wasn't born yesterday,' and that even if she had been poor all her life, that she could manage her fortune for all that. Mrs. Dukes gave them back all the remaining papers, or almost all, representing the rest of her fortune, and told them to keep them for her. She did not trust that big public safe place where they had been kept up till now.

These transactions over, Mrs. Dukes sought her carriage, and returned to Palm Lodge. There a very ornate envelope awaited her, or rather him, for, the seal broken, it was addressed directly to Royal. It ran as follows:

My dear Royal.

Hillington has told me your plan of campaign. I think it is excellent. It is, as you said to him, the *only* one to avoid drawing attention to the fact that you are selling out — *when* the time comes to sell out. The idea of drawing attention more and more to yourself, for the very purpose of making people see less than they even otherwise would do, is worthy of you, my dear Royal. No one else would have thought of it.

I hope you're having as good a time as the circumstances permit. You are quite right to have the carriage, and the extra servants. Things must be done in style.

Perhaps you would send me a word every day or two, telling me some of the details of your work — how things are progressing.

Bien des saluts,

Raza Khan.

P.S. Thank you for sending me Hillington. You are quite right: he would be of little service to you now, and his 'dismissal' fits in well with your plan.

This sugared epistle left Royal very thoughtful. He wondered what Hillington had been saying. He at once sat down and wrote a reply. He said that as soon as he considered that his new attitude had 'taken,' like vaccination, on the sluggish minds of Truman and Hatchett, he would begin selling out, and said that he would need probably a month more.

As a matter of fact, in five days he expected to have all the money he wanted, three hundred and fifty thousand pounds of the whole sum, in his possession. The next four days he was busy laying his plans for escape.

59

As the time approached for acting, for making the dash for liberty with the money Royal had assured them, Lucy became more and more nervous. Above all she dreaded the Khan's getting alarmed and sending his reserve force of Asiatics to assure his interests.

Lucy's story was a peculiar one. She was the only member of the company who knew the Khan's real standing in the world. She had first known him as an Ambassador, and later on as the chief of a set of nefarious 'gangs.' Her father had been British Consul for the greater part of his life at the court of the Khan's sovereign lord and master. He had married a woman of the country, and so Lucy was half Oriental and half English. She had been sent to school in England, but it was only at her father's death, when she was eighteen years old, that she had first come to live in England with her native mother. And so it was that she had never quite lost the faint and not unpleasant trace of a foreign accent that was noticeable when she spoke English. It was not so pronounced as in the case of the Khan, and could even have been mistaken for a personal peculiarity of accent, merely. On arriving in London, Lucy had been taken by her mother to the Embassy of their country, where the Khan had been struck by her beauty and intelligence, and had invited her often to different réunions and soirées. It was at one of these she had met the strange woman that has already twice appeared in this story — the giant-like dancer of the reception at the Embassy some fortnight before, and the huge and muffled figure that Royal had conducted to the house of the three tall Americans. She had come under the influence of this woman in an extraordinary way, and it was through her that she had been drawn into the Khan's secret and disreputable operations. She had wanted very much to go on the stage, and had even made a promising start when the influence of this extraordinary country-woman of hers had directed her energies into another channel. She dreaded this woman above all other beings, she always felt as weak as a child in her presence. And the thing that she most feared in the present conjuncture, was that this woman would appear in the vicinity of Palm Lodge and would paralyse all effort in her by her presence, merely. She was very much in love with Fane, and resolved to escape once and for all with him from her present life. Probably of the three, she was the most eager about the escape, most eager for success, and to be gone forever and start a new life. But she was haunted by the thought of the Khan's power, of his wealth of resource, of his unscrupulousness if too much crossed. She feared above all for her lover. But she recognised that this was their only chance for starting a new life; she knew that by this theft or acceptance of a theft, and at their employer's expense — by this alone could they hope to pass the rest of their lives honestly.

One can imagine the conflict of her feelings when on the third day from the buying of the safe, she had to write a letter to the Khan denouncing Royal. This was a ruse — namely, to draw all suspicion away from her and Fane. It was Royal's suggestion. But she knew that the Khan on receipt of this, would take extraordinary precautions, would at once flood Liverpool with his spies and satellites; and what if this terrible woman came amongst them? Nevertheless, she wrote the letter. She said that from certain indications, she was of the belief that Royal did not intend to act loyally by the Khan. That she believed he had some plan of disappearing, at the last moment, with all the money himself.

She posted this letter so that the Khan should get it that evening.

Royal had not yet told her of the details of his plan. She supposed this was because Royal was always more or less of an improviser by choice, and had determined to make his plans at the last moment. Also he was no doubt waiting to see exactly how things were when the day came – how numerous their enemies would be, etc.

On the following morning, while Royal was sitting in the little room that he had fitted up on the same scale of dirt and disorder, and as nearly as possible to resemble the old room in Marbury Street, Cole rushed in. When we say 'Cole rushed in,' the reader will realise that a most unusual thing was happening. Cole had never before in his life 'rushed.' He came in squinting directly in Royal's face, then letting his eyes roll about the room, sometimes far from each other, sometimes extraordinarily near together, a stream of silent speech was evidently clamouring and raging within him, like a subterranean stream. His lips moved violently as though imitating noiselessly an activity within. He laid a trembling hand on Royal's chest. He was evidently excited to the last degree about something.

Royal did not know in the least what to do. He scolded him in the most approved Dukes manner. He soothed him; but all to no effect. Then Royal took down Cole's Meerschaum pipe from its place on the side of the chimney, filled it, and lighted it, and going up to the still tremulous individual in front of him, forced it into his mouth, as an indiarubber tit is thrust into the mouth of a baby when it is naughty or in any way disturbed. Cole resisted for a moment, then seized the pipe, and sucked away at it with little gasps, desperately. He swallowed so much smoke that he grew suddenly sick. This made him roll about on the floor, holding his stomach for a few minutes. Then at last he quieted down, and remained by the side of the fire for some time in a collapsed and nerveless state.

Royal's curiosity to discover the cause of all this emotion on Cole's part – Cole, always so much master of himself – was very keen. So he began to ply him with questions. What had happened? Was it in the cellar? What was it? Was it a ghost? What had he seen?

Cole made large and vague gestures in the air, gestures expressing vastness and nothing more; and his eyes almost met through his nose, so intense was his squint.

At last he uttered the following cryptic words:

'On my bed! On – '

And here he stopped, making gestures signifying vastness again. He seemed to wish to take Royal upstairs. So up they went together. Cole approached the door of his attic fearfully, then peeped in with an air of intense curiosity. But the next moment he turned back to Royal with the most miserable, puzzled and disappointed expression imaginable. Royal looked in over his shoulder, and saw nothing unusual on Cole's bed or anywhere else. But then, on looking again, Royal saw that although there was nothing there now, something had been there, for the counterpane was ruffled, and bore the deep impress of a human form. The pillow was squashed down in the middle, and the bed itself had a little hollow in the centre.

He could get nothing more out of Cole, whose sulkiness had become quite impenetrable.

What Royal gathered from all this was that Cole, on going up to his room, had found something strange, and, for him, startling, on his bed. Some person probably. Who could it be? And why was Cole's room chosen?

When Royal told Lucy of this extraordinary incident, she turned suddenly pale, but hazarded no opinion.

60

THE REASON OF COLE'S STRANGE BEHAVIOUR

That afternoon, just after lunch, while Mrs. Dukes and her secretary were in the study together, the butler came in and announced that a Mr. Siddon wished to see Mrs. Dukes. This Mr. Siddon was the stockbroker. Royal had not expected anything earlier than the fifth day in any case, and on that day had arranged to call at the broker's offices.

Mr. Siddon had come to ask Mrs. Dukes if, seeing he could not sell certain of the shares at all advantageously for the moment, he should not wait a little. In the meantime he brought her a very considerable sum of money emanating from part of the debentures that he had already disposed of. Mrs. Dukes told him to sell, not at any price, but at anything in reason.

'I don't want any more o' them things; I said to Mr. 'atchett only yesterday, I knew *they* wasn't any good. Can't think what my 'usband was about puttin' 'is money in things like that!'

The stockbroker withdrew, Mrs. Dukes telling him not to trouble to come round any more — that she'd come to *him* on the following day.

When he had gone, Royal looked doubtfully at the wall of the room. He always looked doubtfully at it now. He had spent many odd minutes lately in tapping and pressing it all over; also he had examined the walls in the large bedrooms. But no panel had swung back to reward his pains. It was still pure supposition on his part that there was a secret passage there.

That evening Lucy seemed to him rather strange and nervous. Royal had quite adopted the diet of an old lady, just as he had adopted the voice and clothes. Only an old lady with a huge appetite, of course. Every evening he consumed, before getting into bed, a cup of arrowroot. Mrs. Beechamp, that is the disguised Lucy, always brought this up from the lower regions, where she prepared it for him somewhere under the hall — in the kitchen, the servants' hall, or somewhere or other. Royal used alternately a second floor room and a first floor room to sleep in. On this particular evening Royal had chosen the second floor room. When Lucy came as usual into his bedroom, just before he was going to turn in, the glass of steaming arrowroot was not in her hand. When he asked her if he wasn't going to have any, she replied yes; that it was coming. Royal looked at her in surprise, and asked her why she hadn't fetched it. Had anything happened?

'No, nothing. Only I didn't want to go down there tonight, unless it were absolutely necessary.'

'Why not?' asked Royal.

'Has it occurred to you that my letter may have already sown this house with a fresh contingent of Raza Khan's spies?' she asked in her turn.

'I think it more than likely,' smiled Royal. 'But I don't follow you.'

He looked rather blank at this question of Lucy's. Why should this prevent her going downstairs?

'Well, there's one of the Khan's people that I'm mortally afraid of. It's no good denying it. It was she that made me become what I am. She has an enormous influence over me. I could hide nothing from her. The thought that she may be in the house at this moment, waiting to waylay me, terrifies me — terrifies me, Royal! She of course doesn't suspect me. But she would read me in a moment.' Lucy shuddered.

'Hush,' said Royal quickly. And a servant entered with the arrowroot. 'Go and look outside the door to see that she's not hanging about,' said Royal, sipping his arrowroot. 'I've locked all the doors in front, so that no one could use them as refuges if about to be surprised in eavesdropping.' Lucy looked and when she returned, Royal said, 'No one? that's all right. Well, do you really think that the Khan has dispatched a strong force to watch me? What sort of a woman is this?'

'A Mesopotamian woman, a giant-like – '

'Ah!' exclaimed Royal, his face lighting up darkly, set in a steady frown. 'I know her. Yes, I see. You don't want to meet her. But what kind of influence has she over you?'

Lucy made a vague gesture. 'She frightens me.'

'Well, you mustn't let her!' said Royal energetically. 'If she is really here, things look exciting. Why do you think she is here?'

'What do you think about Coles' fright this morning? It occurred to me he might have seen her. No ordinary being would excite Cole in that way.'

'You think she might have been lying down on Cole's bed – mistaken the room?'

They both seemed reflecting for some moments.

'Do you think then that the Khan would have me killed if I tried to make away with the money?' asked Royal.

Lucy shrugged her shoulders. 'You'd be of no more use to him once you'd proved yourself untrustworthy. I don't suppose that he's sentimental about you. Yes, I should think he'd tell them to kill you.'

Royal laughed at the coolness of this reasoning. 'You intend still to throw in your lot with me, I hope?' he asked.

'Oh yes,' said Lucy, 'I'm not afraid of them in that way. And I believe in you. I think that we will get away all right.'

Royal got up quickly and crossed over to the window, which he opened a little under the blind. He then walked slowly back, and cast himself yawning into an arm-chair. 'Well, I expect I'd better be getting into bed,' he said. He passed his hand over his forehead.

Suddenly he sprang up again, his forehead flushed, and his eyes wide open. He was now without his make-up, and each change of his face could be observed. He seized the cup out of which he had drunk the arrowroot, and sniffing it, put it quietly down. He bent over the table, and pulling out a drawer, chose a small key on a heavy bunch.

'Lucy, no time's to be lost! That stuff' — he pointed to the cup — 'was drugged. I may be bowled over by it at any moment. So listen carefully. Go downstairs and open my large black trunk. In the left hand corner amongst a lot of Mrs. Dukes' things, you will find a small leather case of mine. Bring it up, covered with something, one of her petticoats — it doesn't matter what. It isn't locked. If you find me already asleep, take the bottle with a rag tied round the stopper, mix five drops with a half tumbler of water, and pour it down my throat. Quick!'

Lucy was gone only a few minutes. When she came back Royal's eyes were very heavy, and he was leaning against the wall. But his teeth were set, and he was evidently struggling with the drug.

'Quick!' he hissed.

But before she could bring him the tumbler that she was preparing, he had fallen heavily to the floor. He was not yet quite unconscious, however. She ran to him, and holding his head up, poured down his throat the contents of the tumbler. In a few minutes he was violently sick. After that he mixed for himself — by this time the lethargy had passed — another drink from another bottle, and twenty minutes later he was once more himself, and staring fixedly at Lucy.

'A narcotic! And a strong one! What does that mean I wonder? Well, we shall see, p'raps, in the course of the night. You must go to bed, now, or they'll be getting suspicious. Your bedroom's on the third floor, isn't it? Lock your door, and don't answer to knocking on any account. Good-night.'

She left him without comment. It was useless to guess at the meaning of this drugged arrowroot. That would soon be seen perhaps, as Royal said.

'Go quietly, as though I were already asleep. If anyone asks you, say I'm already asleep.'

Royal blew out the light, and got into bed. It was by that time about eleven o'clock. He was now just as wide awake as the person who had put the drug in his drink had intended him to be asleep. And he lay there, listening to the successive strokes of the clock outside his room until half past twelve had sounded. Nothing happened for a few minutes, and then the door slowly opened and closed, and someone was in the room with him.

61
IN THE SECRET PASSAGE

There was no further sound for a few minutes. Royal could see a tall thin shadow near the door, and that was all. Then the shadow began to move quite noiselessly towards him.

Royal had assumed the set frowning dull look of a man in a heavy sleep. He knew what a sleep such as he was supposed to be in looked like, because he had, in the course of his career, drugged a good many people himself. He was lying slightly on one side, one arm thrown across his cheek, and his right hand grasping his revolver held under the pillow. His eyes were closed tight. He next became aware, through his closed eyelids, of a light playing on his face. Then it faded again.

He waited: a very small rustling sound came from the inner side of the room. Someone was feeling amongst Mrs. Dukes' discarded clothes. It was there that he had left the money that the broker had brought him that morning. A pause, and then the shadow moved towards the door again. It seemed to wait a longish time at the door, as though listening. Then the door opened and shut and Royal was alone.

He slipped instantly from his bed, revolver in hand, and hardly had the door closed before he was at it, listening just as the other figure had before him. He was now dressed in a man's shirt, trousers and socks — nothing more, and completely without make-up.

He opened the door softly, and, his revolver raised, stepped out. There was no one in sight. He stepped quietly along the passage and to the stair head, and saw disappearing immediately underneath him the shadow that had visited his room. Following quickly and silently, he saw it enter the 'state' bedroom, the large first floor bedroom that had been the 'master's.'

So soon as the shadow had quite disappeared through it, he came up to the door, and put his eye to the crack, just beneath one of its hinges.

Nothing appeared at first within. Then a tiny ray of blueish light, shed from a small portable electric lamp, showed a corner of the carpet rolled up, and a brown skinny hand pulling at a nail, which came slowly out of the floor. Then the light went out and there was once more complete darkness within the room. Then Royal distinctly heard a click.

Royal was about to enter the room, convinced that the secret of the passage in the wall was now his, when he sprang away suddenly towards the stairs, for he had become aware in that moment of a dark mass at his feet. He was almost sure that he had seen an arm moving towards him.

Levelling his revolver, he took from his pocket a small lamp, worked with a spring, very much like his visitor's, and flashed it on the thing that lay by the door. It was the figure of a man, apparently asleep. He approached, and, his revolver still directed at this head lying on the floor, discovered it to be the body of an Indian, or Asiatic of some sort — one of the Khan's spies, no doubt. He gave the body a kick. It showed no signs of life. Nevertheless it was gently breathing. 'Drugged' was Royal's comment. He then passed into the room, and going over to where he had seen the carpet turned up, rolled it back in his turn, and pulled at the nail. Flashing the narrow light around the panelled walls, there one of the panels stood open right enough. He flashed his light inside and on either hand of this opening, and found a fairly wide, thickly felted passage, about six feet high and leading along at the left to a door, the other way, following the whole length of the house, seemingly. He clambered in, and pulled the panel to behind him.

Royal sat there for a minute or two, his back against the wall, and then flashed his light along the passage again to the right. There, ten yards away, where a few minutes before there had been nothing, now lay, to all appearance, a human head, with the eyes fixed on him. The next moment Royal saw that there must be a trap door in the floor of the passage, and that this head had but just appeared at the surface. It was quite expressionless: indeed, it was the butler's head. It was as inscrutable as ever, and quite motionless. Royal's revolver covered it — and from his other hand the little ray of electric light just managed to illumine it.

'So you're there!' said Royal.

'Yes, I'm here. I'm all here, too. You can see only my head, but I've got the rest of my body with me too. It's underneath here.' And the impassible butler cast his eyes downwards to indicate where the rest of his body was to be found. 'Would you care to see it?'

'I must reflect a little,' replied Royal.

While Royal was looking at it, suddenly in a flash, the head disappeared. He now saw a black gap in the level felt, and a little door lying on the farther side. His light fixed on this aperture, and he began to creep towards it on his knees — both his hands occupied with light and weapon. He had nearly reached the opening when the butler's voice proceeded calmly from within.

'You needn't shoot the butler. What is a house without its butler? I merely got down into the hole again because your light dazzled me, and I thought I would stay here in the dark till you needed me. Shall I pop up again now for a bit?' All this was said in a very low, quite even voice.

'Yes, do,' answered Royal.

The head shot up before him again like an automatic figure, the expression as inscrutable as ever.

'What have you been up to down there?' Royal asked.

'I've been setting light to a gunpowder train, which will blow us all up within three minutes.'

'Tales like that won't affect my nerves, my friend. You'll find I'll shoot just as straight with 'em as without 'em. Put your hands over your head, or I'll blow your brains out!'

The butler's hands rose out of the depths, and remained, fingers extended over his head.

'Now show a little more of yourself!'

'That's easier said than done, without my hands to help me. But to please a gentleman, I'll do my best.'

And he dragged himself slowly up, step by step, evidently mounting a ladder on which he had been standing. Royal rose to his feet also as the other grew before him. At last they were standing face to face, the butler just on the edge of the pit from which he had issued. His elbows touched each side of the passage. He explained to Royal that his arms were getting tired, and that this was the only way he could keep them in that position.

But Royal also for some minutes now had realised that he could not keep his two arms up forever. And the moment he dropped the revolver arm or when it got tired and nerveless, he would no longer have a very great advantage over his enemy. He let the arm that held the light subside, and flashed the light upwards on the face in front of him. The rest of the man's figure remained in darkness.

Royal was debating as to what he should do next, when he saw a vague movement in the figure in front of him, and in the same moment he received a kick in the stomach, of such violence that he fell over backwards, his lamp, closing of itself, like an eyelid, leaving the passage in complete darkness. But in the same moment that everything rushed into darkness, and that he felt his head strike the soft felt of the passageway flooring, a terrific blow crashed down upon him, just missing his left side, and something snapped where the blow had fallen. He knew, he felt he had known almost before the blow had been struck, that it was a dagger. It had been broken on the felt. He still grasped his Browning revolver in his right hand, and as simultaneously with the blow, and the curse that leapt out with it, a body was flung upon his, he pressed the mouth of his weapon against it, and discharged three shots. It leapt up, and for a moment lying there in the dark, he felt as light as a feather, this sudden weight removed. Then the next moment the weight fell down upon him again, but dully, strengthlessly, a body only half its former weight. All this had passed in two or three seconds. And now he lay for a minute or two where he was, his revolver again against this body pressing on him.

Then he became aware of various secondary and unimportant sensations — among others that his left thigh had, pressed underneath it, a small hard object. He stretched out his arm, and carrying his hand to the place in question, found that it was his little electric lamp. He pressed the spring, and once more a slight ray shot up, making a round space of light overhead. He brought it down to investigate all these mysterious happenings of the last few minutes. He was not surprised to find the butler's head very close to his own, and this time almost unbelievably inscrutable and impassible — with the impassibility of death! There was no doubt about it. Three minutes earlier this man lived, and there was a chance, a very slight one — for while there's life there's hope! — that this inscrutable person would draw aside his mask, and reveal some of his secrets. But now his inscrutability had become quite permanent. Royal knew too well every shade of expression, and had practised dissimulation too often himself to be mistaken in such an expression as this face near his had taken on. This was Death's, that no man had ever succeeded in quite imitating.

Royal extricated himself from under his late butler's body, and going from pocket to pocket, searched for the money that had just been taken from his room. It had been a bulky parcel of bank notes, representing a vast sum. None of the butler's pockets were really big enough to have held the entire bundle.

Anyhow, it was *not* there. What had become of it?

62

LOCKED IN

Royal stepped over the dead butler, and flashed his little bullet lamp down the hole from which this mysterious personage had lately risen. It was a square-shaped narrow shaft, going down apparently to a considerable depth. One side of it was a ladder, descending perpendicularly.

Royal then proceeded, again crossing the butler's form, to the door at the end of the passage. On opening it, he found himself on the threshold of a small well-like room. Two steps led down into it. It was furnished in the style of a century and a half ago, and its old-time owners had left several vestiges of their proprietorship. There was an old faded court jacket, such as was worn with ruffles, and Royal noticed on picking it up, blood marks on the back, and a hole where a sword had entered. Royal examined this first of all, and then looked carefully round the room, appearing to take no notice of his pile of bank notes, which lay there before him on the table. He had seen at once that they were there, that they were safe. That was enough.

He judged that this was the uppermost portion of a large excrescence of the building, like the shaft of chimney, built out beyond the rest of the brickwork, on this side of the house. The lower portion was a linen closet or something. It had never occurred to him to question what this part, which reached up as far as the second storey, might be. A ladder was placed against the wall, and he then noticed an arrangement of rope and pulley, for opening a trap in the roof.

Royal now gathered his recovered riches together, and determining to come back here and explore further later on, made for the entrance. But arrived there it suddenly dawned on him that he had not the remotest idea how to get out again. He let his little lamp play all over the walls, floor and ceiling, but found nothing in the shape of a button, or rail or anything else that might make the panel open again. It was firmly fixed. After a quarter of an hour's search for the key to the mechanism of the panel, he went back into the room he had just left, laid down his parcel, and lighted a lamp fixed against the wall. Then, putting the money into a little cupboard and taking the key, as a measure of precaution, he set out to explore the rest of the passage-way, to see if he could find another exit.

The passage, making two detours, ran along the walls of all the rooms on the first floor of the house, terminating at the further end of the house with the study. There were several peep-holes contrived with great cunning into all the rooms it passed. At the extreme end a ladder led up to a passage-way over head, on the second floor, the same in every respect as that beneath, except that it had no room at the end, and of course no pit in the floor. There did not appear to be any exit upstairs at all, and nowhere did he see anything in the shape of a button, or contrivance for opening a panel. He now returned to the lower passage, and entered the shaft leading down into the depths of the house, if not of the earth. He went steadily on down, down, and at last found himself emerging in a vast vault-like cellar, that must have been several feet beneath the actual cellars of the house. There were three extra size, damp, arched compartments, but no sign anywhere of a further passage-way, a door or exit of any description. He got on to the ladder and began mounting again. He was half way up when turning his head instinctively, he found his eye almost level with a little grating in the wall, through which a certain amount of light was entering. Turning round altogether, Royal looked through the little grating, and his eyes at once fell on a most extraordinary scene. There, lying on camp beds beneath a swinging oil lamp, were four or five swarthy men, their hair jet black upon the white of their pillows. They all were strangely doubled up, all in the most uncomfortable attitudes. But perhaps what would be uncomfortable for Europeans would be the contrary for them. They were evidently of an Eastern race; this was a troupe of the Khan's countrymen, sent to mount guard over him, thought Royal. One, immediately beneath the eye-hole from which Royal was gazing, was lying without any movement, with his dark head thrown back, and the fiercest and strangest smile curling back his lips. So Lucy had been right, and no doubt the woman also was somewhere about. Then there was the man he had found drugged at the door of the great bedroom. He clambered up to the secret passage again, and after another half hour or so of futile poking and pressing in the neighbourhood of the panel through which he had entered, he returned once more to the small room where he had left his money, and stretching himself out on two chairs, was soon sound asleep. The trap in the roof of this room would, could he make a long enough rope, give him his liberty. But the Khan's spies were no doubt watching outside. And in any case, as he thought that probably these other enemies of his were not aware of the secret passage, he did not wish them to suspect its existence; he might wish to utilise it in his escape, in a day or two. Unfortunately all the rooms that these passages gave onto were unoccupied. Fane and Lucy had been given humbler rooms at the back, as they did not wish to attract attention to themselves by being too luxuriously lodged. There was nothing for Royal to do but wait till morning, and then see what could be done.

He was woken up by various dull sounds proceeding from the direction of the passage and house generally. Looking through the eye-hole into the study, he saw a servant dusting. It was still early then. He went back and dragged the body of the butler into the little room, and covered it up with the old laced and blood-stained coat of a former age. So another violent death had occurred in this no-man's-land, between the walls, to consort with this other tragedy, over a century old.

He had been defending his life when he had killed the man before him; and in pursuing him he had been pursuing a man who had just walked off with what he considered as his property. Anyhow, he'd worked harder for it than this other who had wanted to take it from him, thought Royal. Or perhaps he too had worked hard. No one would ever know. He had probably been down the shaft to see if the Khan's people were still asleep. Although his action, that of stealing the money, was plain enough, yet this butler was certainly a mysterious personage. Some weeks later, part of the veil was lifted for Royal. He learnt one or two facts about him.

On returning into the secret passage, he could hear sounds that denoted a very serious commotion in the interior of the house. Had his absence been discovered or only that of the butler? He could hear voices, hurrying about, but nothing definite. What would Lucy think when she found that he had disappeared? She would most certainly think something had befallen him, that he had been killed by the Khan's people, probably. Then what would she do? Would she lose her head? He had thoughts at one moment of breaking the panel open. After a half hour's waiting at the extremity of the passage in the wall, the study door opened and Lucy and Fane entered. Both of them looked very alarmed and they had evidently come here for a council of war.

'What do you think's become of him?' Fane was asking. 'It's terrible! You think they've killed him then?'

Lucy did not answer.

Then Royal called out clearly through the aperture, 'Lucy! Lucy! Come here close to the wall!'

On applying his eyes again to the hole, he found their two faces had changed as though by magic. Lucy came across the room hastily. 'Is that you, Evan?' she almost gasped.

'Yes. I'm safe and sound enough. Only I've been fool enough to shut myself up in this confounded secret passage, and can't get out. Have you told the servants that their mistress has disappeared?'

'No,' Lucy replied, 'but the butler's disappeared as well.'

'Yes. I know all about him. He also is quite safe! Go into the large state bedroom — the first, you know; lock the door behind you. Go to the farther corner, on this side, of course, pull up the carpet and tug for all you're worth at a nail you'll see rather more polished than the rest. Then I shall be free once more.'

Lucy did as she was ordered, and ten minutes later, having waited his chance till the servants were out of the way, Royal was in his room upstairs again. He put his recovered money on the table, and a little while afterwards used part of it as the hump at the top of his back, for impersonating Mrs. Dukes, and the rest to fill out other parts of his fictitious person.

But the first thing he noticed when he had a little settled down to ordinary life again, was the extraordinary pallor of Lucy — not caused certainly altogether by the alarm his disappearance had caused her. And then he remembered her fear of the night before, and pressed her for an account of her adventures.

63
THE KHAN'S FOLLOWERS MAKE UP THEIR MINDS TO ACT

'I have seen her!' said Lucy, and her eyes opened wide and startled, as though she were gazing upon 'her' again at that moment. 'She knocked at my door last night, and when she had said "it is I" I could not keep her locked out; she would have at once interpreted this as a defiance, and would have suspected something. She did not stay long, however. She just asked a few questions about you, and exhorted me to serve the Khan well. The Khan is terrestrial regent for some prophet or other, represents on earth some deity or other, and it is for that that all these people are so devoted to him. I managed I think not to show my emotion too much. The contact of my own people — that is, of my Eastern compatriots — is always invigorating for me. I feel calmer and more mistress of myself when I am with them. And that woman especially always has the effect of turning me into a stone, into a statue, like herself. I'm afraid there are lots of them here,' Lucy added.

'Yes, the place literally swarms with people sent to spy on me. He is determined, your Prince, not to lose his million. From one of those passages in the wall I saw, through an eyehole, half a dozen of your country people asleep — down in the basement there.'

'Then they set guards at night on all the landings,' went on Lucy, 'and this morning, before the servants were up, when they were supposed to return again to the basement, none of them turned up. It was then discovered that they had been

312

drugged. Your door was not locked, and it was soon discovered that you had disappeared. Later on the butler also was missed. It was supposed that you were accomplices, and that you had evaded them. But then those in the street outside had seen no one leave the house during the night. They didn't know what to think.'

Royal was now washed, fresh and ready once more to confront any situation the day might bring forth. He now turned to Lucy with the smile of a confident general on the eve of battle.

'Now, Lucy, my plan is this. It seems to me that the most important thing is that *I* should escape. I'm the person they're after. It seems even improbable that they should so much as suspect you. They might keep an eye on Fane. Well, then, I propose that once I have got all the money from the broker and the Bank of England – a hundred thousand of it is coming from there, you know; old Dukes had deposited exactly that amount in that very safe place – once I've got the money, I'll give you half. Then I'll make my escape. It's useless making plans beforehand. Besides, it's better fun to act on the spur of the moment. In the confusion my disappearance causes, you can make good *your* escape. Pretend even that you are going to join in the pursuit of *me;* or, better still, get them to tell you to go somewhere to mount guard, in a railway station or hotel – let it be them that suggest that you should go in pursuit. I expect tomorrow will be the day. Now go to your room, empty out what remains of your materials for your make-up, damage your paddings in some way. In any case, under some pretext go to the wig-maker's and get the requisite materials for the make-up of two old men; two rather washed-out old men, who've been drinking the waters of various baths and mineral springs for the last twenty years, and who in consequence have captured for themselves a kind of unhealthy, negative youthfulness. Two suits of quiet tweeds. Here, in this envelope, are my measurements, and Fane is about my size. But above all, make sure that you are not followed. Perhaps Fane had better go out just before in an opposite direction, and draw off our guards after him – or some of them. I've counted as many as seven men hanging about the street at one time or another of the day. Then get a room somewhere in the centre of the city. Leave the things – clothes, etc. – there; there we will meet after our escape.'

The hunt for the butler continued all that day. But suddenly, about six o'clock in the evening, it stopped abruptly. Royal was very puzzled by this cessation of anxiety and bustle. He could not guess what it might signify. They couldn't have found him. Or perhaps they had! At this thought he slipped into the large first floor bedroom, and, locking the door, pulled at the nail, and entered the secret passage. When he looked into the little room he found that the lamp had been re-lighted, and the body of the butler had disappeared. So his secret passage had been discovered! He then remembered that on entering the panel that night he had left the carpet rolled back. No doubt someone had noticed the nail head, and so chanced on the secret of the entrance.

While he was standing there, tapping on the table with his finger ends and gazing up at the trap in the roof – turning over in his mind its utilities as a means of escape – he heard a noise in the passage behind him, and then the clicking sound of the panel shutting again. He sprang back into the passage, but was just too late to prevent the panel closing to.

So there he was shut up again, for he had not discovered the whereabouts of the inside spring, by which the panel would reopen. But much more serious for him was the reflection as to what this signified. This was the first open act of hostility on the part of his watchers. The butler had undoubtedly been acting independently, had been 'on his own.' But this time the Khan's emissaries had taken a definite and explicit step. They were now convinced that he was no longer to be trusted; he was to be put out of way and made use of no longer. No doubt they intended, if this were the case, that he should die in these narrow passages. They would wait until he had fallen asleep, then enter and kill him. These reflections did not startle Royal in the least, for he was quite sure that he would get out again, and that pretty soon. He only went over the plans of his enemies, that this act of shutting him in seemed to make clear to him. They might by some means or other have learnt of the notice he had given at the Bank of England for the withdrawal of all the money lying there in Mrs. Dukes' name. Anyhow, they had evidently given up all hope of getting the money with his help. He had been judged as no longer trustworthy. They had a considerable respect for his various gifts; had it been a less resourceful and determined man than himself, they might have waited a little longer, sure of being able to close in on him and prevent him from getting away with the money at the last moment. But with Royal, they had concluded it was too risky to have him at large. So there he was, and there he must stay for the moment.

On going back to the little room and climbing up to the trap, he found it had been fastened, probably from above, and was no longer available as a means of escape.

On making a tour of the passages, he found that all the peep-holes had been fastened up. He could hear in a muffled way what was going on in the rooms on the side of the panelling, but could see nothing. Had he had his revolver with him he would have blown off the lock of the panel without more ado. As it was about eight o'clock, he resolved to make an onslaught on the panel leading into the large bedroom. Placing his two feet flat against the further wall, he tried to break open the panel with his back. But nothing yielded, and he thought that probably they had dragged a wardrobe or something against it.

No indication in any of the rooms behind whose wainscotting he listened that evening, told him anything of what had happened in his absence. With the idea that Lucy might get away from the others and bring him some message, if she guessed where he was, he remained near the study until after midnight. Then he went back to the little room, ever so carefully – for at each step he expected to feel the rush of an unseen murderer – and prepared for rest. He managed to barricade the door successfully, and to prevent the trap overhead being opened from the outside. Then he lay down, as the night before, on two chairs, and was soon asleep. Not so absolutely a prisoner as in the house of the three tall Americans, he was now in a much graver predicament.

64
HILLINGTON'S POSITIVELY LAST APPEARANCE

When Royal woke up he saw by the little watch he wore on his wrist that it was already half past nine. He opened the door very gingerly, and peered out, holding up a lighted match. There was no one in the passage. So he began the day he supposed he should be destined to spend like a rat or a mouse inside these walls. When he got level with the study, he heard a scratching sound inside: someone was writing with a quill pen. This could not be Fane, as Fane never used a quill. He had not long to wait to find out who it was. The door of the study was opened, and the voice of one of the maids announced Mr. Hatchett, who appeared simultaneously, it seemed, for the door at once closed again. The scratching stopped, and in its place his dear friend Hillington's voice could be heard.

'Ah, Mr. Hatchett, how do you do? I did not expect you so early. It was very good of you to come. My dear old friend needed me after all, you see. When she was laid up yesterday and felt she was going to die, as most old women do when they get a cold in the head, she sent at once for me. But seriously,' and his voice dropped to a grave concerned tone, 'she's not at *all* well. Her doctor, a very good general practitioner from London, who's attended her all her life, says that the excitement of the last few weeks and the sudden change of life have told on her severely. If there are no complications, of course — but then with old people one has to be precious careful.' The use of the word precious here was characteristic of Hillington.

'I sincerely hope that she will get over her indisposition,' came the measured voice of Mr. Hatchett.

Royal saw at once, as this dialogue proceeded, how things stood, what the Khan had decided to do. Fane no doubt was going to be requisitioned again, and he was going to leave all his money to Hillington; or, what was more likely, was going to call all Mrs. Dukes' money in, in an invalid's caprice, and then suddenly, everyone, servants, Hillington, Fane, money and all would vanish into the air, disappear as though by magic. He could even see how his own late methods would be utilised for this plan, and the sort of character he had lately read into Mrs. Dukes. This old woman, so miraculously left all this money, enjoying it only for a few weeks, and almost rendered mad by the possession of it, would, on her sudden deathbed, wish to see it all beneath her hands – handle it all before she was snatched away from it forever.

'Will you come with me into another room, Mr. Hatchett? I've fitted up a little room at the back as a study.'

And then Royal heard the solicitor's voice.

'Certainly. Can the patient see anybody – ?'

Ah, so no one's been shown the new Mrs. Dukes yet this morning, thought Royal. At the same moment he shouted shrilly against the wall.

'Oh, yew old rogue, 'illington! You wait till I get out. I'll 'ave you locked up! Don't you believe 'im, Mr. 'atchett. There ain't no Mrs. Dukes upstairs – she's locked up in 'ere. Yew come and let me out this instant – d'yew 'ear, 'illington?'

There was a moment's silence, and then Hillington's voice was heard earnestly protesting to the lawyer.

'Yes, Mr. Hatchett, I have deceived you! I was compelled to do so. The infirmity that has overtaken Mrs. Dukes is even of a more serious nature than we had agreed to give out. Mrs. Dukes – '

And then the voice grew fainter, and the two men had apparently passed out of the door, which closed softly. Royal could see in his mind's eye Hillington closing it slowly and gently, his eyes fixed on the lawyer the while, and talking with hushed volubility.

Royal had been silent for a time to listen for what effect his words might have on the two men within. The lawyer had said nothing. There was no indication to show how he had taken it. But when Royal realised that they were leaving the room together, he clamoured anew. He thought afterwards that perhaps it had been ill-advised to make so frantic a hubbub, as it might confirm what Hillington was trying to make the solicitor believe — namely, that his old friend Mrs. Dukes had gone mad.

Royal once more essayed to break down the panelling; he dashed himself against it at close quarters, but there was not room to take even the smallest of runs, of course. Then he tried as before, with his feet against the opposite wall. All to no avail. The walls were solidly built.

At any moment now the plotters within might bring off their 'coup.' He might even be left there to starve in an empty house, to be found eventually by the police, disguised and unable to account for himself. No, they would not leave him there, though, to betray their gang to the authorities. They would certainly dispatch him before leaving. This was his principal hope. To 'dispatch' him they must enter the passage, and then he trusted to his resourcefulness and to some happy chance to release him. The panel would be opened to admit of the entrance of his murderers. But at present, what would happen between the lawyer and Hillington? If Hatchett were pressing, all might be well yet. No doubt Fane had accepted the role of substitute rather than attract their suspicion to himself. Then Lucy would do her best, if she only guessed where he was all the time.

But the study door opened again, and again Hillington's voice was heard.

'Naturally, she got in there of her own accord, and wouldn't come out again when we called to her. Just like an animal when it gets frightened. The more we tried to coax her out the more terrified she became. I arrived last night. She had sent for me. And then her indisposition took this form. Her son Cole, you know, is not quite all there. It's in the family.'

Then Mr. Hatchett's voice rose, interrupting him.

'Mrs. Dukes, won't you come out since I'm here? I am Mr.

Hatchett, your solicitor, and you have nothing to fear from me.'

Royal at once replied. 'What's that nonsense 'illington's bin feedin' ye up with? I don't want to stop 'ere: it's 'e that put me in — the villain!' Then shrilly and angrily, ''illington, you wait till I get out! What do yew mean tellin' Mr. 'atchett all those lies? You wait till I get out! Mr. 'atchett, go into the big bedroom, *yew* know — the first one; I'll come along be'ind the wall and tell ye what to do to let me out!'

A quarter of an hour later Mrs. Dukes was once more standing in the light of day, and the solicitor was saying, 'I hope Mrs. Dukes, that this will convince you of what I suspected all along. Your friend Mr. Hillington is not to be trusted in any sense of the word. This last action of his is clearly criminal.'

Hillington had vanished utterly by this time. He had slipped away from the solicitor on some excuse or other, and was never seen again.

But now Royal's difficulties had only begun. He was once more free. But he was now in a very different position from what he had been prior to this little incident of the imprisonment in the secret passage. He was now in a house full of enemies. As soon as the solicitor's back was turned, as soon as the front door had closed on him, he would be shot at sight by any of the band of people, English or foreign, who now swarmed over the house. Neither Lucy nor Fane could raise a finger to help him, for to do so would be to betray themselves.

It was war to the death; but obviously, neither he nor his adversaries would invoke the aid of the law. It was an affair between themselves entirely. He had routed Hillington. This was the first move in this game, and he had won it. But there were many moves on both sides yet to come. To secure the rest of the money he must still play at being Mrs. Dukes, and re-main where he was. Yet to pass another night under this roof would be courting death. In this house, cut off from the world, with no interference from outside, with no appeal to anyone outside possible, this game was going to be played out to the finish. Naturally, people from outside could be utilised, as the solicitor had been utilised, to make 'moves' with, so to speak, so long as they were kept in perfect ignorance of the real nature of the case.

The immediate question and a most anxious one, was not to be left alone in the house with nothing but enemies. The two or three servants who did not belong to Raza Khan's contin-gent, had been sent away the evening before.

First of all, Royal ordered the carriage. Then he asked Mr. Hatchett to wait a little longer, as there were several things he wanted to discuss, and said he would drive him to his office. Mr. Hatchett consented. Royal then discussed with him a new investment he had heard about. He also asked him to send at once for the safe in the study. But in half an hour's time he was informed that the carriage had suddenly got out of order, and could not be utilised until it had passed a day or two at the coach builder's. He then sent Fane for a cab, and it was in this that he drove Mr. Hatchett to his office. He had taken Fane with him in it.

He then went to the stockbroker's. The broker himself was not there. He left a note that he had scribbled before leaving the house, asking him to come to Palm Lodge as soon as he returned, and bring the entire sum drawn out of the Bank of England, which no doubt he had received by this time, and as much more money as he had so far secured.

Royal's next visit was to a bureau for the supply of domestic servants. There, fortunately, he at once put his hand on a young footman, whom with whimsical imperiousness, in his best Dukes' manner, he carried off grinning with him in the cab. And then he made for Palm Lodge once more.

Had he returned unaccompanied, he knew that the hall door closing behind him would have been the signal for the attack. Even as things were, it was not at all sure what might not happen. But he thought it likely that they would not, unless they could help it, murder a stranger. They would trust to some other opportunity turning up later on, till the night, for instance. Still, as he mounted the steps of Palm Lodge, he knew he was carrying his life in his hands. It was not absolutely necessary to come back to this house. He could have got the money and made a run for it without ever coming back at all. But the thought of the real uncompromising danger to be found there, that pervaded it, like a heavy atmosphere, that seemed to gleam and glower from the windows, drew him back into it. And then it was a point of honour. He was determined to worst these people in style, superbly.

65
THE FURIES LOOSED

Royal was right in his surmise that the presence of the young footman would give him immunity for the moment. The Actor-Gang were rather like certain populations where stabbing is very prevalent — such as in most parts of Italy. The members of these communities cut each other's throats as a matter of course, but seldom attack a stranger. One of the most remarkable things about the Khan's sinister organisation was that human life was always respected — or rather very little respected — as they would play any tricks with it to arrive at their ends, but it was seldom a 'patient' died on their hands. Royal had never known them kill one of their victims. Even as to killing amongst themselves, he had considered the killing of the Americans a great change and progress in the direction of ferocity and 'going the whole hog.' He had heard once before of a faithless member coming to a strange end, but that was all. But this time with him there was no mistaking indications. Also he read these indications with more certainty, as he had the case of the three tall Americans as a precedent in his mind.

Sure as he was that nothing would happen at once, as he entered the hall door he grasped his revolver tightly inside the muff he was carrying.

But nothing happened. A dark, sleek, silent man-servant in a suit of the late butler's opened the door. The thing that struck him most was the silence that had descended over the whole house. There were none of the vague muffled sounds of servants moving about upstairs, and an occasional call, or medley of distant sounds from beneath. Everyone was waiting hidden, somewhere, for *him*.

The butler was by no means so inscrutable as his predecessor, and he had an evil face of ill-omen.

The footman naturally expected to be handed over to some sort of head of the staff of servants, and to be put through his paces, scrutinised in the servants' hall, expected to find out if there were any housemaid who would answer the purpose of his ardent youth, or whether he would be forced to find a sweetheart without the walls of his new home. These were the thoughts that filled the footman's head, and this was what he expected would become of him, now that their destination was reached. He looked enquiringly at Royal. He had still worn the grin that had appeared on his face on being carried off at once in that eccentric manner from the office. But it faded now, and when Mrs. Dukes told him to follow her upstairs, the deserted air of everything around him, the solitary and 'hang-dog' looking domestic, as he termed it, in the hall, all contributed to make him strangely uneasy. The silence and strangeness, the oppression of the house, was also felt by him; he could not explain his feelings, and so he grew uneasy, and at length almost alarmed.

He was a robust fresh-coloured young countryman of about twenty years old, with a not unintelligent face. Royal took him upstairs to the study, and telling him to sit down and wait a little, as he had some letters he wanted him to take to the post, began scribbling away at the table with the quill pen.

A quarter of an hour passed in this way, and the young footman became fidgetty. At the end of half an hour he spoke.

'Excuse me, mum, but 'adn't I better go down stairs and see about my box bein' brought, and — well — get a little straight like?'

'No, just yew wait there a moment longer. I shan't be many minutes now. These letters is very pertickeler,' and Mrs. Dukes again bent over her writing.

At last Mr. Siddon came. His manner was a little awkward. He suspected nothing, of course, but his client's haste seemed strange. Still, it was her own money. He had brought nearly the total amount.

Royal asked the footman to go and wait on the landing, and said he would call him in a moment. The business was soon over with the stockbroker. Royal told him to bring what remained in a couple of days time.

Royal accompanied him to the door, and telling the young man outside to wait a moment longer, shut the door again. Then rapidly he disposed of the piles of notes all over his person — in inner pockets specially made, some in a little bag round his neck, etc. He did all this in a part of the room where he could not be seen from the secret passage.

On calling in the footman, he found the young man's face very cloudy, and read a considerable determination in his eyes. He did not take the seat Royal pointed to, but stood, flushed, before the table.

'You'll excuse me, mum,' he said, 'but, thinkin' it over, I think I'd rather not stay. I don't mean — no offence.'

'What! Want to go! Why, yew've only just come!' exclaimed Mrs. Dukes.

'Yes, but you'll excuse me, mum; I'd rather.'

'Why, good gracious! What hever's come over yew, boy? Did anyone speak to yew out there while you was waitin'?'

He remained embarrassed a moment, and then spoke.

'I saw enough; that fixed me. One of 'em, a little dark feller, a nigger, showed me a knife, and went like this with it,' and the young footman drew his hand across his throat. 'You'll excuse me, I don't mean — no offence. But I'd rather not stop, if you don't mind.'

This young man had evidently made up his mind to go! And yet, if Royal *let* him go, what would happen? But it wasn't anyway a matter of *letting*. Royal knew, he saw in the young fellow's eyes, which were serious, scared and determined all together, that he would leave the house at once, whatever he said to him. To bully him would only give him a pretext for going away brusquely, for he was not by any means a 'soft' young man. To beg him to stay would be to alarm him still more. No. Well then, he must go. Then Royal must go with him. He had wanted to stay a little longer, and leave word with Fane or Lucy. He had promised to hand over half the sum to them, and he wished to keep his promise. Besides, he must find out the place of meeting. It was entirely beneath his dignity to be hurried, to be forced to give the money later, instead of at once, as he had promised. It was still more beneath his dignity to run away with all the money, and from fear of Raza Khan's people, leave his friends in the lurch — undecided, and not knowing what to do, whether to run after him or not. He had told them to place themselves in his hands. It was his logical conviction that they could do so with safety. And he must not fail them.

He went to the door and called out, 'Mr. Fane, Mr. Fane!' Fane appeared at the stair-head, very white, and came into the study quietly.

'Very well, young man, yew can go,' Royal said to the footman. Fane took a step forward as though to stop him, and looked at Royal with eyes of the most utter alarm. The young footman stopped for a moment. But Royal said sharply, 'Well?' and the young man, who had hesitated at Fane's gesture, then left the room.

'Don't you know?' gasped Fane.

'Yes, of course. Don't worry about that. Here's the money,' and he handed Fane two flat packets.

'But, good God! Man, I can't take them now!'

'Stuff them in your pockets. What's the address — the house where we're to meet?'

'Here it is,' and Fane passed him a piece of paper, tearing it in his haste, as he snatched it out of his pocket.

They were standing in the embrasure of the window, and speaking very low, Fane in a sort of hoarse, excited whisper.

Then the front door banged: the footman had gone! And Fane, as he realised what that meant, stood staring at his friend in horror.

'We'll meet there, then, in an hour or two,' said Royal easily.

There was a sound of many feet on the stairs, and Royal

sprang towards the door and slammed it to. As he turned the key in the lock, it shook on its hinges. It seemed as though four strong men all together had hurled themselves on it from without.

66
MRS. DUKES IS TAKEN AWAY

Royal stood quietly by the door, while time after time it seemed as though it must give way. A kind of low, excited chattering was kept up outside. Suddenly it stopped, and the rushes at the door were abandoned at the same time. Royal still stood with his eyes on the door, and his revolver ready, supposing this silence meant that something new was going to be tried. But hardly had the noise ceased on the other side of the door, when he heard Fane behind him utter a cry of warning, and swinging round found a panel open in the wall. These panels were opened from the little room at the far end of the passage, Royal supposed. Fane had sprung towards it, and had his face at the opening. Then he slammed it violently to. He ran towards Royal. His face was ashen white and he could hardly speak. 'That woman! I saw her eyes! Quick! Quick!' At the same time they heard a kind of rushing within the wall, and a deep voice bellowing in a tongue neither of them understood. 'They're coming back that way,' whispered Fane, pointing to the door. But Royal had already turned the key and sprung out on to the landing. Fane heard two revolver shots almost like one, so near were they together, and on reaching the door he saw an Indian sprawled out on the stairs halfway up, and Royal nowhere to be seen. Then one after the other, a dozen men issued from the passage in front, and in their turn dashed up the stairs. The whole band seemed to have gone in a moment, and in their midst was the giant-like woman, her lips drawn back and her teeth showing like an angry beast. Most of the men with her were Orientals – some three or four only being evidently Englishmen. A clamour of voices came down from the upper landing, and furious blows on a door.

Fane had opened the window a few minutes earlier, as though for Royal's escape. Now he heard a sound from that direction, and found Royal standing on the sill, and pulling in a considerable length of rope. The next moment he slid to the ground, still in every point Mrs. Dukes, as to his make-up, and called to Fane sharply, 'Close the door.' Fane did so, and Royal deposited the coil of rope behind the curtains. Then he gazed round, putting the bonnet straight that had become slightly askew in his descent.

At this moment there was a crash overhead, and a rush of feet, then a silence. The next moment again burst out a babble of voices, and someone was heard calling out something on the stairs.

Royal had dashed across the room to the enormous green safe that was standing on the floor, and, turning the key, had swung open the heavy door and crept in. 'Lock me in, quick, and tie the key underneath – on the inside of the grating – afterwards, when you're alone. Lock it now. No, it's all right – plenty of air comes through,' he said, indicating the key-hole, which in this antedeluvian safe was as open as that of a bed-room door.

Fane turned the key, and, taking some string from the table, tied it on, as Royal had told him. It was standing on two pieces of wood, and he could just get his fingers underneath enough to fasten the key out of sight.

In the meantime there was a complete silence outside on the landing and upstairs as well. Fane was as uncomfortably impressed by this as by the noise that had preceded it. What if they should crowd in here suddenly, and find him standing by the side of the safe? They would guess at once. They would look for the key, and one of those little Indians would see suddenly where it was tied. He would pounce on it, and Royal would be murdered there before his eyes, like a rat in a trap.

This scene flashed through his mind in a second of time, and the next moment he had moved to the other side of the room, and was staring out of one of the study windows that faced the roadway. A few seconds only had passed from the time he had been bending down and attaching the key to the safe. The silence continued ominously within the house. Then suddenly there was a prolonged knocking at the front door — four or five raps — as though someone were knocking who had already knocked several times.

Fane thought he heard a whispering outside on the landing now. At the same time he saw the back of a little van drawn up in front of the house.

Going quickly over to the door, he found, on opening it, two or three of the Khan's countrymen standing impassibly together, their arms folded, and near the stair head the improvised butler struggling into a black coat.

One of the group of three on noticing him smiled civilly, and coming over to him, spoke in a whisper.

'He has got away, and now there is somebody at the door. Wait and see who 'tis.' And still with his brilliant smile, he put his finger up to his lips, and said in a pretty affectation of Europeanism, 'S-sh!' The other arm, still folded across his breast, terminated in a skinny hand holding a dagger clasped to his right side.

Voices rose from the hall beneath, a matter-of-fact, heavy, obviously civil one saying, 'Yes, *that's* right. A safe. Lady give the order that it should be fetched, for Truman and Hatchett.'

'All right, wait a moment, will ye?' replied the butler, and he appeared the next moment, rather put out evidently, and asked the other men standing near Fane where the lady was.

Then Fane saw for the third time that day the gigantic woman from whom all these men took their orders. She appeared on the opposite side of the landing. 'Yes, it's all right, there's nothing in it. I looked,' she said, and turned back again.

Then the butler went half way down the stairs, and called out, 'All right, you can come up and fetch it.'

The Khan's followers disappeared in the same direction their huge leader had taken. Then workmen arrived, and walked round about the safe for several minutes, as though it had been a dangerous beast that they were afraid of attacking at once. They spat on their hands and speculated on its weight. At last they got hold of it, and despite their pessimistic remarks of a few minutes before, seemed surprised at its heaviness.

'It ain't 'arf 'eavy, guv'nor!' said one of them to Fane.

'Yes, I expect it is,' he answered. 'How are you going to get it down?'

The workman explained the process: boards and rope; on the level ground they could carry it — not far, though!

The butler came in to watch operations.

'Whad's this, Bill?' asked one of them, who had come upon the key tied underneath the bottom. He asked his comrade as though it were a problem that it would require their united brain power to solve — Bill's and his.

'Dunno,' said Bill.

'Why, it's the key!' the first man said, astonished.

The butler stepped forward and seemed about to say something, but then changed his mind. This had only interested him for a moment. This was a proof that there was nothing inside, for otherwise the key would not have been left there.

Fane guessed something of this reasoning in the butler's mind, and breathed freely again.

About a quarter of an hour later, the safe was outside on the pavement, yet another five minutes and it was in the van, and then the great front door had closed, the terrible occupants of Palm Lodge no longer interested in it, and it was soon on its way to the solicitors.

67
THE FIRM OF TRUMAN AND HATCHETT PETRIFIED

When the respectable firm of Truman and Hatchett — that is the two Mr. Trumans, and the two Mr. Hatchett — returned from lunch an hour or two later, they found in the centre of their private office a very large green safe. They were at once struck by its unusual size and extreme antiquity, and it was only when one of the Mr. Trumans — not the gouty one — had approached a little nearer to it, that he heard a steady and lugubrious sound issuing apparently from within it.

Mr. Hatchett — the shrewd partner, he who was always sent forth if any particularly knotty question had to be tackled — had been telling them of the occurrences of the morning, at Palm Lodge, and had wound up with the following expression of opinion: 'I do believe that the poor old woman was positively afraid to stay in the house alone; she drove me here simply because she did not want to be left alone. That rascal Hillington perhaps is still on the premises somewhere. It's very strange, all that affair.'

'Very strange,' echoed the gouty member musingly.

'Do you know it's my opinion,' said Mr. Hatchett suddenly, 'that there's something after all in what the papers were saying a few weeks ago about Mrs. Dukes and that house in Marbury Street. Only now the mystery has moved here to Palm Lodge!'

This statement, backed with all the weight and authority of the more acute of the Mr. Hatchetts, caused the other three members to open their eyes wide, and a thrill shot agreeably down the spine and principal arteries of the bodies of all of them.

'Do you think so, Jim?' asked his brother with a half idiotic stare.

Mr. Hatchett, the recognised brain of the firm, was for the other three the only romantic man amongst them. They could have imagined each other as figuring in one of the detective stories they lost themselves in every night, but only as incidental characters. The gouty member would be just a gouty person that came in casually into some story, as the world is made up of all sorts, and a certain percentage are gouty. He indeed would represent Gout, and no doubt very honourably. But nothing more. And so with his two companions. But this fourth one, Mr. Hatchett junior, was a different spirit. Sherlock Holmes, for them the most romantic character in fiction, might have looked like him! As we spoke of a man as representing a class or an abstract idea, such as the idea of gout – we would say that this Mr. Hatchett appeared to them evidently of the class of heroes, the class of heroes of novels. Certainly he would not make the hero of a love story. But there are heroes and heroes. He had in his veins, yes that was it indubitably, the blood of the great race of amateur-detective-heroes. There was something vague, sensational, and romantic about him for his co-partners. There was something of the felicity of touch in the texture and form of his character that awoke their admiration in the many heroes of the detective type that had successively enthralled them.

When Mr. Truman first became aware of the unusual sound proceeding from the safe he remained quite still to listen the better. The conviction then grew on him stronger at each moment, that he was listening to a man snoring, and that this was the sound that, for some reason or other, appeared to be coming from the old green safe. One by one the other members became aware of the sound also, and stopped moving about or talking, and remained quite still to listen. In a minute or two they were all grouped in front of the safe, listening spellbound to the rhythmic snorting and grunting that came softly muffled to their ears.

At last Mr. Hatchett — the young, the penetrating one — went up to the safe, and rapped on it loudly. The snoring stopped, and then for a minute a pin dropping would have positively startled the rigidly grouped firm.

'Where's the key, I wonder?' asked Mr. Truman at length. One of the clerks was called, and informed them that it was tied on to the bottom somewhere. Mr. Hatchett found it at once, cut the string, and with a fearless gesture, turning the key in the lock, flung the door open. The firm stood petrified. For there, into the midst of them, sprang Mrs. Dukes, adjusting her bonnet, but as cool as a cucumber.

'I'm sure I'm very sorry, Mr. 'atchett, to give you a start like that. But it's because of that 'illington. I wish I'd never seen the man. 'E seems to have gone cracked lately, that 'e do! 'E came back when you'd gone, Mr. 'atchett, and was in such a tearin' passion as you never saw. I 'ad to get into that' — she pointed to the safe — 'to get out of 'is stormin' truklent way. I'm goin' to the police. I've 'ad enough of 'is menace. *Menace,* that's what *that* was! But I'll 'ave 'im locked up!'

The firm got out of their petrified attitudes, and assumed each his particular professional manner, frowning slightly at having been taken off their guard. No amount of consumption of detective stories could teach them to be prepared for surprises of this sort.

Mrs. Dukes then informed them that she was in a great hurry, and must bid them good-day, but that she would come to talk over with them some acquisitions of property she had in view, on the following morning.

She was just leaving them — for they had found their customary attitudes but not yet their tongues — when six significant eyes fixed themselves on Mr. Hatchett. It was an occasion for him, evidently, and for him alone. He stepped forward to Mrs. Dukes' side, and spoke to her with an air of quiet comprehension.

'I'm afraid, Mrs. Dukes, that all is not going on very well at Palm Lodge. If we can be of any service to you, you know, Mrs. Dukes, that's what we're here for. Should you not wish to take police court proceedings, for reasons of an intimate character, you could place the matter in our hands. I was afraid this morning —'

'Yes, *there* was a pretty thing to lock me up like that, and say I'd gone orf me 'ead. Did yew ever! No. Mr. 'illington's a wastrel, a wicked wastrel. But I won't 'ave 'im near me any more. Well, I must go now, Mr. 'atchett. I'll drive down tomorrow.'

With a few more sighs and indignant apostrophies, Mrs. Dukes was gone.

At the end of the road Royal took the paper Fane had given him from his pocket, and hailed a distant cab. He was soon at the door of the house whose address the paper bore.

68

FANE BEGINS HIS ESCAPE

When Fane had seen Royal escape in the way just related, his first thought was to escape now himself with Lucy. So far he had escaped notice more or less, but at any moment the Khan's people might grow suspicious, and then they would undoubtedly give him short shrift.

He found Lucy sitting alone in the small room that we have already mentioned, fitted up with becoming dirtiness to please Cole. She had sat there ever since Royal had returned with the young footman. She had thought then that nothing could save him – that he had returned to a certain death – and paralysed by the presence of the giant-like woman who had such a terrible influence over her, she had sat there despondently awaiting the news that Royal had been 'settled.' She had not sufficient energy left to try and help him in any way. Besides she knew that it would be useless. When she heard her countryman's excited voice saying, 'The young man, the new servant he brought with him, is leaving!' she literally stopped up her ears. It was only a matter of seconds now, she felt.

Then she learnt from two men who slipped into the room to wait, that Royal had disappeared somehow; he had not left the house, they said, but was nowhere to be found. They supposed that there were other secret passages of whose secret they were ignorant as yet.

She shook off her torpor at this, and resolved to go and join the hunt herself, and if possible help him. But she, like the others, found no trace of the fugitive. Then she returned to the little room again.

Here Fane found her, and in a few whispered words, told her what had happened, and patting his pockets, informed her that

Royal had given him the money. She woke up to a kind of new and frantic energy at this. She hastily arranged herself in front of the glass, disposing of her charwoman make-up, and becoming again the beautiful young woman she was in reality.

'What things did you bring with you?' she asked Fane.

'Nothing much; a few shirts and a few books and things in my little bag.'

'Well, go upstairs and destroy everything – markings on shirts, your name on books and so on by which, if the police find your things here you could be traced – and then get out of the house as soon as you can. Take this revolver,' she said, handing him a Browning she had taken from a drawer. 'Defend yourself if necessary, but don't, above everything, attract the attention of the police. You will probably be followed if they see you going out. Before approaching our place of rendezvous make certain, absolutely certain, that no one is on your track or anywhere in sight even. They suspect you now. I know because I heard them talking a little time back. If when you come downstairs anyone tries to prevent you from going out at the front door, shoot him and make a dash for it. Those, petit Hercules, are your orders,' she said, smiling rather faintly; then she threw her arms round his neck and with tears rolling down her cheeks she kissed him silently. And he left her there also without saying anything more. There was nothing more to be said until they should meet again, if they were fated to do so ever.

Fane locked himself in his room, and made a little bonfire of several things that might have been traced to him. Then his hands in his pockets, and his revolver ready, he went downstairs. Two of the Khan's Indian bodyguards – tall hill-men, with whom he had talked a little that morning – watched him silently. He walked downstairs as unconcernedly as he was able, but the sensation that these two men were behind him with their knives made his movements perhaps a little awkward and oblique. He found no one in the hall, and left the house unmolested.

When Fane had gone the length of two short streets, he was quite certain that he was being followed. So it was useless to go straight towards the place of rendezvous.

As he felt rather hungry he turned into a comfortable looking foreign restaurant, and ordered a substantial lunch. Before settling down to this, he went into the lavatory at the back to wash his hands, which, after his rapid turning out of his things in his bedroom he had not had time to do. His hands were already immersed in the water of the basin when a man appeared at the door, and entering, lolled against the wall behind him as though waiting his turn at the basin, of which the lavatory only boasted one. Fane kept his eyes fixed on this man in the glass in front of him, and proceeded in a leisurely way to make his toilet.

He was moved all of a sudden to address him.

'I'm sorry to keep you waiting.'

'Oh, don't mention it,' replied the other readily. 'I've plenty of time.' He was a tallish man with a sandy beard and the air of a man who had always been in the habit of having large sweeps of time at his disposal, and who regarded ten minutes spent in watching another man go through his ablutions as a mere bagatelle.

'Take your time, guv'nor,' he added indulgently.

'Fine weather, isn't it?' said Fane. It was as a matter of fact the most detestable day imaginable — muggy, wet under foot, foggy and sunless.

The stranger did not hasten to respond to this remark by any means. He was not the man to answer a curt 'yes' to such an interesting observation. Nor would he answer in the same hackneyed phrase. He wanted to find the exact shade of expression that would convey *his* idea of this absorbing question. He was one of those men who try to make the weather interesting; who put a new life, a fresh energy and subtlety of distinction into the most ordinary topics and themes. He was just beginning to answer Fane's observation when the latter left the lavatory.

Not long afterwards the strange man came back into the restaurant, and establishing himself at a neighbouring table to Fane's, said, grinding the boney part of his palms together with a rotary movement: 'Yes, it isn't too *hot,* and yet it ain't too cold like, either!'

On several occasions they spoke again in the course of the meal, chiefly between the courses. They kept firmly level with each other, and at the end of lunch were both emptying their coffee cups at about the same rate.

When the time came to pay, Fane with a rush suddenly remembered that he had no small money except a few pennies in his pocket, and the two bundles of bank notes were probably for very large sums. He sent every week five of his six guineas of salary to the Post Office Savings Bank, and only kept one. And this was the end of the week.

He only thought of all this when the waiter brought him the bill, and was waiting at his elbow to be paid. He looked at the man at the other table with whom he had been conversing intermittently, and found this individual staring at *him,* evidently very interested in his embarrassment. He went on looking in front of him, and the waiter after a time discontentedly withdrew.

Fane pulled out one of the envelopes from his side pocket, and glancing through the notes found them all for hundreds and tens of hundreds, fifty appearing to be the least. Then it occurred to him with a shock almost of terror that in changing one of those notes he was forging the first link of a future chain of evidence against himself.

He noticed through the confusion of his alarmed perplexity that the man at the next table was still observing him, and then he became aware of the fact that this inquisitive person was straining his neck to see what he was doing – for Fane held the packet of notes beneath the table. He then examined the other packet, and found a postal order for ten shillings, and another for seven and six. This would do. He must use this money now if he was traced by it afterwards or not. He supposed the rest could be changed in the course of the next few days by Royal – who understood all these things better than he did; he would disguise himself probably.

He put the postal order down on the table and asked the waiter if he could change it. This man looked at him and at it very distrustfully. Foreign restaurants do not open their arms joyfully to receive postal orders. But Fane, a novice in the ways of vice, felt a chill run down his back at the distrustful look, and although he was sure that the waiter could not have any reason for suspicion, yet his distrustful look froze his blood. He already felt a panic. The proprietor came up and stood on his heels, and then on his toes, and said that they did not change postal orders.

'Well, you'll have to change that one,' said Fane in desperation, 'for it's all the money I've got.'

The man at the other table, however, intervened. 'For how much is it?' said he. 'P'raps I can oblige you.'

'Ten shillings,' said the restaurant keeper with alacrity.

'Oh, I don't mind changin' ye that,' he said. 'Let's have a look at it.'

The smiling Frenchman handed it to him. It was made payable to Mr. Siddon. Now Fane did not know who Mr. Siddon was, but the man who was now looking at it did. He knew that he was a well-known Liverpool broker.

But while Fane was looking at him, three things suddenly became apparent to him, in such rapid succession that hardly a couple of seconds elapsed between the discovery of the first, and the discovery of the third.

First he thought he had seen the heavy green overcoat the man was wearing before; secondly, he remembered that it had been the first butler's at Palm Lodge; and thirdly he realized with a start that this must be one of the Khan's men. He had not seen him among those who had followed him, and from whom he had taken refuge temporarily in this restaurant. But he had no doubt now, not an atom, that this was one of their comrades. The next question was this; had he seen that he, Fane, was handling bank notes under the table? If so he would at once guess his complicity with Royal, and not only that, would know that he probably had a large sum of stolen money on his person. Could he tell anything from the postal order? The question was startlingly answered at this moment by the man himself.

'It's made out to Mr. Siddon — that's the stockbroker. I know 'im well. He does business for old Mrs. Dukes, Artie Dukes' widow, you know.'

This was addressed partly to the restaurateur, partly to Fane. Well, there was no doubt about it now. He was in for it. Now that they *knew,* practically, that he had played the Khan false and that probably a large portion of the money stolen by Royal was actually in his, Fane's, pockets — perhaps *all* — they would not be likely to let him get away from them.

His lunch was over, and he sat there feeling very blank, miserable and desperate. He had no desire to sally forth again into the street.

69
CHECKED OUT

Fane sat there staring towards the door of the restaurant trying to form some plans. He felt miserably unresourceful. Also he felt the eyes of his neighbour fixed on him. This man was no doubt summing him up, and reading his perplexity and weakness in his face.

'Do you know Mr. Siddon, sir?' It was the voice of this man that had addressed him, whose whole person, voice and all, was an object of loathing to him.

'No,' he answered shortly.

'Well — h'm — excuse me, sir, but 'ow did you come by this? No offence, you know, only as I've changed it, it's only reg'lar — '

Fane sprang up from his chair, and, seized with a sudden fury, shouted at the man, 'Damn you, if you didn't want to change it, what did you offer to for? Give it back! Give it me back, do you hear?'

Fane's violence was such that the man seemed at once startled and cowed and backed to the farther side of the table.

'All right, guv'nor, there's no need to get excited,' he muttered sulkily. 'Can't I ask the question?'

The restaurant people had come forward in an alarmed manner, and again looked at Fane with suspicion, this time largely augmented by dislike. The man who had changed the P.O. now got up and went to the door. He left it open, however, and Fane could see two heads — his and another man's, close together. He came back and sat down at his table, paying his own bill of fare with a half sovereign, and casting sidelong glances at Fane.

The waiter came up and jerked the chairs back into position noisily, flicked a few imaginary crumbs off the edge of Fane's table, and did one or two other things waiters do when they think that a customer is abusing their hospitality and that it was time he left.

'What are you doing that for?' asked Fane quietly but chillingly. The waiter said nothing, but went away with an exasperated expression.

Fane thought, thought, thought. What was to be done? There were half a dozen practised criminals, desperadoes, lying in wait for him. He was like a child to them. They knew every trick of rascaldom, and would stick at nothing.

He shook himself vigorously. Bah! that wasn't the way to face them! He must go through with this now. They couldn't attack him in the open street, or rather they could, but still the chances were not all on their side. The first thing to be done however, was to get these packets into a safer place. In his pocket where they now were they could be snatched at; he could never go out with them there. He got up and once more walked towards the little dressingroom at the back of the restaurant. But at the same time his neighbour rose, and he saw in the mirrors he was following him. Also he saw him slip a coin into the waiter's hand.

Fane entered the lavatory, and shut the door sharply, bolting it behind him. The next moment the handle was shaken and the other man's voice was saying, 'Tut! he's locked it.'

'Vat, locked eet?' The waiter's voice asked, and a rude shake was given to it, this time an authoritative one. 'Open zee door, please!' Fane did not answer. 'Open zee door,' a violent rattling and shaking of the lock. 'Do you hear? Open zee door!'

The tip that the other man had given the waiter was having its full effect; and much more easily since the restaurant people were themselves not best pleased with Fane, and once the staff and patron of a French restaurant begin to dislike you, their dislike does not remain stationary; it grows steadily while you remain there, whatever you do to appease or increase it. Besides, this was an outrage. A man who had already given so much trouble, and already used the place once, goes and shuts himself into the lavabo. It was a little three-cornered cupboard under the stairs, in which they had placed a table, a basin and water, a looking-glass and a comb and brush.

What might he be doing in there? Committing suicide perhaps. For he was evidently a man of no tact or delicacy of feeling.

'Open − zee − door; I say open zee door. My God, open − zee − ' The waiter's voice got angrier and angrier, and now the thicker oilier voice of the master of the restaurant joined his; the door was shaken thrice imperiously, and then, 'Now, no nonsense; open zee door. I fetch policeman! Open!'

'Very well, as soon as I've dried my hands. What are you making such a noise about?' replied Fane.

Fane, within, was frantically trying to get his packets of notes concealed before their impatience definitely boiled over. He folded and refolded them till they formed as small and bullet-like a parcel as possible, and then, taking his shirt together at the left side, level with his ribs, tied it tightly with a piece of string where it was gathered together in his hand, tying the bundle of notes into it, so to speak.

Then he opened the door, and received the full force of the combined anger of his host, the latter's wife, and the two waiters. He walked through this tumult calmly. He realized with an unpleasant sensation of foreboding that this mere Gallic effervescence and ill-humour was a very mild thing compared to what he would have to deal with outside the door in a minute or two. The man of the neighbouring table was putting a few last touches to his toilet in one of the mirrors that lined the wall of the salle of the restaurant – as he had been kept out of the 'wash and brush up' room.

As Fane appeared, he turned round and came towards him with an unpleasant scowl on his face, and said blusteringly: –

'Do you think this restaurant belongs to *you,* you little cub! We all know *your* sort, with your fine airs, my little gentleman. But I for one don't care *that* for you!' And in saying this he snapped his fingers violently under Fane's nose, not effecting this manoeuvre entirely in the air. The organ thus airily menaced received a sharp blow. Although it was essential to keep cool, and not be drawn into a row, as the other evidently meant he should be, this was too much for the young man. He hit the insolent fellow before him squarely between the eyes, and the latter immediately fell full length on the floor. The next moment he was seized brutally by the two waiters, and a kitchen hand who had come up to help a bit, and was flung and dragged towards the door.

As he approached it with such precipitation, he had an impression of several dark, set faces awaiting him there, and quite a little crowd collected round it. Into this little crowd, consisting of some eight or nine men, he was flung by the combined restaurant staff. Without the damp and muggy day had turned to a very foggy one. The dampness was acute.

If the waiters had been brutal, these men amongst whom he had now fallen were even more so. He was dashed to the ground and literally trampled on. He felt hands swarming all over him, entering pockets, palping him all over. Almost

344

immediately one of them came upon the lump beneath his waistcoat – the bullet he had made of the notes. A dozen hands grabbed and tore at this. His waistcoat was torn open, the actual bundle itself, covered by the shirt only, was seized. A knife gleamed past his face. Then the hold seemed to relax, the other hands left him as though by magic, and he found himself lying face downwards in the mud, grasping at the bundle beneath his shirt, which to his relief was still there. But a hoarse voice above him was asking him what he was after – if he were hurt. It was a policeman. He had presence of mind enough to button his waistcoat before getting up, and then with a glibness that surprised himself, he said quickly to the policeman, 'I'm secretary to a rich lady, who has entrusted me with some papers, that I was to deliver to a certain address. Well, I was imprudent enough to leave my cab and come in here to have lunch, before delivering the papers in question. I had been told that there might be some attempt to waylay me, but thought that this was probably only fidgetiness on her part. She is a very fidgetty old woman. You have just seen how these rascals set upon me. Now I must hurry up and get another cab, and get these things out of my hands. She'd never forgive me if I lost them even through no real fault of my own. If you need me in the matter of the prosecution of these men, should you catch them, this is my address.'

And he gave a fanciful name and address. 'Thank you for rescuing me,' he laughed, and with this made away into the fog.

The policeman called after him, but he walked faster, and at length began running and was soon out of sight of the restaurant and the policeman too. But he was not equally out of sight of the man whom he had knocked down in the restaurant. In fact as he was debating as to which road to take

345

next, he found this man almost at his elbow, coming towards him with a very evil look on his face.

70
THE DEEP-SEA DIVERS

'You 'ave a large sum of stolen money on your person, Mr. 'ercules Fane. If you don't give it to me at once, who will restore it to its rightful owner, I will 'ave you arrested. I only 'ave to call a policeman.' The man had caught Fane up and was walking along beside him. Fane shrugged his shoulders and walked more quickly.

'If you do call a policeman, you will get locked up as a criminal with a hundred thefts marked up against you. I am merely, in my capacity of Mrs. Dukes' secretary, conveying a packet she has confided to me to her brokers. So you see it's useless trying that game on. I'm much less afraid of a policeman than you are.'

'Yes, all right, guv'nor. Only s'posin' the Actor-Gang was found out, they'd find out that Mrs. Dukes wasn't Mrs. Dukes, like, at all. See? Then where'd you be? 'Ow'd you prove you weren't in the know?'

'By having you arrested for following me about.'

The man had evidently in the restaurant decided that Fane was in a great funk about the police, and had then, in making suspicious enquiries about the postal order he had changed, tried to work upon his fears. This greenhorn in crime could be managed in that way, he thought. He was rather discouraged by Fane's glibness just at present. So he walked along in silence beside him for some time.

Fane did not know Liverpool at all, except for having

walked down the principal streets once or twice. He was now entirely ignorant of his whereabouts, and for all he knew might soon strike open country. The fog increased if anything. He knew that the original object of his pursuers had been to follow him on the chance of his having a rendezvous somewhere with Royal. Lucy had told him not to go near the house at which they had agreed to meet until he had shaken off these spies of the Khan's. This was easier said than done, though. But now they probably were not sure what they ought to do. For they did not know how much of the money he had with him. But they would still leave him in liberty, and not hurt him too much even if they succeeded in getting the packet of notes away from him, and would shadow him on the chance of his giving a clue to Royal's hiding place.

Two of his late assailants had turned up again and were following them the whole time.

Fane stopped, and the man at his side stopped too.

'Well?' said the young man.

The other did not answer, but stood with a rather bored expression on his face like a man waiting while a friend lights his pipe or does up his boot-lace.

'Well, sir?' Fane said again. 'I don't want your company. If you insist on following me about, you must drop behind with your friends there, and follow at a respectful distance.'

'And s'posin' I don't want to?' asked the other.

'I shall have to knock you over again,' replied Fane.

The newly fledged young criminal, with his booty tied up in his shirt, looked at the old and hardened criminal rather whimsically. For he was thinking, 'All you have to do is to hit him between the eyes and he falls over. I've done it, so I know. I suppose I shall have to keep doing it for the rest of the day if I do it again now.' This bearded man was about fifty-five or fifty

347

years old, and was evidently marked out for one of the hacks of his profession. He now saw before him a young man of twenty summers who at the first try was a rich man – who had plunged his hands into Mrs. Dukes' million, no doubt – and yet he was a shaver, a greenhorn, a raw beginner. This exasperated the older man.

'Well, right about turn!' said Fane. 'Back you go to your friends in the rear – that's your place! Sharply, now!'

"Oo are you?' The man was getting angry.

'It'll have to be done,' thought Fane. He drew his fist back, and with the precision of a habit, although it was only the second time, he struck him between the eyes, and sure enough over he went. As he fell to earth, Fane bounded away in the other direction, running at the top of his speed.

He ran and ran, looking behind from time to time, and saw vaguely through the fog, yet always in sight, two other figures, running just as quickly as himself. He passed people who became distinct for a moment and then, as he looked back over his shoulder, had become indistinct again. As he ran he kept on the look-out for some loophole of escape, and at length he dashed down a narrow street in which the fog seemed to have collected more thickly than elsewhere, and that he chose for this reason. But after having run about sixty yards, he nearly dashed his head into a tall brick wall. The street was only a blind alley, a cul de sac!

The fog was so much thicker here that his pusuers were not at this moment visible. He looked round him hopelessly for a couple of seconds, and then sprang up into the back part of a van that was moving away in the direction from which he had come. He was only just in time for a few moments later the two men who were hunting him passed at full tilt towards the black wall awaiting them at the bottom of the street.

But now the carman had noticed him, and began cursing him roundly, and asking him 'what the devil he meant by getting in there.' Then this surly individual suddenly appeared to remember that a moment before two men had run past, and putting two and two together, he concluded that the man who had climbed into his van was a runaway thief, or something still more dangerous. Under the influence of this brilliant inspiration he became more and more energetic, and Fane saw that if he did not get down himself, he would be hauled or hurled down. He slid off the back of the van accordingly, and saw his two pursuers just visible once more and turning towards him. They had guessed the nature of the ruse by which he had escaped them. So off he started again, and was soon back in the larger street running harder than ever.

As he ran, all sorts of thoughts raced through his head, ran through just as quickly as himself, but jerkily, somehow. He reflected, for instance, that this mad pursuit was like one of the cinematograph pictures that are seen in sixpenny 'Electric Palaces.' And it occurred to him at the same time that if he were stopped or caught he might pretend that this was what was really happening, that he was taking part in a cinematograph 'picture.'

The two men still held him in chase, but they were not quite so near as they had been before the van incident. The street now ended in a broad and tram-swept thoroughfare. He turned the corner at breakneck speed. His way was obstructed by a string of sandwich men coming out of a large red building; they wore huge deep-sea diver's helmets, and a kind of rough umber-coloured Khaki costume, to represent a diver's suit. They were all joined together by indiarubber piping, which was attached to little knobs at the top of their huge helmets, to represent the diver's breathing pipe. Fane, on

349

a sudden impulse, entered the door from which this long string of men was slowly emerging, and found himself in a large hallway. Two or three men were attaching themselves, with the pipe end allotted to each, to the man in front of them. One was still in his ordinary clothes, however, and about to pull on the diver's outfit. Royal went up to him and spoke quickly.

'I have a bet on with some friends, I've just left them, to walk down Bold Street in the middle of the day without being recognized by somebody. When I saw you divers coming out a moment ago, it occurred to me that this would be a way of winning my bet. Let me use your dress. You can put it on before we get back and get your afternoon's money all right, and come tomorrow to a place, I'll tell you where, not far from here — to carry out my assertion, to be my witness, you understand, that I really *did* walk down Bold Street this afternoon. There's five shillings now and you'll have another tomorrow.'

Fane's pleasant face, the fact that he was evidently a gentleman, and the man's appreciation of the joke, enormously reinforced by the five shilling piece, made him reply promptly.

'All right, guv'nor, pull these 'ere things on, and off we go. Ha ha! 'Urry up, mister, or you'll not be in time to go along o' the others.'

In a couple of minutes Fane had entirely enveloped himself in the dark brown suit and buttoned it up — over his other clothes of course — had slipped on the big cardboard helmet, with a square opening in front for the eyes and nose, and had had the placard affixed to his back. Then he attached himself to the man in front by the piece of piping. The next moment he was in the street.

He had told the man whose place he had taken to follow at a

little distance. He tramped slowly, with several stops, through a number of small and quiet streets, but at length emerged on the central thoroughfares of the city.

It was a Public Baths that had sent these men forth to advertise an entertainment — a famous diver who was going to grope about in a tank, fight with a large fish, and find some treasure. They had not got far from the baths when Fane passed within a foot or two of the men from whom he had been running. They stood scowling and perplexed, and were panting hard. Now Fane himself was panting, and, through running through the fog, was shaken now and then with a coughing fit. Once before we have seen how his susceptibility to colds and coughs nearly betrayed him and everybody else in Marbury Street. He knew that if he passed those men panting and coughing that he might attract their attention, and he made truly Herculean efforts *not* to cough and pant. He nearly choked himself, but succeeded in holding his physical nature in abeyance for once. He soon left them behind, hunting about in side streets, and eventually forced to return to headquarters very crestfallen and report that their man had escaped.

In the two busiest streets Fane saw one of the Khan's compatriots and bodyguards parading alertly, and further on another man, an Englishman, also in the great Khan's pay.

In passing down a side street, Fane, having first examined the various horizons, cut himself loose from the man in front, and going beneath the archway leading to a mews, took off his diver's things and helped the man into them. He gave him a place of rendezvous for the morrow, to carry out his former statement, and after asking his way once or twice of benevolent policemen, was soon at the house at which they were to meet Royal, who was already there, testing his new make-up, and munching a sandwich. They sat down before a good fire,

351

and over a glass of whiskey Royal heard Fane's late adventures. He was enthusiastic, and pronounced his friend's exploits worthy of the august man he had been understudying, and then they went into the details of their escape from the city. In this manner they awaited, Fane very anxiously, for Lucy's appearance.

71

THE MESOPOTAMIAN WOMAN BECOMES AN IDOL AGAIN

When Fane had gone Lucy sat down to wait. She knew that in a short time the Khan's people would spread all over the town, occupy the stations, mount guard before the shipping, establish posts on the road leading to the country, not to speak of having a guard at Palm Lodge. How with their rather limited numbers they could accomplish all this Lucy did not know. But she was sure that they would become extraordinarily ubiquitous once they had convinced themselves that Royal had got away and was not hiding anywhere on the premises. She knew of old their capacity for spreading themselves out, for hopping from one place to another, of suddenly concentrating, of suddenly disappearing. They were the most wonderfully disciplined little army of scamps and scamp-catchers in the world.

Now she quite expected to be ordered to march with them, and to get her marching orders at any moment. She would be placed in some station, or sent to some hotel. So when the giant-like Fury came into the room where she was sitting, she got up with alacrity, awaiting orders. But the terrible personage merely sat down wearily before her, and began staring at her stonily. What might this portend? She soon learnt her fate: and it was one she had not reckoned on. She was entrusted with certain books and papers that the Khan had asked for urgently. She alone could be trusted with them. She was to go to London at once.

This news was excessively disagreeable to her, especially as she was to be accompanied to the station by the giantess in person. They were to start without delay. The other lady already had her long hooded cape on her shoulders. There was nothing to be said. She received this order stoically enough.

In driving through the streets to the Lime Street station she looked anxiously into the fog on all hands. The fog seemed to have descended especially as a kind of medium in which the Khan's ghostly followers could better work. Her anxiety did not suggest to her the idea that it was for *them,* Royal, Fane and herself, that it had spread itself so rapidly and well. It seemed rather to be like a dark corner, or a million dark corners, in which watchers and spies lurked and glided. They soon emerged from it, but it was creeping steadily forward, and would soon pervade the city. She felt that could it have been possible, this was the sort of arm that the Khan's followers would have used. It was as though they had started it, and, sown with them, it was gradually creeping forward upon the clearer part of the town to overtake the fugitives – to envelop them and close them in, and when it rolled away, leave them dead in the streets.

They were just in time for a London train – not an express, however. The older woman went to get her ticket, and accompanied her to a first-class carriage, 'for ladies only.' She stood at the window, resting her chin on its sill like a large and meditative animal. When the sluggish guards suddenly became excited and began waving flags, standing on tiptoe, rushing about and blowing whistles, and the engine began its deep, long brusque puffs, as though shaking off its sleep with difficulty, the great Oriental woman stepped back and vanished as the train began moving. Lucy watched her down the platform and drew her head in.

As the train drew up at the first station on its journey, still within the metropolitan radius of Liverpool, Lucy sprang out of her carriage, quite as a matter of course, intending to either get back to her rendezvous in some conveyance or simply take the next train back. But to her intense dismay there stood the gigantic mentor of her youth again before her, quite calm and unmoved, but relentlessly pointing back to the carriage.

Without a word Lucy remounted the step, again placed her things in the rack overhead, and sat down desperately, while this time the other got in with her, sitting bolt upright, enormous and grave, in front.

There was something peculiar in her attitude. She seemed rather sleepy, her expression was very fixed, her large idol's lips seemed more carved out and firm than usual. She had not uttered a word since they had left Palm Lodge. Lucy had the fantastic and very Eastern fancy that she looked like some ghost-like projection of herself, that she had sent after her pupil to bar her way of retreat and to drive her implacably but indifferently on towards her destination – the destination that *she* had chosen for her, but that Lucy herself abhorred, for she wished to be back in Liverpool, where she alone could learn what had become of Fane. She stared at the huge Mesopotamian woman in front of her with some of the tragic awe of her race. Ever since they had left Palm Lodge she had been like some great, vigilant automaton, holding Lucy beneath her spell.

The train started, and the long journey began, each mile covered racking Lucy's heart, and increasing at the same time her terror at the attitude of her companion.

Many stations were passed, and some stopped at, and at length about four o'clock the mid-winter twilight drew in. Lucy had become almost hysterical by this time, and now her superstitious terror was increased tenfold because she could not prevent her eyes from fixing themselves on the eyes of the being in front of her.

Just at what moment she could never tell afterwards, but from shrinking into the farthest corner, all huddled up, and her eyes wide with fear, she became suddenly so overcome with terror that she suddenly opened the carriage door, and flung herself out into the night.

The door swung slowly to and then open again, and then finally closed with a bang. The Mesopotamian did not move, but still sat staring in front of her. At station after station people gazing in at the carriage window, were struck with strangeness at this figure. And the train rolled on with this great lifeless image towards the London terminus.

At Euston the train gradually emptied. All the doors stood open except one. An inquisitive porter, or merely one on the look-out for a job, on gazing in saw a rigidly seated enormous figure of a woman. He called to another porter, for purposes of humorous relaxation. He supposed that this nigger lady was asleep. A third porter of a more curious turn of mind determined that she should be woken up, and, opening the door, vociferated several times. But she remained unmoved by this. Then it occurred to the first porter that he had found a more serious source of relaxation than he had at first realised. Thrills instead of mere amusement for all concerned.

On being prodded she was equally irresponsive. Eventually, now in the midst of the entire station staff, she was carried out on a chair, sitting upright still, like an idol of wood, and deposited in a waiting room. A doctor was sent for, and the word 'trance' soon spread from lip to lip — even more eerie than death. Her limbs were quite rigid, and it was as though she had again become the carved idol that she had almost seemed to be, only with the anomaly of life.

And here, carried about in a chair as though in some procession, first sitting in the twilight of a large station waitingroom, and then removed, in wrappings, to a hospital, as various gods and goddesses are brought in large vans across London to the museum of their destination, we will leave her, and return to Lucy.

72
THE USES OF A GERMAN BAND

Fane had not slept a wink all night. Early next morning there was a ring at the bell, and to his unbounded and vehement delight, it turned out to be Lucy at last. She was very pale, her clothes were rather soiled, but she was otherwise well enough.

In her emotion the night before she had not noticed before jumping out that the train had slowed up. It was nearly stationary when she took her leap, and she was very little the worse for her fall. She saw in the distance the lights of a town, walked there directly, and taking a taxi to the next station along the line — still for fear of meeting the woman she had fled from — had returned by the next train to Liverpool.

With great circumspection she had approached the palace of rendezvous. She had even seen two of the Khan's men posted in the station. But their attention was entirely taken up with the departure platform and the people leaving Liverpool. They had not noticed her. She was reticent about her escape, giving only the bare facts, and with little gusto.

Now that they were all together, Royal was in great good humour. 'What did I tell you?' cried he. 'By far the worst is over. We shall soon be out of their reach now. Fane got away magnificently. Tell your story again, Fane,' and he insisted on Fane telling Lucy of his adventures.

Fear had never been a thing for which Lucy was famed. But now while Fane was telling his story, especially at the parts where he seemed running a serious danger, Lucy's face wore an expression of extraordinary anxiety and fear. Afterwards she kissed him several times to his considerable embarrassment, for they were still beneath Royal's eyes.

'But we must think what our next move will be.' It was about nine o'clock in the morning by this time, and just then from without rose the strains of a German band.

Royal leapt to the window. 'A German band! What can be done with a German band?' he asked. 'Is a German band of *use*? So far it has been one of the real curses of this country. But today it will for the first time be put to a sweet use. It will aid three young and interesting creatures to Liberty!'

After this sententious declaration Royal put on his hat, and disappeared on a mysterious errand. He was seen from the window in deep conversation with the conductor of the band — a black-bearded, deaf, sleepy and dreary-looking West-phalian. This man seemed to be looking at Royal doubtfully, and wiping the mouth of his voluminous and battered instrument. And then he was observed by Fane and Lucy, watching in deep wonder from the window, to open his mouth mechanically and to laugh largely.

Royal came back with the bandmaster, and making him sit

down, turned to his companions with the following explanation:

'I've hired the band for the day. I am going to pay him, this black monster of dreary discord, ten pounds. We, you and I, Fane, are going to put on enormous black and brown beards and wigs, and enlist with these jolly Teutons. As to you, Lucy, I'm afraid we must part company again. If you approve of my plan, will you sail in a boat bound for Cork shortly, and meet us in France, a week hence? I think, with your new disguise, you'll be able to elude the Khan's people; and although you think they are, they are *not*, as a matter of fact, ubiquitous. I don't mind guaranteeing you that there won't be any hanging round the particular dock from which this Cork boat starts.'

He had arranged with the bandmaster that they should tramp to a distant suburb, making a certain amount, but not too much, music on the way. Two of the Germans, returning to their lodgings, brought Royal and Fane two suits of clothes. And somewhat tanned, with large beards, these two little men – Royal and Fane – were soon on the road with the German band. I don't think it should surprise the reader, when he considers Royal's other numerous accomplishments, to hear that he also spoke German a little. Since his escape in Palm Lodge, and especially now that his two friends had also run the gauntlet and rallied to him, he had become quite another man. His exuberance was extraordinary.

Fane and he tramped about for the next six hours, stopping every now and then and playing the *Marseillaise* and the *Wacht am Rhein,* Royal committing a thousand indiscretions and impertinences with his trombone, and guffawing heartily in his beard, while Fane played brisk march accompaniments on his drum in the midst of some of the most touching pianissimos of the German's repertoire. The noise was so frightful that in some of the more aristocratic quarters of the city through which they passed pennies positively rained upon them, and they had people on their knees in the mud before them supplicating them to move on — and on and on, and *not* to tarry!

Beautiful women appealed to their charity. Nervous old gentlemen, speechless with rage and consternation, fixed a terrible eye on them from adjacent houses. 'I have believed up till today that with a good stiff glass of whiskey, and the summoning of all my resolution, I could stand a German band. This was an error. A band came along our way this morning that bent my strength like a reed. I have *never* heard anything like it!' said one old gentleman that evening to another old gentleman. It is true that the Germans played up to Royal and Fane wonderfully. The bandsmen felt it was in a sense a day off. They disported themselves — they enjoyed themselves. They gave rein to their fancy. The French horn no longer waited for the cornet, it began when it pleased and left off as unaccountably.

In the poorer quarters the band passed more insidiously. The poor do not understand the causes and the meaning of things. They were gazed on sombrely and with a pathetic perplexity. Why the wife was beaten by her husband she did not know. A young man who that morning took his life accounted naively for the act in a letter attributing his despair to love.

At a suburban station that evening Royal and Fane, having bought outright a trombone and its case, and a drum, and also the two suits they were wearing from the Germans, left for London.

As Royal had prophesied, the worst of their dangers were over. He had also prophesied that Palm Lodge would not be abandoned for a week by the Khan's people. It was not; it was ten days before a hue and cry was started. But by that time the three young adventurers were in complete safety. Royal had said that their escape would cost them two thousand pounds. Again he was more or less exact in his prophecy.

73
THE FINAL PIGEON HOLING OF
THE DRAMATIS PERSONAE

When Fane and Royal arrived in London, Westphalian musicians grunting at one another occasionally, 'Ist das war?' 'Ja, Ja, das ist war, kind,' 'ein augenblick, junger,' 'So, so,' and such like luminous phrases, they took up their quarters in the Soho district, not far from Marbury Street. The next morning Royal, dressed like a dapper young man of fashion, disappeared at an early hour, and returned that evening with all the money of both of them converted into gold, and from that into paper money again, or some of it, and all crammed into a portmanteau. Then that night they vanished again, bound southwards.

We need not follow the details of the several journeys they undertook in the course of the next week or two. The two old men who walked gingerly across the gangway of the boat at Folkestone, became two noisy tourists in Paris. A week later, Lucy, Fane and Royal were living the student life in Munich with an unmistakable genuineness. A storm of indignation, wonder and curiosity rose in England round the case of Mrs. Dukes and her fortune — the poor old woman so shamefully, so wonderfully despoiled. But the three sedate, serious and unconcerned heads in the Bavarian capital received not so much as a stray raindrop from the storm. It seemed also that the Khan and his followers had again been successful in leaving no traces behind them. Mrs. Dukes was able to supply few indications. Royal sent to the solicitors, Messrs. Truman and Hatchett, a will and testament, a couple of weeks after his flight, from Italy, where he went on a little expedition on purpose to post the letter. In it he, Mrs. Dukes, bequeathed six or seven hundred thousand pounds, the residue of his fortune, to Mrs. Dukes of 21 Marbury Street. This was a very solemn document, and created an enormous outburst of indignation in Truman and Hatchett's office, and an outburst of a mingled nature without it, in the world at large.

Mrs. Dukes managed to content herself with the sum that remained to her. She found Cole under the care of Messrs. Truman and Hatchett, and to find that this poor Cole whom she had believed dead, to be living after all, was the sweetest surprise of her life. She noticed, however, that he was rather changed. She was furious when she first saw him with a pipe, and snatched it out of his mouth; also she confiscated his tobacco. But she became so alarmed at his sulkiness which assumed unprecedented proportions, that she eventually bought him another pipe. But it somehow didn't recompense him for the *first* pipe, the Meerschaum, that Royal had given him. Also Mrs. Dukes abolished the dirty little room near the head of the cellar staircase, and wanted to make Cole wear collars. Cole himself wanted to, it appeared. He became very conceited. But he was not so happy as before. Still we can't have everything. The pride of riches and the joys of poverty as known to Cole in the glorious grimy basement of Marbury Street cannot co-exist.

While the uproar at the discovery of the great fraud practised on the public in this case of Mrs. Dukes' heritage was at its shrillest and basest, Sarandur Khan gave a great reception at the Embassy. He was more quaintly brilliant, more magnificently Oriental, than ever. But the giant-like woman known as the Ambassadress, and who had always received the guests and been looked upon as the hostess, was no longer there. Another woman, of bright vivacious presence, was there in her stead. Sarandur Khan made no comment whatever on this change. This little happening made him more popular than ever. He became incontestably the most romantic of Eastern potentates. The guests were hugely amused. 'He's cut off her head! Yes, that's the new favourite. She's beautiful, isn't she? But she won't live long, you see. Poor girl! The Khan's at the capricious age. I expect we shall see a number of wives now one after the other.' So the guests chatted together.

The giant-like Mesopotamian had not been beheaded, however. She had at last woken up from her trance, and had immediately started on a pilgrimage to some shrine somewhere very far away in the East. It would take her two or three years, the way she proposed to travel, to make this journey. She never returned to Europe.

The Khan is still flourishing. I read of a very ingenious robbery the other day, and had no hesitation in attributing it to him, that is to the Actor-Gang. They have changed their premises. They are no longer in St. John's Wood, but in Well Walk, Hampstead. The reader, in passing down this charming and tranquil street, will gaze up at the houses and wonder which one it is that shelters the infamous Hillington, the discontented Luchars, the little doctor. But I defy them to guess which one it is. Royal heard later on from Lucy, she having overheard her compatriots discussing it, that the inscrutable butler, with whom his relations were so unfortunate, was the person that originally gave the Khan the information that old Dukes was going to leave all his money to the landlady of Marbury Street.

The Khan was not addicted to blackmail, but if he ever heard of any man who had a strange past, the hint of a very big and bloodcurdling skeleton in his cupboard, he very often tried to do a little business with him. He had had his eye, meditatively, on Mr. Dukes for some time because of 'certain information' given him. On hearing that a butler was wanted there, he dispatched one of his best men – a man who had been butler at the Embassy, one of the only men in on all his secrets.

No bodies had been found in the empty house – only Cole. Cole was discovered in the subterranean chambers at the bottom of the secret shaft. It was very difficult to get him out. He had never succeeded in getting so far down in the earth before.

Something of the glamour departed from Mr. Hatchett, the acute and penetrating member of the firm. The blond clerk with the keen look was triumphant. He always knew something was wrong. 'If *he'd* had more to do with their client,' etc. The safe had become historic.

If the reader will kindly pass over two years, crammed with adventures for Royal, but no longer of a criminal sort, we can give another glimpse of this strange young man before finally leaving him.

On a fine autumn day, of *this* autumn, was to be seen Mr. Richard Neal, busy in his shed at Juvisy near Paris at work on his machine. This young Englishman who had lately astonished Europe with the accounts of his amazingly daring aeroplane flights, published by all the papers, was proposing to astonish them still more. It was he who had flitted around the topmost peaks of the Alps in his wonderful biplane, and who had done all the most romantic and most perilous things that the new sport yet had to boast of. He had lived amongst the clouds and snows of mountains like an eagle; he had passed a

363

night at sea, in the Mediterranean, with his machine, especially adapted for alighting on the water. He was, the papers pointed out, like a seamew – this flying man. The love of the waves and a mastery over them, others pointed out, was an English tradition. But it was now an open secret among inventors that he had already prepared a machine which would at last solve all, or nearly all, the problems of aviation, so that at last aviation would no longer be a perilous sport for a few courageous men, but would come within the reach of any man who had money enough to buy a machine. Mr. Neal had not invented this out of his personal desire to have a safe machine, but entirely as a business speculation. He was building extensive works near Paris. If this machine were everything it was said to be, and all the people who had hung back from participating in the new sport because of its dangers, would certainly acquire machines, it was prophesied on all hands that this young man would, besides other things, make a great fortune out of aviation.

But what Richard Neal was now preparing for was yet another feat that would astonish Europe by its madness of daring. Some said it was a descent into the heart of Africa in his biplane, some that he meant to cross the ocean. However this may be, on this particular morning he was working away in his shed, when a fashionably dressed and beautiful young woman appeared in the doorway.

'Richard, take me for a fly!' she exclaimed gaily. 'Fanny's copying in the Luxembourg. Let's fly there, to the Luxembourg gardens, and pay him a visit.'

'Right you are,' answered the gallant Neal.

And soon they were flying for all they were worth over Paris, and to the amazement and delight of the Parisian population, alighted in the open space usually given over to diabolo at the observatory side of the gardens, facing the clock of the palace.

'We can leave it there; no one will fly away with it. She won't let anyone mount her but me,' said Neal, as they started for the museum. Behind them a crowd had already collected, and the name of the 'king of aviation,' the idol of the people, had rapidly run from mouth to mouth. And now a cheer came after them.

The reader, I have no doubt, will have recognized in the inimitable aviator the once distinguished member of the Actor-Gang, and the lady he had thus piloted over Paris was none other than Lucy. And a few minutes later, to make the picture quite complete, they were standing beside Fane – now become Mr. Edgar Pope – in the Museum Galleries of the Luxembourg. Fane was still a poet, only now instead of being a poet in prose, he was a poet in paint. This is after all no more a dislocation of terms than the other.

The knowledge of how he had come by his present riches did not lie so easily on the more delicate conscience of Fane as on that of the more heroical, filibustering Royal. Royal had the conscience, in common with many other attributes, of a Napoleon or an Eastern conqueror. Fane had spent only a portion of his income, and the capital was accumulating. Four years later, thanks to his charming talents as a painter, he was earning considerable sums of money, and he then, in a strictly anonymous fashion of course, restituted that portion of the Dukes booty that had fallen to him. Lucy, of course, was quite of his way of thinking.

The manuscript of *Mrs. Dukes' Million* is an undated typescript, with some handwritten revisions, of 518 pages. The novel was sent by Lewis to the literary agent J.B. Pinker in 1909 or 1910; in the covering letter he describes it, possibly with diplomatic modesty, as a 'miserable pot-boiler' 'done to get ... a little money so that I could complete comme il faut my other novel' (*Tarr*). This letter, and a second evidently written a day later, shows Lewis to be considering 'The Three Mrs. Dukes' and 'Khan and Company' as alternate titles, and seeking a pseudonym ('James Sed' is proposed in the second letter) under which to publish it. A third letter reveals that Pinker felt the novel 'not marketable' and shows Lewis apparently ready to abandon it.

Internal evidence suggests *Mrs. Dukes' Million* may have been written as early as 1908. The US president at the time of the novel's action is Theodore Roosevelt, whose terms ran from September 1901 until March 1909. The technology evident in the novel argues a date late in this period: the London subways are no longer a novelty, motor cars and vans are ubiquitous, aviation has developed to a point where seaplanes, long-distance flying, and high-altitude flying can all be contemplated.

The present typescript, which survives in the Lewis Collection at Cornell University Library, carries the pseudonym John Lawrence; no other copy of the novel is known to exist. This typescript was discovered (according to W.K. Rose, editor of Lewis' letters) in the 1950's in a London junkshop. The numerous corrections and incomplete revisions in the handwriting of Lewis and his mother make it unclear whether this is the copy seen by Pinker or an earlier draft. In editing the novel for this publication, all incomplete revisions have been completed in the direction implied by the existent alterations and excisions. The characters' names have been made consistent, spelling has been regularized and, in some cases, modernized. A gap of two pages in Chapter xv has been hypothetically reconstructed; titles have been given to three chapters left untitled by Lewis.

F.D.